Everything
Under the Sun

A Novel by
Spencer Steeves

ISBN 978-1-64468-384-2 (Paperback)
ISBN 978-1-64468-385-9 (Digital)

Covenant Books, Inc.
11661 Hwy 707
Murrells Inlet, SC 29576
www.covenantbooks.com

Prologue

King Algrith slammed his hands on the table, sending wooden pieces flying off the map and clattering to the flagstone floor. "Does the king of Moonwatch presume to strike our ire still?" Shaking with rage, he tried to calm himself. A king must be composed. "How much more do my people need to suffer for that miserable worm to be sated?"

His most trusted knight, Sir Cassian, stepped up beside him and placed a hand on the shaking shoulder of his liege. "My lord, King Xangrus will never be satisfied until all of the astral lands belong to him. As long as Sun's Reach and Moonwatch share an open border, our people will continue to bleed."

Algrith sighed, sinking slightly in his chair. "You are right as always, Cassian. What are we supposed to do—give in and let him keep mounting attacks? It is no simple matter to close the entire border of Sun's Reach!"

"Especially not with his forces harrying us every step of the way." The knight scratched his chin. "And our latest reports from the spies have the Lunar Legion on the advance once again." King Algrith clenched his fists, sparks of energy flying off from his hands in his distress. Cassian quickly stomped out one of the smoldering bits before it could set fire to the carpet. "This is a tender subject, I know," the knight suggested. "But perhaps it is time we consider declaring war."

"Your suggestion is to make my people bleed more, giving Xangrus another chance to achieve what he wants?" Algrith shook his head.

"My lord, I know this sounds like a bad idea, but look at it this way." He pointed to the map, where the king had recently marked a red X over multiple small settlements. "King Xangrus continues his attacks, slipping past the border to spill blood. If we continue to sit passively by, he will think that he has free rein to do what he wants. If we want to show him we'll not tolerate his attacks, then we must act!"

"I agree with you in this, Cassian," the king conceded. "But is a war the best option? We already know Xangrus's men are tougher than ours, living in the Harshlands."

"I am afraid that it is our only option! Acting in an underhanded manner as Xangrus does will not stop him! We need a show of force, something that will prove we are strong enough to bear assault and avenge those who have died at his hands." He stared angrily at the map, where Sunrise Manor had been crossed out. "Look there for yet another reason why we must retaliate. I cannot stand by after his forces have slain one of my brethren in cold blood!" Cassian's steady voice cracked, and both his and the king's eyes misted. "You cannot allow him to keep killing like this. Avanielle was one of the brightest Lightstriders this land has ever known, and she was like a second mother to your children!"

King Algrith sighed. "Yes, once my son hears of her death, he will urge me to declare war as well." He rubbed at his eyes to clear the tears. Many had already been shed for the brave elf, and though she deserved every last one of them, it would not do to dishonor her name by demurring confrontation.

The Lightstriders consisted of five lords and ladies, honorable as the day is long, and the most elite warriors in all of Sun's Reach. They were the king's closest and most trusted allies. Cassian Brightblade led the elite force. Since the founding of the Lightstriders, there had always been a Brightblade among them, and Cassian was a prime example of the fine and sturdy cloth they were cut from.

The slaughter of Avanielle Tantavaine and her family was painful for all who knew her, most of all her fellow Lightstriders to whom she'd been sister and trusted ally.

"The rest of my brethren will wholeheartedly support any effort you make to strike back against this merciless bastard," Cassian offered. "And we are not the only ones affected by Xangrus's raids. The noble houses have all lost much to him, and I have confidence we can rally the full army of Sun's Reach behind us once news of this outrage is spread."

Algrith skimmed over the numbers on the papers around the tables. "As best as we can hope for." He sighed and scratched his itching palms, which began to spark again. "I wish we had more mages trained here. The magic force of Sun's Reach has never been numerous, and a show of magical power would be enough to show Xangrus that we mean business."

Cassian nodded. "Don't forget that you have the Fyroxi at your disposal. The Sun Mother granted them a fair deal of magic."

"Of course, Cassian." The king laughed bitterly. "I wouldn't dream of going to war without the Fyroxi. I've no doubt Xangrus will call the Chillfang to his aid, which should be enough to rouse the Children of the Sun."

"Agreed, my liege." Cassian held up a finger. "But if I may make one suggestion…"

"Go right ahead, sir." Algrith gestured for him to speak openly. "I have no doubt that I'll be relying on your expertise and training many times in this coming battle."

Cassian nodded gratefully. "I would warn you to be cautious in the use of their race. There are fewer and fewer Fyroxi each year and more fox fur cloaks and scarves in the market, I've noticed. Were the race to become extinct, I doubt Yamaria would be pleased, and we will require the goddess's blessings to win the war. As such, it would not be wise to put her mortal emissaries in peril."

Anger flashed across the king's visage. "Who is responsible for the deaths of the Fyroxi? I will see them hanged!"

"My lord, if it were possible to round up every poacher in the land, the Lightstriders would already have begun the process," Cassian said regretfully. "Unfortunately, this task is near impossible, and some poachers' greed is enough to drive them to slaughter even sentient creatures as sacred as Fyroxi."

"I will never understand the minds of poachers, and yet it sickens me that anyone would think to butcher them." The king's face grew red. "I will see to it that there is a royal decree to stop the unlawful poaching of these brave people, who have lived among us for many years!"

"Yes, we would not want to anger the Sun Mother, would we?" asked a new voice from the darkness of the hall. Cassian clenched his fist. "Planning war without me, I see. I'm insulted that you did not call for me."

King Algrith looked surprised at the new arrival. "Lord Qrakzt! I wasn't aware you'd returned from your trip."

"I apologize, my lord," Cassian bowed deferentially. "I meant to tell you of Lord Qrakzt's return this morning. It must have slipped my mind."

The king didn't seem to catch the subtle hint in the knight's voice, suggesting his forgetfulness hadn't been a mistake. "What are the results of your travels, good wizard? You never did report your intended destination, and you were gone a long while."

"I apologize for the delay, my liege." The robed man bowed obsequiously. "But I bring auspicious news, especially concerning your current plans." He pulled a rolled scroll out of his oversized sleeves and handed it to the king. "I scoured both the kingdom and a few of the islands off the main continent to find personages of arcane prowess. They have been brought here and pledge their servitude to you, o' great sorcerer king!"

"Yamaria truly smiles upon us this day!" Algrith cheered.

Cassian thought it somewhat suspicious this news had come directly after the king lamented the lack of mages within the king- dom. "Lord Qrakzt," the knight asked coldly, "we had no intention of war before your trip. What schemes have you constructed that would require you to gather more mages?"

"Schemes, my lord?" Qrakzt sounded offended. "No schemes here, simply a thirst for knowledge which could not be found here in Sun's Reach. Schemes!" the wizard scoffed. "You make me sound like some sort of mastermind brigand or thief!"

Algrith looked Cassian in the eyes. "I know you don't trust him, dear Lightstrider, but please you must understand how beneficial his aid will be! If he has recruited more powerful wizards to our side, then we can make a decisive strike against Xangrus." The king's face glowed with new hope.

"Yes, my lord. I'm glad you understand." Qrakzt rubbed his hands together. "I shall get my new compatriots to work posthaste. We shall aid your war, and when all is over, we shall give the astral kingdoms a display that will put an end to these horrendous deeds!" With his piece said, the wizard backed out of the room, as quietly as he came, off to begin work on his spells.

Cassian recalled that these wizards had helped the sorcerer king win his throne and knew that no amount of protest or counsel would steer Algrith from those who gave him a chance of winning the battle. With this in mind, the Lightstrider deferred to Qrakzt for the first time in his life, though he did not trust the man. Luckily, Algrith still turned to Brightblade experience when it came to the more mundane war plans. Under the counsel of Cassian and the other advisors, Sun's Reach was prepared for yet another confrontation against Moonwatch. Algrith called his bannermen and all the Fyroxi that could be spared, precluding the Fire-Striders and Bush-Walkers from joining.

The soldiers of Sun's Reach charged in with all the fury of a kingdom scorned. After a bloody and desperate conflict that raged for a year and a day, with thousands falling on both sides, the people of Sun's Reach sent the Lunar Legion scurrying home with their tails between their legs. Algrith was glad for Cassian's advice, as many Fyroxi were lost in desperate volunteer maneuvers. The brave fox folk had sacrificed their lives for the kingdom willingly, despite whatever wrongful treatment they might have received from their fellow citizens.

Lord Qrakzt and his wizards were a massive boon to the army of Sun's Reach. Without them, the war certainly would have been lost. While Sorcerer King Algrith and his son stood proudly, looking over the routed army, Lord Qrakzt's wizards came to the battle site. The king tried to dismiss them, as Xangrus had been dealt an awful blow and would likely not dare retaliate for quite some time. However, the wizards had an agenda of their own, one that had little to do with Algrith's. Casting a stout arcane shield that none of the Redwyn's army could destroy, not even Lightstrider Vedalken, who was trained in the ways of the arcane, the mages began chanting a profane ritual.

This insidious spell created an event that would be known throughout history as the Eclipse. Cassian, who had been correct about the evil designs of Qrakzt, could only watch as the five arch-mages, one for each of the known races besides the Fyroxi—Humans, Elves, Dwarves, Gnomes, and Khindre—removed the magic from the people of the astral kingdoms.

To remove the gift of magic from someone is akin to tearing out their soul, as wizardry, sorcery, and healing gifts are deeply woven into the threads of a mortal's being. Of all the full-blooded mages who came to the fight, only these archmages survived. The king was among the fallen, and the many souls the wizards stole, not least among them Algrith's, allowed them to cast one last spell before disappearing into thin air. With their disappearance, a magical barrier, stronger than any wall ever built, appeared between Sun's Reach and Moonwatch, physically separating them.

While the people mourned the loss of their king and kin and cursed the name of the wizards, Cassian turned to his Lightstriders, surprised to see Vedalken still alive. The elven Lightstrider known as Spellstroke had been studying magic for hundreds of years longer than these archmages and understood the full scope of the wizard's spell enough to guard against it. But he couldn't protect anyone else; he hadn't the time.

Vedalken could see, through the arcane signatures, everything the ritual had done.

It was not enough for the wizards to steal the lives of hundreds of people right after a war, nor was it enough for them to separate the two kingdoms with an arcane barrier, ever there to mock the magic-devoid people; they had to play one final joke on the astral kingdoms. That evening, the sun did not set fully, only growing lower and dimmer in the sky. Nor did it set the next day or ever again. Sun's Reach was now and forever the domain of the sun.

Part 1

Kindling

DURRIGAN
Seeking Salvation

Looking over his tribe, elder Durrigan felt bitter disappointment in himself. He could see the strife of his people, evident in the grim, gaunt faces that at one point in his life had been so cheery, their eyes filled with the fire of the Sun Mother who created them. Now those eyes showed only sadness, hopelessness, as if they knew the end was upon them. Their tails drooped into the sand despondently. *And why wouldn't they?* he thought ruefully. *Many of them have seen their friends and family die from hunger, disease, and raids from our foes. What hope could remain for a once-proud race now cast to the shadows?* Durrigan reflected on the past, when he'd once presided over one of the great tribes of the Fyroxi race, numerous and bright. *Back then, I was young and full of energy.* He cast his gaze over the people that relied on him and their other elders to see them through. *Now, just like me, my tribe is old and weak. I'll not see another two full centuries, and it is likely that many of them will follow me, despite their youth.*

Elder Durrigan stepped forward, out from the protection of his peers. The other elders only had grim looks on their faces. He suspected that they too were reminiscing on the past. He gazed over his people one last time, his tribe which numbered barely over a hundred. He knew it was time to make this announcement.

"Fire-Striders," he called out in his loudest and strongest voice, "today, I call you here to discuss the current affairs of our tribe!"

Everyone looked on with sullen gazes, but Durrigan knew that respect lurked in those eyes. Respect for their elders, able to stay hardy no matter what. *Able to fake it at least.*

"My fellow elders and I have decided that it is time for us to share everything we know of the current situation, for we are not the only ones facing such hardships." This set a murmuring in the crowd, as the Fyroxi realized the strife wasn't just affecting them. "As is known to you all, our current efforts to find food have not been successful. The stores we built up for many years are nearly depleted. So it is across the Scorched Waste. Even the Water Callers, who have pledged their lives to bring aid to the Scorched Waste, have fallen on hard times. Their leaders fear the destruction of the ancient people, who have made their lives in this kingdom since the first sun rose.

"On these sands, many find themselves without sustenance, and some have turned to thievery or, worse yet, murder as a means of survival." The quiet distress of his people set him ill at ease. "Even among our own people, this idea has taken root." Trying to keep the tears out of his eyes, the chieftain called forth the two that had been caught in a raid, killing innocent travelers for no reason but to steal their food. "As much as it hurts me to condemn my own people to punishment, these actions cannot be allowed among us. My children, my Fire-Striders," Durrigan called, "have we fallen so low that we would allow the murder and, worse, consumption of innocent people? No, for if we are like that, we cannot claim to be any better than the Chillfang!"

He saw a shiver of revulsion go through his tribe, and the two condemned next to him flinched at the accusation. The Chillfang were the ancient rivals of the Fyroxi. They had been slaying the Children of the Sun Mother long before poachers and bandits had set their sights. For a Fyroxi, to be compared to the Chillfang, there was no worse insult.

"What shall be done?" Durrigan heard the people shout. "How shall they be punished?"

The chieftain looked at the convicts. One was a mother with a small child at her breast. The second was a young man, possibly the woman's mate. He knew the man to be rash and angry. *And a parent will do anything for a child*, he reflected. *As I would do anything for my tribe, my children.*

"This is not for me to decide! For their crimes, they will be subject to the Sun Mother's whims. We will travel to the Temple of Yamaria, deeper in the desert, where we shall throw them upon the mercy of our mother and ask for her blessings and forgiveness."

"You will need volunteers?" one of the women asked, fearful of losing her husband or eldest son to the harsh travel of the desert.

Durrigan shook his head sadly. "It is not my wish, our wish," he amended, gesturing back toward his fellow elders, "to separate you from the friends you have made among the other residents of the desert or to force displacement, but it has become necessary for all of us to make the pilgrimage to our ancient home."

He waited patiently as the uproar of dissent erupted. He held up one hand, five long tails twitching. Once his people had calmed down a little, he finished speaking. "Many of you will dislike this decision, as I expected. But our numbers have dwindled too far already, and I refuse to willingly put any of you in danger. It is for your safety that we retreat to old homes. There has been news from the capital of Sun's Reach. I regret to say that we are going to war once again, and the king, in his ultimate wisdom, has begged us to take refuge. I feel that returning to our Sun Mother's temple, a place we never should have left, is the best place to make our new lives, away from the warfront."

The Fire-Striders, having made their pilgrimage to the Temple of Yamaria, suffered the least of the war's effects. They recaptured old homes from bandits and sheltering foes, liberating their mother's sacred homeland.

Though life in the desert was no less harsh, the famine no less severe, they were given a promise by their goddess.

Priest Purell, the religious superior among the Fire-Striders, prayed day and night, begging for salvation for their race and for Sun's Reach as a whole. And on the holy days, he led Durrigan's people in the chants of praise to Yamaria.

One day, Yamaria finally answered their pleas. "My children," she said into their minds, "much strife have you seen and many difficulties. Know that these things I cannot change directly nor immediately. But take faith in knowing that salvation is on the way. I cannot say when, but you will know when it arrives, and it will appear at the right time. Until then, know that you have my blessings now and forever."

Knowing their strife and lacking numbers, she showed the two criminals her mercy. After hearing the Sun Mother's voice, the pair were willing to do anything to regain favor in the tribe.

Yamaria commanded patience of them, and this she tested. Many years of toil, strife, and hunting the barren sands were ahead of them, and no significant release from the deaths by causes natural and premature. The tribe lost one elder, an unfortunate number of adults, and many children. But through their grief, they worked and remained in hopeful prayer

After the outcome of the war had been decided, Durrigan sat in a council meeting with his fellow elders, ready to present an idea that would abet the survival of their race. "My friends, I call this meeting today to discuss our future. We have lost one of our eldest members, and there is no telling how many of us will live to see our natural end. We must put plans in place for our survival."

"I concur," Silque, who oversaw the crafting and creation of tools with the tribe, spoke first. "Our place of residence has become even more of a danger. With the increasing dust storms, our protection is not sufficient."

"Who could have believed we would live to see such a change in the environment," elder Purell commented. "Praise Yamaria that we have had the chance to experience such wonder."

"Purell, do you underestimate the death your 'wonder' has brought to our people?" Silque's voice had a tinge of acid in it. "You speak of everything as a blessing of Yamaria, which admittedly most things are, but it seems you feel little remorse for our troubles. Seeing how you are so involved in prayer, it is a wonder you notice what is going on outside of your temple walls at all!"

"Lady Silque, it sounds as if you would call into question the power of our goddess, she who gave us life. Such an act is blasphemy!"

"Both of you shut your yap!" Sigmund, the scarred war veteran interjected. "You squabble about meaningless things. The safety of the younger generations is only in jeopardy because of the enemies that still lurk our sands."

"Sigmund, friend," Copernicus, youngest of the elders, the replacement for their lost ally, soothed with an easy grin. "Since that wall rose, we haven't had to deal with Chillfang, so everything has been much safer."

"You pretend that the Chillfang were the only sentient enemy we have," the veteran growled at the younger man. "Bandits and poachers still roam the desert, killing us for soft furs and trophies!"

"Well, if we were to do as I have suggested and made friends with the other tribes, instead of being so reclusive, we may be better off," Copernicus said easily, waving off the heat with his tails. "Being standoffish never did a friendship any good."

"Are you accusing me of being standoffish, boy?" Sigmund asked dangerously.

"No, no, of course not!" Copernicus smiled, throwing up his hands protectively. "Though you could stand to be a tad more friendly."

"What good is making allies if we cannot even produce supplies enough for ourselves?" Silque postulated. "Not only are we low on food but there is barely enough material for making clothing."

"The goddess did not create us with clothing, so perhaps that is for the best," Purell argued.

"Do you mean to insinuate that we go around indecent?" Silque seemed shocked.

"We do so in our fox forms, so why can it not be so in human form?"

"As full foxes, we have fur, you mad priest! Clothing gives us protection against the sand and sun!"

"Just saying, if we made more allies, we could trade for materials and food," Copernicus interjected. "Solve a bunch of these problems."

Durrigan could take no more. "Enough!" he yelled, cutting off all other arguments in the hut. "Listen to you all, squabbling like a litter of kits! We have all grown bitter in our old age. We've seen so much pain, but infighting will fix nothing!"

The tails of the other elders drooped, and they became suddenly very interested in different things around the room.

"Fools, all of us. As I said earlier, many of us won't live much longer. And you all have valid points. That is why I called you all here. I have an idea that may just save our race." He cleared his throat. "We do need to focus on returning to the proud race we once were. Warriors, crafters, priests, and stout allies." He acknowledged each of the others in turn, appealing to their wishes

Copernicus nodded. "Of course, Chief! You have the right of it. So what's your plan? Mandatory classes? Trading for books?"

Durrigan held up a hand to stay the younger man. "We must start small. We shall oversee the reintegration of training among the most promising members of our tribe. Furthermore, I have decided that when the next litter of kits is born and they grow up to the age at which they can begin proper service to the tribe, we as elders will take one each on as apprentices in our chosen fields. We will teach them how to teach, show them how to lead. The Fyroxi will regain their identity once more!"

"Hear, hear!" Copernicus cheered.

"Yamaria is pleased, I can tell already," the priest exulted.

"This can only mean good things for us." Silque stroked her tails happily.

"About damn time," Sigmund growled, but Durrigan could hear the contentedness in the old warrior's tone.

"The second order of business is far less palatable, but it must be discussed. As I am sure you have noticed, Purell, being the town healer and priest, the mortality rate of children has been extremely high." The cheerful mood immediately dropped from the room. Durrigan cleared his throat again, this time with nerves. "Yes, it is an awful tragedy that is bound to occur in a harsh landscape, but without the younglings, there is no future for the Fyroxi. We must put a focus on their protection and acclimation during rearing. Yamaria has blessed us by guiding us to her temple, which has unfortunately fallen into disrepair in the many years of disuse. I suggest we get our strongest to work on repairing it. This redevelopment will provide work and reinforce the arts we have buried in our times of strife. The kits will be raised within the temple and learn the basics of desert survival before they go through the first transformation."

"You mean to suggest taking the children away from their mothers?" Silque was horrified by the very thought. She pulled on one of her tails.

"The separation will not be permanent, nor will it be complete isolation," Durrigan explained. "The women will be able to see their children whenever they don't have work to be done."

"I understand what the chieftain is saying." Sigmund twitched a tail. "We have grown softer as a race, and that is partly to do with our rearing. Mothers coddle their young, hide them from everything. Then when the time comes for them to start living on their own, they haven't the skills to survive. This desert—with its snakes, bandits, and sand—kills more of us each year. What the chief suggests is wiser than any other parenting strategy."

"When you put it that way, I suppose there is little other option," the female elder said stiffly, causing Durrigan to sigh inwardly. Silque had been the mother of many, and he knew she would present his biggest obstacle in this.

He was thankful for Sigmund, who had at least put him in the clear for now. With the new plans set on the elders' minds, Durrigan dismissed the council and prepared to break the news to the people.

Much to his surprise, they'd taken it quite well. After coming so close to extinction many times in the past, the Fyroxi knew the importance of doing whatever was necessary to survive. Besides, as a race blessed with long years, they had little to fear in losing a few. Durrigan was relieved to know that he would still hold favor among his people, that they would continue to trust his judgment.

*****

With endless sunlight to work by, the restoration of the temple went swiftly, and by the time the tribe's mothers were ready to give birth, it was prepared to host the upcoming litter.

Durrigan only wished that the Eclipse hadn't stolen the magic of the Fyroxi. "If we had magic still available, we could have cast wards around the building, make it even safer." Later, he would reflect if voicing his fears had made them come true, as they still lost far more kits than Durrigan liked, but the numbers certainly did decrease.

*****

A small red-furred fox ran across the sand, darting into a burrow as Durrigan watched. As homage to the everyday creatures from which Yamaria crafted them, the Fyroxi began their life as nothing more than fox kits. A form that they stayed in until their fifth year of life. These being their most vulnerable years, it made sense, Durrigan thought, to have them protected. In his advanced age, he could feel the heat of the desert pressing down upon him. Turning his back to the sands, the chief returned to the shaded interior of the temple. He bowed reverently to the statue of Yamaria, brilliant in her carved red robes and brass sun disk crown. A beautifully carved spear rested in her stone hand, a relic of Fyroxi creation that reminded the old one again of magic long gone. In their prime days, many weapons like this one existed, created to drive off the Chillfang, their mortal foes, and, if one were to believe the stories, some other manner of fell creatures. According to the histories, nothing of their like had roamed the Sunlit Plane in many a millennium. Unlike Purell, Durrigan scoffed at these stories. To him, they seemed like nothing but tales to scare children with. "Like they needed more to scare them while the genuine threat of dismemberment by Chillfang existed."

It had been nearly four years since Durrigan put his new plan into motion. The kits ran around outside, supervised by the watchful eyes of the volunteer caretakers. He walked to the gap in the wall that served as a window, looking out over the children. The storms and snakes had taken more of their mature females, more potential mothers, lost to the elements. *My tribe dwindles, and I can do nothing except watch*, he thought morosely. *Yamaria, you promised us salvation, and yet we lose more by the year. When will your aid come to us?* He chided himself for disbelief, but even his inner scolding was weak.

He wished that he had the faith of Purell, that all would turn out as planned. *Of course, the priest would walk naked and unarmed into the stronghold of the enemy if he thought the Sun Mother would protect him.* Durrigan chuckled at the thought, returning his attention to outside. One of the adults was covered by a bunch of children, barely managing to stay standing, even in her stronger fox form. *Too few. If so many hadn't died, she wouldn't be able to stand against their playful assault.* As awful as having so few children alive was, Durrigan had to wonder if it wasn't for the best. The food situation had only improved marginally, and the Water Callers could only do so much for any one group. Having too many might have just left everyone too hungry. *Was I wrong to bring my people to the desert so many years ago?* He'd always had the peoples' respect and his tribe: a conglomerate of members from other tribes who had followed him willingly into the Scorched Waste, hoping to grow closer to Yamaria, to find the ancient Fyroxi shrine he now stood in. *I'm sorry, my friends. I fear I've led you astray. Will my folly finally kill us after all these years?*

The other elders had watched the kits, just like he was now, and already picked out ones that they thought would make good apprentices. Silque, always one to try something challenging, had her eye on Xio, a lazy girl that spent most of her time sleeping. The chief saw the girl in the corner, dozing as expected, her tail over her eyes. Like her mother, she resembled what the Humans would call a fennec fox, with light-yellow fur, large ears, and beautiful brown eyes.

Copernicus was set on choosing Ren: curious but a little shy, with a coat the color of chocolate.

Purell was enamored with a small frail female by the name of Vienna. "Certainly not going to grow up a warrior, but I'm sure I can make her into a proper cleric of Yamaria!"

One kit pulled harder and bit more fiercely than any of the others: Sigmund's pick, Leif. He was ferocious and would bear watching, but the grizzled veteran was confident in his ability to take the youth and shape him into a respectable warrior. His fur was an equal blend of gray, black, and tan; and the eyes above his pointed snout showed sparks of anger.

As for himself, Durrigan hadn't picked yet. There were a few promising ones, brave and sociable, but the chief knew he had the most challenging choice to make. His apprentice would be training to lead the tribe when they reached the proper status and age. A job much more difficult than fighting or praying and not one he could judge based on physical characteristics alone. However, his eyes kept wandering back to one female who stayed back from all the fighting, sitting near young Xio instead. Unlike any of the others, kits or adults, she had pristine white fur and eyes the color of brass. She sat upright and attentive, long white tail wrapped around her legs. No mother had claimed this one, and she'd not been named, and that interested the chief. When he was available, he'd provide her the company she must surely lack. Durrigan wondered if her mother had died during or shortly after birth. If so, she would go to one of the mature females who were barren or whose children had not survived. *She will make a good daughter*, he knew in his heart, without exactly knowing why that it was true.

Fathers rarely had much involvement with their children's lives. The men seeded the women but then returned to their work, viewing Fyroxi who could be their own children with the same equal respect that they would show any other member. Durrigan had never seen sense in that. And though it might be his age talking, he longed for someone to take care of. *Or someone who can take care of me when I grow too old.*

That had been part of the reason why he'd created the apprenticeship program in the first place. Watching the kit sitting on the border of the playpen, the chief felt an urge to go to her. Shuffling outside, he stepped gingerly over the barrier. A few of the younglings had been daring enough to try climbing the short fence, as evidenced by the claw marks running up them. They'd always been stopped short by the attentive supervisors. Durrigan sat down next to the girl, and with nary a sound, she hopped up into his lap. Her brass eyes stared calmly up at him while he scratched her soft ears. Eyes the same color as Yamaria's crown, he noted. A thought suddenly occurred to him. "It couldn't be…"

Her head tilted slightly at his words, but she made no further attempt to answer. Durrigan chuckled at himself. Maybe he was finally going senile. But even as he walked away, his observation stuck in his mind, and he knew he would be keeping a close eye on this kit.

*****

When the day finally came for the first transformation of the younglings, the whole Fyroxi tribe was waiting with bated breath. This event was one of the most significant in the tribe, the first of the coming of age ceremonies. In the weeks prior, the children had spent a lot of time with their mothers, who taught them about the transformation, showed them what to do when the time was right. Many of the children had probably already transformed a few times. In most cases, Durrigan reflected, calling this the first transformation was inaccurate. Everyone knew that, and yet it was still an important milestone.

A cheer went up among the crowd of Fyroxi. Durrigan even saw a few others on the outskirts of town. By the blue robes, the chief identified them as Water Callers. *Copernicus must have extended an invitation*, he surmised. *That's good, their help will be invaluable if the years continue with such little food.* Before the barrier had been created, severing the continent in twain, his brave Fire-Striders had been able to raid across the border. There had been a rocky stretch past the desert; but after came a dense forest, full of game, and fresh greens. Losing that resource had been devastating for the tribe. While the Eclipse had blocked their enemies, it had also cut off a primary food supply the Fyroxi had come to rely on.

At this very moment, a new albeit smaller litter was sleeping in the temple. While normal foxes were solitary creatures, most Fyroxi decided to stay with their tribes, so until their children had grown to a sufficient age, mothers wouldn't have another litter, for fear of being unable to provide for all of them. He imagined that wasn't as much of a problem for the other races, who lived out in the other parts of the kingdom. With their nearby allies and the fertile ground, they had easier access to food and could withstand larger families.

He turned such thoughts from his head and watched as one by one the children were brought in. They were guided by their mothers, brought to the center of the pen, where they had been playing only a few short weeks before. With a few whispers of encouragement, the young Fyroxi, who was now the size of an adult fox, was coaxed into finally accessing the little bit of power that all Fyroxi still retained, thus revealing their humanoid form.

At a distance, a Fyroxi could easily be mistaken for a human. The same variance that showed among Humans was there for the fox people as well. Fyroxi tended to be on the slim side and grow more lean muscle. It was rare to see a fat one, as their livelihoods depended on being able to hunt well. Even now, in such a small tribe, people who wore out their use were sent out into the desert to fend for themselves. With so little food, nobody could support an extra body. The main physical differences between a human and a Fyroxi were the ears and tails. These two things they retained from their fox form. The sharp ears pointing out above their head gave them a distinct advantage in hearing, and the tails provided their exotic looks as well as a method of silent communication with others of their race.

One by one, the Fyroxi children were led out of the hut, and one by one, they transformed. Each successful shift elicited a cheer from the audience. Durrigan felt proud, seeing these children reaching the new plateau in their lives. Each of the younglings chosen by an elder was joined by them and wrapped in a cloak of a different color, the dyes provided by the Water Callers. Leif was swaddled in red, Xio in lavender, Ren in orange, and Vienna in white. Last to come out of the shelter was the white kit. She had nobody to lead her out and glanced around apprehensively, not moving.

Durrigan wondered whether, without a mother, she had anyone to guide her in the process. Without knowing quite why, Durrigan stood from his seat and approached. He knelt down next to the female and spoke soothingly to her. She had been holding tense, and at his words, she seemed to become more comfortable. He heard the others muttering around the ring. This girl had no mother, no one to take care of her, and she didn't seem to be prepared for such a momentous occasion. Many wondered how it was that she'd survived. There were certainly rumors that Durrigan was taking pity on a doomed child, instead of letting her die for the betterment of the race. The chief didn't care. He knew there was something about this girl, something that drew the old leader to her, and he wasn't about to let her die, no matter what the others said.

Finally, he managed to coax the little one out into the center. He shifted to fox form himself and then, assuring that she was watching, back to humanoid form. She watched him placidly, and her head cocked to the side.

The muttering grew louder, and Durrigan pleaded with Yamaria to show him a sign that he wasn't making a mistake. He was a beloved chief, but if this child who he had marked as important to him were a defective specimen, it wouldn't prove beneficial for his reputation. *If there's anything that we kept from our old days, it's our stubbornness. We base importance on benefit to the tribe.* If this girl didn't transform, she would be left for dead, and that seemed more than just wrong to Durrigan. "Please," he whispered, for the girl's ears only, "please don't fail me."

Now for most Fyroxi, the first transformation is not an attractive spectacle. It often hurts a little and takes time to complete, a slow shift from fox to humanoid. With age and practice, the process becomes swifter and more natural, like slipping into a robe. When the girl finally did as Durrigan pleaded, the old chief was validated in his actions.

She *glowed*. As if she were the sun itself, the girl actually began to radiate bright light and comforting heat that washed over the Fyroxi in the front row. The audience gasped; the newly shifted younglings *oohed* and *aahed*, and Durrigan stared with wonder in his eyes. Finally, when the light died down, a young girl stood in front of them, and the chief let out a breath he hadn't known he'd been holding. The dark mutterings in the crowd became excited, overjoyed in fact. The girl in the center of the pit had an appearance that everybody recognized—shoulder-length black hair, fair skin, and white-furred ears and tail—in an instant. She looked just like her mother.

Durrigan approached the girl, who was looking understandably confused and frightened. He hadn't brought the cloak for his apprentice with him; so instead, he unclasped his own and wrapped it around her, thereby adopting her into his protection. He circled behind and placed hands on her shoulders. Projecting his voice so that all would hear, Durrigan addressed the crowd. "Fyroxi of clan Fire-Strider, our salvation is here, as decreed by Yamaria, the graceful sun goddess, merciful creator, and divine leader!" A massive roar of exultation followed his words. A name popped into his head, no doubt provided by the goddess herself. When the cheer quieted enough for him to be heard, he continued. "I give this blessed child the name Amaru Sunbrand, in hopes that she will live up to the expectations of even the goddess herself!"

He reached out his hand to the small girl and led her back to the hut, promising to return shortly.

*****

When Durrigan walked into the hut where the elders were waiting, he expected to be greeted with cheers and happy faces. The feverish gleam in each of his peer's eyes made him cautious. He was suddenly glad he hadn't brought Amaru with him.

He'd barely even sat down when they all began to speak in tandem. The words were jumbled, but the message was clear. Each had their own variation of "I will take the girl as my apprentice."

Durrigan felt anger flare up inside of him. "You have already chosen your apprentices," he said, managing to keep his voice calm.

That did not deter them, and he could tell that they were all about to start speaking again. Cautioning them, he pointed to each in turn, allowing them to speak; his eyes narrowed accusingly.

"She is the daughter of our goddess," Purell explained. "She would make the perfect cleric!"

"Schooling her in the craft of our people is the only way!" Silque attempted. "She would make things better than any we've seen in centuries."

"You would waste her potential on crafting," Sigmund spat. "Did you feel the heat, see the light? She could have a grasp on magic.

If we taught her the ways of war, we could have a nigh undefeatable power in our hands!"

Copernicus seemed to care the least. "I mean it would be great to have a girl with Goddess's blood to serve as our ambassador, but I have Ren, and I don't want to take her away from someone who could use her better."

Durrigan sighed. *The youngest among us, and he has the best sense.*

Ignoring the daggers in the eyes of the other elders, Durrigan charged ahead. "Unfortunately, if you hadn't noticed, I claimed Amaru as kin and student."

"You knew!" Purell accused. "You knew what she was, and you hid it from us! You want the goddess's child all to yourself!"

The others, save Copernicus, joined in the blaming, calling him a cheat and a trickster until Durrigan couldn't take it anymore. His sudden spike of anger forced the switch into fox form, and he yelled at them in savage tones, utilizing the Fyran tongue that the race shared. "I had an inkling of what she might be, nothing more. Frankly, I am disappointed in all of you. Are you all so willing to drop your apprentices? You have been spending time with the ones you chose; you would just shove them to the side because a prettier option comes along? Have none of you even an ounce of shame!" The other elders sat back, the embarrassment plain on their faces. He backed down, eyeing them down his snout. "You will take your apprentices and teach them in their field. I will take Amaru and give her the training she needs to properly lead us. When she is matured, she will know enough to take the place of whoever follows me as chieftain."

Copernicus had a thoughtful expression on his face, as he played with his wispy mustache. "I agree, of course, that you should take the girl. But what if, to give her the best chance, she learns a little from each of us. If you want to bring us back to our prime, having a chieftain that knows all sides of the race will be necessary. And I think the goddess's child would benefit from all of our skills."

Durrigan considered this for a moment before nodding. "Yes. That is a solid plan. I will plan out a schedule for her so that she can become the best possible." He shooed them away with his tails. "You are dismissed; go to your apprentices."

Durrigan himself collected Amaru and brought her into the temple. "Do you know what you are, little one?" he asked.

"Fyroxi"—came her reply—"of clan Fire-Strider." She looked up at him, her eyes searching for approval.

For a moment, reveling in the fact that he had Yamaria's child in his custody, he'd forgotten that she was still a youngling. *No need to burden her with everything just yet*, Durrigan decided. *Let her enjoy growing up. Teach her why she was so important when the time is right.* He curled his five tails around her protectively. "That's correct."

ALARIC
A Bard Sits on a Rock

Alaric stretched as he closed the wooden door of the monastery behind him. One hand brushed against the stone exterior which was blazing hot. He yanked away his burning appendage and blew on the singed flesh while staring over the dunes. The desert was utterly quiet, totally peaceful.

Absolutely boring.

The tall man sighed. "Happy now, Father?" He could almost hear his tutors scolding him: *Your father did what he did for a good reason. Release the anger from your soul. Bitterness will only distract you from attaining purity.* Alaric saw the sense in the monks' words, but he found he couldn't agree with their message. As far as Alaric was concerned, his anger was completely justified. First of all, purity? If what the monks were training him in was considered purity, he loathed the idea. Second, it wasn't like he'd asked to come here. Perhaps if he'd been allowed to come to the desert of his own will, things would be different.

Part of him had always dreamed of visiting the Scorched Waste for a short stint, see what mischief and interesting experiences he could find, but as Alaric had soon found out, the answer to that was zero. He was no stranger to heat, but the badlands were so *dry*, in more ways than one. In the Scorched Waste, the land was mostly barren of plants and scarce of animals. But more importantly to Alaric, the area where he'd been so rudely foisted had very few people. "A guy like me needs people around!" he called to no one in particular. There were a couple of villages within a few days' walk, but the Solgaele Monastery had been placed in a strategically isolated place. With a sigh, he regarded the empty sands. At least he still had his music.

Alaric unslung his lute and let his fingers dance across the strings. The sweet music he could tease out of instruments had made many a woman swoon and earned him a fair amount of coin. *Most of which Father appropriated before.* And therein lies the main problem with the Solgaele Monastery, where he now lived. It was so secluded that there was nobody besides his tutors to perform for. And of them, only one was pretty, though she'd be more likely to kick him than kiss him if told. He chuckled at the thought. *No respect for her elders, I swear. One would think that she'd learn that at her age. She sure doesn't mind drumming that into the other initiates.*

That he was older than she was something his tutor hated to be reminded of. At nearly forty-five years of age, barren Gemna Noskolla had overseen his teaching personally, at the behest of his father, who had visited the Solgaele Monastery personally to make sure everything was in order. Old Talisin had not enjoyed being here at all, which of course made it perfect for his rebellious son.

Being an elf had its perks, Alaric admitted to himself. Though he had the misfortune of having Talisin Valyaara as father, he had a much longer life to enjoy freedom from the man. Or at least he *used* to have freedom. But that was five years ago, *five years* he'd been stuck at this Yamaria forsaken tower in the sand. For an elf, five years wasn't much of anything, seeing as they could live for nearly a thousand, but Alaric wasn't really thinking for himself.

He wished to travel the grasslands of the Sulfaari Expanse, just as the Plainstrider Elves did, singing music for his many fans. He wished to stand tall on a stool in a tavern, hear the audience singing along to his music. He wished to feel the soft embrace of a pretty fan, taste the heavenly mixture of sweet wine and sweeter passion on her lips.

His keen ears picked up a shuffling behind him breaking into his thoughts, and the elf instinctively ducked just in time to avoid a punch headed toward the back of his head. He twirled on the rock where he sat, toward his assailant. "What the hell was that for?"

Behind him stood a dark-skinned young man with a shaved head, his face expressionless. "Your music interrupted my meditation." His tone was flat, and his face was guarded, betraying little of his actual thoughts.

"And you thought the best way to quiet me down would be to punch me?" Alaric asked incredulously

"It would have shut you up, wouldn't it?" Such moodiness was not out of character, but to Alaric, the boy was an enigma.

"Well, yes, but there are other ways you can get a man's attention!" the elf sighed and looked at the young man. The lean, wiry frame belied terrifying strength, muscles like iron bars. If he made an unwise decision, he knew that the monk could easily be sparked into a fight. Alaric had no desire to battle against this young man, especially considering the soreness of his body after their training session earlier this morning. Alaric shrugged and conceded to his aggressor. "If you are so intent on meditating, I can lower the volume of my playing. Will that be enough to please you, Your Highness?" Alaric thought he saw a twinge of anger in the young man's coal-black eyes and felt a surge of triumph at the small show of emotion.

"Thank you." The young man turned away, heading back into the shaded monastery to continue his meditation.

Alaric almost felt sorry for being snarky, but he felt justified, having come *so* close to being punched in the head. He knew that the monk could hit too. The boy had grown up here and, unlike Alaric, had taken the lessons he'd learned to heart.

Skilled monk or not, the boy unnerved him. Being a musician, he took great pleasure in reading people's hearts with a glance, which he couldn't do with this cold, expressionless boy. "Maybe he keeps so cold to combat the heat of this desert," he'd joked with the other initiates, still receiving no response from the boy.

He was called Sultan, and he hailed from one of the desert tribes, near the Eclipse. Sultan hadn't told Alaric or the other initiatives who he was or what tribe he actually came from, but by his momentary rage at the "your majesty" comment, Alaric guessed that he was higher on the social chain than he liked to pretend.

"Ah well." Alaric shrugged. "Not my place to pry. Though I should try to get to know him better. If he's someone important, maybe I can get him to find me a way out of this place."

Pondering that, Alaric plucked away at the strings of his lute, much quieter this time.

AMARU
The Daughter of the Goddess

Amaru walked outside of the hut, feeling the dry sun's glow on her face. For just a moment, she prayed to Yamaria, her mother, for the bounties she granted her children, both blood and otherwise.

Bowl in hand, she hurried off toward the temple, where the elder priest Purell stored the medicinal supplies.

Within, Vienna was crouched over a book, studying the words intently. Her pale lips mouthed the words, trying to commit them to memory. Hearing Amaru enter, the frail girl looked up and smiled respectfully. "Milady, anyway I could be of service?"

Amaru was already rooting through the barrels of supplies, which she knew almost as well as Vienna. "I just need the medicine for Chief Durrigan again."

The girl's face became more solemn, and she nodded, allowing Amaru to use what she needed. Taking her gathered supplies, she began mashing the herbs into a paste, adding the bitter restorative juices from a couple of plants.

"And if you could spare a little bit of water. His fever was so high, and I'd like to give him some relief."

Vienna could hear the concern in the woman's voice. Durrigan had raised Amaru like a mother usually would, and the two were very close. The apprentice priest nodded and ran off to a dark storage room in the basement, returning, more slowly, with a bowl of the cool liquid.

Amaru thanked the girl and returned to the hut, going as fast as she could without spilling the water.

Old Durrigan was lying on his cot, a thin blanket over his shivering body. He moaned quietly, but when he heard the flap move, the chief stopped. Amaru smiled sadly. Durrigan didn't want anyone thinking he was weak, but everyone knew that he was dying. Purell predicted that before the end of this century, he'd be sleeping in the dunes.

His hair, once chestnut brown, had gone steely gray by the time Amaru was born. Now it was wispy and white. His eyes stared milkily up at the woman as she plunged a rag into the water and spread it over his forehead. "You are too good to me, Amaru," he sighed in relief.

"I wish I could do more." Tears glazed her eyes as she looked down at the man who had adopted and cared for her. Amaru spooned the medicine into the chief's mouth, who took the bitter paste without complaint.

"Don't cry for me." So weak was his voice. So strained with pain. "You'll waste the water!"

Despite herself, a bubble of laughter escaped Amaru's throat.

"See, much better. Now go," Durrigan commanded. "Go outside and see your friends. I know you'd work yourself ragged for me, but I'm sure I won't die without you tending me for an hour or two, and you should never neglect your friends."

Amaru nodded reluctantly and moved the bowl of water over so that the old chief could soak his rag when it dried, as soon it would. The girl planted a kiss on Durrigan's flushed cheek and left the hut.

Blowing sand stuck to the wet spots on her face, where tears had streamed. As they evaporated, Amaru's head cleared. Looking out over her sandy home, over the simple but effective shelters her people used to survive, she felt nothing but pride. "We are surely a strong race that we can make a living out here in the Scorched Waste. Only a daring few people attempt coming here by choice. Those who are brave enough to face such struggle deserve the greatest respect."

As she walked, people called out to her, and she responded warmly, putting the old chieftain out of her mind, as he'd instructed.

The tribe had flourished in the past decades, and Fyroxi milled around, completing chores, fixing their homes, or just talking.

When it came to her, the Fyroxi of clan Fire-Striders had a few mindsets. Most were kind to her, even to the point of reverence, seeing the station and circumstances of her birth. Amaru tried to deflect most of their praise. She knew well that she was Yamaria's own blood, but she only wanted to be seen as any other Fyroxi was. Many of the girls claimed they wanted to be like her, including Vienna. They were all Yamaria's children, were the Fyroxi race, and Amaru tried to get her fellow tribe folk to understand that. They all had the same blood and were all the same. Of course, the fact that she'd appeared among the other kits without a mother to physically give birth to her made that hard to get across.

Some were envious of her, which she understood. She had no desire to steal the spotlight, but in such a small group, being the child of a goddess made her stick out like a sore thumb. Amaru forgave those who tried to swindle or beguile her, understanding that the desire for approval and power drove many men and women, especially in this dangerous environment, where extra skills or allies could mean everything.

And then there were the few that treated her like she was just a normal Fyroxi, even through the respectful deference. Amaru loved these people fiercely. She'd grown up with many of them, and for them, she knew she would give up everything. Lazy Xio, curious Ren, adventurous little Daru, and the half-blood Lily. Lily had been born out of a union between a Fyroxi and one of the Water Callers, who often visited to deliver supplies. If there was anything that Amaru was most proud of, it was her work with elder Copernicus and Ren solidifying the relationship between the relief team and her tribe.

Amaru knew from the elders that the helpful Water Callers had always looked on with pity, even as they came to help with the starving tribe. After the slaughter of the Fyroxi during the Eclipse War, many expected the remaining tribes to dwindle into nothing. But by sheer determination and some level of stubbornness, Amaru believed the tribes Fire-Strider and Bush-Walker had held on. However, the real turning point for the Water Callers was once she'd gotten involved. When the relief team learned that she was the daughter of Yamaria, that the Fyroxi's salvation had finally come, they had been much more eager to help.

Amaru didn't blame them for their hesitance because nobody, not even the most helpful of folks, wanted to risk wasting resources on a dying people. But to have the chance to meet the girl known as the Sun Mother's child had reaffirmed their belief that there was hope for the Fyroxi race. Many of them were glad, as their ancestors had been close allies to the Fyroxi, both outside the desert and in. And not a single person wanted to risk losing the wondrous people.

During her walk, Amaru came upon Lily herself. She was a fair number of years younger than Amaru and looked up to the older girl, both physically and mentally. Both her Fyroxi and human heritage showed strong in her features. Her tail was shorter than that of her year mates and her ears more rounded, but as far as Amaru was concerned, she was still Fyroxi.

A number of "true" Fyroxi had taken offense to Lily's birth, viewing it as a marring of the pure blood of an already-failing race. She'd held her tongue at the time, but she longed to tell them that the joining of races might be for the best. Most Fyroxi lived in the more moderate temperatures outside of the Scorched Waste where the aptly named Fire-Striders had been forced into. If the elements kept taking their toll on the proud race, they would go extinct, just as the Water Callers feared.

Either way, the human blood inside Lily's veins had granted her the adaptability the race was known for. She had fought back astoundingly well against the sicknesses that threatened to take her, and the heat hadn't killed her yet.

Mixed blood may save our kind yet, Amaru thought. *I just have to get to the point where I can convince the others.* Perhaps she would have to lead by example, but the girl didn't want to jump hastily into a relationship just to prove a point.

Lily was always happy to converse with Amaru, and while the older girl searched for her other friends, they spoke. "…And then Daru said, 'Hey, check this thing that I found,' and he pulled out a perfectly round stone. Father told me that it's one of those stones flat enough that Humans use for skipping across the lakes!" She said the last word as if it was foreign to her, which it was. "I wonder what it would be like to have enough water that you could swim in it!" Her eyes filled with wonder at the thought.

Amaru smiled sadly at the younger girl. Lily's father was always telling her tales of the places outside the desert. When Lily grew up, she would probably end up traveling, to see these wonderful sounding places. Especially this lake, which Amaru wished she could imagine. The oases that the Water Callers made their bases in contained more water than most any of the desert residents would see in their life. That thought made her sad, knowing the number of deaths dehydration caused each year. The water with which she'd treated Durrigan this morning was so very precious, and it would cost others dearly if she tried to do that too often.

Just then, her eyes slid over to a nearby tent, where a group of older boys was leaning and talking. One of them seemed to lead the conversation. He had dirty blond hair; and his tails and ears were a mixture of gray, black, and brown.

Her own two tails curled at the sight of him.

"Amaru?" Lily asked. "What's wrong?" She followed the older girl's gaze. "Oh," Lily growled in understanding.

The young woman considered turning around, but it was too late, for the boy had seen her.

Saying something to his friends that made them laugh, he called out to her. "Hey, Amaru!" He strode over, his steps confident if a little wobbly. Lily was standing a little bit in front of Amaru, and the man gave her a disdainful look, nudging her to the side with a foot. "Move, you filthy half-blood."

Lily looked up at the older girl, who just nodded and whispered, "I'll take care of him. Get yourself somewhere safe." The little girl scampered off with a worried glance at Amaru.

Amaru forced a smile to her face. "Leif, how are you?" She fought the urge to slap him for his words to the half-Fyroxi.

"I am doing just fantastic!" Leif slurred. "Even better now that you're here."

"Oh, is that so?" Her voice was sweet and deferential. She knew the beast that slumbered within him.

"Without a doubt. You know, my friends and I were just talking about you." Leif gestured to the men leaning against the tent pole.

Amaru saw their hands move toward belt pouches and watched dry rations change hands. *Some sort of wager? What could they be betting on?*

"It must be fate that led you here."

"If you must know, I was looking for my friends," Amaru replied tersely, getting an uneasy feeling about this whole situation.

"Well, you found me." Leif practically sauntered as he drew nearer.

Amaru found herself backing up at a pace even with his. Trying to buy time, she decided to continue his conversation. "What about me were you talking about with your friends?"

"Oh, wouldn't you be interested to hear?" he drawled.

Not really, she thought. "Nothing would interest me more" was what she said instead.

"Well, since it's so important to you..." He tried to come closer again, but Amaru just kept on the reverse. He worked a different angle, and still, she thwarted him. Or so she thought. Her movement ceased when she backed into something hard. He'd maneuvered her right up against a tree. A short, stunted dry thing, with branches reaching into the skies like claws. One strong arm barred her escape. She was trapped. In that instant, she knew where this conversation was going, and it scared her. "Sweet Amaru, you are so beautiful. Half the men in this tribe would do anything for a night with our goddess's own blood."

She regarded him, trying to mask the anger and fear in her eyes. "What a startling revelation. I thank you for that information. If you'll excuse me, however, I must go tend to the chief. The sickness still has a firm hold on him." Amaru would give almost anything to get out of this situation.

"So eager to escape back to his tent," Leif clucked. "Does *he* honestly give you so much *pleasure*? Oh, wait, of course not," the man corrected. "You're still perfectly pure, aren't you? Don't worry, he'll soon be dead, and there will be nothing left to distract you from what really matters." His tone left no question in Amaru's mind that he was referring to himself at the end.

She flushed angrily as the early insinuations sunk in. "That is our chief you are speaking of! Show some respect for once in your life!"

"Respect? For him? Amaru, I'm a warrior. I don't respect cowards." Before she could answer, he put up a hand and continued. "During the Eclipse War, which of the Fyroxi tribes didn't fight? Fire-Striders, that's who."

She had heard the story from Durrigan many times before. "He had guidance from Yamaria! What he did rescued our people, who even then were hungry and weak, from certain death!"

"And why do you think that is?" he countered, still smirking. "Because he was too afraid to bring his people to a place where they could get food. *It wouldn't be safe enough.* Pah, we used to be a proud warrior race. One that *never* backed down in the face of danger. The tribe will be better off without him. And I hope that the next chieftain is better than him."

This time, when Amaru spoke, there was no hiding the fire or the venom. "You really are a vile man, Leif Kalix. You would do well to pray to Yamaria for forgiveness."

"Oh, trust me. I often pray to your dear mother."

Amaru found that hard to believe. Leif was never at the morning worship services on Sunday, nor did he keep a shrine to the Sun Mother in his hut. "Don't lie to Yamaria's own daughter. It could get you somewhere you don't want." She abhorred lording over people with her heritage, but in this case, she thought it necessary.

His hand crossed his heart in a solemn oath. "I wouldn't dream of it. There is only one place that I want to see you. And therein lies my prayers." Leif licked his lips. "Of course, I've still received no sign of her taking action. I pray every day." He leaned in closer until Amaru could smell the booze on his breath. Alcohol was very rare, like most liquids, only to be used during special events. The dull spark of anger at his wastefulness was quickly overcome by his next words. "And yet here you still stand, denying me."

That is what he prays for? She was appalled by the thought and shivered to prove it. "You presume to have some sort of claim on me?"

"I don't claim anything. I know *exactly* what I have on you. And I have proof." One hand moved toward her hair, as if to stroke it. Her arm flashed up protectively, playing right into his desire. With a cold grin, his hand twisted and grabbed her wrist. She was locked in his steel grip. He pulled her hand under his shirt and moved it down his side, right over the long, raised scar that ran down his chest and abdomen.

All the vehement heat fled her body, as memories of that day only five years ago played in her head. The day they'd both almost died and the one that made Leif what he was today. It had proved to him that even things that were supposed to be stronger than most mortals could be defeated. Amaru still recalled the dull gleam of the sun on scales the color of sand, the leathery flap of small wings, not yet strong enough to fly. The gnashing of sharp teeth and snapping of a barbed tail. And the fear. The wyrm's gaze had frozen Amaru's feet in place. But Leif hadn't been affected, his arrogance and pride allowing him to fly in the face of certain death.

At the end of the fight with that horrifying creature, the other members of their gathering party were dead. Leif had driven off the awful beast but received a nearly mortal wound in return. Back then, he'd been more altruistic. Still a little arrogant, of course, but nobody was perfect. Amaru and he had been friends and often found themselves on the same gathering parties. Amaru thought that a little strange, given that those were supposed to be random draw, but never before had she questioned it.

After he was healed, however, everything changed. The magic Yamaria had seen to put in her blood was the only reason Leif was still alive today, but Leif refused to believe that. He'd rather believe that he'd saved her life, and the healing had been only the first installment of his proper reward. After that day, his heroic antics got to his head.

And see where that's led us? She knew he was moving closer, could feel his hot breath on her neck. Cold fear dripped down her back.

Her mind suggested running, but her feet wouldn't comply. *Even if I did try to run, it would be a fruitless effort*, Amaru thought fearfully. *He's stronger and faster than me. I would be completely at his mercy.* She shivered, not wanting to think about what was to come. Leif had likely been plotting this for a long time, but Amaru had kept her friends around her. Now the boy had his chance to strike and take what he desired.

But luck was with her that day, and a voice angrily peeped behind Leif. "Get your hands off of her!"

Leif barely even turned around. "Go away, twerp. Amaru and I have some private business to finish."

"I'm warning you, Leif, if you hurt her, I will hurt you," the voice growled. Amaru detected only the slightest quiver.

Leif rounded on the interrupting person; his tone was low and dangerous. "No, boy. *I'm* warning *you*. Give me a reason to attack you!"

Amaru craned her neck to see the other person, and her breath caught in her throat. A short, wiry, brown-haired Fyroxi stood in front of Leif, his hands balled into fists. *Ren! Goddess, please no!* she prayed. She wasn't used to hearing her curious friend angry and hadn't recognized his voice. Leif stood over a head taller than Ren, and his muscular frame put the smaller boy to shame.

Ren gritted his teeth and took a step forward. "Back off now!"

"What are you going to do if I don't?" Leif taunted. "Throw one of your pouches at me? Hmm, Trinket?"

Suddenly, Ren slipped into fox form, snarling. Leif laughed and did the same. The second Fyroxi absolutely dwarfed Ren. His multicolored pelt rippled with sinewy muscles. His teeth and claws were sharp and hard, honed by countless days of hunting and training. The two stood their ground and growled at each other, two tails whipping in the air. Amaru knew that if this fight started in earnest, Ren would be left broken physically, and mentally *if* he survived.

Finally finding strength in her legs, Amaru positioned herself between the two fighting boys and threw her arms wide. "Stop it, both of you!" she cried. "Leif, if you want to harm Ren, you'll have to go through me first."

Leif gnarred as if considering it, before looking up to see the small crowd that had gathered, looking on in a mix of confusion and horror. *What must they see now?* They wouldn't have heard the conversation between her and Leif, though some might have seen his movements toward her. Finally, Leif backed off. He took a moment to shift out of fox form and pushed Amaru to the side roughly. He got right in Ren's fox face. "You're damn lucky that I'm not about to hurt Amaru. Don't want to ruin her beauty. Besides, I'm sure she understands that we'll end up together one way or another." Ren bristled at that. "But get in my way again, and I will not hesitate to rip you apart." Leif stalked off, and Amaru heard faint snickering sounds, as his friends laughed at his failure.

Ren, who had also slipped back into humanoid shape, approached Amaru carefully. "Are you all right? Did he hurt you?" Amaru reached out and slapped him. Not too hard, just enough to sting. "Ow! Hey, what was that for?"

"You could have gotten yourself killed; that's what!" she cried.

"What would you have me do?" Ren asked, a little heat in his voice. "Stand back and watch him…watch him do what he was going to do to you? Not a chance in Moonwatch!"

Amaru suddenly pulled Ren into a fierce hug.

"Oh," he managed to get out, and she could practically hear him blushing.

Leif was right about one thing. Half the boys in this village had a crush on her, and Ren was no exception. At least none of the others were like Leif had become. Amaru still had fond memories of the Trial of Blades, a competition between the desert tribes where Leif had competed many times. At the seemingly most inopportune times, Leif would turn his head to smile charmingly at her and then still manage to defeat his opponent, sometimes not even looking back at them. Was that Leif gone, never to return? She released Ren from the hug, and he sat back, studying her eyes.

"Are you sure everything's all right, Amaru? You look like you saw a ghost."

The fading vestiges of her memory of the fateful day flared up once more, pulling a slight shudder from her spine. A thought came unbidden. *I should have let him die that day. Then he wouldn't have turned out like this.* She immediately regretted the thought and sent a fervent prayer to Yamaria for forgiveness. "I'll be fine. I'm just a little shaken, is all."

"Understandably so," Ren commented before sighing. "Man, I always liked the nickname Trinket. Now it's just going to have a sour ring to it."

Amaru allowed herself to laugh at the contrast between their worries. "Only if you let it," she replied. "Be careful of him, but besides that, don't pay Leif any mind."

Ren shook his head. "I don't know how you can stay so calm after he almost just…" He gulped, unable to finish the sentence. "Anyway, I'm glad that Lily found me in time. I ran as fast as I could. If anything happened to you—"

"If he'd tried anything further, I'd have screamed, and the other tribe members would have stopped him." Amaru said this confidently but didn't know whether her vocal cords would have cooperated, or the tribe. Many of them revered her and didn't want to see her hurt, but nearly the same number of them were terrified of the dangerous, violent Leif. Not that she planned to tell this to Ren. She was the daughter of the goddess, there to support the Fire-Striders. She had to be strong. Or at least be able to put on a brave show.

Durrigan had told her that he had to play that part regularly in his time as chieftain. "Showing weakness and indecision often isn't an option for a leader," he'd said. "If your people don't think that you are confident and equal to the tasks set before you, you won't last long."

"Anyway," Ren said, "I wanted to come to talk to you before."

Glad for the change in subject, Amaru nodded and smiled at him. "What about?"

"When I was out doing my gathering"—he hesitated a moment—"I saw something." He got up and began walking, Amaru close behind. "I tried to tell Xio but—"

"Sleeping?"

"Yeah." He laughed nervously. "She's probably still there now. And if I saw what I thought I did, then I'm worried for her and every-one in the tribe."

As Ren had expected, they found Xio over near the outskirts of the village. She was curled up in fox form next to a bush, making use of the minuscule piece of shade it provided. Her light-yellow pelt glistened in the sun, as her body rose and fell in the midst of sleep. As the two approached, her long ears perked and swiveled. She looked up sleepily and let out a wide yawn. "Oh, hey, guys," Xio said when she saw them. "How's it going?" Her big brown eyes blinked a few times, trying to clear the grogginess.

They had decided not to worry her with the story about Leif. Not that Xio was likely to try doing anything about it, lazy as she was. But it was better to be safe than sorry. Leif had a particular sort of contempt for the lackadaisical, and Amaru feared what would happen to her sweet friend if Leif decided to get even. *I'm going to have to check up on them more often.*

Amaru squatted and scratched Xio behind the ears, the other girl's head inclining and eyes squinting in pleasure. "Everything is going as well as usual."

"That's good to hear. Ooh, a little to the left, back a bit. Oh, that feels *good*," Xio purred. Amaru laughed, already feeling much better.

"So did you just come to give my head a scratch, or was there something you wanted to talk about?" Xio was awake now but chose to remain in her fox form, allowing the sun to keep soaking into her fur.

Amaru turned to Ren, who nodded and drew closer. "As I was telling Amaru before we got here, I saw something outside the village borders, and it has me a bit worried."

"Was it a large creature of any sort?" Amaru asked, worried about another attack like the one five years ago. "With scales and wings?"

"No, nothing like that but definitely more mysterious." He pulled out a sharp stick from one of the many pouches slung around his body. Ren liked to collect things that he found and was always searching for new unknown items. "I don't know what I saw exactly since I only caught a glimpse from a distance. But there were two figures. One of them looked like a muscular human, dressed in really dark clothing, not a smart idea in the desert mind you. The other was more animal-like and stood on all fours like we do in fox form." He gestured to Xio as an example. "The only thing is it was huge! Like it came up to the man's chest."

That made both Amaru and Xio blink in worry. Even in fox form, which grew to a substantial size, the largest Fyroxi's body only made it to an average man's waist! Their tails billowed far upward, but those were more for display than anything.

Ren used his stick to draw a crude image of the figure he had seen. It wasn't easy to tell what it was, but still, Amaru got a bad feeling about it. The inkling didn't seem to come from anything she'd seen or experienced, but either way, it was there.

"It could be something, or it could be nothing," she said, biting back the uneasiness. "I'll bring this up with Chief Durrigan." She favored Ren with a smile. "Thank you. For everything."

Xio wasn't sure what had happened between them but shrugged. Whatever it happened to be, it was their business. She knew that Ren was attracted to Amaru; it was unmistakable in the way he looked at her. Maybe, just maybe, he was getting closer to what he wanted. For some reason, that thought bothered her. She dismissed it, sighed, and looked up at the sky. Elder Silque wasn't expecting her until sunfall. She had a few more hours to go. Part of her wanted to follow Ren and Amaru, but the warm sand felt lovely. Settling down beside the bush once more, Xio fell promptly back asleep.

*****

Amaru bid farewell to Ren and returned to Chief Durrigan's hut. The old man was sitting up, a vulture feather pillow propping him up.

There was a cup of water in his hand, which he sipped with the reverence of someone who had lived in the desert for many centuries. Amaru smiled to see him looking so healthy. For a little while, she could almost convince herself that Durrigan wasn't dying.

"Child, how are you?" His voice was still weak and quiet, but at least the cough had died down. "How was your morning out of the hut?"

She hesitated a moment, not sure if she wanted to trouble him with the first of the news. But Durrigan noticed the pause and beckoned her closer. "What happened, young one?"

Unable to keep up her strong front any longer, she broke down and told him the whole story. When she was done, his surprisingly strong hands were rubbing her shoulders while the hot tears she had restrained came pouring out.

"Oh, child," he growled deep in his throat. "I swear, there is no respect in that boy. I'll see that Sigmund hears about this. Next time, he'll think twice before he tries to forcefully deflower a girl before her first century."

Her first century. She remembered just how close she was. Only a few more months now. And once she hit that milestone, she'd be eligible to join the women working to bolster the tribe's numbers, the mothers. One of the last things that Leif had said stuck in her mind: "We'll end up together one way or another." They would both soon be viable mating partners. What union would make a better pair than the child of Yamaria and one of the strongest warriors the tribe had? *No, I'll refuse. I'll never do that with him.* Another voice piped up in her subconscious. *You know you won't give yourself that luxury. You'll do what's best for the tribe, whether you like it or not.* Amaru shook these thoughts from her head. She would deal with that when the time came.

"You mentioned Ren seeing something?" Durrigan asked after silence had stretched for a while.

Amaru allowed her mind to clear and brought back the images that Ren had drawn. "Yes, he said it looked like a burly man and a massive dog, searching for something in the sands. When he tried to approach them, ask if he could do anything for them, they turned away and left," she explained what Ren had told her on the walk home.

"That is distressing to hear, for certain sure." Durrigan scratched at his chin.

Amaru drew a cruder image than Ren had managed of the canine and showed it to the elder. He took it, and his hand clenched. "What's wrong?"

44

He released the tension from his arm and sighed. "Nothing I need to worry you with now. I don't wish to cause trouble over a mere hunch. I'll talk to Silque about this and get back to you."

Amaru was concerned about his avoidance of the subject but decided to trust the chief. Durrigan had seen almost four hundred years more than she, and his head was filled with wisdom.

Something else that Leif had said came back to her at that moment. "Sir, when Leif spoke about you avoiding the Eclipse War, what did he mean?"

Durrigan sighed. "More things that he doesn't quite understand. Did I want to go to war? No. I knew my people were starved and weakened, but I didn't choose to not fight. Had the king commanded it, the Fire-Striders would have been the first ones on that field."

"So what happened? Why weren't you in the front ranks?"

"At the king's command, of course. His advisor Cassian knew our plight, having visited our tribe many a time. He gave the king his advice, and Algrith listened." Durrigan sighed. "King Algrith Redwyn was a good man."

Amaru felt there was something buried in that comment. "What about the current king?"

Durrigan met her eyes. "Well, he's a man."

EMERY
Royal Pains

Princess Emery Redwyn stood outside the door to her father's council room, straining to hear what was going on inside. The large gilded doors muffled all sounds, allowing her only fragments of conversation, most of it in raised voices. Emery looked around fervently. Her father didn't like her snooping around, but she couldn't help it. *I need to know what's happening in my father's kingdom. I think I deserve at least that much.* She still had her own friends to tell her what was happening, and she hung on to their every word. Leonidas in particular. Tears welled up in her eyes, and it took everything she had to blink them back. "Where are you, Leo?" Her brave knight and protector, Sir Leonidas, had left Emery to lead a campaign against some bandits, terrorizing the desert folk. He claimed it would be a simple mission, though all missions could be dangerous. He said he would return as soon as possible. His scheduled return date was one week ago, and Emery missed him terribly. He was part of the reason she now stood with her ear to the council room, hoping to hear some news of her dear knight.

Emery silently cursed the makers of this castle for the thick walls and doors. They were impressive and beautifully made, yes, but they made listening in nearly impossible.

Finally, it seemed the meeting was at an end. That much was plain by the sound of slamming books and the loud yell of "And good riddance!" by some unknown speaker. *What could that be about?* she wondered.

Emery scrambled out of the way, as not to be crushed by the doors. She watched as a group of angry men stormed past her. A couple of younger boys at the end noticed her and bowed respectfully. *Pages probably. Must have been fun to sit in on that meeting.*

Once the last men had left, Emery strode purposefully into the room.

The ceilings in this part of the castle were high, supported by tall fluted columns that punctuated the room at precisely measured intervals. The stonemasons said that it had been built by Dwarves and Elves working together. "No other way it could be so flawless!" Emery saw the sense in their statements. A couple of areas had been added on in more recent times, and the differences were apparent. Even master human stonemasons couldn't get the blocks to lay as flat, the seams to line up as perfectly. Her father sat in his place at the head of a huge roundtable. Tall chairs stood around it, set slightly askance.

They didn't even push in the chairs. Something must have left them quite angry. Even unhappy guests remembered to push in the chairs at risk of angering their lord. A petty thing, she agreed, but sometimes one needed something small to be angry about.

Emery's father didn't even notice her when she entered, so the princess took a moment to look him over. King Godfrey Redwyn had once been an impressive man, to hear the bards and see the paintings: muscular with a chiseled chin, a fiery red mane and beard, and eyes that could strike fear into the hearts of his political rivals.

Age and royalty had stolen much of that from him. His once-tight stomach now sagged, showing a fondness for alcohol and large banquets. His hair was mostly gray, with a few patches of red for accent. And his eyes had gone soft, crow's-feet sticking from their corners. They showed none of the clarity that Emery remembered as a child.

Just then, he seemed to notice her standing there. "Ah, Emery," he said sadly, massaging his temples. "Were you listening again?"

Emery nodded, uncowed by nervousness or embarrassment.

"I wish you wouldn't, my daughter," he sighed. "Some things aren't for your ears."

"I wish you would keep me informed." She kept her tone pointed, but without heat. "I *will* be queen one day, and I need to know the kingdom. If you keep me out of the loop, how will I ever make an effective ruler?" She'd wanted to bring this up for so long, and now she had a chance to actually see her father. No time like the present.

Godfrey's head drooped, his beard touching his knees. "You're right, Emery." He hesitated. "I-I just wanted to protect you. The politics of the kingdom can be ruthless."

Emery approached and lay a consoling hand on his shoulder. "I am a woman grown now, Father," she countered. "I won't go hiding under the table at some veiled threat from a nose-in-the-air, stick-up-the-rear nobleman." She borrowed a line from a favorite poem of hers, written by a famous elvish bard.

That pulled a laugh from him. A deep chortle that made his stomach shake. "That's very good to hear," the king thought for a moment. "I suppose it is about time. You can join me at our next meeting if you so choose. It might be good to have another person on my side during a debate. Lightstrider Casinius is stoic and a stout ally, but his social skills are severely lacking."

"Thank you, Father!" Emery was elated; it felt good to finally have even this small victory. She wondered briefly why her father had taken so long to come around to this decision but thought better than to press the matter. "Since I will be getting a bit more involved, perhaps you can start by telling me what this last meeting included. They seemed rather upset."

"Yes, I suppose it's only right that I explain that much to you," he sighed. "That was Sardan Rainclaw. He had a few offers and a few criticisms to pass my way."

"Rainclaw," Emery pondered. "He runs one of the taverns in the central ward, correct?"

King Godfrey looked mildly surprised that she knew. "Yes, in fact, he does. A prevalent one called Cynderstone. Gives significant contributions to the crown and its events. Well, 'gave' is actually the proper word for it now."

"What happened? What insult was Rainclaw given to drive him from us?"

Her father snorted in a very unkingly manner. "To hear him speak, many. But chiefly on his mind was your little brother."

Emery sighed. "What did Grayson do this time?"

"Apparently, he was terrorizing one of Rainclaw's youngest daughters."

Emery's reply caught in her throat. "Which daughter?" She was close friends with the twins. If Grayson had gotten on the wrong one's side, Emery didn't want to think about it.

"The better-tempered girl, luckily," the king replied. "Sardan gave me some choice words about parenting and then proceeded to offer the other twin's hand in marriage to Grayson, as a truce."

"And?"

"I refused." Godfrey sounded exceptionally pleased with himself.

"No wonder he was so angry!" Emery was shocked. "Father, Sardan Rainclaw has a lot of sway in this city! People of all ranks drink from his casks. Alienating him was not a wise idea."

"Well, I certainly wasn't going to marry my son off to a black witch! Especially not a commoner black witch. I'll find him a proper wife, of noble family, and a good reputation."

Emery groaned. *Father had made a terrible mistake.* She vowed to talk to Grayson and then to the sisters. Perhaps it wasn't too late to make amends. "Anything else?" She was afraid to hear what other things her father had said.

"No, that's all that meeting was about. However, there is something we should discuss around a similar topic."

"And what might that be?" Emery wasn't sure she liked where that was going.

"As you said, you are a woman grown, almost eighteen," Godfrey pointed out. "It's time we started to discuss your marriage."

The princess's eyes widened in alarm. "Father, no! Please I-I'm not ready for marriage yet."

Her father looked shocked. "Correct me if I'm mistaken, but I've never seen you interested in a man. Is that why you don't want to get married?"

Of course, you wouldn't know what man I'm interested in. You've been absent in your children's lives for so long. "Please, Father. It's not that, and you should know it. But could we wait a little longer? There is something I need to know before I am ready to give my hand away."

Godfrey shook his head regretfully. "I've managed to make myself a few enemies within the court and city. I will need strong allies, and a marriage pact is one of the best ways to secure that," he sighed. "It will take me time to find a suitable match for you. You have until then to get your matter sorted out. Am I understood?"

"Yes, Father." Emery nodded meekly, feeling sick in her stomach. "Has there been any news about Sir Leonidas?"

Godfrey Redwyn's mouth thinned as he answered. "Nothing whatsoever. I fear that if no report comes soon, we may have to pronounce him dead. It's unfortunate; he was such a formidable knight. It will be hard to fill his gap."

On one thing we agree, the princess thought. "Will you send out people to find him?"

Godfrey hesitated. "If he hasn't returned, then I would assume that he is likely dead. I see no point in wasting resources to find a dead man."

"Father! He was my personal guardian *and* captain of the royal guard! If he's dead, he could have information on him that would be dangerous in the wrong hands!" Emery was shocked at the anger in her words, but it felt right.

"If he's dead, that information is already in someone else's hands." Not a hint of doubt colored the king's words.

"And you're just going to let it stay there, where it could lead to harm for people in the kingdom?" Emery asked with an accusatory stare. "It is only right for a king to seek to avenge someone important to the crown! And what if he's not dead and he returns? Would you hire a new captain of the guard, after Sir Leonidas has built up such trust with his men? Royal Defender is a position for life. You can't just strip Leonidas of that without being sure that he's not returning!"

"You sound so sure that he's alive, Emery," the king managed. "I wish I had your same conviction. Sending out men would mean less warriors here. I'd rather not do that."

She didn't answer, only glaring at him, her eyes impassioned and flaming in a way he'd rarely seen before. *I would know if something happened to him.* That was clear in her heart.

"You are dismissed, Emery," Godfrey said morosely. "We'll talk more about this later."

Emery knew that was his way of saying, "Drop it, I have no wish to speak of this." *He knows I'm right*, she thought angrily as she stormed out. Emery allowed herself to calm down slightly as she walked toward her brother's room, but she kept some of her inner fire ready, unsure what to expect from Grayson. *Our sigil is the phoenix. Our words "Never backing down, always rising from the ashes" remind us of our inner fire. Has your fire gone out, Father? Are you even a phoenix anymore?* The weight of the revelation slammed down upon her heart. That he would condemn Leo as dead before doing anything to try and save him or salvage his corpse at least bothered her. "He's not dead!" she reminded herself.

"Who's not dead, Emery?"

The princess looked up. She'd reached Grayson's chambers without even noticing it. "Brother." She curtsied.

Her younger brother chuckled at the motion. "No need to be so formal with me, Em. We're family."

"I apologize. I didn't mean to offend, brother," she offered, shaking off her previous thoughts.

"No offense here." He shrugged. Grayson looked much like her father must have at his age. His hair and beard were short and red, though a few shades deeper, russet rather than fire, as she'd inherited. His frame was stocky and muscular, as he spent most of his time out in the training yards with the knights.

Emery recalled watching Sir Leonidas sparring with her brother when they were both younger. Leo was always far more skilled at combat but would often pull his swings to give Grayson a chance. *Though he'd begged me not to reveal that,* she recalled fondly.

"Anyway, I'm sure you didn't just come here for the sake of seeing your brother. Do you need something?"

"Yes, actually. May I come in?"

He nodded and gestured to his bed. She sat down beside him. "I came here from Father. He ran into a tough spot with a citizen."

"Oh." Grayson's tone dropped enthusiasm, already knowing where this was going.

"Grayson, I heard briefly what happened the other day. I need you to tell me what's going on. Reyna is my close friend, and I don't want to lose her because you made a mistake." Emery's words were pointed, but she kept her tone soft.

"Fine. You want to know what happened? I tried to talk to a girl, and the ungrateful night kin rejected me." Grayson's voice was quiet, but Emery could hear the anger simmering underneath. Grayson had never been skilled at concealing his emotions.

She recalled that Grayson had been trying to become romantically involved for quite a while. His violent fits of anger tended to turn off possible suitors. "Explain everything to me, brother. If you offended Reyna, I may be able to salvage the crown's relationship with the family."

"You'd do that?"

She nodded, which seemed to loosen the binds he had on his lips. A long breath escaped from between them.

After a moment's hesitation, Grayson began his story. "I was at Cynderstone, having drinks with some of my friends from the sparring fields. We were laughing, joking, just having a good time, when the door opened and out walked Reyna." Grayson's eyes lit up as he thought about it. "In my half-drunk state, I mistook her for beautiful. She gave cheerful farewells to the patrons as she left for her classes or whatever she does over at the old alchemist's shop. My buddies goaded me on, and I was just buzzed enough to go for it, so I followed her out the door.

"I called out her name, and Reyna turned around, startled. Upon seeing me, she smiled and curtsied with all due respect. But it seemed rehearsed, amicable, but not close and friendly, like she was with you. My jumbled mind felt like trying to warm that formality up. I offered to escort her to her destination, but that seemed to make her uncomfortable," he rumbled deep in his throat. "She declined and said she had to leave, but I… I grabbed her arm before she got away." His fists clenched, and his breathing was growing more labored. "Reyna begged me to let go, said I was hurting her." His eyes burned, and he clenched his fist. "I tightened my grip and asked her to visit me at the palace when sunfall came. Strange and unnatural though she may be, I wanted her. But she shook like a little rabbit, refused me."

"Let me guess, you couldn't let her get the last word?" Emery supplied, appalled at how far her brother had tried to go.

"Of course not! I'll not be turned down by a creature who isn't even fully human!" Grayson's tone held full-on rage now. "Maybe I said a few things in bad taste, but she deserved it. A girl like her should be bloody appreciative when a royal asks for her time! Women of her type don't often get such good offers."

"Grayson!" Emery scolded. She was surprised to hear these words coming from his mouth. "Reyna is a fine woman. Just because she and her sister are different doesn't mean…"

"Oh, don't even get me started on her sister! I swear, I will kill that girl! She appeared out of nowhere and began to attack me from the shadows! Probably some sort of witchcraft, knowing her kind. Wouldn't be surprised if the other one was using some sort of charm to lure me in and cast me away for fun!"

"Brother, please calm down. You sound like a madman. Arcadia was only trying to protect her sister from a man getting too close for comfort." Emery rubbed her temples, hoping that Grayson's good sense might take over at some point. "As for Reyna, it was your drinks that charmed you, not any magic on her part. If you keep this sort of thing up, you'll soil your reputation, Grayson. I don't want to see you do that. I may be heir to the throne, but you are still a prince. You ought to start acting like one."

Grayson's mouth opened and closed furiously, unable to reply as Emery left the room. The princess wiped a hand down her face. *Today is going to be a long day, I can just tell.*

She composed herself. On the walk to where she expected to find her friends, she would be passing many people. She needed to have her best face on, push down her worries about her brother and about Leo. Her mother had taught her the ways of being a proper princess.

"Don't be closed off, but if you are upset, don't let them see it. People reflect the attitude they see from their rulers. If you show them sadness, they will be sad. Be honest and fair, and people will love you." The lessons and attention from her mother had likely saved her from becoming like Grayson, so prone to anger.

Emery walked out into the warm sunlight, onto the stone streets of Searstar, the capital city of Sun's Reach. The pulsing flame in the sky shone down onto her, and she smiled. The light washed over her fiery red hair, which looked to be aflame, and her pale skin. It glittered on the small ruby phoenix brooch around her neck and the silk of her orange gown. Seeing her walk down the steps, the people stopped to watch, breaking off their conversations. She waved politely to everyone, smiling an honest and beautiful smile. Nobles watched her from all sides; the castle ward was always stocked with people of higher class.

Nobody troubled Emery as she traveled through the Castle Ward; she was not an infrequent visitor. When she crossed into the Central Ward, a few commoners were thrown into the mix. They bowed respectfully at her, a few coming to her, kneeling and wishing her good health. It was not hard to smile around these people. While nobles might look on with disdain at the stunning princess, the commoners bore her no ill will. Though most of her time was spent in the Castle Ward, she would often make time to come here. Another lesson from her mother popped into her head. "When a noble sees a royal, their thoughts are of their desire for the seat, so they smile to think of themselves in that position," the queen had explained. "Most low-class people, however, know they will never reach your level. They can be envious, but most are genuine in their respect."

A few beggars sat to the side of the streets, waving their hands along with the rest. They grinned as Emery slipped a silver into their hands. "Praise Yamaria, that she would make such a generous princess as Emery Redwyn," she heard them say.

Finally, she reached the place she was looking for. A small wooden building kept in repair by apprentices. Hanging from a peg above the door was a sign bearing the emblem of a round shield being used as a bowl, green herbs mashed within it. Emery asked her guards to await her outdoors, insisting they stand in the shade, as she'd be awhile. Emery opened the door, and her nose was hit by the mixture of odors from a multitude of crushed herbs. Sour smells as well as sweet wafted through the air, creating layers which the princess walked through as she approached the desk.

"How may I help ye?" asked the short figure sitting at the desk.

"Good morning to you, Berdur," Emery said, curtsying.

The man's face broke into a kindly smile. "Ah, Princess, it soothes an old dwarf's soul to hear your voice again. Been awhile since you last stopped in."

Berdur Longshield, the proprietor of the Shield and Pestle, was a dwarf who moved to Searstar after learning of the city's need for a good apothecary. Unlike many of his race, he'd picked up the herb clippers rather than the hammer. In doing so, he disproved the belief that Dwarves could only forge, fight, and drink well. A talented old man, he'd been working in his trade for hundreds of years and, since the loss of the magical gifts, had become known as the best healer in Searstar, if not the kingdom. Even when blindness took him in his old age, he was only slightly affected. Having worked with potions and herbs for so long, he could brew most things without his eyes.

"I apologize for the delay." She went to curtsy again, before remembering that he couldn't see. "I have been held up with recent business in the castle."

"Perfectly understandable, Princess. I'm kept plenty busy myself, with all the customers I've had. Amazing, you cure the queen of a common cold, and now everyone wants your aid with every little problem." Berdur laughed gruffly. "I have more gold now than I could count!"

"I'm glad to hear that your business is doing well." Emery patted the dwarf on the shoulder and looked around, assuring there was nobody else around. "Are the twins in the back?"

"I figured you didn't just come to chitchat with an old-timer," Berdur sighed. "But yes, they are in the usual spot."

Emery passed through the shop and went around the corner to an inconspicuous-looking door. She knew that it led to an alleyway and eventually a dark plaza. It was here that the Rainclaw twins spent most of their time. As she started to walk, she heard a mystical sound. Coming closer, she listened as it quickly stopped.

"Someone's coming," a low voice said. "If anything happens, I'll take care of them."

Emery smiled and continued walking. It was good that the sisters were so cautious. A trait that would doubtlessly keep their secret hidden.

Suddenly, as she passed through the place where the alley met the plaza, she was greeted with bright light. Emery was wise to this trick, covering her eyes, to save them from any pain or damage.

A sigh of relief went through the room as the inhabitants saw her.

"It's just the princess," the low voice said. "You're safe, Reyna."

From behind the barrels, Reyna stepped, smiling widely. "Emery! I am so glad to see you!" The two girls embraced lovingly. Reyna was like the sister that Emery never had. It didn't matter to the princess that the girl was common born. Nor did it matter that she wasn't human.

Though their parents and eldest sister were full-blooded Humans, Reyna and Arcadia had come out of the womb a little different than most. Where her family was known for white skin and a tendency to tan rather than burn, these two had abnormal coloration. They had the same dark brown hair, but their heads were also crowned by horns, and long slender tails reached out from their backs, curling around their feet while at rest.

By some phenomenon which none in the family or out could explain, the twins were born as Khindre: half devils.

As a rule, the rare Khindre were distrusted, nobody knowing what their infernal heritage might lead them to do. Sardan and Cos Rainclaw had come under fire when they were born and were told to destroy them before they grew up into monsters. But the Rainclaws had refused to murder children, no matter their race. They decided to try and raise the children right. It worked for one of them.

As shown by her friendly display, Reyna had taken well to her parents' teachings and, despite her appearance, was well loved by the people of the ward. Arcadia, on the other hand, had a reputation for a dark mood, and even her own parents remained suspicious, casting her out of the house as soon as allowed. Arcadia had few friends— Berdur, Emery, and her sisters making up the number.

But if Reyna was well loved, why was it that she had to hide out down here in a dark alleyway? Partially, it was so that she could be with her twin sister. With Arcadia's bad reputation, it wasn't wise for the good girl to be seen with her. But that wasn't all. There was something else that they needed to hide, some other trait that had come with their appearance.

The twin sisters could do magic.

Among the races of Sun's Reach, the division of the land had been given the name the Eclipse, like the event itself. This wasn't just to signify the blocking but also the darkness that had fallen upon all magic. With the betrayal of the wizards only one hundred years ago, there was no telling how people would react to two children born with the power to command spell craft. And the fact that it had appeared in Khindre would only give the world less reason to trust them. The twins had hidden their powers from most everyone but their parents and practiced out in the back of Berdur's shop. The old dwarf had been alive when magic was around and trusted the girls not to cause problems.

Emery pulled back from the embrace and looked at her friend. For a moment, she didn't blame Grayson for his infatuation with the girl. Reyna was gorgeous. Her skin was a vibrant sunset orange, her eyes globes of gold. The horns wrapped halfway around her head, looking nothing quite so much like a delicate tiara. The subtle curve of her lips and the sweet smile that liked to play across them only added to her beauty. All this combined with her gentle curves and ample frame made Reyna glorious to behold. The princess looked down at her arms. "Are you all right, Reyna?" she asked. "I heard what happened with my brother."

Reyna cast her eyes down. "I'm fine. A little scared, but nothing more than a bruising." She rolled up her sleeve to reveal a nasty purple ring around her wrist.

Looks like a painful bracelet, Emery thought, flinching. "I'm sorry for my brother. He had no right to do that." She indicated the bruise. "Have you thought about having Berdur heal it?"

Reyna nodded. "I wanted to have proof available in case anything came of this, and Father asked me to prove it. I already had to show it to a few people."

Oh, Grayson, what have you done? Emery worried her lip. "Unfortunately, the king won't do anything about this, but I talked to my brother. With any luck, he'll come to understand his error."

"Have you come to apologize on his behalf then? I know that my father was in a nasty mood," Reyna sounded relieved at the thought of apology. Doubtlessly, she didn't want to lose Emery either.

"Yes, he tried offering your sister's hand in reparation." She nodded toward Arcadia, who scowled and clenched a fist. "My father refused, and I'm sure Grayson would have done the same." The princess couldn't keep herself from giggling. "He doesn't want to admit it, but I think he's in love with *you*, Reyna."

A light of amusement flickered in the Khindre's eyes. "Oh, really? Could have fooled me. Sounds like he was just trying to use me for carnal pleasures and nothing more."

Emery nodded and shrugged. "His impulsive anger tends to disguise his feelings when he can't purposely do it himself. Whether he is or not, it doesn't excuse what he did to you."

"No, I'll not forget this," Reyna promised. "But I see no reason to beat him up for being attracted. Despite the affliction of my race, I'm sure that there are a few boys who would like carnal knowledge of me." She winked at Emery. "That's the curse of being beautiful."

Emery blushed and turned to Arcadia. "One final matter, I am sure that my brother was overreacting, but I need to be sure. What did you do to him?"

"Just scared him a little bit. Moved a few shadows, gave him a tiny nip from one of them." She moved her thin fingers, and the darkness at the edges of the plaza began to dance. "Nothing that could actually harm him. Usually that, combined with the sight of me, is enough to send people scrambling."

It wasn't that Arcadia was ugly or terrifying by any means. While not as pretty as her sister, the darker twin still had a share of exotic features. A few inches shorter and a fair bit slimmer, thin and bony. Her tail ended in a scythe-shaped protrusion, which poked out of the silver-trimmed black shroud that she wore. "Every silver lining has its own dark cloud," another line from that elvish bard. Where Reyna's skin was sunset orange, Arcadia's hue was a deep purple, which some old members of the mystical races, those who'd been alive before the Eclipse, found similar to the night sky. With thoughts of Moonwatch, their bitter rivals on their minds, it was no surprise they didn't much care for the second twin. The small twisted horns that jutted from her temples made her look far closer to the devil of people's imaginations. Her eyes also served to unnerve those who came close enough to see them. Where Reyna had two pools of mystical gold, Arcadia possessed mismatched orbs, one pale pink and the other purple. Even Emery, who had known these two for many years, had to admit that the darker twin gave her chills sometimes.

"I figured as much. I am just glad that both of you are safe," Emery said, relieved. "I know that my brother can do awful things when angered."

"He doesn't scare me," Arcadia stated. "He tries anything more, then he'll just have to deal with the consequences." Her frown subsided slightly, the closest Arcadia came to smiling. "Same with that man who calls himself my father."

"Anyway," Reyna broke in, not liking the way the conversation was heading, "Let's have some fun before you bring the apology to our father!"

AMARU
An Unexpected Visitor

Amaru sat on the roof of Durrigan's hut, Ren and Xio by her sides. They had become constant companions in the recent days, Ren refusing to leave Amaru alone in case Leif decided to make a reappearance, and Xio happy to join them when she wasn't sleeping.

Leif for his part didn't confront Amaru again but always seemed to be lurking in the background, waiting and watching. She could feel his eyes on her wherever she walked. She loathed to bathe by herself, often inviting the other girls to join her. Those from her age group talked excitedly about the quickening arrival of their first-century celebration, only bolstered by those that had experienced it. They gossiped in hushed voices about what the night would be like and which boy they wanted to be paired with. A few had already asked the males they were interested in, mostly receiving positive responses.

Most of all, they wanted to know how Amaru felt about all of it. They were envious of her. "You're ravishing and the child of the goddess. You'll have your pick of any man in the tribe!" they exclaimed.

"Have you put any thought into which man is lucky enough to have your divine maidenhead?" one of the more experienced women, Shiara, asked.

Amaru blushed and shook her head. "I'm sure I don't know. When the time is right, I'll decide."

The others laughed good-naturedly at her embarrassment. Amaru had then another strange premonition. Like the one about the four-legged creature before, it had come out of nowhere. It was as if something was talking to her, and her subconscious was repeating it. She felt no excitement for the celebration, as most seemed to. *I have a duty that must be done for this tribe. But I don't feel like having children is part of it,* the voice said. *At least not yet.*

So there she sat, watching the sunfall. It had become the three friends' own little ritual. The sunfall was a mystical and strange event, and the Fyroxi, like most inhabitants of the Scorched Waste, could feel when it was coming by the breaking of the suffocating heat of the day. As at last, a cool breeze began to blow through, ruffling through their ears and tails, the three friends huddled close together. The sun commenced its gradual decline through the sky, moving in a near-perfect diagonal. As it neared the tip of the mountains that surrounded the desert, its light became soft and orange rather than the blinding white hot it burned all day. With it, the cloudless blue sky drifted to a deeper shade with a layer of light orange underneath. Suddenly, it would stop, resting at the tip of the mountain, like a crown atop the stony head. There it would idle, sending comforting arms to swaddle Yamaria's children in warmth until the morning came, when it rose again to reflect her fiery, piercing glare.

"The two moods of the Sun Mother," Xio muttered sleepily, her head resting in Amaru's lap, where her pale blonde hair was stroked lovingly. "I wonder if you inherited that, Amaru?"

The white-furred girl nodded. "That much I know I did. As a healer, I care for everyone in this tribe." *Even Leif. I know if he were hurt, I wouldn't let him die, no matter how much he scares me. He's too good of a hunter for the tribe to lose.* "But if anything were to happen, I know I would fight to the last to protect you."

"And we'd do the same for you," Ren assured, looking up into the taller girl's eyes. A flicker of sadness ran through his. "A lot of Fyroxi leave to wander the desert after their first century. Are you going to leave, Amaru?" His melancholy tone made it clear he didn't want her to.

For a moment, the goddess's child couldn't see Ren as anything more than a youngling. *That's wrong. He is my age and brave too. He stood up to Leif when he could've been killed for it.* Even so, she ruffled his ears and kissed him on the forehead. He blushed deeply, even at the chaste show of affection. "Only if I have no other choice. Besides, I'll likely have to stay and provide children for the tribe."

"Oh, true." Ren seemed to notice the pang in her voice. "Amaru? Is that not something you want to do?"

Amaru hesitated a moment before replying, "No, Ren. I suppose you are correct."

Xio's face turned up to hers. "Most mothers say that it's the greatest joy, to have a child of your own. And with Lily, you proved that women don't just have to exist to make children but start a solid family. Look how her parents kept each other happy and provided services for the tribe. What would keep you from wanting a family?"

She stopped stroking the fair-haired girl for a moment, trying to figure how to word it. "Have you ever felt like something was waiting for you?" she asked at length, slowly at first, before picking up momentum. "Some destiny, hanging just out of reach, that calls in the deep recesses of your mind? The past few months, I've been wondering. Yamaria sent me here to be the salvation. She said that I would come at the right time. What did she mean by that? Is it actually my lot to live like any other Fyroxi—give the men children, try to keep the tribe alive? Or is there something else, something bigger that I'm meant for?"

None of them knew the answer, so they allowed it to hang open in the air. Ren snuggled closer to Amaru, and the three friends twined their tails together.

Unbeknownst to them, the question would be answered soon. Sooner than some would like.

*****

Over the following days, Durrigan's condition grew even worse. He lapsed in and out of consciousness, spending more time in the latter state. When he was awake, he rarely recognized his surroundings, and his mind was fogged. His conversation grew incoherent, and it became apparent to the tribe that his days as leader were over. The moment Durrigan was dead, Amaru knew a new chieftain would be voted in. She was almost surprised nobody had suggested replacing him, but many of the founding members had fond memories of Durrigan and refused to disgrace his name by letting him die anything less than a chieftain.

Amaru found herself in his hut more often than not, watching over him, wiping the drool off his face, and feeding him. Xio and Ren practically had to drag her away to rest.

In his brief moments of clarity, she would speak with him. During these, it was still hard to believe he was dying; he was so civil and calm. When he devolved back into his spacey silence or flew into his fits of terror, Amaru couldn't keep the tears from her eyes. This man had raised her like a father, and she didn't want to lose him. She wished her healing spells could cure him but, at the same time, was glad they couldn't. He'd lived a successful long life. Nearly five hundred years of seeing the world, understanding it and leading his people fearlessly. If she extended his life any longer, it would just be unnatural, terrifying. He shivered, and Amaru pulled the blanket around his shoulders.

So absorbed was she in caring for Durrigan that she never heard the commotion outside in the village. It wasn't until Ren ran in, telling her to come quickly, that she noticed that anything was off.

"I came as fast as I could! Someone is coming, and they're going to need your help."

"Is someone hurt?" She sprang to her feet. "Who is it?"

Ren shook his head. "I don't know. I've never seen him before in my life. But he has two younglings with him, and he's limping."

That got Amaru moving. Shaking herself out of her reverie, she ran for the border, where everybody was gathered around the unfamiliar Fyroxi dragging himself toward the group.

Amaru gasped in shock when she saw his injuries. Only one tail flagged tiredly in the air; of the other two, there were just stumps. A multitude of scratches ran across his pelt, and his thick russet red fur was torn and patchy in places. And his leg! His back left leg was shorter than the rest, and it wasn't by birth defect. Another bloody rag wrapped around the end of the jointed piece, and there was no flesh or bone past the knee. Two younglings yipped next to him, running circles around the older man.

Without hesitation, Amaru slipped skin to fox form and went to support the man. "Clear the way!" she barked, not caring about the blood that was staining her white fur. "He needs attention quick!"

One of the Fyroxi living near the border gave up her cot, allowing Amaru to bring him in. "He might not make it back to the temple," the woman said.

"I'd rather have blood on my floor than my hands." Yamaria's daughter thanked the woman and made the injured Fyroxi as comfortable as possible.

He tried to growl out a few words, but Amaru had slipped back to humanoid form and closed her hands around his muzzle. "Hush. You're severely injured and probably nearly killed yourself walking through the desert. We'll make sure you are healed and rested; then you can talk." His eyes gleamed as if he wanted to tell anyway, but the stern look he received in answer made him calm back down.

Amaru took a moment to examine his injuries. His injured leg was still wrapped, though it was thoroughly soaked and would need to be changed if she didn't get to heal it quickly. Amaru had her friends run for water and a few other basic healing supplies. While she waited for them to return, she busied herself on the tails. Simple clean cuts had removed them, but all the same, it was a shame to see. The brushes were a part of Fyroxi pride, and to have them chopped off was a tragedy.

The wounds were raw and red, with grains of sand stuck to the top. Taking a dagger off her belt, which she was careful to keep with her always, she began to slice off some of the hair around the stumps. It would be much easier to clean and fix them that way.

When the water finally arrived, she was able to flush and clean the wounds, binding them up for further consideration later.

She turned now to the leg. The male gritted his teeth as the old bandage was peeled away and revealed the cruel wound. It looked as if the end of the leg had been twisted and torn off, and ribbons of flesh hung down, kept wet only by confinement of the pressure. "At least this one's not full of sand," Amaru said, extremely relieved. "You were smart to bind it so well. Had it been dry and cracked, this would be far more painful."

As it were, the process would be bad enough. Amaru's hand hovered over the herbs that had been set beside her. Picking up a funnel-shaped yellow flower, she ripped off a petal and stuck it on the man's tongue. "Chew. It will help with the pain." He chewed and swallowed gratefully, and Amaru crushed and combined a few herbs while she waited for it to take effect. The man grunted when he felt numb enough, and Amaru went to work.

Cleaning and sanitizing the knife, she sliced the ribbons of flesh away. She would need a clean closure, and those were likely to mess it up. Using a fresh cloth soaked in an herb mixture, she cleaned out this wound as well. The ripped appearance made it seem to be the work of a wild animal, and Amaru wasn't going to risk any infection.

By this point, the injury had stopped bleeding, and Amaru wrapped it up in a fresh poultice. Her command of the healing magic was still minor, so she wanted to ensure that as much was done manually as possible, lest she failed to fully cure an awful wound.

She wished she had one of the sleeping drugs or something, anything to distract his mind while being healed, but she had used the last of the supply to calm Durrigan after his most recent fit had escalated to screaming. The feeling of flesh reknitting itself was a strange one, and she didn't need her patient squirming while she worked.

"This is going to tingle a bit," she warned the Fyroxi. "But once it's over, you will feel much better for it. I just need you to keep yourself still." He nodded tersely and tensed himself, unsure what to expect. Amaru drew closer, placed her hands on the Fyroxi's side, and offered a prayer up to Yamaria. "Mother, grant this man your mercy, that he may help us better understand the world you have gifted us."

Warmth and faint light blossomed out from her splayed hands, washing over the injured man. The smaller gashes below her hands thinned and healed. Moving her hand over to the tails, she felt the magic flowing through his system, as new skin and fur grew over the stump ends. Stumps they would remain, without the old tail to meld on, but at least they wouldn't provide further pain to him. Finally came the leg. With one hand, she removed the herb poultice and the other, still glowing, moved over. The wound almost seemed to resist healing, being so gruesome, but she pushed through. The fractured bone knit itself back together. Surface damage was an easy fix; bones were harder, and flesh was nearly impossible. Forcing a body to grow something in moments that would usually take it weeks was never a simple task. Shaking, Amaru let her mother's power work its magic. When she felt her work was done, she stepped back. The man was staring at her, questions burning in his eyes.

"You rest," she told him. "We'll talk later." With that, Amaru leaned against the wall of the hut and promptly fainted.

*****

When she finally woke up, Ren was standing protectively over her. By the seemingly random items decorating the wall, it was clear she was in Ren's hut. To the side, Xio was playing with the two kits that had come in with the stranger.

Hearing her awaken, Ren rushed over, the relief evident in his eyes. "Thank Yamaria, you're all right." He nuzzled his face into her shoulder as she sat up. "We feared the worst."

Amaru's skin still tingled, and she felt a little woozy. "I've not often had to use my healing magic so much." *Not since Leif.* "I must have overexerted myself. How long was I out?"

"Only a few hours," Ren answered. "The man asked to speak with you whenever you are ready."

"His healing?" Amaru asked worriedly. "How did it go?"

"Masterfully done. He says there's no pain left."

"Has he given any other information about where he comes from?"

The brown-haired Fyroxi shook his head. "Claims he'll only speak to you."

"I'll go to him then." She started to swing her legs out of the cot, but Ren pushed her back down.

"No. You were tending to Chief Durrigan before, and you worked on this new guy for almost two hours, plus used all that healing magic. I heard you tell him to rest. Now I'll say the same thing.

If this man refuses to speak to anyone but you, he can wait until morning." Ren's tone brooked no argument.

It was late the next morning when Amaru finally stirred into consciousness. *Ren was right. I really did need that rest.* The tingling and headache had died down. Amaru worried about Chief Durrigan but doubted that the tribe would leave him unattended in her absence. Making her way back to the hut she'd worked in the day before, she found the strange Fyroxi man staring into space. He snapped into attention when she walked in, his eyes hazy and confused for a moment. Then he seemed to recognize her from the day before.

Using the low growling Fyran language that was comfortable for the fox form, he spoke to her. "You *healed* me." The emphasis on the middle word was strong. "I wasn't expecting to survive."

"Well, you are alive, and that's what matters," Amaru said simply.

"Does that make you Yamaria's child?"

Amaru nodded. "You don't seem to have come from here. You know of me?" The thick pelt of his fox form made it clear he lived in a somewhat-cooler environment, and his shade of red fur wasn't common among desert dwellers.

"Only recently. When I left my home, I knew I was searching for Durrigan's tribe. Some people in an oasis told me about you. They didn't mention the magic though."

"You know our chieftain?"

The Fyroxi nodded. "I was young when he left with his own tribe, going back to the Scorched Waste to grow closer to the Sun Mother. I reckon he managed, by your existence." He smiled as much as he could manage with his tooth-filled snout. "How is he now? The years must be creeping up on him."

Amaru nodded numbly. "I fear he won't last long." They sat in silence for a few minutes, reflecting on the past. "Enough about us. Let's hear your story. You came from the south?"

"Yes. My name is Weylin, previously a member of the clan Bush-Walker."

"Previously?"

Weylin sighed, melancholy filling his eyes. "Me and those kits that came with me," he muttered, "we are all that remains of clan Bush-Walker."

Amaru mouth dropped open in surprise. "All that remains? What happened?"

Weylin bared his sharp teeth. "We were betrayed."

Amaru thought for a moment. "Bush-Walkers… They were the ones who banded together with the Humans, correct?"

The older Fyroxi nodded bitterly. "We lived with them, in a settlement called Fyrestone. Everything was friendly between us, or so I thought."

"What did they do? Was there an argument between you?" Amaru's head buzzed with questions.

"No argument," Weylin answered. "Nobody expected anything. One day, we were bartering with them in the market, and the next, they were cutting off our tails to wear as trophies."

"And they killed everyone?"

"All but us." Weylin's voice was hoarse. "Those two kits are siblings. I was helping their mother with some chores when the blades were unsheathed. I saw Humans who gossiped in the square drive spikes through their companion's heads. I watched as the husband of one of the mixed couples dashed their child's head on the floor and dug out the wife's heart with a dagger!" Weylin's eyes were moist, and his voice choked now. "I killed the man who killed their mother and two of her other kits. With her dying breaths, she begged me to escape, to let somebody know what was going on. I fought my way through the men and women. That's how I lost my tails. Then when I was at the gate, the children on my back, one of their dogs got me by the leg and tore it off."

"Did you have to travel far?"

"A few days, most of it through the desert," he answered. "The only thing that kept me alive was the thought of the kits. If I died, they would die, and I would fail their mother's request."

"What are their names?" Amaru asked, trying to change the subject to something more positive.

"The girl's Savannah. She's old enough to transform, but she's wise enough to know that staying small keeps her hidden and safe." Weylin smiled. "The boy is Jarrah. A fur sack full of energy, that one. By the fact that I haven't heard his yipping all day, I'd think the desert air tired him out." He searched the hut, wondering where they were.

"My friend Xio was keeping them entertained last I saw," Amaru assured him. "I'll personally make sure that they are taken care of, even if I have to bring them into my own hut."

"I appreciate that. I would be willing to take care of the little rascals if you are too busy, however."

"I'm too used to taking care of Chief Durrigan," Amaru said with a sad smile. "When he's gone, I think the hut will be too quiet. I'll be glad for the company."

"And I suppose I'll be glad for the peace and quiet." He laughed bitterly and seemed to recall something further. "There was one thing, just something that caught my attention as I was walking the streets in the days before. Thought nothing of it then, but the lord, er...human leader," he added for her benefit, "was standing all peaceful like in front of some massive black dog thing. Wish I'd got a better look, but I had no special relationship with the lord."

"So you saw that, and shortly after, you were attacked?" Amaru asked, now worried. *Ren saw a large canine creature outside the village. Could the appearances be related?*

"As I said, it could be a coincidence, but I'll not dismiss any evidence."

"As long as your wounds are in acceptable condition, I will go have a talk with my chief." She ran a hand through her long black hair. "Perhaps we can find some meaning in this."

Weylin excused her, asking only to see the children when the time permitted.

Amaru was glad to comply, relieving Xio of her duty. She and Ren were sitting in the tent, in fox form, using their tails to lift the children playfully. The little ones were yipping in excitement as they bobbed up and down in the air, and her two friends were smiling warmly. It gladdened her to see them getting on so well.

As she led the two back, Amaru turned to the girl, Savannah, who walked along beside them, in fox form still. She was still small, around the size of a normal fox. "I hear that you are of transformation age."

The girl yipped, stopped in place, and squeezed her eyes shut, and after a few moments, a young girl stood in front of her. Savannah had a wild head of light brown hair and intelligent eyes. Amaru wrapped a cloak around her.

Savannah's voice was high and quiet. "Yes, ma'am. I apologize for any inconvenience our sudden arrival may have caused."

Such manners! Amaru had never heard such formality from one so young. "It is only common courtesy to save the life of a desert traveler," she answered. "For they might one day return the favor." *Leif saved my life, and I rewarded him by returning his own. Not the gift he'd have of me but a valuable one still. That is how this game called survival goes.*

"That is a good way to live," Savannah agreed. "Either way, we deeply appreciate it, even if my brother cannot express it in words yet."

Amaru ruffled the fur of the Fyroxi kit, who was lying on her shoulder. He was a little heavy, but she found she didn't mind the weight. "Do you know why you are here, little one?"

"No. Mr. Weylin says we were escaping from something. Why haven't we returned home?"

Amaru felt a wave of sad sickness run through her. These two poor children had even less idea than she did about what was actually going on. In a way she couldn't understand, she felt *responsible* for the deaths of their people. *You weren't there*, she told herself. *You didn't know any of clan Bush-Walker before today.* The logic was sound, and yet the feeling stuck. She decided it would be better to let Weylin explain it to them. They seemed to like the injured Fyroxi well enough, and he was their last connection to home. He might know how to tell the two without it being too painful.

Once she dropped the two children off, Amaru made a path straight for the chief's hut.

Inside, Durrigan was once again sitting up, as if he'd know she was coming. "Daughter," the dying man had started calling her this recently. A sign of affection but also one of the deteriorations of his mind. At least he seemed to be in a good state.

"Durrigan. How are you today?"

"Well enough, for my condition." He swished five tails back and forth, face darkening. "Though I doubt I will live much longer. I can feel the weakness taking over. I'd be surprised to see another two weeks."

Amaru knew it already, but it was a shock to hear him say it outright. "The tribe will be sad to see you go. *I* will be sad to see you go," she admitted.

"I know, dear. But you have grown very strong. When your time comes, I know you will make the right decisions." That struck her as odd, but she kept the words in her heart, even if they were nothing but an old man's ramblings.

She now turned to the business of her visit. "Besides coming to check on you, I wanted to update you on the happenings within the tribe. You are still chief after all."

He gave a mock groan, smiling the whole time. "More reports? I thought that taking to the sickbed would get me away from those." They both laughed lightly at his humor.

"This one is of serious consideration to all the elders, but I thought you should know first." Amaru quickly grew serious. "Especially since it relates to something I asked you before." His eyes registered curiosity and concern, sensing that all was not right. "We have a new resident in town. From clan Bush-Walker to the south."

Durrigan's brow scrunched in concentration. "Bush-Walker... Bush-Walker... Oh yes! That's young Osmund's tribe, I do believe," he grunted in satisfaction. "How is that rascal doing? He never had any of his brother Sigmund's discipline."

Amaru's gaze found the floor. "He's dead, sir; they all are. Only our new resident and two kits that he saved remain."

"Oh, Yamaria above..." The smile was gone from his face.

"Betrayed by people they lived alongside," she explained everything as Weylin had told her. Durrigan tried to grasp it but couldn't get out any words. "That is why I wanted to come and speak with you. Weylin, that's the new man, said that he saw a large canine figure with the lord."

This shocked the ability of speech back into Durrigan. "Yes, you came to speak to me about a similar sighting before. One outside our own borders." He looked into her brass-colored eyes. "I have more information."

Amaru kept her gaze locked on his. "What have you learned, Elder?"

"I should have recognized the description immediately. I shouldn't have forgotten. These are memories I would sooner forget, but doing so may have put my people in danger."

"What are these creatures?" Amaru prompted.

Durrigan sighed. "I have no idea how they may have gotten here, but my best guess, especially after hearing what happened to clan Bush-Walker, is that they are creatures we have hoped to never deal with again." The girl hung on his every word, worry and curiosity dueling in her beautiful eyes. "Chillfang."

EMERY
Council Disapproval

"Emery, my girl!" Godfrey Redwyn's face was absolutely jovial as she walked into the throne room where he sat. She bowed in front of him, showing proper respect to the crown. "I have much pleasing news to share. Sardan Rainclaw came to make a formal apology for his outburst. He agreed to continue supplying our cellars and providing transportation for any trips we need to make!"

Emery smiled contentedly to herself. "That is indeed good news, Father. I am glad that Sardan had it in him to see sense." Convincing to the barkeep hadn't been a simple matter. Sardan and his wife Cos doted on her like a fourth daughter.

"More than he loves me, no doubt," Arcadia had commented under her breath. But the severity of the matter had made it a complicated situation.

"You have further news?"

Godfrey nodded. "Tomorrow afternoon, there will be a meeting between myself and a few representatives from the Sulfaari Expanse. As I expressed before, you are welcome to join in the proceedings."

"What is being discussed?" Emery knew that Leonidas had to pass through the Expanse on his journey. Perhaps they might have some information about his whereabouts.

"I honestly couldn't tell you." Godfrey laughed. "I suppose they'll tell me on the morrow."

Emery was shocked. If there was a meeting planned, shouldn't the king know what to expect? "Did they not tell you what they want to talk about?"

"The Plainstriders are strange people," Godfrey said as if that were a proper answer.

The princess shook her head. Sometimes her father's lack of attention to business matters was infuriating. She knew her mother ended up handling most of the work to keep everything running. "Either way, I will be here at the proper time." She had a feeling that her father would need her there, which was unsettling.

The Sulfaari Expanse was home to multiple nomadic tribes, some of which tended livestock on the move. There were a few settlements, but with the temperatures milder than the Scorched Waste and dryer than Kindol Woods, the inhabitants generally enjoyed moving around. With people on the move, they found it easier to defend themselves against the outlaw tribes that wandered as well.

*****

The next day, when she walked into the council room, most of the attendants were already in place. Her father had the head of the table, and the right-hand seat was empty beside him. Lightbringer Casinius glared at the empty spot. Emery understood that the position of honor was usually his, but with the princess joining the meeting, he had been downgraded to the left side. Around the table, a few different figures sat. Most were dressed in simple, rough garments, clearly handmade and ornamented with various items. Though she couldn't recognize the meaning of any, Emery knew that they denoted rank and honors among them.

The wearers were just as varied as the clothing. Three other people sat in the chairs opposite to the royal party. One was human, a man with a longbow slung over his back. His sharp eyes glanced around, at the chamber, taking in every detail. The next was taller, and his clothes seemed more refined. From the pointed ears, Emery gathered that he was one of the Plainstrider Elves. Short sharp hair poked up from his head, and glasses sat on the bridge of his nose.

This seemed unusual, as elves were known for having better eyes than Humans, but she had to admit that he looked impressive with his eyes enlarged as they glared down his nose. The third member of the delegation was propped up on many cushions, to be at the same height as everyone else. She must have only come up to the knees of the Humans in the room at the very most. With a broad nose, waxy chestnut hair, and more colorful clothing than the other delegates, she made an unusual sight.

Emery took her seat, and her father passed his gaze around the table. "Is this everyone?"

"Hold on one moment! I'm here," a gruff voice responded. Looking toward the door, Emery heard a grunt escape Casinius's mouth. Coming in through the door was another human. Tall, pale skinned, and dressed in all black and gray, Emery wasn't sure what to make of this man. His dark eyes were sunken into his face, which was rough with stubble. He was slightly stooped over, and Emery noticed the gleam of multiple daggers on his person. Most surprising, however, was the messy shock of white hair that erupted from his head. He sat and stared around the table as if daring anyone to call him out on his disheveled appearance. Nobody did. "Had to finish a letter."

Unable to help herself, Emery turned to him. "Sir, who are you?"

Her father turned to her, gesturing toward the sullen man. "Daughter, this is Ignis Duskwalker."

Emery gasped; she knew that name! This strange man was called the Secretkeeper. Very little was actually known about him, even by the king himself, but that level of secrecy made him perfect for his job. If you needed information on someone or something, Ignis was the man to speak to.

"No surprise you didn't know me," Ignis said, his voice a rough whisper that Emery had to strain to hear. "I've not done much work around Searstar since you were born. Most of my information has been sent by letter." It was then that Emery noticed the raven sitting on his shoulder, which Ignis fed a couple of kernels of corn.

Her father cleared his throat. "Well, I suppose that introductions are in order." He pointed to the human with the bow. "This is

Gage Fletcher, of the Arrowhorn tribe." Next came the elf. "Faenith of Krael, an elf of the plains." Finally, the small woman. The king faltered. "And you are?"

The girl glanced up from the papers she had been fiddling with "Odala Wala, at your service. Orator for the Gnomes of Sulfaari!"

"I wasn't expecting a gnome; that's for certain!" He shrugged. "Either way, you are welcome in our hall."

"Thank you much." Odala Wala bobbed her head.

"I'm sure you all know who I am," the king continued. "And of course, my head Lightstrider, Casinius. But you may not have had the pleasure of meeting my daughter and heir, Emery Redwyn."

The delegates all gave their polite salutations.

"I've not seen you in meetings before," Faenith said. "Though it seems you certainly are of age, as you Humans classify it."

Gage agreed, "Yeah, she's almost half my age, and I've never seen her before."

Ignis chuckled darkly. "So are the rumors true, my liege? Have you been keeping your daughter from the political front?"

Godfrey had the grace to look embarrassed. "Ah yes. This is actually her very first meeting."

"Strange, I would think you would want your daughter in on these sorts of things. So she could, ah, learn the ropes as you people say," Faenith said critically. Apparently, Faenith had a generalized view of what Humans said and did. For all Emery knew, nobody around Searstar used the term "learn the ropes." If anything, maybe the people in the port towns might say it, but not up here in the capital.

Godfrey cleared his throat once nervously and then again more loudly. "I assume we aren't here to discuss my parenting style? Let us move on to the business."

Gage and Faenith both shot queer looks at each other, and Emery decided to speak. "My father simply wanted to ensure that I was in the best possible condition for one of these meetings. Now as the king says, we should get on to the discussion. We are all curious to know what news you bring."

Gage shrugged and turned to Odala. "I'll let her begin. She still hasn't told us why she came."

Odala promptly stood on her chair and unrolled a scroll, cleared her throat, and read. "This is a message from Ellep Bult, Gnommaster of Sulfaari. It is my humble request that trade be started between the Gnomes and the people of the Sunne Steps, including Searstar. We Gnomes are always looking for fun new materials to use in our free time, and we are willing to trade clothing material, medicine, and other things that we have available. My father, Yellek Wala, helped train Berdur Longshield, the dwarf apothecary, so he will know our word is worth trusting. Your approval is much appreciated." The orator bowed thrice, her nose almost hitting the table.

There was a momentary silence before Gage began clapping, cutting off quickly when he realized nobody else was joining. "I thought it was very well done," he said defensively.

The king was stunned for just a second before he threw his arms wide. "I wish you had told me this was a trade alliance meeting! I would have gladly brought in some delicacies and other fine works for sampling. I would be glad to trade with the Gnomes. Young orator, I hope to remain."

Faenith cleared his throat sharply, breaking into the king's speech. "I apologize for…bursting your bubble, but I'm afraid this delegation is not all here for such…lighthearted matters."

"Oh? Whatever could you mean?" Godfrey turned a questioning look upon the elf, who sniffed.

"You see, Gage, Ignis, and I were supposed to be joined by two others today, residents of Fyrestone, one Fyroxi and one human. That would have made our party an even five since this gnome wasn't supposed to be part of our group." He cast a sharp glare at Odala Wala. "Foul luck that we travel without the full number. There is good fortune in five, but less seems wrong by all the light of Yamaria."

"What happened to your other people, Lord Faenith?" Emery asked gently.

Another sniff. "One refused to join us, and the other couldn't join us."

"Care to explain what that means?" Godfrey asked.

"Have you received no word?" Faenith seemed angered. "We sent a letter by raven before we left!" He gestured to Ignis's raven. "And by the fact that it is on our messenger's shoulder, I know the message was received."

"Please, milord Faenith," Emery spoke calmly to the delegate, "my father received many a letter through the week. If he doesn't remember the contents of each one, he cannot be blamed." In her mind, Emery wondered what could have happened that had made these people all so angry.

Faenith glared at her father. Gage was taking an extreme interest in a piece of fur that had affixed itself to his cloak, and Ignis just looked grim. Only Odala didn't seem to understand what was going on.

"Hmph. I suppose that is a logical explanation," Faenith grunted. "Though seeing his lack of competence with including his own heir into the kingdom's business, I wouldn't be surprised to find a false ring to that." He added the second part under his breath.

Emery cast her eyes to the table. Casinius growled, but King Godfrey didn't even seem to notice.

Gage crossed his arms. "Had you read the letter, sent to you at our own risk, you would know that Lord Phaser of Fyrestone decided not to join us, on account of being *too busy*. Unfortunately for him, we were delayed in our leaving, by the arrival of this gnome." He nodded to Odala. "So we were in the area during the attack, which resulted in the inability for the Fyroxi chief to join us."

"Attack?" Emery asked, worry creeping through her mind. "Did outlaws attack Fyrestone?"

Faenith grunted, "I suppose if you wanted to label the entire human population of Fyrestone as outlaws, you could explain it that way."

"So what happened?" King Godfrey asked, not sounding as stressed as Emery thought he should. "What did this attack entail?"

Gage raised a hand. "I was in Fyrestone when it happened, hoping to give Chief Osmund another chance to join us. I saw the lord speaking with someone who had a massive dog beside him. Then while I watched, the man blew a long note from his horn, and the slaughter began." The archer shuddered at the memory.

"A slaughter?" Casinius growled. "What is the meaning of this?"

"It means," Faenith answered, "that people not unlike you all decided to turn on those that had been their closest friends for many years. What the reason is, we couldn't begin to fathom, but either way, it is a heinous crime that must be dealt with!"

"On this, we agree, Faenith," Casinius assured, backed up by Emery.

King Godfrey, on the other hand, seemed skeptical. "Are you sure this is what you saw? Perhaps there has just been some…misunderstanding here."

Emery was appalled to hear her father say this but kept her face composed. "I don't understand your meaning, Father, and I'm certain our guests don't either. If you were to explain, we could come to a consensus."

"Well," the king blustered, not expecting to have to explain himself, "I am only saying that when this sort of thing happens, there is usually some…reason behind it. It's possible that we don't see a piece of evidence that justifies this."

"Justifies the slaughter of an entire clan of people?" Casinius questioned. "No less the emissaries of our great goddess above? Emissaries that are already numbered, thanks to their *willing volunteerism* in a war in which they had little stock!"

Emery shook her head. "In this matter, Father, I must disagree with you. I think it is only right for this to be investigated and the people who started this attack to be imprisoned for murder and treason. The Fyroxi and Humans of Fyrestone lived together in peace for generations. There is nothing about this that can be justified!"

"At last, somebody speaks some sense at this table." Faenith slammed his hands flat on the table. His voice lowered in a nearly threatening tone. "It would seem that the previously excluded daughter has more wisdom than the king himself."

Gage grimaced and responded at full volume. "My king, we have come here on behalf of the people of the Sulfaari Expanse and in the memory of the people of clan Bush-Walker to ask you for assistance with, as your daughter says, investigating this tragic happening."

"I fought during the last War of Sun and Moon," Faenith growled. "I saw the wisdom of the king Algrith Redwyn when he excluded clans Fire-Strider and Bush-Walker from the battle. Would you do your ancestors a disservice by turning a blind eye to this massacre?"

Ignis finally spoke up again, Emery noticing a hint of amusement in his tone as he watched the argument unfold. "My king, I have been doing research into the Fyroxi tribes. As Faenith says, your ancestor saved the lives of clan Fire-Strider. Now with the death of Osmund's Bush-Walkers, the desert tribe is the only group of the Sun Mother's people still alive. I'm no god and cannot claim to understand them, but I would be sore wroth to learn of this injustice, were I Yamaria."

"Yamaria has watched over us for thousands of years. I'm sure she has seen many…injustices," Godfrey said defensively.

Gage and Faenith were both fuming now. "Are you denying us the assistance we ask for? Will you not arrest the outlaws who slew a miraculous and rare race?" the elf yelled. "What if this isn't an isolated incident? What if more attacks like this happen? Will you sit back and continue your lavish feasts as if nothing is going on?"

Gage joined in as well. "In all of my people's knowledge of the known world, the Fyroxi race only exists here! All we request is that you send one of your Lightstriders with a small force to clear out this evil that has tainted beautiful Sulfaari!"

The king hesitated, and Casinius turned to him. "My lord, we act on your command. I am bound to stay here to protect and advise you. Lightstrider Vedalken is currently patrolling the forest, and we are awaiting a report from Tinco Anar and Raerizen on the Sunne Steps, but you still have Galbraith ready to fight. Or I can send word for the others to make for Fyrestone immediately."

Godfrey wiped at his brow. "The captain of my guard, Sir Leonidas, is missing in action. Without him, I don't want to be rid of Galbraith." The king said this, not realizing his accidental sleight at Casinius, who was his personal retainer and guard. "And the other

Lightstriders are in strategic locations, assuring the safety of the neighboring people. No, I'll not have them moved either."

Casinius was clearly bothered by this and was about to argue but bowed his head. "Yes, milord." Going against the king's will was treason, and Godfrey had made up his mind.

Faenith's tone grew venomous. "So is this the pronouncement of our king? He will leave his own people in the rut because he is too scared of his own shadow?" He spat on the floor as he rose, turning to Emery. "It pleases me that at least one member of the royal family has some brains in her head. I look forward to the day you ascend to the throne. Perhaps then, crimes won't go unpunished," he stormed out of the room, Ignis following behind.

Odala Wala looked very confused. "What does this mean for our trade deal? Is that still on?"

Casinius was red in the face. "Go. I will send someone to discuss with you later. For now, speak with your fellow delegates. I don't want our alliance to endanger you with their hackles so raised."

Odala bowed deeply and scurried out of the room.

When Emery was sure that it was just the three of them, she rounded on her father. "What in the name of darkness was that? Why did you deny them aid?" The whispers about her father hadn't eluded her. She knew that the servants called him the Do-Nothing King. She wondered if there were others, out in the kingdom, who thought the same. The servants had to get those names from somewhere.

Godfrey flinched. "I was only doing what seemed right, Emery."

"What seemed right?" The princess's tone filled with heat. "The right thing to do would be to avenge the Fyroxi who were slain! The right thing to do would be to fight back!" She spoke the words that she'd asked herself prior. "We are *phoenixes*, Father. We are supposed to rise from the ashes and strike back at injustice. That you would act in the manner you did today is appalling! No wonder you have enemies!" With that, the princess stormed out of the room, blinking back hot tears that threatened to spill forth. *A princess shouldn't cry. At least not in public.*

"I ought to arrest those two for speaking treasonously to me," King Godfrey said.

Casinius pulled at his mustache. "No, my king. You know that I hate to contradict you. But in this case, both the delegates and your daughter are correct." Shaking his head, the Lightstrider left the room.

*****

Emery collapsed into her soft mattress and soaked her pillow with tears. An entire tribe of people decimated and her father wouldn't do anything! *He will leave his own people in the rut because he is too scared of his own shadow?* The weight of Faenith's words crashed around her. She had never known her father to leave the castle, except to make his speeches or other announcements. The elf had been right. The king, the most powerful man in the land, was scared of death lurking around every corner. It didn't matter that Casinius rarely left the king's side or that the Lightstrider captain had descended from a long line of warriors, tracing back to Cassian, King Algrith's chosen warrior, and many before him. It didn't matter that his son was a formidable warrior or that his daughter was well loved by the people. Her mother, Queen Lysaria, had spoken at length to her about his great deeds, and Emery had hoped that he would live up to these stories, not the rumors that the castle servants swapped like currency. Unfortunately, it seemed the latter held more water than the stories of old Godfrey Redwyn.

Emery wanted to go find Reyna and Arcadia, to tell them everything, let them console her with magic and kind words. *I cannot do that*, she realized. *No matter how much I trust them, they can never learn how weak their king is, at least not from me. Besides, Mother would tell me to be strong. I can't go out in this state, lest I upset my people.*

Instead, her thoughts turned to Leonidas. Emery wished for his comforting presence. She realized that in the tension of the moment, she had forgotten to ask about her knight. She doubted that the delegates would have remained in Searstar long, given their anger. Perhaps the Secretkeeper would still be around. He worked for the crown, so it would make sense for him to stay in the city. She needed to know whether her knight had even a chance of returning, no matter the damage the answer might have on her heart.

AMARU

To Honor the Lost and Celebrate the Rising

Durrigan died less than a week after planting the knowledge of Chillfang in Amaru's head. The young woman knew he had gone peacefully, with his adopted daughter at his side, but still, it hurt to see an impressive and wise man succumb to the everlasting darkness of death. In the days leading up to his funeral, the whole tribe was left in a somber mood, as everyone reflected on the man they had grown under and pushed through the difficulties of the desert for. As the heat of the day began to break, everyone gathered for the service. Amaru stood beside Ren, Xio, and Weylin.

The older Fyroxi gestured toward the wooden altar upon which the chief was being placed. "What is that for?"

"That is a funeral pyre. Here in the desert, we burn our dead, to ensure that they become one with the world of Yamaria and, as such, live on. You will see during the service," Amaru assured him.

"Interesting. Back in Fyrestone, we had a cemetery, where we buried the dead." Weylin scratched at his ears with one paw. "Their bodies were returned to the earth and their names recorded in stone for all eternity."

"With the winds that we experience here in the Scorched Waste, there is no telling whether a body will remain interred. And in such a sterile place, their nutrients would simply go to waste in the sand. In this way, we free the deceased spirit to return to Yamaria and reap the rewards they've earned in their time on the mortal plane."

Weylin nodded his understanding, and the service began.

Vienna emerged from the temple, garbed in red, white, and gold, holding holy implements which she waved in the air. As she walked, she prayed for all to hear. "Radiant Yamaria, you send your light down upon your children each and every day. For this, we thank you! Along with your light, you see to it that we are provided with people that enrich our lives! May today your soothing light shine down and dispel the darkness of death."

All the Fyroxi in the tribe bowed their head in reverence to their creator. They held a moment of silence before Vienna turned to face the Fyroxi

"We gather here today to honor the life of Chief Durrigan Lanneo and to send his soul up to the Sun Mother, where he shall reside from now until the day the sun fails to shine! We give thanks for his life's work, guiding us to be closer to Yamaria, and for his never-ending strength. For all of us, there will be loss, grief, and pain. Whether his impact was large or small, Durrigan's life mattered to us all. With his passing, life will not be the same, and it shouldn't be. Today, let us open our hearts to honor this man."

She gestured toward the pyre behind her. "As we light the fire to send Durrigan to our Mother, let us raise our voices in song!"

As the flames licked up around the pyre, growing and expanding, the sound of the tribe's song flowed through the air. A haunting but beautiful melody that sounded complete without any music to accompany it. "Now, as his physical body is burned away and his spirit is freed, I would invite you all to send your good wishes to our beloved chief, to see him across the barrier between this world and the next." She paused while the flames reached higher and higher.

"We also lift up to Yamaria prayers for the souls of clan Bush-Walker, who were unjustly killed in the middle of peace. We hope that our words will guide them and convince Yamaria to send her wrath down upon the betrayers!"

Amaru felt Weylin go rigid beside her. He hadn't been expecting these people, who didn't even know his people, to pray for their vengeance.

As sunfall began, the small altar of sticks burned down to ashes, Durrigan's body with it. Vienna scooped up these ashes in a cloth and held them in the air. "Now, as we release his remains into the wild, let us all remember that now he roams with us in spirit and in mind, as we tread upon the sands, which will always have part of him in it!"

As if on cue, a gust of wind rose, blowing the ashes out into the desert. They mixed with sand in the wind and were carried far and wide, a physical representation of the impact Durrigan had on his tribe, his Mother's children and his.

"From this moment on, as we live our lives, let it be known that our chief and all the chiefs before him are watching over us, guiding our paths with their collective wisdom!" Vienna finished.

A deep-throated chant broke out among the gathered Fyroxi. A song honoring the ancient ancestors and all they had built for the current world.

For days after the death of the chief, a somber mood hung over the Fire-Striders. In the end, it was quietly decided that Yarena, a rational and respected elder, would replace Durrigan as chieftain. Much to Amaru's relief, she allowed the girl to stay in the chief's old hut, setting up her main office in the tent used for council meetings. Yarena was wise and, in proper respect of the leader who had persuaded them to leave their homes and move here to the Scorched Waste, named his death day a holiday, to celebrate Durrigan and all the great leaders who had come before him.

Amaru watched as Weylin taught Savannah and Jarrah the ways of the desert, which he caught on to relatively quickly. Despite his missing leg, he adapted well to hunting, as it was a natural instinct of the Fyroxi. Often, she talked with the wounded man, wondering what life in a walled town had been like. Through his explanations, Amaru learned a little about gardening and the so-called civilized lifestyle. While there was currency in the Scorched Waste, it mostly consisted of tokens of wood or dried grass, traded in for food and water. When Weylin introduced her to the coins of Sun's Reach, she was in awe. They were so beautiful, so mysterious, and the things Weylin said they were used for intrigued her. The lowest value was the copper dim, a small triangular coin, stamped with the face of the king on one side and the words "All Things under the Sun" on the other. Next up was the silver bright; this one was square in shape and, like all the rest, was marked in the same way as the dim. Next was the golden radiant.

"Is this made of real gold?" Amaru asked in surprise. Gold was a rare element, which many of her kind had never seen.

"Yes," Weylin answered. "The Dwarves bring it up from below, and we turn it into coins and jewelry, which we then purchase with the coins."

"So your currency is made of the same material as your valued decorative items?" Amaru mused. "One must wonder why nobody just wears the coins."

That coaxed a laugh out of the older man. "That would simplify the process," he admitted.

Finally, he pulled out the most valuable currency of all, the brilliant. It was a three-dimensional pyramid of a transparent substance, a small orb of precious red metal hanging in the center. He only had one and regarded it with sadness in his eyes. He had received it from his wife before she'd been taken by a sudden sickness, her family heirloom, passed from generation to generation.

"Her death is awful, as all deaths are," Amaru tried to comfort him. "But at least she didn't live long enough to be betrayed and massacred. I doubt you would have left if she were there. Then nobody would have warned us of the possible Chillfang danger." She wasn't sure if her words had the intended effect, but Weylin swallowed his grief.

He nodded and handed the coins to Amaru. "You seem passionate about the Fyrestone issue. Keep these and keep the people in your heart, now and always."

Part 2

Trouble Brewing among Scorched Sands

AMARU
Blood, Ice, and Sand

If Durrigan's death had been a low point for the Fire-Striders, then the Hundredth Sunturn celebration became an equivalent high. Yarena quickly set people to work, preparing their settlement for the upcoming festival. Excited chatter filled the streets, as it had the bathtubs Amaru had shared with the other women. The crafters made decorations of all kinds, stringing up lanterns, woven grass ribbons, and painted stones wherever it could be found. With materials borrowed from the Water Callers, a giant tent was constructed in the center square. This was where the feast and dance would take place. All around the pavilion, small sectionals were erected, filled with woven grass cots and hung with fine silk. Scented candles, which the crafters toiled long and hard to make, stood ready to fill the air with intoxicating scents when sunfall came on that fateful day.

Though nerves were expected leading up to the day of Hundredth Sunturn, Yarena noticed that one of the participants seemed to grow more tense with each passing day. The new chieftain called in this one to speak privately in the tent. "Amaru, you don't seem to be very excited for your Hundredth Sunturn," Yarena said directly after they had sat in silence for a few moments. "Most women your age are tittering with joy, but you have become even more reclusive than when you would spend days caring for Durrigan."

"I apologize, Matron Chief. I understand that this is a rite of passage and a grand celebration for most, yet I can't help but feel... wrong."

Yarena chuckled. "Now, now, young one, there is no shame in having misgivings about the body. And sharing flesh is something that all must do at one point."

"N-no. That's not what I mean. I just don't feel like this is how my life is supposed to play out."

Yarena became suddenly serious. "Do you think that being of the goddess's blood makes you any different from the rest of us?"

"No." Amaru shook her head. "I am just another Fyroxi, no matter what my heritage." She related her concerns about being the so-called salvation and wondering after her purpose.

"You aren't thinking of trying to get out of the ceremony, are you?" When Amaru nodded, Yarena let loose a long sigh. "Girl, I understand how you feel. You are pressured to be something more powerful than you are. You have your magical healing powers, but you feel like something's missing. I used to feel like that, too, minus the magic, of course. However, this tribe has grown exponentially with you here, these past hundred years. Would you leave them behind when you could help bolster their numbers?"

"I have no desire to leave them behind, as you say. I only wish to do what the Sun Mother, my mother, has asked of me, and I feel as if my thoughts are mirrored by Yamaria."

"So there is nobody in the tribe that you would join in this celebration with willingly? I know that young Leif is rather excited about the ceremony."

Amaru shivered, and Yarena looked at her sharply. "I'll do my duty to the tribe, whatever you may decide that to be, but if I had my choice"—Amaru shook her head—"there is none that I would say I was close enough to give my desert flower."

Yarena sighed again and glared disapprovingly at the girl in front of her. "Amaru, I *won't* withdraw you from this event. I understand how you feel, but you must see it from a different point of view. If you don't join the people, they might begin to feel wrong about their duty as well. They all look up to you, Amaru. Were you

a little older, it might very well have been you sitting in my place."
She scratched at her ears. "Besides, your being matched with Leif is
no coincidence."

Amaru blinked in surprise.

"Honestly, you didn't actually believe that you would end up
in the same events as him so often by pure chance of luck, did you?"
Yarena snarled out a laugh. "No, we have set you up to be with Leif
since we first saw his potential."

Amaru could hardly believe what she was hearing, but Yarena
wouldn't let her get a word in edgewise.

"This sunfall, you will enjoy the celebration, and when the time
comes, you will give yourself to Leif Kalix. After that, what you do
with your life is up to you."

Amaru nodded obediently and bowed out of the tent, preparing
herself for the evening.

*****

Despite her worries, Amaru found it easy to lose herself in the
way of the party. The Water Callers had provided a few traveling
bards to perform that evening, and the air came alive with music.
Around the tent, Fyroxi and Water Callers alike danced and swayed.
Food that had been stockpiled for months was revealed: large casks
of ale, bowls of figs, dates, and other fruits, some of which even Ren
couldn't name. Platters were full of roast meats: ostrich, grouse, venison, rabbit. The Water Callers had also brought in pastries and loaves
of bread, baked on flat rocks in the sun. It was all delicious, and more
was provided than what the tribe were used to eating in a week, let
alone a single night.

Everyone was dressed in colorful fabrics, loose flowing gowns,
scarves, and ribbons. Ren had told her of a phenomenon called rain-
bows, which Copernicus had him read about. Amaru figured that
there must be all the colors represented here, plus many the rainbow
would have never seen. As the light of the sky turned from white
to yellow to deep orange and the ale flowed, the nervous energy
increased as did the fervor. Amaru made sure to eat plenty but drank

only a little, for some reason, thinking that she needed to be sober this evening.

Amaru watched happily as Ren and Xio passed themselves between different dance partners while Savannah and Jarrah played with the other kits in the corner. She wondered whether her friends had chosen their partners yet for this evening. She knew that Ren had still harbored thoughts of being with her and had been devastated to learn that Chief Yarena had ordered her to go with Leif.

"I'm sorry, Amaru. I wish you didn't have to take a man you didn't want. It seems unfair that we all get to choose, but you are arranged for someone."

"That's my lot as the child of the goddess, Ren," Amaru had explained glumly. She would have rather taken Ren up on his offer than be with Leif tonight. "Just be glad that you don't have to fulfill that role. Now go, have some fun. You deserve a good time this evening."

Time seemed to slow for Amaru, as the music wound down and the lights began to dim. She saw a few couples already sneaking off to the cubicles. Soon, the trickle became a stream, and steadily, everyone began to file out of the tent. Amaru took a deep breath and steeled herself as Leif appeared behind her, grabbing her shoulders roughly. "You'd better be ready." Amaru nodded numbly and allowed the boy who'd saved her life to drag her toward their cubicle.

Within, the candles already burned, lighting up the silk hangings and filling the air with their sweet incense. The walls were decorated with symbols of Yamaria on one side and weapons on the other. The beautifully carved spear had been removed from Yamaria's hand in the temple and given to a second smaller statue. It seemed to fit perfectly in the statue's hand. From her training with Sigmund, Amaru recognized it as a medium-length thrusting spear, made for one-handed use alongside a shield. In the desert, it was a favorite weapon for most, its usefulness in hunting unparalleled. If a boar was running a hunter down, they could trust the spear to stop its charge before the deadly tusks could gore them. Plus, it was easy to throw as a distraction while the hunter slipped into fox form.

This particular spear had a head of a red mineral that Amaru couldn't recognize. The tip looked deadly sharp and stronger than any steel. It was shaped like a flame, and the light of the candles seemed to refract through it. Its haft was made of sturdy black wood, hardened by age but not left brittle by some miracle. Runes and symbols were carved on it, some of which Amaru could read as prayers to Yamaria, and others which held no meaning to her. The girl could feel slight magic woven into its crafting, which attested to how it had lasted so long and remained in perfect condition. This was the work of Fyroxi thousands of years before the Eclipse when the race had been rivaled in magic only by their ancestral enemies, the Chillfang.

Pulling her eyes away from the spear, she forced herself to turn toward Leif. "If you're finished drooling over ancient artifacts," he drawled, "there is something much less dusty and much more alive for your eyes to feast upon."

His shirt was already off, and Amaru could see the long scar that traced down his side. No amount of healing would make that go away, and as long as it stayed, Leif believed he had a claim on her. His mottled tails flicked restlessly, as Amaru commanded herself to walk toward him. Was she really about to do this? Was she going to give this arrogant man everything he had desired, prove that his claim held power? *Yes, I told Yarena and myself that I would do anything for my people. This is just one more duty.*

"Come on," Leif urged. "Let's see what I've earned."

Hesitating only slightly, Amaru sat down on the woven mat and prepared to disrobe.

Before she could, however, a sound pierced the air. A long, low noise that sent a shiver down Amaru's spine. Never having heard it before, she was surprised to realize that she recognized the sound. Maybe it was the instincts of her race, or perhaps it was knowledge supplied to her by her mother; she didn't know either way. What she did know was that the shivering noise was a howl...a wolf howl. But there weren't any wolves in the desert.

"Did you hear that?" she asked Leif, fear in her voice.

"Don't know, don't care," the boy growled without a hint of worry. "Just lie back, don't worry about it, and let me have my prize."

He approached and lay his hands on her chest, pulling at the fabric of her gown. Lifting her feet from the ground, she kicked him square in the chest, pushing Leif away. "Get back here! You are mine, and no fake howl made by one of your stupid, jealous friends is going to change that!" Amaru dashed to the side of the room, and as Leif stood to try and rush at her, he found himself confronted by the tip of an ancient artifact. Another howl pierced the air.

"Leif Kalix. You are unarmed, but if you try to stop me, I will not hesitate to spit you on this spear. My friends did not make this din, and I am going to investigate it. If you want to make yourself useful, you can grab your swords and prepare for a fight. If not, you can run out to whatever made that howl and feed yourself to it. You might even manage to buy us all a little more time!" There was an unmistakable force in her voice, a commanding power enough to cow even the most arrogant man. Leif nodded, gulped, and stepped back, running outside and in the direction of his hut. Amaru sighed, momentarily allowing pride to wash over her for standing up to him.

The scream that split the air broke focused her, and gripping the ancient spear, she stumbled out into the low light. The thought of having to use the weapon scared her

The cry had come from one of the cubicles to the left, and now Amaru could see which one. Ren was huddled over a frail figure, which she recognized as Vienna, Purell's apprentice.

Ren looked up, shaking and sniveling with fear. "Amaru! I-I was w-with Vienna, and we-we were about to…" he snuffled. "Suddenly, something big and gray ripped through the tent and grabbed her in its mouth. It shook her like a rag doll and…and…"

Amaru only had to look down at the girl to finish the sentence. Vienna's body was a bloody ruin, her stomach ripped apart, one arm bent at an awkward angle, the other missing entirely. Hair was scattered everywhere, matted with blood. Ren looked into her eyes, his own brimming with tears and a silent question. Amaru shook her head in reply. No magic could cure this. She looked closer down at the body. "No…" She couldn't believe what she was seeing. There were tiny red crystals floating in the cooling blood of the young priest. Suddenly, something clicked. The howl and something that

Durrigan told her before his death. The creatures were wolves, and unless she was mistaken, those were ice crystals. "Chillfang!" she shouted. "Ren," she said with confidence she didn't have, "are you prepared to fight to avenge Vienna and save the rest of the tribe?"

The small Fyroxi nodded, and Amaru reached out a hand to pull him to his feet. She looked down to him and held his hand in both of hers. "You'll do amazing. I know you will." Ren gathered his confidence for a moment as he watched Amaru run down the street calling warnings to the air. "Chillfang! Chillfang! Every able-bodied Fyroxi, prepare to fight!"

REN
Nearly Overwhelmed

Taking a deep breath, Ren shifted skin. His sense of smell was the first thing to kick in. He could smell the piney, musty scent of a mangy wolf, singling it out among the host of familiar aromas. He angled himself toward it, running as fast as he could down the trail. He traced the wolf to another of the pavilions. One ruined body had been flung to the side, and a girl sat bolt upright on the bed, her pale skin quivering.

In front of her, a massive beast stood slavering, saliva dripping from its curled lip. The thick legs were tipped with long claws, and the hair on the bottlebrush tail stuck out in sharp spikes. In the dim light of the candles, Ren could see some sort of glassy glaze on its fur. The creature growled and spoke in a language that sounded disturbingly similar to Fyran. "She's not the one. I can smell it. Herrr death is allowed."

"Allowed by who?" Ren was surprised to find that he had spoken.

The giant wolf turned on him, his piercing yellow eyes seeming to stare straight into Ren's soul. "Look, a little herrro fox. Come to save the girrrl." A harsh barking sound that Ren realized was laughter followed. "That otherrr boy was no fight. Perrrhaps you'll prrrove a betterrr amusement beforrre you die!" Without warning, the wolf pounced, barreling into the small Fyroxi.

The pair went flying, rolling into the wall of the tent, held secure by the stakes in the sand. The wolf snapped at him, Ren barely pulling his head out of the way in time. The wolf's cold breath puffed against his fur. Cold. That seemed wrong. Shouldn't its breath be hot? In fact, Ren realized the wolf's entire body seemed to radiate cold. Where their fur collided, ice crystals formed, causing them to stick together. When the beast jumped back, the frozen hair ripped painfully from his body. Ren cried out involuntarily, and the wolf let out another barking laugh. They were both covered in scratches, but his foe hardly seemed to notice them.

"Is that all you have, Fyroxi? Your kind has grown weak in the yearrrs since we last fought!"

"So you are Chillfang!" Ren replied stupidly. "Amaru was right!"

The wolf perked up at the name. "That name sounds similar to the hated She-Fox." If wolves could laugh, the Chillfang did now. "Tell me now about this Amarrru. Is she imporrrtant to your trrribe?"

Ren shook his head, refusing to say any more, knowing he'd let something dangerous slip in his nervousness.

"I'll get it out of you one way or anotherrr. If you know the Sun Wench, you could just tell me wherrre she is. Could save us a lot of prrecious time. Might not even kill you, as a rewarrrd."

"Even if I did know, you would have to break every bone in my body to get me to tell you!" Ren realized his mistake as the Chillfang bared his teeth in a terrible smile and tensed his legs to pounce.

"All rrright, thrrreaten me with a good time!"

In moments, the two were rolling in the sand again. It was clear that the Chillfang had the advantage; Ren was quickly weakening. He wasn't bred for fighting, and he'd not taken too many classes in combat past the necessary basics. Right now, the young Fyroxi was only doing whatever he could to keep those cold, sharp teeth from his throat. As he thought that, the Chillfang lunged, and Ren jerked to the side. The bite missed his neck, but the fangs found purchase in his shoulder. Ren felt the flesh harden, and crystals started to form in his blood. He gasped in pain as the Chillfang began to pull backward. Skin and muscle stretched, and a layer of frost began to cover him. In another few moments, he would lose the arm and bleed out, or he'd be frozen. Ren thought, *I'm done for. This is it! This wolf beast is the last thing I'll ever see! Xio, Amaru, I'm sorry I disappointed you.*

Suddenly, he noticed that the pressure on top of him had disappeared. His wound throbbed, but the Chillfang was no longer ripping at it. Looking in front of him, he saw Weylin now tangled up with the enemy. Unlike in the battle with Ren, the older Fyroxi definitely seemed to be controlling this battle. Even with only three legs, he pushed the wolf around the room, snapping and clawing at the face and causing deep red blood to mix into the sand.

The two separated for a moment, snarling at each other.

"This one's much betterrr at fighting," the Chillfang growled.

"You're not half shabby yourself, wolf," Weylin replied. "How does it feel to be matched by a cripple?"

The wolf seemed to notice the missing back leg and cursed. "Soon, they won't be able to call you crrripple because therrre will be no limbs remaining to be called norrrmal!"

"That's what you think," Weylin muttered as the Chillfang leaped again. He went low, sliding forward and kicking his good leg up into the bottom of the wolf's jaw. It whimpered and keeled over. Before it had a chance to move again, Weylin was on top, plunged his muzzle toward its neck, and tore out its throat.

Weylin returned to Ren. "Can you still fight?"

Ren nodded. "They're looking for Amaru!"

"What?" the older Fyroxi blinked.

"I don't know why, but he said something about wanting to find the 'Sun Wench' and reacted when I accidentally said her name."

The older Fyroxi cursed to himself. "You damn fool. Doesn't matter now, we have to find her quickly and protect her. If these really are Chillfang, then nothing good will come of them capturing the child of the goddess."

Without any further words, the two bounded out across the sand. They came across multiple bodies: Chillfang, Fyroxi, and Water Callers alike. Following their ears, the pair tracked down solitary wolves and killed them together, allowing their intended prey to escape.

They finally saw Amaru across the field, surrounded by three of the creatures. A couple of other Fyroxi stood by her side, pushing back against the wolves whenever they drew too close. It was three against three, a fair fight in terms of numbers, but the Fyroxi were tired, full of food and alcohol. And they were afraid. They hadn't seen their rival race in over a century, and now they were fighting for their lives. The Chillfang circled their prey, watching the Fyroxi with hunger in their eyes. Amaru stood in the center of the others, one hand on her spear and the other ready, Ren knew, to heal her allies.

One of the Fyroxi near Amaru stumbled, his pounding head getting the better of him. The Chillfang wasted no time, immediately hounding the weakest link. With the ease of a skilled hunter, the wolf ripped at the fox, slicing open one leg gruesomely. The Fyroxi managed to jump back in time. Amaru went to reach for the wound, but the Chillfang wouldn't give her a chance. They closed in, forcing the Fyroxi to tighten into an easily killable knot. Amaru jabbed out with her spear. The wolf that it struck yipped in pain and bounced back, but there was no fear in its eyes, only murder.

Weylin smacked Ren with his last remaining tail. "Stop staring and start attacking. She can't hold off forever!"

Shaking the daze from his eyes, Ren leaped into the fray. These Chillfang were smaller than the one that had almost killed him. Small, yes, but still savage beasts. They tore in without heed to their injuries, acting on their hatred for their opposing race.

Ren and Weylin fought together, surrounding the spear-struck wolf and keeping him confused. Ren could feel the pain in his shoulder, the muscles still tense from the icy jaws of the Chillfang in the tent. Through the pain, he kept fighting, knowing that he had no other choice. It was either fight or die and let Amaru die. The latter was not an option. With thoughts of Amaru in mind, Ren pounced and locked his jaw around the snout of his opponent. He wasn't strong like Weylin and couldn't toss the wolf to the side, but the pain from the tearing teeth did cause the beast to fall to the ground, and Weylin moved in to savage the Chillfang's stomach, ending him.

They turned to the confrontation behind them just in time to see one of the remaining wolves finish the job the first started, a wet sound and a howl of pain emanating from the previously injured fox, as his front leg was torn off. Immediately, the wolf went for the throat and rolled, finishing the job.

Seeing that spurred Weylin into action. The older Fyroxi yelped to gain the attacker's attention and pounced. The Chillfang didn't have a chance to stand, as all of Weylin's weight pounded him into the earth with a crack. Weylin's powerful front claws slashed back and forth as if he was trying to dig through his enemy. The beast on the ground straightened his legs, positioning them under Weylin's stomach, pushing his crippled foe off. Weylin righted himself and made to pounce again but never got the chance, as Amaru's spear flew through the air and took the Chillfang in the side. The wolf fell to the earth, dead.

*****

The alpha male of the Chillfang, a tremendous black wolf named Frax, snarled a toothy grin as he looked around at his pack. They had waited so very long for this day. Those foolish wizards had ruined the race's chance at revenge against the Fyroxi. They had both taken considerable losses in the war, but Gaarhowl was not appeased. He knew his pack was ready to destroy this little desert village, the final living Fyroxi.

Frax had never tasted Fyroxi blood before but soon got his chance. A youngling, walking with his mother back to the hut where he lived. The boy never made it more than a few steps before Frax was upon him and tearing off those furry ears, claiming the first kill of the night.

Frax dug his muzzle into the succulent flesh, praising Gaarhowl for giving him this opportunity, the chance to end the Fyroxi once and for all. Raising his head to where the moon should have hung and snarling at the orange sun for good measure, Frax let out his most haunting howl, signaling the attack.

The gleeful yips of Chillfang rose around him, and they charged in.

All around him, Frax could hear the giddy cries of Chillfang as they brought down their prey and the joy-eliciting screams of dying Fyroxi. How Frax wished he could join in the rest of the bloodshed. But Gaarhowl had chosen him for this most sacred of missions. Within this village was a girl, a girl that Gaarhowl wanted: the Sun

Wench, child of Yamaria. And Frax would ensure his spot among Gaarhowl's most honored, by delivering his lord the prize he most desired.

Frax cast his gaze around the settlement, hoping to find something that would lead him in the right direction. "If I werrre a stinking goddess's girl, what hole would I be hiding in?" His eyes caught a tent near the village head, where a few of the Fyroxi had run. He started to pad over; surely, the Fyroxi would want to protect someone of great importance to their tribe! A few of his fellow pack members, caught up in the bloodlust and seeing the children that had taken shelter in the tent, were also en route. But before they could reach the vulnerable flesh, another Fyroxi stepped from the tent. He was large and covered in scars. The big fox growled, and the ferocity of it caused the approaching Chillfang to retreat a step. Gathering up their courage and knowing they had others from their tribe to bolster them, the wolves charged. Unfortunately, they underestimated their enemy's skill and experience. The elder fox fought tooth and nail and, with a swiftness that scared even Frax, slew all three of his opponents.

Frax knew who this was now, seeing the missing tails and the ferocity; the alpha cursed himself for not recognizing the man sooner. All knew the stories of Sigmund, brother of Osmund, who had commanded the Fyroxi force in the war. All Chillfang hoped him dead, either by age or battle, but it was clear that all he'd gained was a few more scars.

Frax quickly turned around. He would take his chances that the Sun Wench wasn't huddling in the tent. Alpha or not, Frax wouldn't tangle with Sigmund if he had the choice.

Frax ran through the camp, rejoicing in all the bodies he passed, the corpses of the long-hated foes. The alpha saw his second entering tents and tossing out dismembered corpses. He was glad to see Cracktooth enjoying himself. The fool had suggested attacking while the Fyroxi were still in the midst of their celebration. Frax had dismissed his idea, with a great deal of grumbling from the giant wolf. It took only a nip on the nose to remind Cracktooth why Frax was alpha and Cracktooth was second, not the other way around. Though the second's idea was tactically sound, it would eliminate most of the fun of the hunt for scattered foes!

The closer he moved to the center of the village, the more bodies of his own he found. Frax grew distressed at the sight. This was supposed to be a simple fight: in and out, kill the tribe, capture the Sun Wench, and leave. But Frax could see that his pack was going to be thinning out more and more by the moment. The alpha spat out a curse meant for Yamaria, for making her people so damned crafty and bolted forward. He could smell the fresh blood in the air and the pheromones signifying danger. Looking back, Frax saw two Fyroxi running out one of the cubicles, killing Chillfang as they went. That was the cubicle that Cracktooth had been in last! Was his second dead? A feeling he'd not expected to feel on this joyous evening appeared within him—a twinge of fear. Frax cursed again and refocused. "I must find the Sun Wench. For Gaarrrhowl!" It didn't matter that his whole pack would die here. As long as he captured the girl, his gains would outclass anything he'd lost this day. A horde of Gaarhowl's most favored would be placed under his control! Once-dominant wolves would bow at his paws, and he would have more females than he could count.

Frax sniffed at the air and caught the scent. The sweet aroma of Fyroxi blood, freshly spilled, mixed with far more favorable pheromones, those of triumph. He darted toward the smell and saw precisely what he wanted to see.

Standing among a group of Fyroxi was a girl. Frax did not know the girl personally, but every Chillfang knew the look of the hated Sun Mother. This girl was the spitting image of the enemy goddess, and she held a dangerous weapon. The Chillfang knew instinctively from the smell and the way that his fellow pack members flinched away from its touch that it was one of the ancient magical artifacts of the Fyroxi. Though going up against one of those weapons made Frax afraid, it did confirm that he'd found his quarry. Who else but the goddess's child would hold that caliber weapon?

Frax loped in, gritting his teeth as the two Fyroxi who had killed Cracktooth slew yet another of his pack. The alpha's teeth snapped in anger. *No matterrr*, he thought. *Once I bring Gaarhowl his prize,*

I'll returrrn and give those Fyrrroxi their due payment! The thought brought him joy, even as he watched the spear of the Sun Wench pierce the side of one of his last. The death howls of the others had already stained the night sky.

Frax was rightfully scared by the weapon, and by the odds. *But* the alpha reminded himself, *Lord Gaarhowl has granted me gifts of my own. A reminder of the magic we once all possessed, to signify my prestige among his ranks.* The Chillfang tapped his tail against the icy shell over his fur, and his secret weapon twitched within the matted bush, awakened by the sudden movement. *Be rrready.* He warned the thing with his mind. *Soon, I shall have use forrr you.*

Frax crouched, his powerful muscles compacting, readying him for the attack. Like a spring, he unwound and soared through the air, landing atop his quarry as she bent to pull her spear from his dead comrade.

The girl cried out at the sudden attack, and Frax heard a crack followed by a stifled squeal of pain. *The girrrl is frrragile*, he thought regretfully. *I must be carrreful. Gaarhowl would not be pleased with a corrrpse.*

He shot a sidelong glance at the other two: a cripple and a diminutive little Fyroxi. How had they killed Cracktooth? The little one's mouth was held open in a silent scream, and both had fear in their eyes. *She is significant in theirrr minds. They will get their nerrrve up enough to fight me if I'm not careful. I have no intention to kill her.* A plan suddenly formed in his mind. *But they have no way of knowing that.*

"Make one wrrrong move and the girrrl dies," he growled. For good measure, Frax placed one of his paws on the girl's throat, deadly claws mere inches from severing her windpipe. *Now how do I get her out of here?*

Frax cast his gaze around the village, trying to find a point of escape. Of course, he had to find his quarry in the *center* of the settlement. Anywhere else might have made this far too easy. *Gaarhowl trrrusted me with this mission. I cannot fail; I will not fail.*

If he went toward the two Fyroxi, they would not hesitate to pounce on him, and no threat to the girl's life would keep Frax alive, not when she was out of any immediate danger. *She will have to be if I want to get her out.* Frax supposed he could lift her onto his back. She didn't seem like the heavy type. But any encumbrance would slow him down. Dragging her along might also slow him down and would leave him vulnerable to attacks from behind. He almost preferred the first option and prepared to get underneath the Sun Wench. But then he recalled his icy armor. *That would put her in a precarious position, which she could use to get off of me and ruin everything.*

Frax sighed, *Dragging it is!* But thoughts of his icy armor gave him an idea. The alpha shook his tail and growled at his secret weapon. He lowered it down toward the girl's stomach and felt her shudder as the fangs of the ice wraith, which lived in his thick tail, pierced flesh. Skin tinged blue, and muscles froze as subzero saliva mixed with her bloodstream. Now she wouldn't fight. He grinned his wolfish smile and turned to the others. "The Sun Wench is dead!" he announced, reveling in the gasps of despair from the two at the apparent death of their friend. *Now to get her out of here and to Gaarhowl, before her end truly comes.*

But if Frax had expected to make a clean getaway, he was a fool. The alpha hadn't expected another Fyroxi to enter the fray.

"All right, wolf. You're the last of your miserable kind, no small thanks to me," a smug voice boasted behind him. "And I'm going to have to ask you to get off of my prize."

Frax made the mistake of looking behind him and saw a tall Fyroxi male with blond hair and mottled fur, with a curved blade in either hand. He casually scraped their edges against each other while waiting for a response. Frax turned back around and wrapped his tail around the Sun Wench's leg, allowing the ice wraith to latch its jaw around her ankle, and began to lope away.

"Hey!" the smug one protested. "Don't you ignore me! She belongs to me!" When he didn't answer, the Fyroxi clicked his teeth. "Your funeral." Frax barely had time to react before the sharp blades pummeled onto his back, once, twice, thrice! The weapons slid harmlessly off the armor, but the alpha could feel chips coming off his pelt. He spun around, smelling the fresh blood enter the air as the ice wraith's teeth ripped out of his captive's leg.

Frax crouched low, growling fiercely, hoping to dissuade the cocky Fyroxi not to continue the offensive, but if anything, it had the opposite effect.

"I see you're not *as* cowardly as I first thought." He sniggered contemptuously. "I admire that, but you still have to die." Leif hopped forward again, stepping on the woman sprawled on the floor in his haste.

Frax momentarily heard the diminutive one growl, but then all his attention was taken by the scimitar-wielding Fyroxi in front of him. The blades weaved a dance of death, one that marked a skilled warrior, and the red crust that already lined their edges proved that Leif's words before weren't just idle boasts. The weapons clacked and cracked on his icy armor, shearing off shavings with each swing. It was all Frax could do to stay on the defensive; he couldn't get an attack in edgewise! And the alpha knew that his armor wouldn't last too much longer against this assault. *It's fine. I'll tirrre him out and then kill the idiot and take the Sun Wench back to my lord.*

But Frax had forgotten about the other two. Whether it was their unwillingness to let Leif get all the glory or the sight of Amaru on the ground that spurred them on, Frax soon found himself surrounded on three sides. Two snarling foxes and one grinning swordsman. The swordsman shot a dirty glare at the other two and scraped his swords as if claiming the kill for his own. Frax used the momentary distraction to burst forward out of his crouch, like he'd done with the girl before, except this time his momentum was all forward. His forceful attack knocked the cocky fox off balance, and Frax beat the scimitars out of the way, before flying into his own combo. Clawing and snapping at every piece of skin he could reach, the alpha bloodied the chest of the cocksure bastard.

Using the momentum from his body's desire to escape the pain which burned and froze at the same time, Leif leaped backward and regained his feet. But Frax wasn't alpha by chance of luck. It was all skill. While Leif was still resetting his stance and remained off-balance, the wolf spun and kicked out with his back legs, slamming the boy to the floor once more, with a pleasing spray of blood as a bonus.

Now the two others, who had been harrying his hindquarters, were right in front of him.

Weak one firrrst. Frax sprung forward, in a similar move as he'd done with the first. But Ren had been watching the battle unfold and rolled out of the way. Frax's rough landing gave Weylin the chance to jump in and pummel against the alpha's cracking armor. Frax was growing desperate now; he snapped his fangs shut on the cripple and shook him savagely, tossing him to the side with a grunt. Weylin fell hard to the sand and didn't rise, still breathing but out of the battle. *Now back to the little brat.* Frax padded over to the growling brown fox and smacked him with a paw, drawing a red line across his muzzle. Ren snapped out and grabbed the alpha's leg, which Frax quickly pulled out, earning him a painful scraping of flesh. "You're going to die forrr that!" he growled ominously. He pounced once again, but this time, the elusive little creature went under him! Ren kicked up with his hindlegs, causing Frax to whiff out his held breath. Oh, how the alpha wished that they were back in Moonwatch! The snow there crunched under his feet, making it hard to sneak up on perceptive prey, but at least he wouldn't have this damnable sand sliding under his feet. These Fyroxi were in their element, and the ice wraith wouldn't leave his tail, for fear of the killing heat.

Frax approached Ren, his annoyance at this foe quickly snowballing. He went for another bite, hoping to remove him from the competition, as he'd done with the older Fyroxi. But the alpha wasn't the only one doing repeat tricks; Ren tried once again to slip underneath the attack, but Frax was wise to the strategy this time. The massive wolf dropped to his stomach, pinning the smaller foe beneath him.

The two combatants began rolling, snapping futilely at each other, in hopes of severing something important. Had Frax been fighting a stronger Fyroxi, he might have been at a disadvantage. But as Ren had noted earlier, he wasn't bred for fighting and was tiring very quickly. It didn't take long for Frax to secure his place atop his winded foe and prepare to end his life. A triumphant grin on his muzzle, Frax raised his head to deliver the killing blow!

He howled in pain as a spear was thrust deep into his side. The alpha swiveled to see the source: the girl! The Sun Wench had been frozen solid! No amount of sun should have been able to fix that! But there she was, fire in her eyes and that hateful burning spear in her hands.

"Off of him!" The spear, still embedded in his flank, twisted and pushed forward, forcing him from the small one.

Ren smiled appreciatively up at Amaru, thrilled that she was still alive, but the glance went ignored, and Ren nodded, refocusing himself. Frax tried to stand, pain lancing through his side. The alpha Chillfang breathed raggedly, glancing around, once again searching for a way out. The scimitar wielder was up anew. The cripple was still down for the count, but the sly little one showed no intention of letting him through. And there was the Sun Wench, the spear still dripping red with his blood.

"So," Leif said, approaching with his blades scraping again, "does the wolf still want to fight, even when he's clearly outnumbered?" He smiled at the little growl that escaped Frax's throat. "I commend you for being so very brave, even if it's not smart." The boy actually had a tinge of *admiration* in his voice, and Amaru shot him a glare. "Fine," Leif sighed and lunged forward, biting his two swords into the back of Frax's legs simultaneously. He pulled them out, and Frax whimpered, effectively hamstrung and unable to move.

Amaru stalked forward with her spear held high. Frax knew he'd been beaten. There was no escape, no way out for him. *Oh well, might as well strrrike a little more fearrr in theirrr hearrrts; maybe Gaarhowl will give me crrredit and let me into his rrranks.* "You think you're safe, Sun Wench?" He managed a laugh, blood gurgling out from his previous wound. "You'll never be safe. Gaarhowl will have you!"

Amaru finished the deed, piercing the skull plate of the Chillfang alpha and destroying his brain.

The battle was won.

Then Amaru let out a deep shuddering breath. "That should be the last of them." She turned to Leif. "Go make sure. Check that all of them are actually dead." The boy nodded and ran off, knuckles white on his swords in anticipation. Amaru shifted her attention to

Ren. There was no smile on her face, only a strange mixture of anger and sorrow. "Are you all right?" Ren nodded. "Good," she said and turned to Weylin, dropping her spear and laying her hands on the older Fyroxi's neck. They glowed white for a moment, and Weylin groaned, coming back into consciousness. Once she was sure his head had been gathered, Amaru looked into his eyes. "Xio and your two kits are safe with the elders. They have Sigmund to protect them, so I harbor no fear for them." Weylin mumbled his thanks and began to lope over in the direction that Amaru indicated.

Ren slipped back to humanoid form and ran up to Amaru. "What about you? What that Chillfang said—"

She cut him off, "I know. They wanted me. Or rather, their god wants me." Her brass eyes were guarded, not blocking whatever emotions she was harboring. The white gown she had worn at the party was colored red with blood and had lost a ton of fabric. Small scratches marked her body, but no serious wounds. The spear she held, however, was drenched in the blood of the Chillfang alpha. Small shards of ice dripped off the haft, melting in the still-warm desert air. "Durrigan was right; the Chillfang are here, in the Scorched Waste. Why? What would possess them to come here? For beings as cold as they are, this whole kingdom must be unbearable."

"I wouldn't even want to think about what their home is like!" Ren replied. "And I just did." He shivered involuntarily.

Amaru gazed numbly around at the corpses littering the sand. "So many dead. I worked so hard to increase our numbers, and now…"

Ren knew what she meant. On the way over to her, he had counted five corpses at least. All her life's work had been undone in a single night. "At least we killed them all, right?" he asked, trying to sound hopeful.

"This was only the first attack. There will be more." Amaru wasn't sure how she knew it, but there was no doubt in her mind. "I don't want to let this happen again. I'm going to talk to the elders." She turned around and stalked off, Ren left trying to reach out a hand to comfort her.

Eventually, Xio came out of the elder's hut and buried her face in Ren's shoulder, crying profusely. Ren, still stunned by the night's events, held her tightly and tried to speak soothingly to his frightened friend. They stood outside of the tent, listening to the muffled sounds erupting from within. Voices were raised, and a heated argument seemed to ensue before finally everything calmed down. There were successive grunts of approval, and after a while, Amaru came out of the tent. She barely spared a glance at them, but Ren was sure he glimpsed sadness in her eyes. Amaru lingered for a while in her hut, before finally coming out. In one hand, the girl held her new spear, using it as a walking staff. She wore a new red robe with white trim, a deep cowl tucked over her head, hiding everything but her face and the bottom of her hair. No tails were visible behind her back, buried as they were under her cloak. A small pack sat high on her back, filled with provisions and other necessities.

Ren took in her outfit. If he hadn't known any better, she could have passed off like any human girl. "Wh-why are you dressed like that, Amaru?" he asked, though he likely already knew the answer.

The guards were back around her eyes, and she kept her voice even. "I'm leaving."

Ren's eyes widened, and he reached out toward her. "No! You can't leave!"

She gritted her teeth. "I have no other choice!"

"You could stay here! I don't see what is possessing you to leave!" Xio whined. "We don't want to lose you, not after this!" She gestured to the bloody field.

"This is precisely why I must leave," Amaru explained. "The Chillfang are trying to capture or kill me, and I doubt that they'll stop at anything until they do." She began to walk away, her two friends on her heels. "I don't want to be the cause of another event like this. I know I can't stop the attacks, especially since it's still Chillfang fighting Fyroxi, the age-old conflict. But if by leaving, I can find some way to protect you. Remember what I said before: 'I'd do anything for you, my friends, my people.'"

"And if they do come back?" Xio peeped quietly.

"Then you'll be prepared," Amaru assured. "Those dogs won't catch you off guard again. Next time they attack, you will kill them."

Ren and Xio agreed only half-heartedly. "Where will you go?"

Now standing at the fringe of the village, Amaru turned to face her friends one last time. The worry was etched deeply in Xio's face. The same was true with Ren, but he also showed a deep longing. He wanted to go with her, she knew. "Even if I knew that answer, I wouldn't tell you. It is unsafe for you to know where I am, what I'm doing. This is goodbye, for now. Perhaps forever. If so, I will see you in Yamaria's sunlit halls!" With that, Amaru stuck her spear butt to the sand and traveled away from the place she had spent her first one hundred years.

Xio could see the conflict and the pain in Ren's eyes. Standing next to him, she put an arm around his back, leaned her head on his shoulder, and wrapped their tails together. Seeing one of his closest friends deeply hurt and driven away, the brown-haired Fyroxi needed comfort, and Xio was just the one to give it to him. Standing like this just felt right to Xio, two close friends holding on tight, after their world crashed down around them. Amaru was right: they would fight, and they would kill the Chillfang, no matter what it meant.

ALARIC
Meeting a Perfect Stranger

Alaric regarded his opponent critically wishing, as he always did, that Sultan would show some emotion, give some betrayal of his moves beforehand. He was an elf, able to move with the grace of a water nymph and strike with the speed of a wind sprite, but all of Gemna's training would be for naught if he didn't have the necessary information with which to decide his strategy. *Or perhaps, that's precisely why Gemna keeps pairing us together*, Alaric realized. *She wants me to be able to fight an enemy I can't interpret.* Though to be fair, he never understood why it was they had to learn to fight in the first place. The Scorched Waste was dry, dusty, but most of all empty! What around here needed to be challenged, especially hand to hand?

As an elven lad, his father had tried to make him learn the ways of the long sword and longbow, though he never saw much use in any of them. He much preferred winning battles with the strings of a lute, and the only bow he planned to pick up was used on a fiddle. Besides, who needed a blade, when you could drive mental nails into someone's head? *You see, Father? Music can be useful in fighting. Self-defense is part of bardic training!*

Sultan stood slack in front of him, his body not even in the ready position. Taking the opportunity he saw, Alaric leaped forward, planning to deliver a jarring blow to the boy's head, as the desert dweller had tried to do to him. Uncoiling like a spring, Sultan intercepted the blow and retaliated. His bare fist thumped into Alaric's chest, and for a moment, the elf thought his heart had stopped. *That's going to bruise.*

When he was sure that his heart was still beating, the elf attempted another attack and then another. Each pass was blocked by some part of Sultan's arm. *He'll barely even show the bruises, lucky bastard*, he thought ruefully.

Keeping his perceptive eyes on Sultan's flat ones still did Alaric little good, as the blows kept flying. Alaric stepped into the defensive procedures he had learned in his time. Though Sultan's unexpected attacks were startling, very few could get passed the elf's defense when he really tried. As he blocked, he chose certain parts to leave open, hoping that Sultan would take the bait. And like a sandfish, so he did. As Alaric flashed an opening between his arms, the dark fist came sailing in. Without a moment's notice, the forelimbs clapped together, trapping the wrist. One of Alaric's long legs swept under, taking Sultan's legs out from under him. Alaric shifted position as he fell, and the satisfying "oof" as his elbow drove into the boy's stomach made the bruises all worthwhile.

Gemna's slow clap filled the tall spires of the Solgaele Monastery, as Alaric put one foot on his prone foe and raised a hand in triumph. "Congratulations, you've passed lesson one for the day. Let's see how you do with the rest of them," Gemna said dryly.

Like most nights, Alaric went to bed sore and bone-tired, though feeling accomplished. For what little there was to do around here, he did it all to the best of his ability. The rest of his days and nights followed the same pattern: wake up, eat breakfast, train, meditate, eat supper, sleep. *Wash, rinse, repeat.* Occasionally, visiting monks would stop in, and the training would get a little more fun. New techniques, new stories, and sometimes new girls. Some of the trainees and trainers who dropped by were undeniably pretty. Sometimes it didn't even take much; a smile or an impressive round of stylish combat and they would fall all over him. *Ha, they always say that monks are special and full of self-restraint.* He chuckled at the thought. *Nonsense, they are just like any other person.*

Alaric wasn't surprised to find out that Gemna knew what he was up to at night. He knew that when his training was extra strenuous in the morning, it was supposed to be a punishment. *I really don't see why I should be punished. Most of the time, it's not even my fault. They almost beg for it, especially if they come from the wider kingdom and know who I am. I simply follow the rules of your training.*

"If it is within the parameters of your mind, soul, and body to fulfill an ally's desire, then do so with gratefulness and know you will be in their good graces." Gemna *loved* to say that, but when it came down to his late-night excursions with the initiates, she seemed to forget it right quick.

*****

One night while Alaric was out practicing his fiddle playing, the distant strains of music caught his ears. Stowing his own fiddle on a rock, he sprinted to the top of the dune, from which he could see the desert laid out before him. Off a ways from the monastery, he saw lights and music. He could only imagine what sort of celebration that would be! There would be people, excellent food, colors, and most importantly: people! Alaric stayed and observed until the music eventually died down, his cue to leave and head to bed. As he fell asleep, he heard a high-pitched whine that gave him an eerie feeling, but he was fast asleep before he could think any more about it.

The next morning, he confronted Gemna. "There was a party going on last night. We had no special training or meetings last evening. Why didn't you tell me about it?"

A light laugh burbled from Gemna's throat. "It's hard enough trying to keep you faithful to your oaths while you're here under our roof. Had you gone into that village, you may have never come back." Without realizing it, her words had a double meaning. "Far too much temptation for a man like you."

Alaric realized that fighting her on that was pointless and changed the subject. "And that howl last night? You heard that right?"

Gemna's brow scrunched up in confusion. "Yes, what a strange sound. I've not heard of wolves anywhere in these parts."

Alaric stared northward, in the general direction of the Eclipse. "Even Kindol Woods didn't have wolves," he said, referring to his old home. "You don't think they could have come from the other side of the Eclipse?" During his time as a traveling minstrel, he'd heard many tales about the wolf-beasts from Moonwatch. Was it possible that these were more than just tall tales? He'd been so very young at the time of the war, and Kindol Woods was quite far away from the front lines, so he had no personal way to prove or disprove them.

"I doubt it," Gemna sounded completely assured. "The Eclipse has kept us separated for over a century. Why would it break now? That seems like it would ruin those mad wizards' plans, whatever they may be. Besides, with its dimensions, no wolf could make their way over or through it. If anything, it was someone playing a joke, mimicking the sound of that baying creature."

Alaric shrugged and returned to his training, satisfied with that answer.

For the next few days, he continued his work, breaking the meager wood for the cook fire and assisting with making the bread on the rocks, whatever he could do to keep busy. He knew that Master Kellick would be around on his circuit soon, with one of his star pupils, Nadia. Alaric awaited her arrival, for the two got on famously, much to Gemna's and Kellick's chagrin. Or at least he did wait for her, until the day when he saw the most beautiful woman in the world.

It was a day just like any other, less than a week after hearing the festival music and the "wolf howl." Alaric was tuning his fiddle, drawing the bow across the strings, to ensure the music was sweet when he glimpsed movement in his peripheral vision. Looking in the direction of the shadow, he saw a figure cresting the tall dune he'd run up only a few nights prior. A solitary figure, which meant it wasn't Master Kellick arriving early.

Always one to entertain a possible guest and draw them in, Alaric began to play. Casting his eyes up to the person, he saw them turning toward his music. He smiled, another one caught by the masterful web of music. Returning his eyes to the instrument, he awaited the visitor's approach, his sharp elven ears picking up the sound of their sandals shifting in the sand. As he drew to the end of the song, he dropped his hands to his lap and turned a smile upon the visitor.

His eyes studied her face as she drew nearer, and his smile melted into a look of awe. There was no doubt in his mind. This woman, moving toward him now, was more gorgeous than any he had ever seen. Thoughts of Gemna and the apprentice girl—what was her name again?—dropped from his mind, as he took in her beauty.

A calm, deeply tanned face, with eyes the color of brass. *Such a unique color!* Soft lips sat underneath a small, straight nose. Her face was framed by luscious black hair that fell down a little past her shoulders. The hem of her red-and-white robe flowed around her ankles in the hot breeze. To Alaric's well-trained eye, even the concealing garb showed hints of a lovely figure. A masterfully crafted spear rested in her hands, but Alaric barely spared it a glance, too absorbed in the girl who held it.

After he had stared for a few precious moments, she looked at him curiously. "Hello?"

Her voice is clear and sweet, like bells. He shook himself. "I'm sorry, milady." He bowed deeply to her. "I was distracted for a moment."

"I could see that." She cleared her throat. "I wasn't planning to stop here today, but I heard your playing. It's been a few days since I've listened to any good music. Could I trouble you for another song?"

"For you, my lady?" Alaric straightened himself out. "I will play whatever you wish. It gets so incredibly dull out here."

Alaric thought for a moment. How best to impress this woman?

He looked into her eyes once again, holding himself back, so as not to get lost in them. His heart called for playing one of his best, right off the bat, but his entertainer's sense warned him otherwise. *You fool! Never start with your best work! Lead up to it, with slow, gentle steps. Like a dance, starting simple and growing more complex, more* intimate *with every verse.*

And so he did; he played a short set of songs, simple but naturally beautiful. When he finished and bowed, she applauded politely.

That wasn't even very good, easy music, and he'd missed a few notes. Alaric vowed to practice more.

"It seems that you are quite a fair hand at the fiddle. Not many in this desert choose to learn string instruments. In the hot air and grating sand, they are difficult to maintain."

He smiled and nodded. "It is a constant task, but it is a challenge I take pride in. As of yet, in my years here, it has not managed to beat me, and I refuse to give up!"

She chuckled at the airs he put on. "You must be a very resilient man to put up with all of that."

"It is why they call me the Indomitable Alaric Honeytone!" He said the name as if it was something she should recognize

She rolled her eyes. "Oh, is that so? Who exactly calls you that?"

"My fans, of course!" He looked around sheepishly and lowered his voice to a whisper. "Though you won't find many of them around here. Unfortunately, I have been trapped! Isolated from the people who beg for my appearance!" The edges of her mouth quirked upward in a little smile, which Alaric took as encouragement. "You would honor my fellow monks and me by supping with us this evening."

She looked into the sky and shook her head ruefully. "It was a pleasure meeting you, but I must return home for now."

Alaric sighed in disappointment. "Well, my music will always be here for you, should you desire to hear it. Will I see you again?"

"Perhaps" was her only reply, as she began to walk away.

Before she could travel too far, he called out to her. "My lady?" She turned. "I don't believe I caught your name!"

She hesitated for a moment as if deciding whether to answer. "Amber," she finally replied.

"Amber." The name felt sweet on his tongue; Alaric couldn't help himself. "You may believe me too brash or perhaps even a fool, but I believe that you are the most radiant woman I have ever seen!"

She gave no response to that, except to turn back from whence she came.

You idiot! he reprimanded himself. *You'll drive her away if you don't guard your tongue!*

AMARU

Indecisiveness

Amaru cursed herself for being too trusting with the man at the monastery. *Anyone could be working with the Chillfang.* As she'd told him, she was planning to pass it by; but only a few days after leaving and wandering the desert, she'd quickly grown lonely. She'd known it wouldn't be easy to drop everything she knew and loved, but it had to be done, for the sake of her people.

But, Mother above, hearing the sounds of music playing had tugged at her so firmly that she couldn't avoid going to meet the player! "Alaric Honeytone," she said aloud. Amaru had to admit it rolled well off her tongue, and he'd played so stunningly. But Amaru could tell that she hadn't even scratched the surface of his talents.

The way that Alaric spoke of himself, he sounded so confident, and he certainly enjoyed putting on a show. He talked as if he were performing for a full crowd of adoring fans, instead of one stranger. As much as she hated to admit it, she found *Alaric* amusing. *I should leave, continue my journey, get as far away from my home as possible,* the rational part of her brain argued. *That way, fewer people will be put in danger.*

But the other part, the wistful and already-lonely piece of her, countered with "Where's the problem in making a friend? Alaric seems nice enough. Are you going to remain suspicious of everyone who might be able to help you? You'll end up a hermit, and you know that's not what you want."

"If I must," she answered the voices in her head.

*****

Despite herself, she found her way back to the monastery the next day and the day after that. By the end of the week, visiting became a part of her regular schedule. She'd wake up, check the area for anyone who might be watching, slip into fox form and do some hunting, preparing the meat and setting it out to dry and cook on a hot rock. Usually, by early afternoon, she would be on her way toward Solgaele Monastery, where Alaric would be waiting for her. She was introduced to some of the other vital people: Gemna, one of the masters, a woman past her prime but still spry enough to keep up with the trainees. Sultan, a queerly detached boy, not quite two decades old. Vrain, a large man who was undeniably more brawn than brain.

Amaru continued to introduce herself as Amber and made sure to conceal her Fyroxi parts as best as possible. She hated the feeling of tying up her tails and ears, but she had to keep herself a secret. A white-furred Fyroxi girl traveling around the desert after the attack of clan Fire-Strider would be way too easy to distinguish. Though she didn't want to have her tribe be attacked, Amaru also didn't want to single herself out as a target.

If Alaric noticed her reservedness, he had the social grace not to mention it. He kept a smile on his face, a song ready in his throat, and a caring look in his eyes. It had been clear from the day they'd met that he was interested in her for more than merely a cordial relationship. Amaru couldn't be sure if his first parting words were actually meant to plant the seed of his affection or whether it was a casual slip of the tongue for him. Talking to Gemna, it seemed like the latter, with his "appetite for women," as she put it. But she was careful not to give him anything that might be taken the wrong way. Alaric was a fine man, but she didn't see him that light. Not after what she'd just managed to escape from. Alaric was a refreshing and entertaining change of pace, both from the sterile sands and from the people she'd known in her old home; that was all.

EMERY

Shadows and Secrets

E mery walked briskly down the dark stone hallway. Her inquiries to the servants had led her farther beneath the castle than she'd ever been. The thin silk of her dress did little to abate the chill that presided in the passage. Keeping one hand on the wall, she wondered why there were no lights, no fires. A sudden gust of wind from an unknown source had blown out her candle, leaving her in the dark. *This place gives me the creeps*, she thought. *It's like unseen eyes are watching me.* She considered going back up for a torch. Some of the earlier passages had sconces stocked with them. *A torch would provide both light and a small bit of warmth*, she added, shivering. No, Emery knew that if she left, she might never work up the courage to return again. Thoughts of Leo were all that allowed her to continue walking. *I must know what happened to him. And Ignis Duskwalker must have that information.*

So on she went, not stopping until she finally reached a door. She couldn't see if there were any distinguishing features to it, as the darkness was blacker and thicker than pitch. The sound of her knock echoed through the hall. No immediate response came, but Emery kept patient. Just as she was about to knock a second time, the door swung open, and her fist dropped through empty air.

"Princess? What are you doing here?" a gruff voice answered.

"How can you see me?" she asked, surprised that he'd recognized her in the darkness.

"I have my ways," Ignis answered vaguely. "I ask again. What are you doing here? This is one hell of a place to get lost in."

"I wanted to speak to you, as the crown's Secretkeeper."

"Ah." She heard him shuffle his feet. "Come in then." Emery hesitated for a moment. The room looked just as dark as the hall, perhaps even darker, if that was possible. "I conduct all of my meetings in darkness...in secrecy."

Emery nodded and went inside. "But you can see people in the darkness?"

"Consider that our little secret. You were the last person I expected to see here, so my tongue slipped." They walked together in silence, the only sound the scuffing of feet on the stone and light breathing. Emery marveled that they didn't encounter any furniture. Either the Secretkeeper kept a spotless room, or he had very little. She imagined that such a useful role would be well paid, so were his chambers barren by choice?

Finally, the two reached the only items in the room. A small table and a set of chairs. Ignis guided the princess into one and sat on the far side himself. Emery heard joints cracking and the chair squealing slightly on the stone floor as Ignis sat down.

"So what did you wish to speak of? Your father? This morning's meeting?"

She almost said no, but if the Secretkeeper was offering, then there might be something worth hearing. "Yes, and another matter as well."

"Then let us converse." Emery heard a fluttering as something flapped through the air, as Ignis's raven landed on his shoulder. "Your father was...not quite what you expected, I take it?"

"No, not at all," Emery admitted. "I knew that he'd changed while in power, but so much? It was disappointing to see."

"I understand, Princess," Ignis said, the same way he said everything, grimly, darkly. "I've tried to tell him that he will appear weak and foolish, but he never listens."

Emery swore under her breath. "What will happen if he doesn't fix his reputation or change his ways?"

Ignis Duskwalker chuckled. "Then I suspect his rule won't last as long as he might like."

"And what will happen once he's no longer king?" Emery was worried for her brother and mother.

The tone of his voice made Emery think Ignis was shrugging. "I cannot see the future. With any luck, you will end up on the throne, left with your father's burdens to carry and his mistakes to remedy."

Emery sighed. "My father has enemies, plenty of them, but what about friends? Are there any allies who might come to his defense?"

"The nobles like him plenty, and many of their families have gold and power."

"And beyond the castle walls?" Emery pressed. "Anything out there that will be friendly to us?"

"That number grows smaller every day. The king won the Gnomes today; but he lost one tribe of Humans, one of Elves, and one of Fyroxi. He will want for protection within, soon enough."

"The Lightstriders, any information on their progress?"

"Many rumors, none from reliable sources. The crown's warriors can be notoriously hard to track down if they are let out of your sight."

Emery's heart caught in her throat. *Leo...* "And what of another warrior loyal to the crown? Could you find them?"

"You ask of your lion. The Braveheart, I believe they call him."

"Y-yes." Emery felt her stomach lurch, and her heart skipped a beat. As if Ignis knew what was going on inside her, he waited. Emery could hear a faint scratching sound like he was using one of his daggers to clean underneath his nails. "Tell me what you know of Leonidas Braveheart."

Another few moments, he paused before replying. "Nothing."

"What do you mean nothing?"

"I mean nothing when I say nothing, Princess," Ignis answered at length. "The Braveheart went into the desert and seemed to disappear off the face of the continent."

"I'm sure a man like yourself has sources in the desert," Emery protested. "How could you have no information whatsoever?" The princess realized that by not having a light in the room, Ignis and his client would both be left in the dark considering the emotions of their conversation partner. *Or at least the client is left blind. I'm not quite sure about the Duskwalker.*

"Even my spies are mortal. It is not my fault that they didn't catch sight of one specific man." His words sounded more like a shrug than a defense.

"If we have no basis of information, my father will never authorize a search for Sir Leonidas. Am I just supposed to give up on our Royal Defender? Is it our place to just step away without trying to recover him, or his corpse?" Thinking of the latter made her stomach lurch again.

Ignis cleared his throat. "I will give you one piece of advice, Princess. You are allowing emotion to cloud your judgment. Sometimes, when it comes to someone you love, it is best to step back and try to view the situation with a clear head."

"Someone I love." Emery bolted upright, immediately on the defensive. "H-how did you know?"

She could imagine his sly smile. "I *am* the Secretkeeper, Princess Emery. That makes your *secret* affection for your knight my business. You don't make it far in my position without knowing a little bit about everyone."

Emery blew out a long breath. "What do you suggest? How do I go about finding Leo?"

"This may not be the answer you want to hear, Princess, but it is the best one I can give." He waited for a moment, to ensure she was listening. "Just push the whole ordeal to the back of your head. You need to focus on these council meetings, learn everything you can about the people of the kingdom that will one day be yours."

"And what about Leonidas?" Emery couldn't help herself from asking.

"Like I said, Princess, have patience. I've never been much of one for the gods most people keep, but sometimes, it seems that there are fated plans for people. Perhaps everything will work out in time."

From Ignis's lips, that sounded just cryptic enough to come true, so Princess Emery sighed resignedly. "Fine."

"Good." The chair scraped on the stone floor again as he rose. "Now, you were never here to visit me, Princess. You were only taking a nap." With that, he snapped his fingers, and Emery woke up in her bed.

ALARIC

Irresistible Temptations and the Danger that Comes with Them

After his comment on the first day, Alaric was worried all night about whether Amber would return. When she crested the dune the next day, cool relief spread through his body and mind. From then on, he was more careful with his words. He wasn't sure what it was about her, but she seemed…special, and he didn't feel like giving that up.

As days turned into a week and a week into two, Alaric grew ever fonder of Amber, and not just for her beauty. He knew he had to temper his expectations, as it was clear that she wasn't going to fall into his arms at the slightest compliment. That was certainly frustrating, but he accepted the annoyance in stride, just as he had accepted being dumped at the monastery. Actually, for the first time in the five years he had lived in the desert, Alaric realized that perhaps he didn't resent his time at Solgaele, didn't resent his father for trapping him here of all places. *I'd never had gotten to meet Amber had I lived in Kindol Woods the rest of my life. What a stroke of luck for me!*

*****

Amber was late. Alaric stared out the hole in the stone wall that served as a window. His sharp eyes caught every movement in the sand: a slithering snake, a scuttling scorpion, but no beautiful

human girl. Alaric could be patient when it suited him, so he waited. He didn't want to consider the possibility that she wasn't showing up. They'd been talking about the spear she carried the day before. Though she seemed sweet enough, Alaric surmised that she couldn't survive if she didn't know how to use that weapon. Finally, she'd given in and promised to show him some moves the next day. Now she hadn't shown up. He wished he'd asked where Amber lived. It had to be within a morning's walk from the monastery, and Alaric didn't know of any settlements that close. The monastery was meant to be secluded, and even the village that he could see from the top of the dune, the one that had held the party on the night of Wolf's Howl, was at least three days' brisk walk away from Solgaele Monastery. A sudden thought occurred to him. Does Amber live alone in the Scorched Waste? If she'd had other friends, she would have introduced them already. *And she wouldn't have a reason to show up here every day.*

Gemna finally strode over and put a hand on Alaric's shoulder. "It's possible she got caught up hunting." She'd made the same guess as Alaric had. "She wouldn't want to leave herself out of a meal when she returned home."

"Why do you think she refuses to stay with us? You and I both have offered to let her remain for supper, or for the night."

Gemna shrugged. "I'm sure she has her reasons for keeping away. Whatever they are, you need to respect them."

Alaric turned halfway to his mentor. "You don't think..." He didn't want to think about the possibility. "She ran afoul of something?"

Before Gemna could answer, Alaric caught movement at the top of the sand dune. "There she is!" Amber was running at top speed down the sand dune, her robe flapping wildly in the momentum. "Why is she running?" The elf ran out the door and called out to her.

Catching sight of him, she motioned for him to get inside. "Alaric! Please," she cried, "get back to safety!"

Safety? Why safety? Amber wouldn't be saying that if there wasn't something wrong! Just then, something else crested the top of the hill. Multiple men in mottled brown clothing and masks of some sort that gleamed in the sun. They all charged down the hill, straight toward Amber, most with swords and one with dual daggers in hand. The last man raised one hand, taking a moment to aim. Alaric's legs started to move on their own, the world seeming to move in slow motion, even as he bounded up the hill. He was faintly aware of Amber yelling at him to turn around. Was she a fool? He wouldn't abandon her to the mercy of these heathens! Doing so would make him no better than they, and that was something he refused to allow.

As he had the thought, the man jerked his hand forward and released. It should have been an impossible shot. She was running downhill away from them; the sun was right in his eyes. But the dagger flew through the air and stuck right into Amber's left leg. At the impact, the beautiful girl stumbled and fell, her spear going flying as she rolled down toward him. The scream of pain that escaped her sweet lips gave Alaric a burst of supernatural strength. He closed the gap in mere seconds, it seemed. As he came closer, he realized he didn't have a weapon of any sort on him. *Oh well, I'm here now.* He did the first thing that came to mind. The elf leaped forward, the full driving force of his palm smashing into his enemy's nose. The mask wasn't made of a sturdy material, so it bent easily at the hit. There was a sickening crunch as the mass of cartilage was forced to the side. He didn't even think as the knife slashed upward, leaning back, so the blade only made a shallow scratch. The elf grabbed the wrist of the knife hand and twisted it. His foe's grip on the knife weakened, and it fell to the sand. The wrist was a surprising position of control, and with his grip, Alaric only needed one sharp jerk to bring the bandit to his knees. The elf's knee came up with a jarring force, delivered straight to the bottom of the chin. The man was out cold before his head hit the ground.

Alaric turned his attention to the others. They now stood right above Amber, yelling in some unintelligible language, as she tried to roll away as fast as she could. Alaric scooped up the man's knife and charged down the hill, carefully placing his feet so as not to stumble. Falling on his blade now would make him no use to anyone, and Amber would be killed. His gut roiled again at the possibility.

Alaric had the high ground; he needed to do something smart. Amber would be tiring quickly, and those men would be all over her when she did. He wondered why they hadn't pounced yet, but he decided not to question it any further. *Count your blessings and save the girl.*

He jumped down, launching his whole weight on top of one of the men. He swept the knife toward his foe. Alaric couldn't aim in the tumble they were in now, but now, anything could help. He could feel the muscles rippling under the skin and knew this man could break him apart if given half a chance. The blade whiffed through the air and jabbed into flesh, eliciting a yell as it punctured his foe's stomach. Alaric released his hold on the man and rolled backward, clearing himself from danger. He spared a look back at Amber. Her robe was ripped in multiple places, but besides the knife still in her leg, she seemed unharmed. He shot her a confident smile, unsure where the self-assurance came from.

He shouldn't have looked back because in that instant, another of the men was on top of him. If they had shown reluctance to kill Amber, he had no such restraint with Alaric. He was just barely able to move his neck out of the way of each sword jab.

He tried to roll away, but the human's weight had him pinned. *Is this the tragic end for Alaric Honeytone? I can hear the town criers now.*

"Talent dried up! Beloved bard dies in the desert, murdered by a malignant, jealous fan!" They always had some way to spice these stories up.

Amber, my sweet, do as you asked me and get yourself to safety.

Just then, the man rolled to the side, snarling, and Alaric was shocked back to reality. Out of his shoulder stuck the wooden shaft of a bolt. As he rolled, he saw Gemna standing at the door of the monastery, a crossbow in hand. She loaded another bolt and prepared to fire again. Alaric took the opportunity to check on Amber. "You all right, my lady?"

"Why didn't you run?"

"And leave you to die? Unthinkable!"

She started to struggle to her feet, keeping as much weight off her injured leg. "This should be my battle. I shouldn't allow you to fight it for me."

Part of Alaric wanted to push Amber down and force her to rest, but the logic in the situation demanded otherwise. The knife hadn't done any critical damage to her leg, and he would need all the help he could get. Gemna could only have gathered so many arrows on short notice.

The man was enraged at the stinging shafts whizzing toward him and yelled at the monk mistress, who snapped off another shot, followed by another, until the foe fell prone to the sand. Alaric walked over to Amber's spear and slammed his foot on the butt end, flipping it to his grip and handing it directly to the proper owner.

Alaric finally got his wish, to see the girl in action with her spear. Ignoring whatever pain her leg was in, she stepped forward, using the reach of the spear to keep the last foe at bay. Gemna continued to fire at the injured one, eventually killing him. Alaric wished for a moment he had taken weapon training seriously as a lad but then realized he wouldn't be here if he had. So instead, he served as a distraction while Amber went in with the spear. He couldn't help but notice that she was hesitant with the attacks, even though this man had nothing but malign wishes. Still, even her tentative strikes showed more than just a few ounces of skill in her gorgeous body. But her assailant was quick. He dodged around the attacks and prepared to make his own advance. He punched forward with the hilt of his sword, driving it hard into Amber's stomach. The girl fell back, and her spear instinctively swung up. That instinctive move saved her life, as the wooden haft slammed into her foe's head, dazing him for just a moment and stopping his blade from driving through her stomach. Just one moment too long, as one more bolt protruded through that man's throat, ending his life.

Amber lay on the ground, clutching her stomach and sucking in air to recover what the man had blasted out of her. Alaric too fell backward. He could hear Amber crying next to him. He propped himself up on one elbow and reached his other hand to stroke her arm comfortingly. "Hey, it's all right," he cooed. "We won; they're gone." Alaric let out a low whistle. "And you were fantastic with that spear. If you hadn't distracted that one, Gemna and I might both be dead now."

"If it weren't for me, you never would have been attacked. I should have stayed away; I almost got all of you killed. I refused to let that happen again," she whispered implacably.

For once, even Alaric was at a loss for words. *Again? What darkness weighs down her beautiful conscience?* "My lady..." he trailed off, looking for the right words. "'Almost' is the operative word. Nobody died, so you needn't feel ashamed. Would you rather you hadn't come to us and been slaughtered without a chance to survive?" He shook his head. "No, you don't want that, and neither do I." Alaric sat up and put an arm around her shoulders. "Frankly, I've grown quite fond of you over the past weeks. Had I lost you today, I never would have forgiven myself!"

"You'll have to forgive me then." Seeing the alarmed look in his eyes, she scrambled to explain. "While I won't die on purpose, I'm afraid that I cannot continue coming here." Amber's eyes showed signs of a hurting heart, and Alaric wished he knew the way to comfort her.

"About that." Alaric shook his head. "Not happening."

She looked sharply up at him. "What do you mean?"

"My lady, Amber, if you think I am going to let you go back out into the Scorched Waste alone, after what I just saw today, you have another think coming."

"But—" Amaru started to say, but Alaric held up a finger; he wasn't quite done.

"Besides"—he favored her with a winning smile—"if I lost you, I wouldn't have anyone to share my music with." He gestured to the other residents of Solgaele Monastery, some of which had joined them out by the dune. "None of these people appreciate it the way you do." He pointed to Sultan. "Did I tell you that this one tried to punch me in the head for playing my music a little too loud?"

That got a laugh out of her. Never had a laugh sounded so sweet.

"I suppose you did save my life," Amber admitted. "I would be remiss to just leave you without proper thanks."

"Well, if you're looking for a good reward, me thinks a sweet kiss for the dashing hero would serve."

"Don't push your luck," she said, but she was still smiling, and to Alaric, that was worth more than all the gold in the world.

EMERY
A Wonderful Gift

After meeting with Lord Ignis, Emery took his suggestions to heart. During the day, the princess would try to push Leonidas from her mind and convene with her father and Casinius at council meetings. And as insightful as those were, a much less frequent activity caught her attention more soundly. Finally, after years of waiting, Emery was allowed to attend court. The princess had never known what her father did in the morning hours until she was allowed to join King Godfrey.

As the heir of Redwyn sat in the throne room at her father's side, she was amazed by the mass of people. The stone walls, hung with tapestries and paintings, were lined by guardsmen, who stood solemnly with spears in hand. Sunlight streamed in through the tall windows and poured from the glass dome that capped the room. It washed over the supplicants who came to present their problems to the king. Their clothing and walks made clear the difference between their classes. Nobles swished in wearing fine silk and cloth. Middle-class folk wearing fairly average pieces walked in with deference but confidence as well. There was even a smattering of commoners some of whom limped or dragged weak limbs up the steps to the throne. Emery was distressed to see their torn woolen shifts and scratchy rough spun robes. *Do they not have any better clothing for court?* Even worse was the shape they seemed to be in. She made a mental reminder to ask her father about it after they were done here.

As each person came into the room, the king's page, daughter of one of the noble families, spoke to them. "You stand before His Majesty, Godfrey Redwyn, Sixth of His Name, King of Sun's Reach and Lord of Searstar, and Her Royal Highness, Princess Emery Redwyn! Come forward and make your plea."

Emery sat patiently and listened to the nobles' gripe about increased prices of fine cloth and wine (Emery had negotiated an increase of pay per cask to the Rainclaw family to ensure their continued cooperation to the throne). "Not only did I have to pay more for my wine, when I went to Cynderstone to pick it up, but some filthy commoners also refused to give me their place in line," one of them complained.

Emery saw that her father was about to agree with them and was appalled! How could he turn a blind eye to such blatant disrespect of his subjects? Struggling to keep her voice even, she addressed this complaining man directly. "Lord Errig? If I may, I believe that Cynderstone is located in the Central Ward. Am I correct about this?" Lord Errig, an older scrawny man nodded. "As far as I recall, the Central Ward was made for people of all backgrounds, not just nobles."

The nobleman spluttered, "Yes, but—"

Emery silenced him with a sharp wave. "Lord Errig, those 'filthy commoners,' as you call them, are just as much subjects of the king as you are. They have equal access to products such as wine as you." She paused a moment, her finger on her chin. "If access is equal, then whoever shows up first should be served first. Does this sound correct?"

"I suppose," he stammered. "However—"

"Lord Errig," Emery sighed, "you are making this harder on yourself than you need to. From now on, you can wait a few minutes for your order of wine."

Lord Errig seemed embarrassed. "I-I understand, my lady." He bowed. "Forgive me for this intrusion. I shall keep these points in mind." Flanked by his servants, the nobleman and his family exited the throne room.

Emery saw her father gaping at her. "I told you, Father. I won't be cowed by a nobleman." The princess turned to the page. "Call in the next one please." The young girl seemed shocked by the turn of events but nodded hurriedly and hollered for the next supplicant.

A variety of different troubles were presented to the king that day. Everything from petty crimes to neighborly squabbles. Each matter, the king dealt with, though Emery could see that very few actually left satisfied with the solution. Still here to learn, Emery stayed quiet and observed, only speaking if addressed or if some conversation included something she had insight on. As the morning dwindled on, the princess could see that her father was growing weary. At first, Emery wondered how this could be so exhausting but then took a step back. *Having to deal with this all the time could grow tiresome. However, it is part of a monarch's duty.* She knew by her father's schedule that rarely held court like this more than once a week unless there were many urgent matters to attend to. He left it to Casinius and his other advisors to take care of these tasks. Emery once again saw this as a mistake. Wasn't it a king's job to know about the kingdom he ruled? Emery vowed that when she took the throne, she would hold court far more often than her father, even if it wasn't every day.

As they neared the end of the line of visitors, the supplicants became more pleasure based. After all the squabblers came singers and merchants. One of the latter came in with a small cart filled with fabric. This merchant was age worn, with milky skin, wrinkled hands, and hair worn long over his ears; but his eyes were still sharp, and no shakes dulled his ability to work. Emery did not miss that he bowed to her, instead of the king, but decided not to say anything. "My lady Emery"—he smiled—"a pleasure to see you again."

"Again, sir? I don't recall meeting you." Emery wracked her brain to remember this gentleman but came up blank.

He held up his hands placidly. "No worries, my princess. You may not remember, but I will never forget the day you stopped by my stall in the Central Ward. My son was actually running the booth that day, but I sat back watching." He gestured to the cart behind him, where Emery saw the young man from the booth.

Now Emery remembered. One of her favorite dresses, the silk one colored like Reyna's skin, had come from that merchant. The older man looked content telling the story, so she allowed him to finish describing the day.

"We, like all of your people, were admiring the fact that our princess would come among us, with only one guard in tow. Of course, when that one guard is someone like Leonidas Braveheart, who needs others, right?" Ignoring the stabbing pain in her heart, Emery smiled and nodded. "But imagine our surprise when her Royal Highness actually stopped by our booth to examine our wears!" The princess recalled just how nervous the son had been, but he'd managed to keep his composure throughout the whole affair. "You picked up one of my best pieces," the merchant continued. "It had taken me weeks to perfect, and it was my proudest work at the time. I was expecting to be haggled down to a paltry sum by one of the nobles, but you came and asked the price. Most nobles don't, declaring a price instead and then haggling down from there." He shrunk a little. "No offense meant."

"None taken," Emery assured him.

"Being the princess and heir to the throne, my son rightfully thought that you should get a discount and gave you a lower price." The old man laughed gleefully. "You immediately answered no, looked at the dress again, and said, and I'll never forget this: 'Such masterful work is worth far more than a handful of brights. I would be paying you naught but an insult to accept that price.' Then you reached into your coin purse and pulled out a radiant! A coin worth more than double our original asking price!" When my son scrambled for change, you closed his hand around the coin." The merchant seemed on the verge of tears. "You said: 'I'll accept no lower sum. The only thing I'll take from you today is the dress.' My lady, that radiant kept my family fed for the month, and I will never forget the kindness you did us."

Emery smiled wholeheartedly. "I said nothing that wasn't true on that day. I'll not watch merchants go hungry from being shorted on their wares."

"Infinite blessings upon you, Princess." He snapped his fingers at his son, who began to remove a delicately folded piece from the cart. Hoisting himself upon the frame of the wagon, the son unfolded the dress, leaving the hem floating just above the red stone tiles.

If the garment that Emery had bought from this merchant before had been a masterpiece, this one had to be his magnum opus. Made of flowing red fabric, the sleek dress reminded Emery of fire, of a phoenix. The cut of the garment was just low enough to show a little skin but not reveal too much. Long tapered sleeves and flared body were shot through with red, gold, and orange fabric; and the bottom hem had tassels of swirling red. When he turned it around, the princess could see a swath of material connected to both sleeves, pleated to make a design like wings. When someone walked in that dress, Emery imagined, it would be like they were dancing through flames.

"It's amazing! How long did it take you to make that?" Emery asked, her heart filled with pride and joy for the old merchant. She recalled his name from the stall: Barnio Boome.

"This design has been in the works for over a year. It has been through many different installations, but only this one turned out the way I wanted it to. And I know in my heart of hearts there is only one person fit to wear such raiment." Barnio bowed before her. "Your Highness, you would do me an honor to take this dress as a gift." He cleared his throat nervously. "Of course, I would like to be the one to tailor it to your measurements, and you would need to pay for that service, but—"

"Nothing would make me happier than to wear this dress," Emery replied honestly. "It is the most perfect piece I've seen in my life."

"I hope that in your time, you get to see fashion that will dwarf my own," Barnio said humbly. "But I thank you for your compliment either way."

"I will come to you tomorrow morning to have it fitted, if that's all right with you," the princess offered.

The old merchant bowed nearly as fervently as Odala Wala had. "Consider it done. I will see you on the morrow." Both father and son had a noticeable skip in their step as they left the room with the dress.

If the cloth merchant was a highlight to Emery's morning, the final visitor was a favor to the king. Down the red carpet strolled a nobleman, with a woman close to Emery's age at his heels. Emery recognized the girl, with her dark brown curls and doe eyes. She wore a soft shirt and skirt of striped animal skin and high heels. While not close friends, Mia Rothsster and Emery had grown up with each other. While Emery had gravitated more toward friendships with castle workers and the inhabitants of the Central Ward, Mia had taken to the other young nobles, with their more lavish lifestyle. And it showed in her fashion choices, with her face beautified with makeup and the exotic clothing she chose to wear. It was said that House Rothsster had been among the first families to support the original king of Sun's Reach in the battles against the invasions of Moonwatch, and as such, they had the honor of being one of the high houses. With the vast amounts of money the family had, they could afford to buy clothing and leisure items from distant lands and often did so just to show off to the lower families. The red rooster that they'd chosen as their symbol was surprisingly similar to the phoenix of Redwyn, which many took to believe the high house had aspirations for the throne. It was true that for a couple of generations, House Rothsster did boast sitting on the Highsun Seat, by rights of conquest. But in the end, a jealous queen had assassinated her husband and children, thus ending their reign. With the complicity of King Rothsster's brothers, the remainder of the family was either placed in jail or forbidden from taking the throne, and once again, a Redwyn was elected to sit on the Highsun Seat.

Whether they still thirsted for such power or not, the rooster was displayed on every outfit the family wore. Today, it was mounted on Lord Rothsster's breast and Mia's gloves.

"My lord, my lady"—Lord Nestor Rothsster bowed to each of the royals in turn—"I come in front of you today to share some exciting news."

"And what is this news, Nestor?" the king asked, the weariness in his voice evident.

"I have come to tell you that my daughter, Mia, will be getting married soon to solidify the relations between my house and that of Lord Bernard Leygrain. His son, Ferrin, asked for her hand just a week hence, before we left the Sulfaari Expanse!"

Leygrain was another great house that had set itself up in the Agrarian Pass and became the foremost producer of grains and flour. They churned out a steady stream of farmers and stable hands. The princess knew that Ferrin was yet another of these, thick of arm and wise in the way of animals and farmwork. To marry a Leygrain meant marrying plenty of money and a hard worker.

Emery smiled down at the newlywed. "My humble congratulations for your marriage. You must be proud to have won the heart of such a reputable figure."

Mia blushed. "Y-yes, Princess. I couldn't be happier with my fortune."

Emery stole a glance at her father, who didn't look quite so happy as he should at this news. The wedding of nobles was a momentous and joyful occasion, representing the building of strong relationships between the great houses. *Then again, the man I want to marry is not of one of the great houses.* She felt a twinge of shame but banished it. *Dropping Leonidas from my mind is harder than I expected,* the girl reflected. *When every little thought brings him to mind.*

"Y-yes, I can see that this is great news, indeed!" Godfrey said at last. "Is there something you ask of the crown? I'm sure you can handle the dowry on your own!"

Lord Rothsster looked slightly miffed by the suggestion that he couldn't pay for his own daughter. "I just thought since it is the union of two major houses, it might be nice if we held a celebration, a grand ball of sorts. I'm sure the people have been waiting for a high-scale wedding, so why not give them what they wish?" At the last part, he nodded pointedly at Emery.

The king gave a single loud clap. "Why, of course, Lord Nestor! That is a perfect idea! I will get to work on having it planned right away!" The change in attitude was sudden, the mention of a party making Godfrey far more excited.

"Excellent!" Nestor Rothsster exclaimed. "We, of course, will assist in the payment; never you fear. We've no desire to leave our king in the lurch."

Assured that there were no more supplicants awaiting the king's pleasure, the three went off to finish planning the feast, leaving Emery with free time to visit her friends in town. With the scale of the party the lords were discussing, most of the noble population would be invited with their significant other if they provided help with the decorations. But Emery noticed that they didn't speak about allowing any commoners. She already knew who her guests were going to be.

AMARU
Ready for a Journey

That evening, Amaru sat on a soft cushion, her legs folded under her, around a low table. A teapot sat in the center, and ceramic plates were filled with food, cooked fresh from her own hunt earlier and the Solgaele Monastery's pantry. Their meals were supplemented by sweet water and fun stories from Alaric. The general mood of the monastery was so joyful one might forget about what had happened earlier that morning. Amaru absentmindedly touched her injured leg. Gemna had wrapped it up for her, and as much as she wanted to, Amaru knew it wouldn't be wise to heal it. If she hadn't been trying to hide her identity, she would have fixed up all of Alaric's scratches and bruises from the battle. She'd been fortunate to have the sense to pull her hood up over her head before the monk had a chance to get a good look at her. *No one must know. Not until the time is right.*

Only now did Amaru really appreciate how nice it was to have friends to share a meal with. Back home, she'd always had Durrigan, Xio, or Ren to sit with. She hadn't expected the utter isolation and loneliness that came after sunfall. There had been evenings where she'd considered returning to the monastery to seek succor, but her pride and protective nature won out in the end. *And now here I am, sitting at their table, sharing their food.*

Amaru looked around at the people sitting with her. Good-natured Gemna laughed along with Alaric. Sultan, on the other hand, didn't seem to be interested in such diversions. His normally placid, steady gaze kept flicking back to the man tied in the corner. The mask still sat on his face, obscuring his features, but familiarity showed in the young monk's eyes. Amaru wanted to ask questions but knew that Sultan would hate to have it said that he was anything less than composed. *He's hiding a secret, just like I am.* So she kept quiet, making polite conversation with each person in turn.

As the evening wore on and the sun stalled in the sky, casting its orange glow over the sands, the conversation began to turn away from lighthearted topics.

"So, Amber," Gemna began tenderly, "those men, why were they chasing you?"

Amaru was honestly unsure. Whether this was just a random gang of bandits or if it had something to do with the Chillfang, she couldn't tell offhand. "I don't know. I'm just glad I saw them in time and was able to get to safety. I'm sorry to have involved you in… whatever happened. I was just so scared."

"As well you should be, my lady," Alaric soothed, patting her hand across the table. "It is unfortunate that we have no information. I'd like to know who needs to be punched for trying to hurt you!" His fists clenched, and Amaru saw the bruise from where he'd hit the first man.

"If we really want to know why she was followed"—Sultan jerked his head toward the bound captive—"we can just ask him."

Gemna gave the boy a knowing look. "Do you have information on this man, Sultan?"

Sultan nodded tightly. "As well you know, Gemna. You understand my past." His voice held no smugness, though the words called for it. "The metal mask and roguish attire label him as a Venomsting member."

"Venomsting," Alaric mused. "I know that name. Aren't they—"

"The assassins for hire, correct," Sultan said, wanting to get the last word. "Someone wants you dead, Amber." He said it with such certainty, but his face remained deadpan. "Unfortunately, the Venomsting are smart enough to burn their orders after memorizing them, so there's no way of telling any details behind this event."

Gemna nodded and went over to the tied man. "You, who are you?"

The assassin spoke to her in a tongue that none of them understood. Seeing the confusion on their faces, he laughed.

"Speak common, damn you!" Gemna swore. "Tell us who you are and why you are here!"

The man just kept laughing, pointing his chin at his chest, where the scorpion symbol was embroidered. He spoke slower, knowing perfectly well that Gemna didn't understand, and spat blood into her face.

The monk returned to the group, grabbed a rag, and cleaned off her face. "Rotten man, he is. Know what language he spoke? Sultan, Alaric?" Both shook their heads.

Amaru looked on with despair. *So much for that clarification.* As much as she didn't want her secret getting out, she wanted more to know why desert-dwelling men had tried to kill her today.

"Amber?" Alaric snapped to call her attention back to the world. "I assume that you still don't want to stay here longer than necessary."

"Correct. I still plan to leave tomorrow," the Fyroxi replied.

"And if you recall, I told you that there was no chance I was letting you leave the semblance of safety."

"I do," Amaru answered hesitantly, not sure where this was going.

"Well, it seems to me that with the knowledge of these Venomsting folks, we have something to investigate and someone to go after for daring to attack a beautiful lady."

"What do you mean 'we'?" Amaru asked.

"I thought it was quite obvious," the elf said, pausing for dramatic effect. "I'm going with you." He held up one finger to forestall her. "Don't even consider protesting. I have been thinking about how to win this argument all day." He took a deep breath and began. "I know that you want to keep your friends safe. Trust me, I understand. As irritating as Sultan and Gemna can be at times, they are still important to me. But if this seemingly random assassination attempt is more than it seems, then it could portend serious dangers to come. And I'm not letting one girl go out and possibly get herself killed, as I'm sure you won't just sit back after being targeted yourself. I'm really not the type to leave a damsel in distress to wander the land alone."

Amaru folded her hands in her lap. "And what role would you serve, Alaric? Entertainment?"

The elf grinned unfailingly. "I would hope so! Far be it from me to leave a girl unsatisfied with my performance." He moved his face back as if he expected her to reach out and slap him. When she did no such thing, he continued. "But though I can't swing a blade and my punches are subpar at best, I have plenty of other talents, besides amazingly good looks." Amaru found herself chuckling at that. Then Alaric looked her straight in the eyes, his tone becoming suddenly serious. "Also, I know that you don't actually want to go out by yourself. As much as you want to deny it, you hate the thought of leaving friends, even new ones, and you are scared about being beset by more dangers. Amber, you understand that there is safety in numbers, and that, more than any other reason, is why you will accept my proposal."

Amaru resisted the urge to gape at him. *He read me like a book!* He'd told Amaru that bards were good at understanding people, but it was still unreal to hear him repeat her exact worries, which had just gone through her brain many times!

Amaru smiled sweetly, knowing she'd been convinced. "Very well, I suppose having a companion along will be a benefit to me." Her acceptance earned a glowing smile from the elven bard. Though Amaru expected he would have pushed the point until she acquiesced. There would have been no way for her to win that argument. *Oh well*—she shrugged inwardly—*Alaric was correct.* She had no desire to leave the company of those who had undoubtedly saved her life against the Venomsting.

Alaric grabbed his fiddle and played a joyful tune, glad for a quick solution to the predicament.

> Fiddle de dee, fiddle de day,
> On desert wind, we'll get away,
> Glad to go, we'll not whine,

Not when life seems so fine
Courage we'll need, for our path to find
But nevertheless, we leave home behind!
Adventure's only a night away,
so early we must hit the hay!

Everyone applauded his impromptu music, and after only a short discussion, they all heeded the wisdom of his closing words and found their beds.

*****

The next morning while the sun rose in the sky, Gemna woke them and led them outside. She presented Alaric with a smooth wooden rod, one end wrapped in oilcloth. "Alaric Valyaara, as of this day, you have completed your training at the Solgaele Monastery. You have learned much in your years here. Though not quite as much as your father might have hoped," she added as an aside. "Either way, the Sun Mother Yamaria has called your name from her warm halls, proclaiming you worthy to walk the earth which she has breathed life into." She gestured around to the sands. "To mark the end of your isolation and training, you must now complete the final ritual." Gemna pointed to the roof of the monastery where a brass gong sat, suspended from a sturdy frame. "Make your way up the stairs and light the braziers, then strike the gong with all of your might. Only with this will you finally be freed from your commitment to the monastery."

Alaric bowed and held out the torch for Gemna to light. Once it flared to life, he strode proudly, his chin high in the air. As he ascended the wooden plank stairs that surrounded the building, he reached out with his long arms, lighting up the torches on the sides. At the top, he climbed on top of the railing, leaning precariously out over the edge. Amaru was worried he might fall, but the elf didn't seem to care in the least. He teetered on just his toes and juggled the torch, passing it smoothly hand to hand. As he caught it the last time, he did a backflip and landed squarely in the center of the roof platform. He went to each brazier in turn, each one flaring up in a different color: red, blue, green, and finally white. Once this had all been finished, he made his way over the gong and smashed the still-burning torch into it. A booming crash reverberated through the air, seeming to shake Amaru's very core.

When he finally returned to them, Gemna was clapping and shaking her head. "Is nothing sacred to you?"

"As Amber said, I am the entertainment, so put on a show I must!" Alaric replied airily.

Sultan approached and handed Alaric the pack he and Gemna had packed for the travelers. "You'd best leave soon. The Venomsting won't hesitate long after they realize their first attempt failed." The young man held out one hand. Alaric grasped it, surprised. "Good luck. Keep in mind what I've told you about the Venomsting and be careful if you encounter their camps. No matter what you feel, show them no mercy, as they won't extend the same courtesy."

"How is it that you know so much about them? You've been here at least since you were three." Alaric wanted this one question answered.

Unfortunately, the young monk had picked up a few traits from Alaric, one of them occasional cryptic speech. "They are as tied to my past as your blood is to yours." Sultan waved them off and turned off to the monastery, likely to continue meditating. Alaric shrugged and watched the boy stalk off.

With final farewells, Amaru hoisted her own pack and made way toward the dune which she'd fallen down the day before. She and Alaric climbed up the slippery sand, allowing the warmth held within its grains to soak in through their shoes. Reaching the top of the dune meant passing through a large shadow. Amaru imagined this shadow like a door and crossing through it like an opening to a broader world. She couldn't be sure where that feeling came from. *I felt something similar when I left clan Fire-Strider, though I didn't recognize it at the time. I wonder how Ren and Xio are doing. Would they laugh to know I was allowing myself to go out alone into the desert with no protection except a musically inclined elf? Ren might, though more likely he'd just be jealous. Xio...knowing her, she's probably sleep-*

ing, having good dreams. I hope that Ren helps her as I used to, giving her the information that she misses during her naps. I know that would make her happy.

Alaric was having thoughts of his own. *Finally, it seems my luck has turned around! I can leave Solgaele Monastery, return to traveling, and finally see part of the Scorched Waste! And of course, I can't forget Amber. It would seem that she is my savior, stealing me from the tedium of monastery life. Having a capable traveling companion will make the road much less boring, and safer to boot, that's for sure. Still, I spoke truly when I said I'd miss the monks. They taught me well and kept me alive. Gemna was far more lenient than Father would have liked, and I think, in the end, that Sultan may have actually liked me somewhat. Not that I have any proof, that deadpan face thwarting me at every turn.* He shrugged to himself, putting a cap on his inner monologue. *Doesn't really matter now. I suppose I get to see how the world has changed in five years. A long time for a human, but nothing for an elf like myself.* He stole a glance at Amber. She looked to be in her midtwenties, likely at the peak of her beauty. How would the years change her? He supposed he'd see when the time came, for Alaric had no intention of leaving her behind.

As they topped the dune and looked back one more time, they each saw their pasts behind them. Amaru directed her attention toward her village, which she could see in the distance across the windblown flats, while Alaric saw the monastery and, in his mind, the woods in which he grew up and the Sulfaari Expanse through which he'd traveled. Little did they know that walking over that dune meant their fates were sealed, for better or for worse.

REN
Unpleasant Business

R en stepped out into the early morning sun and looked over the village. He'd always loved that his home was so close to the central plaza. But now, looking at the view in front of him, he felt only sadness and anger. The land in front of him was a slurry of blood, sand, and innards. A few corpses were strewn on the ground directly in front of him, which he'd stepped over last night. He sighed at the prospect of the task ahead of them. The tribe would be burning so many bodies there was no way they could hold a proper ceremony for each departed soul. *I hope Yamaria doesn't mind a mass burning.* Ren shifted into fox form and walked over to the first corpse, dragging it to the central plaza and laying it out. He couldn't even tell who it was, her face and body so severely ripped apart. It was a woman; Ren could tell that much from the style of the torn rags. He could see others rousing themselves from their huts as well. Most of their eyes were tired and their expressions grim as they set about their task. He doubted anyone had slept well with the sickly sweet smell of fresh corpses permeating the air or the thoughts of what had happened in the dim light of sunfall. Nobody had been prepared for the attack of the beasts. What was supposed to be a celebration of vitality and procreation had become a nightmare.

Ren couldn't get the image of Vienna out of his mind. He'd been in the corner, just about to disrobe, when the howl shivered through the sky, and moments later, the fabric of their tent had been torn apart. Before either of the Fyroxi had much of a chance to react, the

146

wolf had pounced. Poor, frail Vienna hadn't even stood a chance. Ren heard the snap of her arm bones as the creature's jaw clamped around it. Her scream had jarred the camp awake and spurred the animal to action. It had clamped down and shook her viciously. More bones snapped, and the girl's body went crashing to the sand outside, sans one arm. Cowering in the corner, Ren had escaped notice, as another high-pitched whine broke through the night, calling the wolf out. Before it left, it took a few moments to make a meal of Vienna's stomach. By the quiet moans he'd heard, he figured the girl hadn't died until that point. Ren wanted to avoid thinking about the sweet priestess being in excruciating pain for her last moments.

The remaining members of the tribe worked silently and numbly, collecting what bodies could be recognized and piling up the pieces that couldn't be. At one point, Ren was dimly aware of Xio working next to him, but the two didn't speak. The burning heat of the sun above them made the odors of the carcasses worse, and any attempt to converse was just inviting the stench into their nostrils. Survivors as always, another pile was made for salvaging equipment that the massacred Fyroxi had on them. Very few had anything, seeing as they'd been at the party, but every little tool had its use in the harsh desert. Only the most personal items were left on them, as mementos to comfort them in Yamaria's sunny halls when their spirits were lifted on the smoke and wind.

The corpses of the Chillfang were left where they lay. Nobody wanted to touch the accursed beasts, not after last night. Not after seeing so many of their friends ripped apart in…what had it been less than an hour. Ren stepped cautiously around them, remembering the cold, numbing sensation that had come over him on contact. When he'd passed one of the critters earlier, he'd noticed a dark, wet spot by the top of its head and another circling its body. The blood came from its stomach, and the moisture had burned off quickly in the heat of the day. That would make it water or some similar liquid. *That was why that alpha was so hard to kill. He was covered in ice.* Ren shivered reflexively. *I guess their name makes sense now.*

*****

Days later, the smoke billowed in the air, thick and greasy, bringing a queasy feeling to all who sniffed the noxious fumes. The final count was a little over thirty dead. Nearly one-third of their people, gone in less than an hour. As many as could be identified had been marked down, their possessions sorted according to their families' wishes.

Amaru did so well, returning our tribe to respectable numbers, but after losing so many... The thought of Amaru sent a pang through Ren's heart. Her eyes had been stone masks that night, concealing her pain and hurt. Despite her explanations, Ren wanted to believe that she could have stayed, she could have been safe. He reached an arm around Xio's shoulder. She flashed a sad smile at him and drew closer. The sleepy girl had become his closest confidant and had helped him in more ways than could be imagined in the past few days. She was always glad to have a conversation, and she allowed whatever topic Ren wanted. He managed to coax a little out of her as well. When the Chillfang attacked, she hadn't been in the tents, having grown tired hours before and snuck off to the elder's hut where the Fyrestone children were being kept, to get a bit of sleep. The howl and following screams had woken her up, but she stayed with the young ones to keep them calm. It wasn't until elder Sigmund arrived that she had any idea what was going on. At first, Ren was a little angry with Xio for leaving but then realized just how brave she'd been. She'd been stuck in a small hut, with two young children, and not one of them had made a peep. And Jarrah was known for making quite a bit of noise when it suited him, so keeping them quiet couldn't have been any small effort on Xio's part.

"I know you were tired, but why did you go off without telling anyone? Many of the others were worried when they didn't see you," Ren pressed. Xio had turned her face to the ground and murmured something about seeing him go off, but Ren was unable to get a clear answer out of her.

*****

"Men and women of clan Fire-Strider," Yarena addressed the crowd as they stood watching the smoke of their friends and tribe-mates fill the air. "I apologize for the length of time it took for me to speak with you. I wanted to make sure that my facts were sorted out before I informed you." The chieftess cleared her throat. "We have all seen our share of loss due to this attack, and after careful examination and lengthy discussion with my fellow elders, I will report to you now that the attacking party was most certainly Chillfang." A murmur went up from the older members of the tribe. "Quiet!" Yarena yelled. "Listen to me for a moment; then you'll be allowed to speak. As I said, those wolf-beasts were indeed Chillfang. How it is possible that they have come here once more, I'll not claim to know. Nor can any of us lay a finger on their intentions. We were fortunate that young Amaru reacted so quickly to their arrival. Had she not, many more would be dead, so we must all be thankful for her contributions." Yarena paused for a moment, and an angry voice called out from the crowd.

"Where is she now? Where was Amaru while we cleaned the village? Has our goddess's child abandoned us?" The sarcastic swagger sent a whisper through the people, as they tried to figure out who had spoken.

Yarena looked over the throng of Fyroxi in front of her, finally locating the source of the voice. "Leif Kalix! I would expect that you would know where she would be! Weren't you slated to fill her divine belly with a child?"

Leif growled at her bluntness, and every eye drifted in his direction. "The wench ran before I could take what was mine!" he yelled. "She threatened my life and then fled the tent!"

Yarena did not raise her voice to match his. "You speak as if she did not aid us. I'm sure you must have seen her in battle; she stood alongside us and fought our enemy, ancient spear in hand."

Leif snorted, "Just because she cried the name of our ancient enemy and fought them means nothing! Amaru Sunbrand avoided her duty on that night, and you all would do well to remember that. Just because she has some healing magic, it means nothing! She is just like any woman, weak and afraid!"

Some of the whispers grew to angry protests. Ren couldn't make any specific words out, but he figured he could understand them well enough, as the same thoughts were running through his own head. *Arrogant bastard to put down the name of Amaru, who is beloved here among the Fire-Striders.*

But Leif wasn't done. "Where is she now to defend herself against my claims? Amaru, if you genuinely are some goddess reborn, come out here and prove it!"

Everyone went silent, as they waited for Yamaria's blood to accept the challenge. When she didn't, Yarena was forced to speak. "Amaru is gone. She left in the night." Ren hoped he imagined the fear in the chieftess's voice. "The Chillfang were after her—"

"And she ran," Leif finished for her. "She left us for the sake of her own safety. Durrigan told us that Amaru was our salvation, yet in our time of need, who fails to stay around? To me, this is proof that she was nothing more than a farce. Durrigan was a fool for trusting her, and we were fools for listening to him. And we shouldn't put our trust in some woman whose mind aligns with theirs. The elders speak the name Chillfang, and you all whimper like kits!"

Ren tensed at the utterances of agreement that he heard among the gathered people. He wondered with dismay if he'd misjudged some of the whispers before. Xio pulled closer to him, shaking with fear. "Why shouldn't we be afraid?" The crowd whirled toward the voice, and Ren was stunned to find himself speaking. "I agree that we shouldn't be idle with the Chillfang at our door. But the massacre proved that they are a force to be reckoned with."

"You see, a prime example of our weakness!" Leif retorted. "And he's one of the elders' apprentices too. A clear sign that they are fools and afraid."

Ren paid him no mind, speaking louder to drown out Leif's poisonous words. "I cannot claim to know anything about the Chillfang, but I fought during the Hundredth Sun Massacre. I heard them speak, saw them go hut to hut, methodically killing people. And I felt the hard, cold power of their ice magic." He bared his shoulder for all to see his scar. "When that creature bit me, I felt my blood start to freeze. Had it not been for Weylin, *whose life Amaru saved*, I would have been killed by cold ice in the land of the hot sun! We may be a powerful race, but we cannot match the strength of the

Chillfang when they have the sheer numbers that we've lost. We need to learn how to defend against them!"

The agreeing whispers were quiet, tentative, but at least he had support. Ren felt more confident than he ever had as he strode up to the tall Fyroxi trying to whip up discontent. "And how dare you question Amaru's name and heritage! You saw as well as anyone how she glowed during her first transformation. After the Eclipse, the gift magics ceased to exist. That Amaru showed up among us, that she can heal wounds, bring people back from near death"—he gestured toward Weylin, who everyone had seen drag himself across the sand—"it is irrefutable truth that she is Yamaria's child. Even if she wasn't, she is still an amazing person. She treated us with kindness and bolstered the tribe's numbers, yet some of you are willing to just cast her into the sand?"

"Listen to Lover Boy over here defend his precious Amaru's name. Everyone knows that Trinket here is enamored with that woman. What good are his words?" Leif looked around at the people who had supported him before. Many nodded along with him, but after Ren's words, others seemed unsure. Leif spat in the sand. "We were once a strong, proud race, but now we've become sniveling wimps." The larger male got in Ren's face. "This isn't over," he growled, his voice dangerously low. "I was denied what I deserve many times, but it won't happen again." Leif Kalix raised his voice for all to hear. "To defend against the Chillfang but refuse to seek them out and enact revenge only proves that our race has become frail. Those who wish to listen to the elders may do so, but know what you support before you blindly follow. A disgrace to our ancestors, every last one of you!" With that, he turned away and walked back to his own hut.

Ren sighed deeply. He knew that Leif had reached a significant number of people. *He would start a mutiny, replace our elders with people of his fiery spirit. We will all be doomed if he does.*

EMERY
Family Issues

W hen Emery entered Cynderstone Brewery and Bar, there was already a large party of people within. The area directly in front of the bar was filled with people, guards by the look of their uniforms. Most had the red rooster of Rothsster on their breasts.

The attendants that came along with Mia Rothsster must have heard the news that her father had persuaded the king to assist with the wedding and were drinking healths to Godfrey Redwyn. Loud, boisterous laughter reverberated off the stone walls. Lanterns hung from wooden beams casting a red glow over the room, which shook slightly as the men slammed their fists on the bar.

Emery was surprised to see that chief among these was Grayson, her brother. He stood atop the wooden surface, with mug held high, leading the procession in some bawdy song.

Emery sighed. She pushed through the crowd of men, smelling the alcohol and sweat that clung to them. So caught up in their discordant singing they were that none of them seemed to notice as the princess forced her way toward her brother. When she came close to the bar, she pulled at Grayson's pant leg. Her brother looked down, his eyes slightly bleary. It took him a moment to recognize her, but when he did, his face broke into a grin.

"Sis! Didn't expect to see you here." Grayson stomped on the bar. "Everyone, raise a toast to my beautiful sister, Emery Redwyn, crown princess of Sun's Reach!"

Mugs clacked, and a general roar rose to the ceiling. Emery saw Sardan Rainclaw wince as two soldiers toasted too enthusiastically and fragments of ceramic spilled amid a shower of ale. Emery pulled on Grayson's hand and gestured to the corner.

"My sister requires a word. I shall return shortly! Don't miss any toasts on my behalf," he said, before climbing down.

When the two were secluded to the corner, Grayson turned on her, his eyes already registering annoyance. "What's wrong? I'm a little busy here."

"Brother, what are you doing here so early in the morning?" The princess gestured to the window. "It's not even noon yet, and here you are drinking with soldiers." She looked at the crests on each man she could see. "I don't see any Redwyn men here. Where are your guards?"

"I left them at the castle, just like you," Grayson countered, noticing her similar lack of attendants. "I know that you only just tolerate the guards Father insists stay around you. Unless Leonidas is around them. Guards are meant to protect you, not be your friends."

Emery sighed in exasperation. "You don't know what you are saying, Grayson. You are drunk and are coming close to making a fool of yourself."

"Why? Because I came out in public?" Emery was suddenly glad for the raucous singing from the group, as her brother's voice grew heated and angry. "You go out among the people all the time. I don't see why I shouldn't be able to do the same!"

"Brother, please calm yourself." Emery lay a hand on his shoulder. "When I go out, I do so to help improve the public opinion of the royal family. When you come out and allow yourself to get drunk, you are allowing the people to see you in a way that they never should. There will be stories of whatever you have done this morning, just as there are whispers of what you did to Reyna. You are fortunate that Arcadia was there to stop you at that time. Now I am here to stop you from starting bad rumors. I told you last time we spoke to start acting like a prince, and yet you come here to do this." Something that Ignis had said still stuck in her head. *Father has enemies everywhere. There is no telling who might decide to take advan-*

tage of a prince. Anything he says or does can and will be used against him at some point.

Grayson glared at her, not speaking, but his red-brown eyebrows scrunched together at an angle.

"Brother, why did you come here this morning?" She kept any anger out of her voice, not wanting to provoke him. "Was it solely to drink with these men?

"No, I came to see Reyna, but Mr. Barkeep said she was busy." Grayson's face turned a little redder. "I wanted to apologize to her. I shouldn't have hurt her."

"And when Lord Rainclaw didn't allow you to see her, you decided it was a smart idea to get drunk?" Emery asked pointedly.

Grayson had the grace to look embarrassed. "That may have been the wrong thing to do," he muttered.

"Oh, brother." Emery shook her head. "Look, I plan to spend the day with the sisters. If you want, I can bring her down for a moment and allow you to speak to her. Would you like that?" Grayson nodded wordlessly. "Fine, it will be done. Go splash some water on your face and try to sober up a bit."

*****

"You know, Emery, I think you might have been right about Grayson," Reyna admitted quietly as the two walked down toward the house of the twins' older sister. "He really might be in love with me." She let out a nervous giggle.

"And," Emery prompted, "how does that make you feel?"

"I don't know," Reyna said honestly. "He's rather handsome, and he's a prince, but…well, that's just the problem."

"The class difference does make it an issue." *How would Father react to learning that both of his children were in love with people unworthy of their royal station?*

"And with his anger issues already, I wouldn't want to provoke anyone. I'm sure that if the prince—even if he has little chance of sitting the Highsun Seat—were to be seen with a Khindre like me, it would bring all sorts of unnecessary trouble." Reyna sighed as they reached the door.

A few moments after they knocked, they heard some shuffles from inside. A panel slid open, and a single hazel eye looked out at them. "Who is it?"

"It's me, sis. And the Princess Redwyn," Reyna answered.

The panel slammed shut, and the door opened to reveal a tall woman with brown hair tied back from her face. She wore a simple tunic underneath a leather apron cinched tightly with a belt. Placid hazel eyes stared forward out of a bronzed face. A small hammer swung on her belt. *Not a battle hammer like Leonidas uses, more like one for crafting.* Lean muscles flexed underneath her sleeves. She must work with her arms, and by the slight smell of coal and iron, the princess surmised that it was the smithy that claimed her as employee.

"I apologize for the rudeness." She bowed stiffly, obviously not accustomed to the action. "I wasn't expecting this sort of visit. Not after all of the other visitors I've had these past months," she finished, rolling her eyes slightly.

"And what sort of visitors are those, Caitrial?" Reyna asked politely. The woman at the door shot a furtive glance at the princess. "I know you're not used to speaking to nobles, but Emery is safe to talk around."

Caitrial seemed mildly surprised at how Reyna used the princess's first name. Shrugging, she answered her sister. "I've had quite a few men coming around. Some folks were plain about their intentions, but the nobles claimed desires to 'enact a courtship ritual.' I think the current count is six different ones."

"Ah, I can see why that could be annoying to deal with. I'll have to come by later and hear the stories." Reyna giggled, and Caitrial grimaced. "But for now, we are here for Arcadia." The second twin had been kicked out of the main Rainclaw household, but Caitrial had taken Arcadia in, so now the twins lived apart.

"What business do you have with her?" The woman's tone immediately became guarded. Arcadia rarely left the house, often times staying in her room except when called to meals. As far as

Caitrial knew, she, Reyna, and Berdur were the only people her sister actually talked to.

"Reyna and I are going riding, and we were wondering if Arcadia would join us." Princess Emery smiled at the eldest Rainclaw sister. "These two have become my closest friends in the city, and I'm sure the fresh air would be good for her."

Caitrial nodded and only then seemed to notice that Emery was wearing simple riding leathers. She hesitated for a moment before turning back and calling up the stairs. "Dreamer, you have visitors! Put on your riding clothes!"

A few minutes later, Arcadia appeared on the stairs, cloaked and hooded. "Princess," she said curtly, "let's go then."

Caitrial gave Arcadia a quick hug, which the Khindre accepted rigidly. Emery figured if anyone else but her sisters tried to do that, they would likely feel the sting of Arcadia's bony tail. "I'll probably be at work when you return. I left some food for you in the icebox. Try to have some fun for once. And be safe."

Arcadia rolled her eyes. "Yes, *Mother*."

Caitrial tapped the Khindre's cheek in admonishment. "You know how important your safety is to me."

"I know, sis. Thanks."

Emery was touched and surprised to see such genuine contentedness and respect in Arcadia's eyes. It was a sweet sight, the love between sisters.

*****

The three friends walked through the streets of the city. They were met by conflicting shouts. Some called out to Princess Emery, praising her name, but more spat names at the Khindre traveling behind her. Emery furrowed her brow and looked as if she wanted to protest, but Reyna put a comforting hand on her shoulder. "Don't worry about them. We are used to dealing with worse." There was a faint snapping sound from behind them. One of the more vehement dissenters yipped in pain, his feet leaving the ground for just a moment. He frantically began to search for the dog or large rat that had just bitten him, before running off. "As my sister has just proved." Emery couldn't suppress her laughter as the men ran off, searching in vain for the source of the attack.

One particular cluster of dissenters tried blocking their way, small knives brandished in their hands. Emery saw Arcadia begin the motions for another spell, but the princess waved her off subtly. She stepped up to the man who seemed to be their leader by his frontmost position. "These two are under my protection," she said evenly, staring directly into his eyes. He couldn't be much older than she was, the princess realized, by the smoothness of the skin around his eyes and the slight stubble of a stubborn beard that he couldn't quite grow. "By threatening them, you threaten me!" she spoke loudly enough so that any others could hear her. "And threatening the crown princess of Sun's Reach is a grave offense. If you got off lightly, you may find yourself with jail time, though I'd expect an execution might be in order. King Godfrey would not take kindly to a dangerous man in the streets at any point! I'd suggest that you step back and return to your daily business, before I call for the guards." The man's eyes were wide, and the knife clattered to the flagstones as he and his friends scrambled back to the alleyways.

Emery smiled tiredly back at the two Khindre, who nodded their thanks.

Whether the group she'd sent scrambling had been the last of their kind or Emery's words had dissuaded any further dissent, the three friends arrived at the stables owned ironically enough by Cos Rainclaw, the sibling's mother, without another issue.

The Rainclaw family was prevalent in Searstar. Sardan served good ale and wine at acceptable prices. Cos was a stable hand made famous by her husband's success, and Caitrial worked in the smithy, making building supplies and tools as well as horseshoes for her mother, plus weapons, little use though they had for most citizens. By covering such a wide variety of talent, they made a definite presence in the capital city.

I could do no better than having them as friends.

Cos Rainclaw curtsied roughly at Emery's approach. "Princess, it is good to see you again. I'm glad to see you spending time with my daughter!"

It was not lost on the princess that Cos used the singular daughter and barely flicked her eyes over Arcadia.

"We are going riding outside of the city. I wouldn't dream of getting my horses anywhere else," Emery said honestly. Searstar, being a large city, was well stocked with stables, but the care and pride that Cos Rainclaw took in her work were never in question. The stock of well-fed, well-trained horses that she kept was rivaled only by the castle's own purebred stock of warhorses. The Rainclaw stables had a wide range of horses, from comfortable steeds for short rides to hardy horses able to survive long arduous marches.

Cos got to work quickly, pulling out harnesses, bridles, and bits. She allowed Emery to come up to the horses and hold her hand up to their muzzles. Their noses snuffled in her palm, searching for food. Not finding any, many of them turned away, but others were willing to accept a stroke on the nose or a scratch behind the ear. Madam Rainclaw saw one that seemed especially receptive and pulled him out. The stable hand gave him the name Cloudy Day, for his gray coloration, covered in soft white spots that looked like nothing quite so much as clouds. Once she'd finished harnessing and securing Emery to Cloudy Day, she went around the back of the stable and came out a few moments later leading two horses. One plodded along peacefully while the other seemed to struggle against the reins. The calm horse was tan in color with dark hair and tall ears. She knickered softly when she saw Reyna. The Khindre smiled and strode over to take the reins. Reyna thanked her mother and put on the harnesses herself, seeing her mother's difficulty with the other horse. The orange-skinned twin shot a doubtful glance toward Cos, as she handed the reins to Arcadia. The giant horse was so dark brown he was almost black. As Madam Rainclaw set up the securing pieces, the horse bucked and turned. Arcadia sunk deeper back into her cloak. Emery felt sorry for the girl. She'd heard how the parents didn't respect the second twin, but to go this far, it left a roiling feeling in her gut.

"No offense, milady Rainclaw, but do you have another horse available for Arcadia?" Emery queried. "It seems like that one isn't quite ready for a rider."

Cos smiled up at the princess. "Nonsense, Princess, begging your pardon. But Blackheart is the perfect steed for Arcadia."

Emery wanted to protest, but this time, Arcadia held up her hand. "Don't bother. I can manage with this one. A challenging ride will only make this more fun." Emery could hear the stiffness in the Khindre's voice, but also there was a willing acceptance as if Arcadia was used to this sort of treatment. Emery felt a small flash of anger spark in her stomach, but her friend had told her to leave it alone, so she did, not feeding the flame.

*****

Cos led them as far as the gate leading out onto the plateau upon which Searstar sat. A thick iron portcullis blocked the wooden door, providing an extra defense against intruders. Two rotating ballistae were situated on either side of the door, and more lined the walkway. Only one on each side was manned at any time; most of the guards spent their time patrolling the streets or walking on the top of the walls. Searstar was a plenty large city, leaving more than enough places for the patrols to protect. Cos strode up to the door and called up to the sentries. They hesitated a moment, but the moment Emery's name was mentioned, they scrambled to open the gates. The portcullis scraped against stone as it rose, thick anchoring spikes pulling out from their holes in the ground. The wooden doors pulled open, and the landscape outside the capital walls was revealed.

Red stone cliffs jutted out from the earth, descending down to the flatlands. From above or below, it created the illusion of a stairway up to the capital city. This vision lent the plateaus their name: the Sunne Steps. Smaller towns and villages rested on these steps, providing a chain of safe havens for travelers as they made their way to the capital. Emery had no doubt that Faenith, Gage, and Odala Wala had stayed in a few of those villages as they came to their mostly disappointing meeting with the king. She hoped that their reception in these other settlements had been better than their treatment within the king's council chambers.

At the bottom of the Sunne Steps, a sizable forest called Kindol Woods—home to elves, centaurs, and other sylvan creatures—reached into the sky. Around the forest and stretching as far as the princess could see was the Sulfaari Expanse, the savanna where the delegation had come from.

Emery imagined she could see the city of Fyrestone, standing solid and proud, despite its recent actions. Fyrestone was one of the five cities. The five were the pinnacle of civilization in Sun's Reach—Searstar, Mirshiall, Cystur, Bellepon, and Fyrestone. One city for each of the beloved races of the land. Now Humans commanded two of the cities because of the massacre of the Bush-Walker Fyroxi.

Did the residents feel remorse for what they did? Emery wondered. *Or did they feel justified in their choices? Would they expand their slaying outward, or was it just the Fyroxi they wanted to destroy? If they did continue, Father would* have *to send someone to help. Failing to retaliate would only promote similar actions across the kingdom.* "Then we'll be no different from Moonwatch," the princess commented aloud. Every story she'd ever heard put down the residents of Moonwatch, the opposite kingdom to Sun's Reach, as lawless savages. Tales of terrible wars between the two nations had ruled their evenings whenever their maids wanted to give the children a scare. Grayson had taken a liking to these stories, but they always made Emery sick to the stomach. She wished there would be some way for peace between them. She supposed with the Eclipse, there was now. The magical barrier that had been placed in the deepest part of the desert, known only as the Desolation, for no mortal creature could make a home there upon the sands burned black by the mages in the last war. Now nobody from either land could make their way through. But if that wall fell, would there be war once again? For even in the century since the last battle, it seemed that tempers had not cooled. The only ones that the citizens of Sun's Reach hated more than Moonwatch were mages. And *that* made Emery worry about the Rainclaw sisters.

"Princess?" Reyna spurred her horse up next to her question, pulling Emery out of the rabbit hole of worry she had quickly been spiraling down. "Everything all right?"

"Yes, nothing to worry about." Emery pressed her feet into Cloudy Day and continued trotting down the trail. "Just thinking about things I've heard around the castle."

"Anything particularly interesting?"

Emery considered for a moment. Reyna wasn't the type to spread rumors, but if she learned about the attack on Fyrestone, the obvious next question would concern what was being done. That could lead them to a dangerous conversation. "Only that there's to be a wedding soon," she said instead.

"Are you finally tying the knot, Emery?" The Khindre sounded excited at the prospect. "I had no idea that you had been seeing boys behind our backs!"

"No, not me." Emery laughed at Reyna's instant assumption that it was her that would be getting married. "But it will still be a high-scale wedding. Two of the great houses are being joined."

"Oh." Reyna's tone dropped from the prior excitement. "And here I was hoping you'd finally found the one."

"Not yet, but I'm sure it won't be too long," the princess remarked with dismay. "The king will soon be sending out invitations for suitors. There will be men writing me love letters before the month is out."

Struggling to keep hold of her wild mount, Arcadia grumbled. "Someone doesn't sound too excited about her predicament." The Khindre shrugged her shoulders while she bounced in the saddle. "Not that I blame you, most of the nobles in the city are vile people, and there's no telling if they'd be any different in the greater kingdom."

Emery nodded in agreement. "Being the crown princess is nice and all, but I just..." She hesitated for a moment, unsure of how much to say.

"You just what, Emery?" Reyna prodded.

"I wish that I could have more of a say in who I marry, is all," she finished, heaving a sigh of exasperation.

"She has a point," Arcadia growled. "People like us get to meet a wide variety of people and then get to know someone before giving ourselves permanently to them." Arcadia sighed. "Well, not us, seeing as we are Khindre, we will be lucky to find a man who doesn't want us banished to Carrion Cove. But those of a lower status in the city don't have to worry much about that issue. Their parents aren't always trying to sell them off to another family for money since none of them have much to spare as it is."

Reyna nodded, a sympathetic look passing over her beautiful features. Arcadia had summed it up nicely, though it wasn't a pretty picture. Emery was relieved that her friends understood what she was feeling. They were stuck in a similar boat as she was, as Arcadia had mentioned, due to their race rather than their societal obligations.

The horses trotted along the trail they knew so well. Rocky cliffs rose above them, where the upper level and, thus, the Castle Ward would be located. The shadows they now passed into seemed fitting given the darker turn of the conversation. A few bushes grew to the side, doubtless an addition by gardeners hoping to earn the king's favor. Unfortunately for those gardeners, their king rarely left the castle, even in his spare time, so they went unseen by him.

"What if the royal happens to love someone else?" Frustration seeped into Emery's tone. "They have to push those emotions to the side while living in wedlock with a man they barely know."

"Princess, I'm sure your father will choose a perfectly suitable match for you," Reyna offered tentatively.

"Reyna, until only recently, I barely even saw my father, except in those few times I talked to him after one of his meetings. I'm not even sure if he knows me well enough to make a 'suitable match' for me," Emery complained. "And unfortunately, this is one of the few decisions he won't delegate to my mother!" The princess realized that she might have said too much in her anger and clamped her mouth shut. *I let the phoenix out of the cage. Deep down, maybe I'm just the same as Grayson.*

They rode in silence for a while, Reyna sidling up next to the princess and stroking her tail comfortingly down her friend's back. After letting the air clear for a while, Emery took a deep breath. She hadn't meant to ruin this outing with her gripes, but they'd managed to slip out, and she reprimanded herself for that. "Anyway, about the wedding, between the nobles."

"Yes?" Reyna leaned over, glad for the change of subject. "I am excited to hear about what it's like in there. You can still tell us what goes on during the parties, right? I'd hate to lose that little window into the good part of highborn life."

Emery grinned coyly. "I *could* still weave the tale of the night. But I figured that you might want to experience it for yourselves." She fished in her tunic for a moment and produced a tightly rolled scroll, sealed with wax and stamped with the official seal of the crown.

Reyna took the papyrus, breaking the seal with her thumb. Shooting one final curious glance at Emery, the Khindre unraveled it and glanced down at the script. Apparently, she couldn't believe her eyes, as she went back multiple times, her lips moving silently as if the words were foreign to her. "Em…" she breathed, "you don't actually mean this, do you?"

By this time, Arcadia had moved next to her sister. "Just spit it out. What does it say?" Too impatient to wait, the darker Khindre swept her tail in and pierced the empty top of the paper, dragging it to herself to read. "Oh." Arcadia had a similar reaction as her sister. "That's unexpected."

"Our kind is never allowed to your highborn events," Reyna said, indicating both her social class and race. "And now…"

"Now, you two and your sister Caitrial, if she wishes, will be attending as my guests."

"I can't believe this." Reyna could barely contain her excitement. Even Arcadia's face had moved into something slightly less than a scowl. "We can finally see the inside of the castle!"

Emery had tried inviting her two friends to visit her multiple times, but every instance, Casinius or one of the other guards turned them away at the gate. They said they would never allow something so impure as a Khindre to pass their gates, and nothing that Emery said would persuade them to change their minds. Leonidas had often told her that if it was up to him, he'd allow the girls in, as he knew that good souls rested in the flesh that they had unfortunately been bound to.

This time, she'd decided to draft the invitation and sign it herself, stamping the letter with the royal seal. No guard could deny a legitimate seal, not even a Lightstrider; Casinius wouldn't be able to turn the Rainclaws away, no matter how much he wanted to.

"Yamaria," Reyna exclaimed, "I wouldn't even know what to wear! Everything we have would be rags to the highborn."

Emery personally believed that Reyna could make rags look like a silk dress but kept the observation to herself. She didn't want to embarrass her friend. "If you two have tomorrow morning free, I am going to be fitted for a dress. You could join me and see what the vendor has."

"That may be a little out of our price range, and we refuse to ask you to buy our clothing for us," Reyna sighed.

"Price won't be an issue. The man who made my dress is very fair. I believe his name was Barnio Boome. We have a number of weeks before midsummer when the wedding will be held, so you have time to choose."

Arcadia's eyes widened. "That's the name of the tailor in Central Ward, isn't it?" She turned to Reyna. "The half-bred veteran? Didn't he fight in the Last Astral War?"

Emery was shocked to hear this. "Half-bred? And the Last Astral War was so long ago! He must be alive by some miracle!"

"Some miracle indeed." Reyna laughed lightly. "A human girl married an elf and bore him a child. That's Barnio." She leaned in conspiratorially. "And keep this one a secret, but I've heard that his father was a moon elf of some high ranking, but he was trapped on this side when Qrakzt's wall went up."

Moon elf? Emery was shocked. *That meant they originated from Moonwatch, which everybody hated intrinsically. He was Lunian, and nobody could tell!* "I never knew! And the people of Searstar have no idea that partial moon elves live among them to this very day," Emery mused. "It makes you wonder whether those who live in Moonwatch are really any different from us here in Sun's Reach."

Reyna tapped her nose knowingly. "You see, this is why you deserve to be queen. Most people, if they learned that Barnio was a moon elf, would rip him apart. But not you; I'm sure that it almost made you more excited to own clothing made by him."

Emery nodded in agreement. "I'll be watching him and his son closely on the morrow, though I'm not sure if I'll bring it up to him quite yet. I have a theory I want to test now, but I don't want to risk bringing trouble to his doorstep." Reyna and Arcadia both agreed that it was a wise decision.

The rest of the day was peaceful, despite Blackheart continually trying to rid himself of Arcadia's presence. Once they had assured themselves that they were far enough from the city, Arcadia and Reyna practiced their magic, tendrils of darkness and flashes of light mingling in the air. Emery stood by the horses, keeping them calm as the two sisters flung their spells. At one point, the princess thought she heard someone moving in the bushes behind her, but Arcadia cast a spell of detection, finding nothing of the sort. By the time they returned to the stables, the sun was sinking in the sky, but their spirits soared high with joy.

ALARIC
Water Caller

When Alaric had decided to join Amber on her journey, he hadn't a clue what to expect. In retrospect, he thought he knew little about the land in which he'd been so unceremoniously dumped five years ago. That was partially his own fault, Alaric decided. He'd not done much to learn about the local landscape during the few chances he had. The elf realized now how foolish that was. Had he actually expected his father or some other member of his family to come and retrieve him? Alaric snorted derisively. Old Talisin believed him an utter disappointment and more likely than not would have been content to let him shrivel up and die here in the Scorched Waste. That realization cleared up so many things in the elf's mind. Alaric was Taliesin's oldest child, which gave him a measure of power in the family. If he wasn't in the way, that left the spot open for Viari, Alaric's younger sister, to take Alaric's inheritance, therefore, ensuring that the Valyaara family name stayed "in good standing" as Talisin saw it.

And if I die out here in the desert, then my father won't have the blood on his hands, won't have to answer to the Sylph Court of Mirshiall.

Despite how the plan was supposed to end in death for Alaric, the elf couldn't help but applaud his father for his foresight. Talisin's strategy had been a sound one. *Unfortunately, Father, you chose a safe place for me in Solgaele Monastery. Five years and I'm still kicking!*

Now he'd left the relative safety that the monks had provided, going out into the Scorched Waste.

At the very least, he wasn't alone. He had Amber, and the beautiful woman had lived in the desert for all her life. If anyone were able to keep him alive, she would. Alaric had the utmost confidence in her skills.

Amber proved that his trust was well-founded very early. Whatever home she had come from, Amber still would not tell him anything about the people who'd had the pleasure of her company in the previous years of her life; it was clear that her time and livelihood had granted her knowledge of the surrounding desert. Amber walked confidently across the sands of the Scorched Waste. During the hottest portion of the day, when the air shimmered with heat and the sun-warmed sand seemed to burn the soles of Alaric's feet as if his sandals weren't even there, Amber had them rest. Living here for as long as she had, Alaric reasoned, she probably didn't feel the heat so keenly. Though he had no way of knowing that Amber's resistance to the weather was as much a benefit of her race as the long period during which she'd lived at the mercy of sand and sun.

Either way, they walked during the night and early morning, when the light was dimmer and the heat somewhat less intense. When they stopped to make camp, Amber would occasionally use her spear for hunting, though far more often, she would only gather fruits or other strange desert edibles.

"Why is it that you rarely desire to hunt, my lady?" Alaric asked as they were settling down for the evening. "I thought that hunting was how your people survived in this barren land."

Amber stopped unfolding the small ground tarp—part of the set that Gemna had provided in lieu of a proper tent, which they slept on to save themselves from burning on the hot sand—to look at her elf companion. "Fires can be seen from a long way off in the desert," she replied simply as if it were common knowledge.

Alaric couldn't deny that, for sure. He'd been able to see that village where the music had been playing the night of those strange wolf howls, even though he suspected that it had been perhaps a two days' walk, at the very least, from Solgaele. Still, Alaric wondered why that mattered to Amber. He recalled the events at the monastery, the very same day he'd decided that he would not allow Amber to go off alone. *I almost got all of you killed. I refused to let that happen again.* That was what she'd said after the fight. Something similar had happened to her before. Was she on the run from something? Was that why she'd never wanted to stay the night? But Amber hadn't told them why the men were after her. Was she lying then, or did she really not know what purpose the men could have had in trying to kill her?

Alaric shrugged. From how tight-lipped Amber had been about the subject, he doubted she would appreciate him bringing it up. The elf took a swig from his waterskin. Gemna had gifted them two large waterskins that had sustained them thus far in their travels. "Keeping alive someone who has slept under your roof is no charity," she'd explained, and Amber had agreed. "The desert gives no charity. To provide you water and food, which we could just as easily use for yourself, is nothing more than the necessary treatment of one who is like kin to you." Alaric had been pleasantly surprised by that last remark: proof that Gemna had been fond of him after all. The water-skin was light—much lighter than it had been when Alaric had first slung it over his shoulder—and tasted faintly of leather.

"We are running low on water," he called out to Amber. An understatement as he reckoned he had perhaps a few small swigs left in his skin, and he doubted Amber would have much more.

She nodded and pointed to the west, in the general direction they'd been traveling since leaving the monastery. "We'll arrive at an oasis sometime early tomorrow by the grace of Yamaria," Amber assured him. "We can refill our skins, and with any luck, there might be a few trees bearing fruit."

The mention of fruit got Alaric's mouth watering. It had been *ages* since he'd bitten into a sweet, soft peach or crunched an apple. The figs and dates that Amber had provided for their meals just weren't the same.

"If you want to make it there tomorrow, without keeling over, you need to sleep now," Amber ordered him sternly. "The day will only get hotter, and you'll want to be asleep before then."

"Yes, ma'am," Alaric said respectfully with a salute. He moved over to where Amber was sitting and lay down in the shade of their makeshift shelter.

Amaru waited for a few minutes while she made sure that Alaric had indeed drifted off. The oasis was a bit farther off than she'd hoped. But Alaric wasn't suited for desert travel, after so many years living in the comparably wet Sulfaari Expanse, so she had to pace herself. Tomorrow would be the third day since they'd left Solgaele. So far, they'd seen nothing, no signs of anyone following them, though Amaru wasn't foolish enough to believe that they were safe. She hadn't noticed the Venomsting operatives watching her as she traveled to Solgaele, so they could be on her trail right now, and the companions would be none the wiser.

But the two couldn't keep living on fruits and desert grass, and Amaru wanted to save their dried rations until they were needed. She sensed that there might come a time when they wouldn't have the luxury of hunting and gathering, and Amaru wanted to visit as few settlements as possible. The fewer people saw her, the fewer people would recognize her. Yamaria's child knew that if the Chillfang had managed to get operatives all the way out into Fyrestone, then they would undoubtedly have allies within the desert. They would need protein, fresh meat to survive. So Amaru left Alaric's side, whispered a prayer to Yamaria that no trouble would come upon the resting elf, and slipped into fox form to go hunt.

*****

Alaric woke shortly before sunfall that day to a surprising combination of sounds and smells. The crackle of a small fire came from the center of their campsite, far enough from the tarp shelter so that they wouldn't risk burning it down but close enough that the wonderful aroma of roasting meat could reach his nostrils. After the conversation earlier that day, this was the last thing Alaric expected. It still seemed so strange that he'd gone to sleep, and yet it was the same day. With the shaded interior of the monastery, the monks of Solgaele kept the same hours as most out in the kingdom proper.

He'd get used to it in time, Alaric knew, if for no other reason than to not disappoint Amber.

"You lit a fire," Alaric said in disbelief, folding and stowing the camp gear.

"I did," Amber agreed expressionlessly. She'd skinned two hares and rotated them on a makeshift spit over the flames. The juices hissed and sizzled as the hares cooked, releasing that mouthwatering scent that had awoken him. "We must travel today, or else we'll not survive the day," she explained. "It makes sense that we have proper energy for the walk."

And, Alaric filled in mentally, starting to get the hang of Amber's mindset, *since we will be traveling, we can cook early and then head off. That way, any pursuers we may or may not have won't be able to catch us unawares as we sleep.* He had the tact not to mention that fact since to do so would admit that he was worried about being attacked, and Amber did not need anything more to worry about, what with keeping them both alive and finding her destination.

It then occurred to Alaric that he hadn't a clue where Amber was planning on going. He didn't know much at all about the places within the desert, so he'd placed his trust in Amber that she wouldn't lead them astray. But they had been heading straight westward, with little variation. The companions had passed a few distant villages or clusters of tents, but Amber never stopped long enough to consider them as places to go. Furthermore and far more critical, Amber had not given him any clues of their ultimate destination.

It wasn't that he didn't trust Amber because he did, but still, "Where are we going?" Alaric asked suddenly.

"To the oasis." Amber furrowed her brow, as they'd discussed this before Alaric went to sleep. "To fill our waterskins."

Alaric shook his head in exasperation. "No, not today. I understand that much. I'm asking what your ultimate destination is. What place are you aiming towards? Somewhere we'll be safe from the Venomsting, I hope. I don't mean to be pushy, but I do feel that as I am traveling with you, it only makes sense that I have some clue as to what's going on."

Amber sighed and silently continued turning the rabbits. The meat was turning golden brown now and soon would be ready to eat. When Amber did not attempt to respond, Alaric wondered whether she'd heard him or if she was going to ignore the question.

She pulled the turning stick off the fire and broke it in half, handing one side, and, with it, one rabbit to Alaric and taking the other for herself. "There are no seasonings, so you'll have to make do with just the flavor of the hare." As far as she was concerned, having eaten meat raw in fox form for many years, the hare was delicious by itself, though on occasion, some desert herbs and goat butter never hurt. The Fyroxi weren't farmers; they kept no herds and grew no crops. The Fire-Striders were hunters, sustaining themselves off only what Yamaria saw fit to provide them. Only by trading the furs, antlers, and other miscellaneous useful parts of their prey could the Fyroxi obtain such luxuries, for luxuries they were.

They ate in silence for a while before Amber finally answered Alaric's question. "I don't have one."

"What?" Alaric asked, having thought the conversation over and done with by Amber's silence.

"I'm not heading for any city or village," she mumbled quietly. "I have no location in mind."

That gave Alaric pause for a moment. "Have you had no plan from the very beginning?"

"N-no," Amber admitted. "I didn't know where I was going. That's why I stopped at Solgaele."

"Wait!" Alaric touched his chest right over the heart in mock disappointment. "I thought you came for me? I'm hurt!"

Amber smiled wanly, stood up, dusting the sand from her robe, and turned toward the west. "We have to leave. The oasis isn't getting any closer."

Alaric unfolded his legs out from under him, strode quickly in front of the girl, and braced his arms on her shoulders, staring steadily into her brass eyes. It would have been so easy just to get lost in those entrancing eyes. But he would not, *could not* be distracted at this moment. "Listen to me, Amber. I know that I don't know everything that's going on here. All I know is that you came to Solgaele and granted me my freedom. Now under normal circumstances, I'd be all for living out in the desert with a beautiful woman, especially since I know you could keep both of us alive. But this is no ordinary situation. You were sought out by assassins." Alaric shook her a little and made sure her eyes were focused on him. "They wanted to kill you!" he cried desperately. "Sultan didn't tell us much, which is unfortunately just what I expect from him, but I'll be damned if I'm going to let you wander aimlessly around this desert, giving them all the time in the world to make a trap to ensnare you and end your life!" He could see faint traces of sadness in Amber's eyes, so he softened his voice. The last thing Alaric wanted to do was make her cry. "Please, Amber," he begged instead, "don't let yourself get killed by carelessness. The Venomsting are assassins, skilled ones, who have been doing their dirty work for who knows how long! The longer we stay out here in the desert, the more opportunities we give them to get the drop on us. It might be safer for you to return home."

"I can't return home," Amber asserted, her tone forlorn. "But what you say is wise. Which is why we should get moving to the oasis."

Alaric sighed but released Amber's shoulders. She was correct; they needed water and soon. But the elf was worried. Would Amber take his words to heart?

He sure hoped so.

*****

As Amber had said earlier, visibility across the flat, bare desert was something marvelous, and Alaric saw precisely what his travel partner meant shortly after their journey had begun once again.

Even from a distance, the sight of the oasis was bizarre. For miles all around him, Alaric saw only sand, rocks, and tough, dry desert grass. Miles and miles of dun and brown.

One moment, Alaric was cresting a dune behind Amber, wishing that the desert's heat allowed for conversation. He couldn't tell whether Amber was angry at him for the argument they'd had earlier.

The little talking they'd done was simple, nothing more than Amber pointing out facts about the sparse vegetation or animals they saw.

And then, all of a sudden, the shimmering air revealed something green! Up ahead, spiky fronds and grass taller than anything Alaric had seen since leaving the Sulfaari Expanse shot out of the dun landscape. The sight was a shock, and it took everything the elf had to resist the urge to run toward the familiar color in the hostile landscape. Trees, similar to those he'd seen near the shoreline of Sun's Reach, poked out, their long leaves eagerly drinking in the harsh sunlight while the roots absorbed the water that had to be there for the plants to live.

Green was the color of life, and with the sight came a wave of relief. Amber had given him the last of her water, saying that he had spent far less time in the desert and would need the water more. Alaric had thought that notion was outrageous, but Amber wouldn't take no for an answer, so the elf had reluctantly accepted the drink. Now that they could see where the water was, Alaric was assured that Amber would survive.

Despite the gift of water, which deeply touched the bard and which he promised to pay the girl back for, Alaric couldn't help himself. When he saw the deep pool of water, he sprinted through the grass and threw himself to his knees. His throat was so very parched, his voice scratchy. The bard dunked his face into the oasis and began to drink deep gulps of the sweet water.

Only a few blissful seconds later, Amber had a hand on his neck and yanked his head from the pool. "Do not drink too quickly. You will make yourself sick!"

Alaric sat down heavily, wincing as his tailbone impacted the hard-packed dirt beneath him. "Thanks," he said sheepishly.

"It's nothing to be ashamed of," Amber comforted, patting his shoulder. "It's the natural reaction of someone who hasn't seen an oasis before. I likely did something very similar when I was young, and my"—she hesitated for just a second—"my father showed me my first one."

Alaric wasn't sure how to reply to that. Amber's voice was wistful as if she recalled something sad. "Do you miss your home?" he asked softly. "You've neglected to tell me much of it. To be honest, I thought that I would be joining you back to your family." The elf laughed. "But I do believe that we've gone in the exact opposite direction, judging by the way you came to us."

Amber looked momentarily alarmed after hearing that but quickly recovered. The sadness returned to her face as she recalled Xio, Ren, Weylin, and the two Fyrestone kits. "I miss them terribly," Amber admitted. Though she couldn't worry Alaric with it, the Chillfang haunted her dreams most nights, scenes of the carnage they had brought upon those that she considered her family. "But I cannot return home," she said again, hoping to convince both herself and Alaric.

The notion of leading a Venomsting clan or whatever Chillfang might be following her into the heart of the Fire-Striders was unthinkable. Amaru was sure that they had more than enough troubling them already. Undoubtedly, the Chillfang would not be quite finished with them, not until they learned that the one they searched for was not among the tribe. Then what would they do? Would Amaru return to see the bones of her friends and family, scoured clean by predators and sand squalls? No, she couldn't think about that. She had to believe that they would survive. That they would prevail against their foes.

Alaric crawled toward the shore of the oasis, undoing the ponytail in his hair as he went. The elf massaged long fingers through the wheat-colored hair, spreading it until it hung in a long sheet down past his shoulders. He silently cupped water in his hands and washed out the sand and dust of desert travel. He could sense that Amber was thinking about something. Though he couldn't be sure what it was, he got the sense it wasn't pleasant and refused to be the one to force any unhappy emotions to the surface. The bard felt foolish for suggesting home. She'd spared him no explanations of the dangers that the desert hosted, all of which made Alaric glad he'd chosen to join her. If a trek through the desert was so deadly and her home was a safe place, why would Amber be here?

She wouldn't. Alaric wished he knew why she'd left, but he supposed that Amber would favor him with the truth eventually.

Darkness, he thought. *We haven't yet known each other for a month. I can stand to wait a while longer.*

The elf dipped the waterskins in the oasis, filling them with clean, sweet water. He carried one over to Amber and pressed it into her hands. "Come now; you must be thirsty by now. Giving me your water was an appreciated gesture, but not if it means depriving yourself."

"Thank you, Alaric," Amber muttered appreciatively. "If Yamaria smiles upon us, then we shouldn't have to worry about that again. Now that we are here, I have an idea of a route we can take. With some luck and a little hard travel, we should be able to reach an oasis before our supplies wear out. The Sun Mother blessed us by placing plenty of life-giving oases around the Scorched Waste."

"Of course, that's not the only favor that the great Yamaria granted the people of the desert!" a new voice said from behind them. They both whirled around to see a gray-bearded man dressed in faded blue robes. He had a friendly smile on his face and hands stuffed in the folds of his robes.

"A Water Caller," Amber said, a hint of apprehension hidden in her voice.

Alaric noticed it and how the reaction didn't line up with his companion's explanation of the Water Callers' kindness. He filed the information away to ask about later.

If the stranger heard the inflection, he had the good graces to ignore it. "Yes, child of the desert," he replied. "But we can talk about that later. I wish Yamaria had told me she'd send me guests today. I'd have taken those figs I saw earlier! But no matter, I should have enough stew to go around." He looked at them for a few moments, and when nobody made any move, the Water Caller sighed. "Come, come; the stew will be ready soon, and my tent is plenty large enough to host three for a time!" Without waiting for them to respond again, the elderly man gestured and walked back in the direction where his tent presumably was.

"Can we trust him, Amber?" Alaric asked, touching his lute case and realizing just how useless of a weapon it would make. *Should have asked Gemna for more than just the belt knife*, he thought ruefully but quickly dismissed the thought. He knew nothing about weaponry, which was why he'd fit in so well with the monks.

"I've never known a Water Caller to deceive someone, for it rarely gets them anything," Amber answered slowly and contemplatively. "A traveler in need of a Water Caller's assistance usually never has anything a brigand could want to steal. But"—Amber paused, scratching her chin—"he's old! People in the Scorched Waste rarely grow old; unless, of course, they are specifically cared for." *Like Durrigan.* A terrible sense of loss ran through her at the thought of her surrogate father.

"Well, if nothing else, that has to make you curious," Alaric said, secretly deeply relieved to see another person. "And he invited us into his tent; it would be extremely rude not to take him up on that offer."

"You're right, of course," Amber admitted. "We must accept his invitation. At the very least, it will save us the effort of hunting dinner." With her mind made up, she stood and strode off toward the old man's tent, with Alaric only shortly behind.

EMERY
Distressing News and New Hope

Emery escorted the Rainclaw sisters back home after their appointment at the dress shop. A cozy building hung with half-finished works and filled with bolts of cloth, lace, and silk. Small buckets of pins, needles, and clips sat near both worktables, one for father and another for son, Emery guessed. Barnio had been more than happy to accept the Rainclaw sisters' business and made no remark about their race, which Emery was quite glad for. For the first part of their meeting, they had debated which colors would match their skin best and which cut of dress they would like. Reyna decided that if she wanted to push her commoner rank from the eyes of the nobles, she would have to dazzle their eyes and capture their hearts.

Barnio suggested a blue gown slashed through with pink might be just what she needed. He decided to go with something simple for the Khindre, choosing to accentuate her natural beauty rather than create anything new. "It would be impossible for a man of my talent to make something that rivals divine beauty such as yours." The old dressmaker had a real way with words and made everyone in the room feel like the most gorgeous person on this side of the Eclipse.

Arcadia, in her usual fashion, went with her signature colors of black and silver. She knew how people viewed her, but unlike Reyna, she saw no reason to warp that assumption. "Because of what I am and how I act, people tend to be afraid of me," she explained to Emery as they walked home. "I don't have Reyna's charm to keep them from assaulting or even killing me. Nor do I have my parents' support. You saw what my dear mother did yesterday. That slight tinge of fear is the only shield I have against my enemies, both identified and secret."

The dress fitting itself took little more than half an hour, but all the while, the Rainclaw sisters, or at least Reyna and to some very small part Caitrial, gushed over how the princess wore it. Arcadia wasn't one to gush, but she did nod discreetly at Emery to show her approval.

*****

By the time she returned to the castle, it was well past midday, and servants shuffled through the halls, cleaning absentmindedly. As she wandered through the corridors, making her leisurely way toward the castle gardens, one of the men stopped her. "Excuse me, Your Highness, but the king said he wished to see you in his chambers when you returned home." He bowed as Emery nodded her understanding. "Will you want anything to eat? Most of the midday meal has been cleared, but I'm sure someone in the kitchen should have an extra portion set aside somewhere."

"No, thank you," Emery said. "I ate while I was out."

"As you say, Your Highness. I trust your meal was satisfactory, at least?"

"It was." In fact, the meal she'd purchased from a restaurant highly recommended by Barnio Boome had been excellent. Though perhaps not as rich or fancy as the food served in the palace, Emery found she almost liked the simple fare better. "You may tell my father that I will attend him shortly."

"As you wish, Your Highness." The servant scurried off with a bow.

Emery didn't bother changing her clothing; only a little dust had found her way onto the simple garb she'd worn for the meeting. She'd known that it would be necessary to undress to pin and fit the garment and didn't want to be struggling to escape fancy clothing.

This answer still didn't suit her father, whose eyes had a mote of fear in them.

"What will the people think, seeing the princess go into a commoner's shop and in rags no less?!" He massaged his hands nervously. "You should have requested Barnio to come here to do the fitting!"

"Why does that matter, Father? So what if I went into someone else's shop, and so what if I was wearing simple clothing?" Emery would not call what she wore rags by any means. The plain garment was still expertly tailored and made of premium material.

"Appearances are everything, Emery!" King Godfrey replied, unconsciously smoothing his red-dyed ermine robe. "If we don't keep up the right appearances, then we risk portraying that something is wrong with our family. And there is nothing wrong with our family!"

If only you knew, Emery thought to herself. *If only you saw just how many things were wrong in this castle, in your kingdom.* The list was extensive already, and Emery was sure she didn't know the half of it.

He took a series of deep breaths to calm himself. "It's fine. It's fine. We can still save face. I received some news today that may redeem us yet."

"What news is that?" the princess asked apprehensively. "Something that concerns me, I'm sure, since you called me here."

"Yes, in fact. It's in perfect timing too since we planned the wedding with houses Rothsster and Leygrain."

Emery's heart dropped as he unrolled a long, thin scroll that must have come by a raven.

"I have received several responses from different nobles across Sun's Reach since my proclamation went out. But none more promising than this one." Godfrey waggled the scroll, almost giddily. "I'll admit that I've never heard of their family name or anything about them, but the report he sent along with his allied lands and the men in his service is very impressive. I've not heard of many of them, but your old tutor assures me that they exist, and he seemed as impressed by their acquisitions as I am."

"Who are they?"

"They claim the family name of Gardstar, and they are offering their son Tarus's hand, forming an alliance between our families."

"And you're just going to hand me off to some family you don't even know?" Emery asked incredulously. "Based off of some numbers on a paper?"

"No, of course not!" King Godfrey protested. "What do you take me for, some sort of fool? No, they are coming to court to present themselves. We will wine and dine with them, and then if I deem them suitable, the announcement of your marriage will be made official."

"And if I don't find them suitable?" Emery had noticed that her father hadn't even bothered to ask her opinion on the matter.

"I'm sure he will be. But if not, you'll do what is best for the family and for our reputation. They'll be here a week before midsummer. You are dismissed, Emery."

Best for your reputation maybe, Emery thought as she left the room. Her steps led her to her mother's chambers. The king and queen of Sun's Reach no longer shared a room, a symbol of a royal relationship gone sour. And her father wondered why the princess wasn't enthused about this betrothal. She knocked on the door and an irritated "Can I help you?" rang out sharply.

"Mother, it's Emery. I wanted to talk."

There came an audible exhalation, and her mother's voice immediately became softer. "Just come right in, darling."

Emery opened the door to see her mother sitting at a desk, quill in hand, spectacles over her eyes. A candle flickered dimly beside her, burned nearly to the stub. A weary smile lifted Lysaria Redwyn's wrinkled face. Lysaria was a few years younger than her husband but certainly didn't look it. If being king had been hard on Godfrey, it had been brutal to his wife. While the king focused on the public affairs of the crown, Emery's mother handled most everything else. The tall stack of papers to her side proved this fact. Even in the low candlelight in the dark room, Emery could see the thick stripes of gray in her once-glossy hair. Wrinkled skin was the only crown on Lysaria's brow. Staying mostly in her room, handling the king's paperwork, she had little need of the tiara collecting dust on its pillowed pedestal.

"Open the shades, dear," Queen Lysaria told her daughter. "I'm sure it's wrecking my eyes, but I've grown more accustomed to candlelight for reading." She squinted and blinked as a blade of sunlight struck back the darkness. When her eyes finally adjusted to her surroundings, she looked over her daughter. "Somebody chose not to look like a princess today."

"Don't you start too!" Emery begged.

"Did you approach your father in such clothing?" To Emery's relief, there was none of the same disapproval in her mother's voice. "I can't imagine he took that well."

"He didn't." She explained the reason for the simple tunic and leggings, and her mother nodded. "You should have seen the dress, Mother; it was gorgeous!"

"I'm sure I'll see it at the wedding." Lysaria waved. "Your father will have to let me out of my cage for that much at least." She pawed at her face. "Though it will take a miracle worker to make this look presentable."

"What are you talking about?" Emery teased. "You wear your age well."

"Are you calling me old, Daughter?" Lysaria asked with mock stiffness.

"Never, Mother."

"Good. Now what was it that you wanted to speak about?" Lysaria crossed the room and sat down on the soft featherbed, patting the empty space next to her.

"I wanted to consult you on marriage," Emery started.

"Ah yes, your father has told you about Lord Gardstar then." She cocked her head at Emery's glance of bewilderment. "I am practically your father's scribe. The raven keeper came to me with the letter first."

"And what are your thoughts on the contents?"

"I can certainly see why your father would be taken with the idea. Godfrey sees enemies in every shadow, and if Geurus Gardstar has even half the number of men he claims, we could fill in the sparse patrols that we have around the city."

"But what are *your* thoughts? You've only talked about the king so far."

"Honestly, Emery?" Queen Lysaria rubbed at her temples. "Until I've met them and spoken with their matriarch, I cannot judge them. My guess by your questions is that you are having misgivings about this marriage."

"I'm not really sure, to be completely honest," Emery explained. "I don't quite know what to feel."

"And that's why you're here," Lysaria stated matter-of-factly. "You want a second opinion on this whole arranged-marriage business." The queen took a deep breath. "Emery, one should always be honest with their family, and so I shall be with you. Arranged marriages…don't have a high success rate. It is not, however, impossible to find a successful match."

"You believe that Tarus Gardstar could be worthy of my affection then?" Emery asked reluctantly.

Lysaria chuckled grimly at that. "No mother with her wits about her will ever consider a suitor worthy of their child, but it is not my approval that matters, and unfortunately, yours is much the same. The only one this Lord Gardstar has to win is your father."

"And if I end up in a loveless marriage because of it?"

"So quick to jump to conclusions, Emery. Such pessimism about love won't do you much good," Lysaria reprimanded.

"I don't want to end up like you and Father," Emery whispered.

"Daughter," the queen crooned sympathetically, wrapping an arm around her, "what you see here is a result of neglect and business on both ends. When your father was still the prince and not the king, our relationship was far better. It was him taking the throne and becoming paranoid about his seat that doused our flame. If you can put aside your doubts and go into this with a clear and open heart, then problems will be less likely to occur. But I will tell you that it will be difficult to do that if you love another."

Emery let out a long spiraling sigh. Her mother was the one person she'd trusted with the knowledge of her affection for Sir

Leonidas. Much to the princess's surprise, Queen Lysaria had taken the news well.

"I don't blame you," she'd said. "Leonidas is a good man and a skilled knight. He's proven his way into the king's good graces, but he is not noble by any means. Just be cautious about your choices. I don't want you walking into the proverbial lion's den and be torn apart because of it."

"Mother, I want to give this Tarus a chance. Truly I do," Emery answered at length. "But what if I can't get over Leo? What happens if he comes home? I'm just supposed to betray my heart to do what's best for the family! Why is it such a crime for me to marry the man I love?"

Now it was the queen's turn to hesitate. "Because you are the princess of Sun's Reach, Emery. Once Sir Leonidas returns home, you will have to ask him and your father about that matter."

"Once he returns home?" Emery quoted hopefully. "Do you mean to say…"

"I don't wish to get your hopes up, Daughter," Queen Lysaria said. "But I do know that at least one of Braveheart's band survived, a dwarf by the name of Dalphamair, who contacted me recently. There is a chance that your guard will find his way home as well, if he still lives."

Emery was nearly overcome with excitement and joy. There was little doubt in her heart Leo would be coming home. The Secretkeeper had been right; things would work out in the end.

AMARU

A Strange Desert Savior

When they reached the tent of the old Water Caller, he was already rummaging through a pack within, pulling out utensils for eating. The campsite, like all such sites made by a true Water Caller, was small and tidy. One tent, with just enough room for two people to sleep comfortably or three in close quarters, was pitched a few feet off the shore of the oasis. Next to it, a stake was hammered into the ground, where a long-legged and hairy creature was tethered.

"Camel," Amaru explained to Alaric, seeing his confused glance at the ugly creature. "They are preferred over pack mules and horses in the desert, as they can withstand the heat and go for days without water."

A ring of stones surrounded a fire over which the aforementioned stew sat bubbling in a pot. The aroma wafting off toward them was divine. Amaru could smell the familiar odor of venison. Though they had eaten rabbit earlier, the possibility of a well-cooked and assumedly well-seasoned meal brought joy to the companions' hearts.

The old man was mumbling to himself as he collected the last of the supplies. "Glad I listened to my mentor, yes, I am. 'Always bring at least three bowls and three sets of utensils,' he always said. 'Being a Water Caller can be very lonely work, but you never know when you'll have guests.' And now look at me, with two guests for dinner!" He stood and returned to the fire, where Amaru and Alaric were standing warily. "But it would not do to be so overwhelmed by the prospect of guests that one forgets to acknowledge them," he scolded himself. "You look as if you've been traveling all day and long before that." He beckoned to them, pointing to flattened logs placed around the fire. "Please come and sit!" the man said jovially. "I'm glad that Yamaria finally answered my wishes for company."

Amaru and Alaric still weren't sure what to make of the man. He seemed to enjoy talking to himself.

"I think I may have received some form of communication from the Sun Mother this morning," he said conversationally, his eyes focused on the stew that he was giving a final stir and taste. "Though I didn't realize it at first. I don't usually make such large portions since I'm only ever feeding myself, but this morning, I had this…inspiration, and a smallish desert antelope presented itself to me. I wasn't just going to let my luck pass me by! I figured that whatever meat I didn't use, I could dry and salt for later." He ladled the thick stew into the wooden bowls and glanced over toward the companions. Seeing that Amaru and Alaric were still standing, bewildered by his speech, he pulled a sour and impatient face. "Oh, please you two, just sit!" he said crossly. "I made all of this food, and I'm not going to eat it all of myself." The Water Caller gestured toward the camel. "Diarth certainly won't eat it! He prefers vegetation."

The two companions, chagrined, folded their legs underneath them and gratefully accepted the bowls of stew.

"But where are my manners!" he exclaimed suddenly, dropping his carved wooden spoon in the bowl with a small splash. "My name's Ephraim," he introduced with a bow, only slightly diminished by his sitting position and the drips of red stew in his beard. "As I'm sure you've figured out by now, I am a Water Caller. And you are?"

"I am the renowned bard, Alaric Honeytone," the elf said theatrically.

"Who?" Ephraim asked, scratching his head. "That's not a name I've heard around these parts. And what business does a bard have here in the desert? The Sun Elves don't have many bards as far as I know; I wouldn't expect the sand to be good for the throat."

"I've noticed." Alaric seemed visibly deflated by Ephraim's lack of recognition. Amaru wordlessly patted him on the back, hoping to console his easily bruised ego.

"He's Alaric, and I'm Amber," she hastily finished, as she was not clear about why the elf was in the Scorched Waste either. *I suppose that makes two of us with pasts that are mysteries.* "We are…" Amaru wasn't sure what story to give. She most definitely couldn't tell the truth; Ephraim wouldn't believe them, would he? Even if he did understand and accept their story, that would mean another person who knew Amaru's whereabouts. Another person that the Chillfang or the Venomsting could hurt. She couldn't avoid the question and knew that Ephraim would get suspicious if she didn't say anything, but she hadn't thought about this. Luckily, Alaric saved her.

"My lady and I are out on an adventure to get to know each other better," Alaric said quickly when it was clear that his companion wasn't going to answer.

Ephraim nodded in understanding. "A kinship trek! I should have guessed that was what you youngsters were up to!" He chuckled knowingly. "I'm sorry if I'm spoiling your fun."

Amaru resisted the urge to gape at Alaric. Had the elf actually known about the kinship treks, or had his quick thinking just produced the perfect answer to the question? Amaru didn't know, but either way, she was impressed.

Kinship treks were part of the marriage ritual among the nomadic tribes in the desert. Since marriages were often forged between members of different tribes, it was essential to ensure that the couple would be compatible before inviting them into the family tents. Once a marriage was approved by elders and parents, the couple would go out to journey through the desert. The arduous journey would prove that a union could withstand tough situations and that both members were competent in the necessary skills for survival. If by the end of the trip, the two decided they were not as compatible as they first hoped or one declared displeasure with the other, the pact could be broken quickly and cleanly without causing tension between either tribe; it was seen as a sign from the sun goddess that the two were not meant to be together.

The daughter of Yamaria nodded politely and rested a hand on Alaric's shoulder, deciding it was best to play out this part. "Yes, my beloved and I have only just begun the journey, but I hold little doubt in the outcome."

"Ah, young love," Ephraim said dreamily. "I can remember it as if it were only yesterday." He stared off into space as if stuck in a reflective trance. Amaru and Alaric watched him in bewilderment. Finally, after many long moments, Ephraim woke from his reverie. "Ah, good memories," he reflected. "The pair of you make a good match if I do say so myself!"

"I couldn't agree more!" Alaric leaned in slightly toward Amaru, resting a slim, bark-colored hand on her tan one.

The old Water Caller looked appraisingly at them, worry in his gaze. "But you two are either very brave or very foolish, doing your kinship trek at such a time as this, especially since one of you is not of the desert." Ephraim gestured toward Alaric. "This one is *clearly* not of the Sun Elves that live deeper in the desert than many a human tribe would dare or think about daring, for that matter!"

Amaru cocked her head. "What do you mean, graybeard?" she asked, respect evident in her voice. "About the danger, I mean." Dread filled the pit of her stomach, weighing heavily on top of the antelope stew. Could the Chillfang have already started menacing other people as well? And if they were, what did that mean for her tribe? Amaru could hardly imagine the horror.

Ephraim's next words didn't exactly comfort her but at least dispelled the worst of her fears about the Chillfang.

"I've heard only idle rumors and haven't seen anything myself, so perhaps take these warnings with a grain of sand...or many! There is plenty to go around!" When the two didn't smile at his joke, Ephraim plowed onward. "Anyway, I've heard that there have been a few sightings of strange creatures." Amaru's mind immediately jumped to the scaly beast from years earlier. That creature had survived the fight with Leif, for all that the Fyroxi knew. What if it had found another of its kind and reared offspring? And what if it grew stronger? That thought was nearly as bad as the Chillfang. "I've heard everything from giant scorpions to spear-wielding killers which brings the Venomsting to mind, knowing the dangers of the desert."

Alaric was quick to jump on this comment. "What do you know about the Venomsting, good sir?"

Ephraim chuckled humorlessly. "More than I'd like to but less than I should," he answered. "They do little without specific orders and the proper payment; that much I can tell you." The Water Caller's words confirmed Sultan's belief: somebody had paid the Venomsting to go after Amaru. "But once they have been paid to eliminate someone, they don't tend to let up, unless they figure they can take the wrath of their leaders and, some say, their gods. I do know that the Venomsting don't pray to Yamaria, though what god they aim to please is a mystery to me."

Amaru clenched her fists. The people hunting her weren't followers of the Way of Yamaria, and that angered her. "Whatever the dark being is, it has tainted this desert folk into savage murderers."

"Murderers indeed, though I don't think 'savage' is the right word for them," Ephraim said, stroking his beard thoughtfully. "I've heard that they plan their kills very methodically. There is a reason you never hear about a *survivor* of a Venomsting attack!"

Alaric continued to eat his stew, hoping that Ephraim wouldn't realize that his fingers were white from gripping his spoon. He couldn't help wondering again why anybody would want so desperately to kill Amber!

"But now is not a day to be talking of such depressing topics!" Ephraim interrupted their private musings. "Unless this wondering about the Venomsting is more than just an idle curiosity?"

Amaru shook her head and waved off Ephraim's claims. There was no reason that this old Water Caller needed to be involved. If she were right, the relief group would have to get involved at some point, but not yet.

"Very well, just remember, if you ever need somewhere safe to go, Oasi Sanctus is open to all." Ephraim seemed pleased with the response and the chance to change the subject. "Then perhaps we should change to something lighter. I am interested to know why a woods elf would find himself in the desert."

The three talked until the heat became too oppressive for any-one but Diarth the camel to stand. Then Ephraim invited the two into the tent. He chose to sleep outside, underneath a canvas canopy and on a rug, ignoring Amaru's attempts to switch with him. "I have been sleeping in that tent for quite a number of years now. I don't think that a rest or two on the sand will kill me. I've survived this long!"

An hour past sunfall, Amaru and Alaric woke on their respec-tive sides of the tent. The air had cooled to the more tolerable travel-ing temperature, and the oasis was silent.

Amaru got up to thank Ephraim for everything, but when she left the shelter, she found that he was gone! There was no trace of the old Water Caller anywhere, no trace except for the canvas tent and a couple of pouches laid on a rock under the small awning. Upon fur-ther inspection, Amaru found them filled with dried antelope meat and fruits.

"What's wrong?" Alaric asked, coming out of the shelter with a languid stretch.

"Ephraim left," she answered simply. "And we have a tent."

They bundled up the tarps that Gemna had given them and concealed it in the brush, not well enough that it couldn't be found but just enough so that wild animals might leave it be. Amaru explained that it was only right to leave it for another traveler, who might happen upon the oasis and be in need. Besides, it would be impractical to lug around both tent and tarps when they would only be using the former.

With another silent prayer of thanks to Ephraim, the two started their journey again. This time, Amaru had decided where she had to go. Though she didn't want to put anyone else in danger, if the people were dealing with strange creatures already, then somebody needed to be alerted about the possibility of a Chillfang threat and everything that could mean. And the Water Callers would be the best for that. Amaru took a deep breath of the warm air.

She would have to go to Oasi Sanctus.

AMARU

Close Call and a New Companion

Alaric followed his desert-dwelling companion as willingly as ever, glad to see that she now seemed to have found a new purpose. With Ephraim's unexpected appearance at the oasis and the news of the new dangers in the desert, Amber had resolved that they would search for Oasi Sanctus. It must have slipped Ephraim's mind to tell them where to find his fellow Water Callers. He did, however, inform them that he planned to go farther out in the Scorched Waste, in the opposite direction of his brethren. This, he said, was to ensure that somebody took care of the more widespread desert tribes that very few Water Callers made out to visit. More often than not, those tribes would make contact with Oasi Sanctus, sending notice that one of their brave number had fallen to privation. Amber had been worried about what might happen to Ephraim if younger Water Callers didn't survive the journey. But Alaric had been quick to remind her of Ephraim's age.

"You said yourself that it's uncommon for people of the Scorched Waste, even Water Callers, to survive to such a ripe age. If he's gone on this long, I would imagine that he knows what he's doing."

"What you say makes sense," Amber said, still a trace of doubt in her voice. "I worry. He left his tent with us, and I worry what the heat of the day might do to him."

Alaric pat Amber on the back, feeling how tense her muscles were. "Amber, is something wrong?"

She shook her head but gave no further answer. Amber was, of course, thinking about home again, as she often did these days. Durrigan was ever present in her mind. Ephraim had made the memories of the old chief resurface, and the pain of his loss filled her heart again. Amber took a deep breath and cleared her head. She couldn't afford to be distracted if they wanted to reach the next shelter before their water supplies ran out.

So on they went, traveling after sunfall and sleeping in their tent during the hottest parts of the day. Occasionally while they rested, Amaru would go out and hunt for fresh meat. She missed being able to shift freely into fox form, the feeling of being able to run across the desert, at speeds that most wouldn't dare to go in the Scorched Waste. She hated the need to be so cautious, but at the same time, she was glad for it; only a week after they had left what they dubbed Ephraim's Oasis, they started seeing the signs of danger that the old Water Caller had warned them of.

The sun was beginning its steep climb to the sky, already tinged with the searing white that it took on during a desert day. The sands in the area they had just reached were more like a thin, light powder and often slipped under Amaru's and Alaric's feet, slowing their progress. Up ahead, they could see a cave: the oasis they hoped to rest in tonight. The shaded shelter of the cave would be a blessed boon for the two of them. The tent Ephraim had left them kept them safe from the sun, but the fabric still grew hot, even with its purposeful openings. Alaric was glad that it never rained in the Scorched Waste. This sort of tent would be useless at keeping water out.

They approached the oasis; Amaru informed Alaric that the symbols cut into the rock designated it as Shalsen Oasis. They followed their regular procedure, Alaric washing the sand from his hair and the crusted salt from his face while his companion went behind the bushes to a different part of the pond to wash. Alaric wondered why Amber was so shy as to avoid even washing her hair near him, but he was a gentleman and gave the beautiful woman all the privacy she required.

But only a few minutes after Amber had gone off, Alaric heard her calling him. "Alaric, you'd best come to see this!" Her voice was tinged with fear. The elf, his hair still hanging down around his shoulders, quickly stood and ran over.

Amber was kneeling next to a bush; the bard gave her a once-over before anything. Seeing that she was unharmed, he crossed over to her side, to see what she was staring at. In the sand near the bush was something that glistened in the sun. It had been pulled from the sand, but the grains still stuck in the grooves proved that it was previously buried. In front of Amber, the sand had been shifted hastily, and other similar items protruded partially from the powder. He glanced first at the stricken expression of Amber's face and then back down at the ground where the offending item sat.

And then he realized why she was so worried.

"Remind you of anything?" she asked.

"Yamaria's mercy," Alaric breathed. The yellowish mask was indeed familiar to him. "Those are the same masks that the Venomsting used when they came to kill you!" Alaric handled it. The smooth, gleaming surface was not metal as the elf had expected. It felt like the shell of some insect. Chitin masks certainly made more sense than metal. Alaric had wondered why anyone would be stupid enough to wear metal in the desert. Besides weapons and small trinkets, there was little done with metal in the Scorched Waste. The sun made that nearly impossible without risking singeing flesh.

His companion nodded. "We can't stay here."

"I agree, but where would we go?" Alaric asked, gesturing widely to the desert. "Let's say that the owners of these masks return today," he reasoned. "Mind you, we don't have any clue where they are or how long it's been since these masks were buried. If I were one of them and I saw two figures walking in the desert, shortly away from a place that I've claimed as a base…" He didn't need to finish the sentence; Amber nodded her understanding.

"So we'll have to wait here and hope that nothing happens," she concluded.

"We collect our water and then go as far back in the cave as we can. With any luck, the Venomsting won't notice us." Alaric smiled at her. "We should know soon if anyone's going to come. Even people as deranged as Venomsting won't want to stay out in the desert heat."

*****

The two arranged themselves far back in the cave. The narrow section required Amaru and Alaric to sit very close to each other, which at the very least Alaric didn't mind. But neither of their minds were on that. They sat there, as still as could be and tense. They kept their breath shallow and soft, worried of the close confines. It was all Amaru could do to keep her tails from twitching from nerves. While they waited, the Fyroxi girl became keenly aware of how sore her tails were.

She wanted with all her heart to know that she could trust Alaric with her identity. Amaru knew that was she on her own; she'd have gone insane on this desert trek. Alaric's companionship and the stories he'd told her while they rested made her heartache less painful when she thought of Ren, Xio, and the others. She didn't want to be Amber the human anymore, not really. It felt like she was lying to herself; it had from the beginning, but her sense of caution had buried those thoughts.

If I can't trust Alaric, who can I trust? Amaru wondered. But then again, it still wasn't safe. How would Alaric react to learning that she'd been lying to him the whole time? *I wouldn't blame him if he hated me. I can't forget about my magic either.* She hadn't been able to practice her spells in a while. A few days after they'd left the monastery, she'd healed the knife wound on her calf, but just as Amaru was wary about revealing her identity, she was afraid that something would happen if she told Alaric that she could do magic. *I am likely the only person in Sun's Reach who can do healing magic since the Eclipse. The Fire-Striders took it well, but who knows if anyone else would? What if Alaric thinks me a monster? What would I do then?*

Before she could worry any more about that, something interrupted her reverie—a laugh from outside. Alaric's eyes went wide, and he scrambled for his lute. Amaru gripped her spear tightly, drawing the tip out of the sunlight, where the strange red material might reflect. The sound came from many throats, and the following voices spoke in a foreign tongue. A foreign language but a familiar one—their Venomsting had returned. The noise was growing closer. Then they heard a heavy thump and a groan as something fell to the ground. Something living! There was a second thump but no second grunt. That elicited another laugh from the Venomsting. Amaru heard the sounds of water splashing and knew that the assassins were washing in the oasis.

Amaru looked Alaric in the eyes. *What do we do?* the gaze asked. Amaru knew that Alaric had trained in bardic magic and hoped that he had something that would save their lives. Alaric nodded to say he had something, but the elf was worried. Amaru remembered then that most, if not all, the bardic magic required music or sound of some sort. It would be a terrible risk; the Venomsting might hear them and then be able to kill them.

But it was either that or leave themselves open, and when the Venomsting decided to come into the cave, which was inevitable, they would die. She nodded quickly, and Alaric took a deep breath.

The elf scrunched his brow in concentration, recalling what he needed to do. Then as softly as he could manage, he pulled strings on the lute. The tones reverberated against adjacent walls, shockingly loud to their ears; suddenly, the air before them seemed to take on a shade of gray. Alaric made a pointless hushing gesture, and the two waited in high-strung tension.

The voices outside had stopped, and Alaric's ears picked up the trickling of water. There was a slight rustling as one of the Venomsting wrapped himself in cloth. The sand crunched quietly underfoot as the assassin approached, and the breath caught in the throats of both of the hidden squatters. The man appeared around the corner, his red face scarred and bruises showing all the places the cloth didn't cover; Alaric did not doubt that this one was being sent to investigate the noise due to some disgrace during the day's feats.

The man scowled into the cave, his staff—a long blackwood pole with a chain wrapped around the top, the end of which was ornamented by a metal piece shaped like an enlarged scorpion sting—preceded him menacingly. The Venomsting took a few paces into the cave and called out something in his harsh language. He peered into the darkness, and Amaru felt her heart stop as his eyes seemed to fall right on hers. He held the stare for an agonizingly long number of seconds; he rapped his staff threateningly on the stone floor and called out again, stepping farther inside and squinting. Finally, the moment passed, and the Venomsting shrugged, turning back outside and calling foreign assurances to his allies.

The relief in the room was palpable, but still, neither of the two moved. Alaric's hand fumbled and grabbed onto Amaru's hand. His palm was clammy and slick with sweat. Amaru was sure hers were the same, so she didn't let go. They both needed the comfort the other could provide. Alaric had to reset the spell twice more before the Venomsting finally came into the cavern to sleep. One of them carried something in his arm. It was just over three feet long and wrapped in a burlap sack. When the assassins threw the bundle to the ground and it made the grunting noise they'd heard earlier, the two realized that the package wasn't an *it* at all. It was alive!

Shortly after, the Venomsting had all fallen asleep, their breaths falling into a gentle and even rhythm. They had been sleeping for about fifteen minutes—Alaric and Amaru couldn't get a wink of rest themselves; despite how tired they were, they couldn't risk it—when the prisoner began to move again. The knot around the opening started to come loose; Amaru and Alaric looked on with amazement as whatever was inside seemed to pull at the rope, and shortly after, the bag extruded a head.

The woman panted quietly, taking fresh air for the first time in what must have been hours. She had short flaxen hair which was a mess around her head. Big bright green eyes shimmered with relief over a nose that was perhaps a bit longer than was normal for a human. That's because she wasn't human. Alaric knew it for certain. The long nose, big eyes, short stature. This woman was a gnome. And she was looking at them!

The gnome pulled herself quietly from the bag and stared at the two, winking and giving a small smile. Gnomes were known for being hard to put down, but even Alaric found this situation hard to smile at. It occurred to Alaric and Amaru at the same time. The gnome had looked at them; she'd seen them and winked! Amaru glanced nervously around. The gray tinge was still present in front of them; the spell would be active for another few minutes. The gnome made a hushing sound and then beckoned to them. Alaric shook his head and pointed at the Venomsting.

The gnome shrugged and folded her hands together and under her head, silently miming sleep. She waved again, this time more impatiently, and plodded out of the cave.

Their hearts in their throats, Amaru and Alaric extricated themselves from the cave and crept past the sleeping Venomsting. They followed the strange gnome outside. She was stretching and rolling her joints, getting the stiffness out of them.

"Oh, man, that feels so much better!" the gnome whispered. "I hate being stuck in sacks."

"Do you do that often?" Alaric asked, matching her volume.

"Not if I can help it!" The gnome stifled a grin. "But more on that later. Now I need your help." She gestured toward the cave. "We need to get out of here, but I'd rather not have to do the stealth thing for too long if I can avoid it. Instead, we're going to trap them inside!" A wicked grin played over her shrunken features.

"Won't that kill them?" Amaru asked, berating herself for being worried about the assassins. She reminded herself that they'd tried to murder her.

"They've got food and water in there, and it shouldn't get too hot," the gnome said sincerely. "Besides, I'll send more Water Callers this way as soon as possible." Only then did the two look down past the girl's face and see that she was wearing the blue robes of a Water Caller!

Amaru nodded at that. "What do you need us to do?"

"Simple." She looked at Alaric. "Bard, you have magic that can keep them asleep, right?" When Alaric nodded, she rubbed her hands together. "Great, do that, and I'll take care of the rest."

"Take care of the rest" was a straightforward way of saying, "I'm going to cast a very impressive druidic spell that took me months to learn!" As Alaric started his playing and the three men inside curled up tighter around themselves, the gnome chanted and moved her arms in strange directions. Suddenly, the stone at the lip of the cave entrance began to move! It slid downward slowly, like a door closing, releasing a shower of dirt and dust. Though the process was loud and the rumbling certainly noticeable, not a single one of the Venomsting even stirred, kept in dreaming sleep by the elf's magic weavings.

When she had finished, the gnome's spell left no indication that there had ever been a cave here, just a rock. The sliding top of the cave fused joined seamlessly with the bottom, and only a few minute gaps for air existed, perhaps enough to fit a little finger through.

The gnome turned back to them and flashed a winsome grin. "The name's Celwyn, by the by!"

When the prisoner came out of the cave by herself, the camouflage-wearing Venomsting stationed as guard, the same one that checked the cave earlier, was startled. He was under orders to kill anyone who tried to escape, including his own allies. He had a hand on his staff and planned to rush in and kill the foolish gnome, but then two more came out of the cave. One looked elfish and carried a musical instrument, and the other, similar to a human, held a spear. At that moment, the assassin's priorities changed. He couldn't fight these people outnumbered, angry though he was that he'd been fooled earlier. So when the gnome started casting a spell and the ground shook beneath him, Zossttak took it upon himself to flee. It was time to report back to one of the bases anyway.

So absorbed in their task that none saw the elusive Venomsting escape.

Part 3

Love and War

EMERY
Tarus Gardstar

As midsummer grew nearer, the mood within the capital grew increasingly more excited. Guests from the far reaches of Sun's Reach made their way in. Lords from the cities and tribal leaders from Sulfaari Expanse alike came bearing gifts for the king and ordered provisions for the wedding. The Sunne Steps, close to the kingdom's center of command, was where the main force of nobles and settlements under their control was located. Out in the Sulfaari Expanse, only a few lords actually resided, most people living in plain wandering tribes. Fyrestone had been one of the significant cities of note, and its walls, built in the times of Fyroxi and human prime, boasted the best protection against outside threats.

Not inside threats though, Emery thought ruefully, remembering the news about the Fyroxi.

Past the Sunne Steps, most of the people were either farmers or members of some sort of tribe. They followed the food and resources, only making temporary settlements. This was what gave Sun's Reach its reputation for freedom. Those few people that decided to travel here would take up a nomadic life out in the wilderness, breaking away from the classic life under subjugation by the noble lord.

*****

With the financial backing of houses Rothsster and Leygrain, the noble wedding was looking to be a massive affair. House Leygrain was set to provide most of the food with their farmer connections. A ten-course meal was planned for the guests, and wine from the king's own cellar would be served—rare and expensive drinks from all over the world to hear her father speak of them—for all to drink. Not exempt from the mood shift was Godfrey, who almost seemed more excited than Mia and Ferrin themselves. Emery wasn't sure if that had more to do with the big party or the nearing arrival of the Gardstar family. It almost seemed to the princess that her father was already in love with them, despite not having even met them. Not even Emery, unenthused with the idea of her own marriage as she was, could say that she wasn't looking forward to the ball. Since the Rainclaw sisters would be there, Emery knew she'd have an escape from this Tarus Gardstar if he turned out to be an awful person.

Most of her time was spent with the bride-to-be, by her father's command. The king wanted to put on a good show of being around for Nestor, or any of the lords of the great houses, during their good times. Then they might also be persuaded to turn to him during the bad times.

*****

It was a cool rainy day in the city of Searstar when the first news reached the castle of the approaching large host. Their reports said that a significant number of men were approaching up the Sunne Steps to the north, not stopping despite the weather, apparently not even slowed by the slippery conditions. Two days after the first sighting, they arrived at the city gates.

The sun had finally come out, after a long rainstorm, blown in from the sea to the west. Steam curled off the stone tiles as warm light beamed down, turning the water into moisture which clung to Emery's face as the family rode their wain through the streets. Watching her mother dab at her face with a handkerchief, the princess was glad that she didn't wear makeup. The sweat from warm weather and wet from rain always ruined such falsely crafted beauty.

Emery held open the curtains that veiled the cart in which they rode, letting the people see her face and gifting them with a smile. As would be expected, the people had initially reacted with fear at the arrival of a great force of men outside the gates. Showing them a relaxed expression would prove to them that, in fact, they were not about to be invaded and nothing was amiss. More numerous than the worriers were the people curious about what could have made the king leave the castle, as he hadn't in quite a few years. So thus did a small host of noblemen and commoners alike follow the rumbling carts of the royals of Redwyn to meet the men and women of House Gardstar. Finally, with anxious hearts and curious minds, the group crossed the threshold of Searstar to behold those waiting outside. Sunlight glinted on the tips of tall spears, wielded by proud, straight-backed men. Fully clad in black armor were the men of the host; the mass of warriors seemed to absorb the very sunlight but did not show any sign of discomfort. Emery thought they must be extremely disciplined to stand without weariness in all dark armor. And what a strange color they wore too. Already a muttering had begun from the small gathering behind them, wondering what sort of people from Sun's Reach would allow themselves to be clad in such a color. Not even in mourning did the people of the Sun's Reach wear black, for it was the color of their enemy in Moonwatch. Instead, solid garments of dark blues and purples stood in.

Emery saw the excitement in her father's eyes looking over the men in front of him, any fear that might have tinged them in the recent months washing away. She wondered exactly what was racing through his mind now. After only a few more moments of nearly drooling over his thoughts, Godfrey Redwyn clapped, and servants threw aside the curtains. With some help from Lysaria, the king stepped out and moved to the front of his host. Casinius offered his hand to the princess and helped her out of the wain. It would seem that her father had directed the head of the Lightstriders to serve as her retainer during this trip since Sir Brightblade would be at Godfrey's side during any other occasion. Once the whole royal family stood in front of the wain, flanked by Casinius and Galbraith Severesse, there began a movement in the ranks of the rigid men. In a fluid motion, the lake of men parted, allowing the figures in the center to walk through. Each of the center group was garbed richly in black-and-gray velvets. In the heat of the day, their cloaks and hoods had been left behind, allowing pale blond hair to show. In such stark contrast was their hair to their clothing that their heads seemed to shine.

At the head of the family was Lord Geurus himself, resplendent with long hair flowing in the breeze. His hair seemed more silver than yellow, and a thick beard and mustache combo covered most of his lower face. He wore a broad smile, white teeth gleaming like the spears behind him. Next to him stood his graceful wife, Cereos. Her skin was milky white and smooth, with deep dark eyes. Behind them, arm in arm came their children. Velara ever had a smile on her features, which sat above a body many girls would die for. Graceful neck and arms hung with lace ribbons and wrists heavy with ivory jewelry, she was quite the attractive sight. No doubt, she was used to turning heads, as she strode calmly up the dirt path. Linked with her was the twin brother and the boy that Emery was likely to marry. Tarus, unlike the rest of the family, didn't wear such a broad smile, which for Emery almost seemed to ring false on their faces. He had a straight nose set below pale eyes and thin lips, slightly upturned at the corners. Broad shoulders and sizable muscles filled out his uniform nicely. His raiment was styled with spots of white, creating a wondrous effect like none she'd ever seen before. She'd heard old Berdur talk about the stars; back when he could see, they were the most beautiful thing to him. Small points that gave the night sky a light source other than the hateful moon. The lord's clothing put her in mind of those vivid descriptions. Tarus's pale hair was shorn shorter than his sister's, but both had the little ringlets that bounced up and down as they walked.

"Godfrey Redwyn." Geurus's voice was tinged with a strange accent, which explained why Emery had never heard of his family before. She wondered where in the world they were actually from; that would be among her first questions to Tarus when they got the chance to speak later. "I'm glad we finally get the chance to meet in person. Letters never give a good judge of character, don't you agree?"

"Most certainly, Lord Geurus. I'm glad to see that you are, in fact, real. I started to worry that maybe you were too good to be true."

Geurus laughed, a deep gusty sound. "Well, here I am, in the flesh." He turned around to give the king a good look at him. "One hundred percent real. And my children are much the same." He motioned for Velara and Tarus to come forward. Allowing his son to step in front, he braced the young man's shoulders with his large hands. "My son has been very excited to meet your daughter." Lord Geurus gave Tarus a gentle push toward the princess.

Kneeling in front of her, Tarus took her hand and pressed his lips gently to the back. "My lady, I've heard tales of your beauty, but it is difficult to trust tales. Unless some sorcery is tricking my eyes, I know that they were all true." Emery felt her face flush. If nothing else, Tarus Gardstar knew how to flatter.

"When I first heard about you, my lord, I wasn't sure what to expect," the princess said honestly. "But now I can say with certainty that you are both chivalrous and handsome." Though her words were born mostly of necessity, they weren't necessarily untrue. Tarus *wasn't* difficult on the eyes.

"Would you look at that!" Geurus exclaimed. "They're already getting on famously. Now, my friend, I believe you were interested in my men?"

"Oh yes, definitely," Godfrey answered with palpable excitement. "Quite an impressive selection you've brought in front of me. Though I wish I'd known the color of your banners and armor. I might have cautioned you to clad yourselves otherwise. You aren't from around here, so we'll forgive you for not knowing, but the colors of the night are not well taken here."

"I suppose I should have guessed, with your kingdom being called Sun's Reach. Of course, I thought the whole 'nothing but sunlight' thing was a myth. But as I've seen in my short time here, the only thing that stops that ball of brightness from showing its magnificence is a rain cloud."

That sounded strange to Emery. Lord Geurus said that he'd not been here long enough to know about the kingdom's customs, and yet he had a sizable force and managed to learn about her hand being open for suitors. If the reports Lysaria Redwyn had shown the princess were true, House Gardstar also had many allies. How could he amass so much support so quickly?

"That is the truth, Geurus." Godfrey laughed. "Now let's take a closer look at these warriors."

"Gladly. Follow me; I only brought a small portion of my forces as not to overwhelm you. I've heard that you have your hero captain working double duty with your Royal Defender missing."

"Ah yes, it is unfortunate that he's not turned back up. But Casinius is a stable man, more than equal to the task I've put him to," Godfrey said proudly. "Galbraith, on me. You aren't a traditional knight by any means, and I'd like to hear your perspective on Lord Geurus's troops."

"My liege." Galbraith bowed her head and followed, fingers ever curled around the handles of her dual hand axes. The Lightstrider came to them from the desert and was the youngest of her team, though nonetheless skilled.

Queen Lysaria and Lady Cereos joined their husbands, speaking quietly behind the men while they discussed battle affairs. This left Emery and Grayson alone with Tarus and Velara. The young lady detached herself from her brother and quickly moved over to Grayson, chatting while they waited for their parents to return.

Casinius turned to Emery. "Princess, your father has granted permission for you to return to the castle if you wish to. There is a second cart prepared for you and Lord Tarus to travel there."

The princess considered for a moment. "Leave the cart for Lady Velara and my brother. We shall walk; it has been many days since I walked among my people."

"As the princess commands." The Lightstrider allowed the two nobles to walk ahead, signaling their intent to the cart driver. Casinius fell into place a few paces behind them to give them the illusion of privacy, though Emery knew that he would be able to hear every word they uttered.

Taking Tarus's arm, the princess led him back through the gate, urging the man to wave to the nobles who'd followed them. Chief among them were Mia Rothsster and Ferrin Leygrain, pressed so tightly together that they looked like only one body with two heads. Tarus sniggered at the observation and made a snarky comment about true love.

As they passed the outer gate and into the Commoners' Ward, Emery saw that there were increased numbers of beggars on the streets, coaxed out by the procession of nobles. Emery delved into the purse at her waist and placed a silver bright in each of their dishes.

Tarus looked at her queerly as she returned from paying the latest batch. "Do you plan to fill the bowls of each commoner we pass? The princess would make herself destitute, trying to feed all the people in a city this big."

Emery looked evenly at him. "As only one woman, I know there is not much I can do, but House Redwyn has more than enough money. The way I see things, it's better to help wherever I can. If I could convince my father to do more, I would. But until that day comes or I sit the throne myself, this pittance will have to do."

Tarus suddenly looked ill at ease. "The princess is very generous," he said, stroking his chin with a free hand. A fine layer of wispy hair covered it, promising to become a beard much like his father had. Tarus was quiet for most of the walk, focused more on the buildings around him and occasionally glancing with furrowed eyebrows at his arm within hers.

"Are you nervous, my lord?" Emery asked. "Or perhaps just a man of few words."

"Hm? I'm sorry, I was just…lost in thought," Tarus answered. "As I'm sure you've guessed, we aren't from around here, and there is just so much to take in."

"Don't strain yourself too much on your first day to the capital," she advised. "There is much for you to see, and I will take you around for sightseeing. But that reminds me I was wondering where exactly you came from."

Tarus nodded. "Fair advice you give, my lady. As for my home, we were living on an island a ways off the coast of this continent. But that is only a recent location for our family. My grandparents came here with my father from a distant land to the far north. Apparently, it is home to frigid temperatures, which explains why the constant warmth here is slightly strange and uncomfortable." The blond young man chuckled. "The first day I came here, I received the worst sunburn."

Emery couldn't help but notice the distinct change in mood as they moved farther away from the gates. While his smile wasn't as full as Lord Geurus's, it did actually reveal itself. His teeth were as white as his father's. "What would people from the far north hope to find here?" Emery mused aloud. "So far from their original home, away from everything they know."

"I'll admit it seems a strange choice of location," Tarus said. "My father claims they were following some sort of legend, though he's neglected to tell us which one."

"There are thousands of those the world over, so divining which one could be the work of years," Emery pointed out.

"A bit of magic could also do the trick," Tarus said. "See into the past with nothing more than a bowl of water."

"You'll be hard-pressed to find anything of that sort around here," the princess commented.

"So the rumors we heard were true?" Tarus asked. "Most kinds of magic in your land were lost?"

"Indeed, milord."

"Ah, I see," Tarus sounded disappointed. "My father had hopes that this would be mere conjecture by uneducated sailors."

"None of what we call the gift magics have been seen in the kingdom in a century," Emery lied, thinking of Arcadia and Reyna. "Whatever outlandish stories you may have heard, I'm sure most of them are true."

Tarus was clearly bothered by that news, but he didn't choose to elaborate any further.

After an excruciatingly long, quiet walk, Emery stopped Tarus, right before the final corner. "I'm unsure what sort of places you'd have seen on your island home, but what little I know about architecture leads me to see this castle as a true marvel."

Rounding the corner, Emery allowed Tarus to see the home she'd lived in for her whole life. At the end of the street, a bridge made of white stone and golden wood that had been imported from a faraway kingdom had been built. This bridge spanned a vast, rapidly flowing river of white water, which emitted a soft, high-pitched whine. Emery warned Tarus not to touch the water, knowing it for one of the few magical wonders that still remained in the kingdom, though she only had a vague idea of what it could do. The enchanted river had been directed around the castle and gave it an extra level of defense outside the walls. Past the river, sprawling steps climbed up to the castle itself, met at the top by the wall and portcullis which was hoisted open for their arrival. They passed through the long tunnel, lit by torches that lined the wall, allowing the noble pedestrians to see the arrow loops and murder holes throughout.

"A defendable palace, that's for certain," Tarus said. "I'd hate to be leading an invading army in here."

"The original builders were very wise in their construction, and the later occupants only improved on the design," Emery explained. "It always interested me how castles were once fortresses for war but have now become homes to nobles."

Tarus said, "Yeah, it does seem a bit strange when you think about it. I suppose it's just the architecture that drew them, but one must wonder who the first lord to claim a castle as a permanent home was."

"The histories have nothing to say about that unfortunately," Emery said in answer. "Though I'm sure everyone would claim their own distant ancestors had that privilege."

Past the tunnel was a green lawn sporting multiple paths that led off to the villas meant to house lords of particular importance to the king. Currently, House Leygrain was hosted in an empty one, adjacent to Nestor Rothsster's. Leygrain's temporary home was designated for Lord Ignis, but the Secretkeeper preferred his chilly dark cellar room instead.

The castle itself was a beautiful sight. Made of red and golden stone, it rose high above Searstar, glorious as the sun itself. A drum-like main keep provided the main housing for the royal family and the other castle personnel. Radiating around the courtyard within stood five tall towers, settled equidistant to the keep. From above, this made the castle looked like a shining sun, with rays reaching out. The two frontmost towers belonged to the Lightstriders and, according to the history books, the arcane masters called Sunseekers who served the crown. The latter tower had been abandoned after the wizards left during the Eclipse, and Emery seriously doubted that anyone had been inside since then. The Lightstriders had been sure to take a frontal tower to be the first ones to act in the case of an attack. At one time, all the heroes had remained within the keep to protect the king and castle, but her father had decided to send most of them out to the broader kingdom to survey and protect when duty called. For a man so intent on keeping himself safe, Emery had to admit she didn't see the logic, but it had been his decision "for the betterment of the Sun's Reach." At least on the last point, the two could agree.

One of the two other flanking towers held storage of the king's goods and supplies as well as the king's own smithy and clothier. Most of Emery's clothing was made by Lady Manaba and her daughters, but the princess took far more pride in the garments made outside, like the dress from Barnio. The smithy, a gruff man by the name of Jorjen, supplied most of the weapons and armor for House Redwyn's fighting force. Jorjen was rigid in mind, and his work displayed that, utilitarian rather than gilded. In her time with the Rainclaw sisters, Emery learned that Caitrial apprenticed in a midcity forge that served nobles and commoners alike. It was run by two master smiths—a dwarf and an elf, once rivals in the business who swore a pact long ago, sharing tips and tricks and combining their skills to the benefit of their customers. Emery often wondered why Godfrey never invited them to the castle since their every piece was a work of art. She figured it had something to do with their apprentices' heritage, for Caitrial would ask for her sisters if not her whole family to move in with her. That would mean allowing two Khindre to reside permanently within the castle walls and Yamaria forbid he allow that to happen.

The fourth tower held the stables, kennels, and rookery. The fifth and final tower was dedicated to Yamaria, maintaining rooms for the high priest and his droves of clergymen and women. Most of the priests did not actually live in the tower, usually out on the road, spreading the Way of Yamaria. This tower was made of a dull bronze stone and was split into two pieces. The slit down the center of the buildings allowed Yamaria's sunlight to peek through. A half circle was missing from either side, the edge surrounded by thin slabs of stone. When the sun shone through this design, a golden beam of light was cast over the castle, enhancing its glory. The final details of the castle had been brought in by Godfrey himself. On top of the drum tower, which he called the Roost, was a golden statue of a phoenix. It stood proudly, wings outstretched, a flame burning eternally within the statue's stomach. He had doled out quite a few radiants to have it watching over the city. Emery had heard much from Reyna and Arcadia that said people hadn't taken too kindly to the creation. So much of their tax money had gone into it—despite what they might say, nobody believed that Godfrey had used his personal savings for the extravagant piece—that could have been used elsewhere. There were far too many who thought that all their king did was drink, feast, and use their money on trivial tasks. For much of her youth, Emery had denied these claims, justifying her father to the sisters and others. *But now,* she thought, *now that I've seen his work, can I still do that? No, it's all I can do to remain silent about what I know.*

"Wow," Tarus breathed, breaking the princess from her reverie. "You were right, this palace is gorgeous. I can't imagine growing up like this."

"But you're a noble family, right?" Emery asked, confused. "Though I admit you'd not have half of what royalty claims, you would have had some taste of this life."

Tarus glanced back as if checking to see if somebody was there or not there. "It's easy to style yourself as lord when you and your army are the only people on an island."

That admission surprised the princess, but she tried not to give anything away. "That must have gotten boring," she said mildly.

"Unbelievably so," Tarus agreed. "You might not be able to tell, but my father's warriors are not the most sociable of people."

"I only saw them standing at attention in the field. I'd imagine they're different in a less rigid circumstance."

"Perhaps some of them are. But others, particularly the ones my father brought with him today, are his proudest find. They'll listen to his every command and never talk back, even among themselves." The blond man shrugged, his curls bouncing as he did. "But I'm afraid that's enough talking for now. I'll need to get used to being around people who'll actually talk to me sooner or later, but I just had many days of long marches. Perhaps you could lead me to my chambers?"

"Of course." Emery nodded and guided Tarus Gardstar, this strange boy, to the rooms Godfrey had designated for him. "You should find everything to your liking within here, but if you need anything or you'd like to continue our tour, just tell your door guard to call for me."

It was Tarus's turn to nod. Before Emery left, he swept up her hand and kissed it one more time. "Thank you, Princess. And thank you for considering me as a possible suitor."

Emery curtsied and walked away, straight-backed, unsure whether a response would be wise. Instead, she walked. The princess walked down the stairs to the main floor of the Roost. She slunk around a corner and over to a dead end in the corridor. Then assuring there was nobody of importance watching, she continued going down. Down the steps below the trapdoor. The spiral stairs led her to the familiar eerie hallway: the Secretkeeper's hallway. She'd surprised him before with her arrival. Hopefully, she could do it again.

"Princess, I've been expecting you," Ignis said as she reached to knock on the door. She cursed herself for not noticing him, leaning against the wall, arms crossed, a bemused expression pasted on his face. With nary a move of his legs, Lord Ignis stood up straight and regarded her. "What pressing question brings Emery Redwyn to my chambers this time?" Emery glanced warily at the still-closed door in front of her. "No need to go in there," Ignis said in his whispery voice. "The room is more for people making an official visit. The Secretkeeper shouldn't be having official meetings with the crown princess of Sun's Reach. That privilege comes when you sit the Highsun Seat."

"Are you refusing to answer my questions?" Emery asked, her tone a mixture of disappointment and heat.

He waggled one finger, barely visible to her in the dark hallway. "I said, nothing official. I also said the *room* was for official business."

"We are not in the room," the princess said, finally catching on.

"The princess *is* smart." Emery could hear the wry grin in Ignis's voice.

"Good, then I have a request to make, as a fellow citizen who knows your skills."

"Ask away."

"What do you know about House Gardstar?"

Ignis was silent for a long while. "Honestly, Princess? Nothing," he said finally. "I specialize in secrets of this city and the kingdom. This house has just arrived in the kingdom."

"So you can't help me," Emery answered evenly.

"Now, I never said that," the Secretkeeper said slyly. "I *can* give you my judgments. I often keep those out of the picture, as they tend to spoil the information. But I believe this much is pressing. I know little enough about Tarus Gardstar, who I imagine is the reason you're down here. His father, on the other hand, is a smart man."

"What do you mean?" Emery asked, wondering what Ignis was getting at.

"I just mean that your father is not exactly popular, and he's worried about enemies. Most of his trusted advisors are currently not in the castle, and the people know that he's scared. It's why they were so interested when he left today. Geurus Gardstar understands this, I'm sure." Ignis shuffled and cleared his throat. "No offense meant, but your father bartered your hand like a prized broodmare for the best ally he could get. Lord Geurus brings a veritable army to your gates in response."

"So you're saying I shouldn't trust the Gardstars?" Emery asked, surprised to be getting so much information from the Secretkeeper.

"On the contrary, Princess," Ignis said mildly, "Lord Geurus is smart. He knows about things that you will learn soon enough. His strength may be the key to keeping Sun's Reach shining." Ignis's voice sounded strangely strained, almost as if he didn't believe his own words or didn't want to.

"What?" Emery could hardly believe his last nonchalant comment. "Explain yourself! What do you mean *keep Sun's Reach shining*?"

"I'm afraid I cannot answer any more questions without a proper appointment. I wish you much happiness in your betrothal and subsequent marriage." With that, the Secretkeeper entered his room and closed the door with naught but a whisper of air.

ALARIC AND AMARU
The Sand Squall Assault

With that, they began the nearly weeklong trek to the City of Tents. Though the desert didn't become any less dangerous with the presence of a Water Caller, Celwyn, who knew the ins and outs of the Scorched Waste just as well, if not better, than a local. Amaru had a general sense of the tells that the sandy waste provided to give water, but Cely knew shortcuts through the desert, which would make them marginally harder to track. Even on those days when they couldn't reach an oasis or they found one that had been tainted by bandits or other natural occurrences, the gnome knew how to extract water from the desert cacti safely, causing no harm to plant nor animal.

Much to the party's relief, they didn't meet any resistance from either Venomsting or any other strange creatures. In fact, they rarely saw another living organism, besides the desert hares that they hunted for dinner and the occasional sighting of sand shifting from some burrowing creature.

Though to Alaric and perhaps Celwyn this seemed like a blessing, Amaru didn't like the feeling it gave her. That they barely saw anything, even on the nearly barren desert, seemed wrong. To the Fyroxi's sharp senses when it came to hunting prey, it almost seemed like the animals were perhaps hiding from something. But what they could be hiding from, Amaru had no clue. She recalled Ephraim's warning: strange creatures were surfacing in the desert. Could that have something to do with the sudden lack of game? If there was something, it certainly didn't make any attempt at the traveling party, and finally, their journey neared its end.

The distance between the last two oases on their trek was farther than usual, so despite the heat that had begun to swell, Celwyn urged the two onward. They were all exhausted, thirsty, and in desperate need of a meal; Celwyn was growing distressed as she couldn't see the oasis on the horizon. Seeing as the gnome knew the desert, her flagging morale affected everyone. "There's sand in the air," Celwyn explained shortly, though there was an air of confusion about her. "I fear a sand squall."

Amaru made a worried grunting sound. "It isn't storm season. How can there be a sand squall coming?"

"I don't know." Celwyn wiped at her eyes. "But I don't like it. It doesn't feel natural."

Amaru chose now to share her worries with the others. "Has anybody else noticed the lack of animals?"

Celwyn nodded vigorously. "I'm glad I'm not the only one. For a while, I thought I was going crazy."

"No, there is definitely something wrong, though what it is, I cannot say." Amaru peered ahead, and suddenly, she caught something through the veil of sand. "Up ahead! I think I saw a flash of blue! The tents of Oasi Sanctus?"

Celwyn followed Amaru's gaze and gasped. "Yes! That's them!" Her brow furrowed then. "If you can see them through the sand, we must only be a few hours away."

"This sand squall will not hold off that long," Amaru warned. "And if it strikes us…"

"Don't forget who you're traveling with, Amber!" Celwyn said, somewhat reprovingly. "As a Water Caller, I specialize in keeping people safe during sand squalls. The only problem is, with this storm incoming, we'll never find our oasis. Besides, I need to be awake to keep protective spells going. With Oasi Sanctus so close, we ought to go through."

"That seems like a terrible idea," Alaric said. "Even with a Water Caller's protection, I don't think it wise to walk through a divine's damned sand squall! Besides, what if we get lost?"

"We won't," Celwyn said. "Trust me!"

Somehow, the gnome saying that didn't inspire much trust in Alaric. But then she began chanting quietly, using one arm to gesture vigorously while the other blocked the sand from her mouth. When she finished, she pointed forward, and a small glowing figure erupted from the tip of her finger. The creature ran bravely into the sand, which Alaric could feel picking up speed and ferocity, and disappeared. Before Alaric could wonder what Celwyn had done, he got his answer, as a bright blue ball of radiance burst to life ahead of them. The blowing particles in the air slightly distorted it, but nonetheless, the ball glowed brightly. The bard didn't need Celwyn to tell him to go toward the light; he already was, plodding forward against the wind, as the particles of sand and rock began to fly fast enough to cut at his skin.

Visibility was soon down to almost nothing, as the three companions plodded forward. Celwyn's spells were keeping out a majority of the sand, but a few stray particles and rocks came through. Amaru was still worried, knowing that one poorly placed shard of stone would be all that was needed to knock one of them out. If she or Alaric were hit, they would be as good as dead. If Celwyn got caught, they would *all* die. Amaru sent up a fervent prayer and felt a strange sensation of sudden enlightenment as if Yamaria herself were conveying her wishes to keep her daughter safe. Hopefully, that would count for something.

Walking through the sand squall was a bizarre experience, having no sense of time or place in the world. The only things that kept Amaru feeling anchored were one hand tight around the shaft of her spear and the other in Alaric's. The two provided support to each other that they both desperately needed. Endlessly, they plodded toward that glowing blue light, focusing only on taking their next step and holding on to each other. Celwyn's chanting let them know that they hadn't lost her yet, and after a time, the group began to feel somewhat safe.

Then the noises started.

It started as little more than a whisper, nearly lost amid the all-encompassing winds, but Amaru—who already knew the wind

had bared her ears—could feel the wind rifling through hair and fur and swore she heard something.

Alaric, whose sharp ears caught the same thing as Amaru's, thought he heard a ticking sound. It reminded him of a wooden windlass, like the one in Mirshiall. But they weren't in Kindol Woods; they were in the Scorched Waste, the farthest thing from the forest! But Alaric thought more about it as the sounds continued, cutting off at random intervals then returning a few seconds later, just as suddenly as they'd stopped. To the bard's trained ears, the sounds almost sounded like insects of some sort: the whirring, clicking sound had a droning kind of undertone to it. Then Alaric's mind provided something that he hoped wasn't right. The variation in the sounds—sometimes low pitched, occasionally high, short, and long notes, varying in intensity—almost sounded like some strange language!

But what could make those sorts of sounds? No sentient creature that Alaric had ever heard of, for sure. And by the way that Amber's hand tightened in his, he guessed that she was thinking the same thing. Either that, or she recognized the signals and knew they were in danger. As a precaution, the elf pulled the desert scarf Celwyn had provided him from her dead partner's gear farther over his nose, hoping that Amber would do the same. She'd lived far longer in the desert, so he had to imagine that she was going to do the right thing. He pulled on Amber's hand, signaling her to speed up. He wanted to get to shelter as soon as possible.

A moment later, Alaric was very glad he'd adjusted the desert scarf, as from ahead came a muffled squeal, and the protective spells dropped.

All at once, the clear air filled with sand, which flew into the elf's eyes and nearly blinded him. Squeezing them as tight as he could and still be able to see, the elf gripped Amber's hand as if nothing else in life mattered. He somehow knew that if he lost contact with that hand, he would lose his lifeline.

One step at a time they went, ensuring that they didn't trip on some unseen stone and lose each other. Both wondered what had happened to Celwyn. Why had the spells dropped? Was there something more in this sandstorm to worry about?

Alaric learned that answer quicker than he would have liked.

The light from Oasi Sanctus was growing intense; they had to be close! But the noises, those strange alien noises, they were getting closer and louder as well. Alaric's ears noticed something different then. There was a sudden pause in the clicking sounds and then the faint whisper of shifting sand. Fear crawled up the elf's throat, and he felt the creeping sensation of hair raising on the back of his neck. The clicking languagelike sound reverberated in his ears again, and then there was a whooshing noise, and Alaric felt something jab into his stomach.

All of a sudden, as Amaru and Alaric were trudging along, Amaru cried out in fear, as Alaric's hand was ripped from hers. Following immediate instinct, Amaru grabbed her spear in one of the fighting forms she'd learned from Sigmund and jabbed outward tentatively. She heard the *clack*, as the tip impacted something hard. A hiss followed, and Amaru just managed to jump back in time, as something drove into the dirt, lightning quick. She could feel the size of the creature, whatever it was. Ephraim's warnings popped back into her head. This had to be one of the strange creatures! And now it was attacking her and Alaric, during a sandstorm, a sandstorm that came during the wrong season. Things started to fit into place now, as Amaru frantically searched around, waiting for the next attack. She felt the shift in the wind a moment before the strike came and swung her spear to deflect it.

As it came in, Amaru saw a flash of color: black, a black shell of some sort. By the way, it reflected the light that still shone through the sand. Black carapace, that reminded her of something! Something that she'd seen not too long ago. A chitin mask at the Venomsting hideout! It hadn't been crafted of many pieces of crushed shells; it had been a single piece! That meant it had to come from a larger creature. Amaru distinctly recalled the attack of the Venomsting when she visited the monastery. This wasn't just any random sandstorm and a random attack within it. This was deliberate, Amaru knew, and whatever this creature was, it had come after them. That was likely the thing that had forced Celwyn to stop her spells and what knocked Alaric away. Amaru felt a burst of fury, though she wasn't quite sure where it came from. How dare this creature attack her friends. How dare it tried to kill defenseless creatures making their way toward shelter!

Amaru jabbed again with her spear, this time with full intent to kill. She wasn't sure where this thing was, but rest assured, it would die!

The creature let out a scream as if Amaru had struck flesh and stalked forward, allowing the Fyroxi to see her foe. It stood perhaps seven feet tall, the humanoid torso looking for all the world like an armored knight clad in gleaming black chitin. Its arms were segmented, and grasping claws, split into three serrated parts, snapped menacingly in the air. The creature leered down at her with dark beady eyes staring out from a head curiously shaped like a knight's helmet, with a brush of what looked like hair along the top to boot! But it was the lower half of the creature that really terrified Amaru. At the waist, the figure melded into a scorpionlike body, complete with eight insectoid legs and that deadly barbed tail, which Amaru didn't doubt was filled with poison, ready to pump into her veins, paralyzing and slowly killing her so the monster, whatever it was, could have its meal. The tail struck out again, arcing over its back to land right in the ground before Amaru. Sand exploded out from the impact site, and Amaru shivered at the thought of that striking her. Then she recalled what had happened just before the creature appeared. Alaric had been thrown backward by some terrible impact. Could this creature have gotten him? Amaru's heart caught in her throat at the awful thought. She had to kill this thing quickly and find Alaric! But where to start? How could she possibly kill this massive terrifying beast? It was unlike anything she'd ever hunted. And nobody was foolish enough to hunt in the middle of a sand squall. By the clattering, Amaru realized that it was only this thing's bulk that was sparing her from the storm. If she kept the scorpion-man ahead of her, she could at least aim without debris in her eyes.

But she still had to find a weak spot, a chink in that armor. So she began to circle slowly, and the monster matched her movements. *This is more than just any predator. This thing is intelligent, and that makes it dangerous.* That deadly stinger shook in anticipation, waiting for the monster to line up a killing blow. Amaru had seen just how fast that tail could move, and she didn't like her chances. For a brief moment, she wished her magic had developed into something more useful for combat. But before that thought could stick, the child of Yamaria berated herself. She'd never before needed magic for killing. She was a healer and a hunter; that was all. But this was no prey, as Amaru had already figured out. It suffered her methodical strikes, swiping at her with closed claws each time she drew near, forcing her to retreat. Each time her spear lanced into soft flesh, Amaru could feel its anger. As soon as it decided it was fed up, Amaru was done for; she could feel it.

But luckily, the creature never got the chance. From behind came a muffled war cry, and right before Amaru's eyes, a javelin pierced through shell and skin, the point erupting from the monster's midsection. As it reared in pain, Amaru took the opportunity, as any good hunter would, and jabbed her spear into the vulnerable flesh. Then came the sound of hooves stomping on the sand, and the scorpion-man hybrid turned toward the direction of the greater pain.

Amaru never saw how the battle ended, as the bulb end of the scorpion tail glanced against her head in its whipping turn, and everything went black.

REN
History of a Rivalry

Ren shuddered inside his hut, waiting for the sandstorm to end. Nobody expected something so strong to come out of nowhere, but luckily, the years the Fyroxi had spent in the desert had taught them to be wary of changing winds. Xio slept in the corner of his hut, with the two children curled up by her side. Ren marveled at her ability to fall asleep anywhere because he couldn't catch a wink. The sand pattered against the wood and hide shelters, punctuated occasionally with the sharp rap of stone. Not for the first time, Ren was glad they didn't use glass windows, as he'd seen in some other villages. According to elder Silque, who trained Xio, glass was made of super-heated sand and used more often for its beauty than practicality.

It was always the most fragile things that were most beautiful. Ren's mind flashed back to Vienna, the pretty priestess, ripped apart like an old scroll. He'd danced and talked to many that evening, but only Vienna had come to him. She'd been so shy in approaching him and nervous for the event. *If anything, that probably saved my life*, he reflected. *If we'd been in the middle of it, that Chillfang might have come through and killed both of us before we had a chance to react.*

Ren shook his head, banishing the thoughts. He had to stop being stuck on those memories. It was okay to grieve, and he would never forget the decimation the Chillfang had brought upon them that night, but if he dwelt upon it for too long, he risked digging a hole too deep to get out of. Elder Copernicus had told him time and time again not to allow misfortune to affect him. He was still in training to take Copernicus's place, which meant being the face of the village. And with Amaru gone, that job would fall squarely on his shoulders.

Once the storm had finally cleared, Yarena had the tribe gather to get a census on the damage. A few damaged huts, ripped tents, and worn statues. The crafters had sustained the most damage, unable to properly store all their pottery in time. But ceramics could be remade; lives could not. Luckily, despite some of those near the borders claiming to hear Chillfang howls amid the wind, no further attack came upon the village. When the Water Callers visited the next morning, having traveled all night, medical boxes on their backs, they were dismayed to hear of the recent happenings. Apparently, no word had gotten back to them from the callers who had left the Fire-Striders after the first attack.

"Did any creatures come with the sandstorm?" one asked. "Anything scorpion or snakelike?"

"Not as far as I know," Ren answered honestly. "Why? Was that a common occurrence across the desert?"

"From our reports, yes. Even Oasi Sanctus was not safe from their assault. Luckily, we were alerted to their presence by two people seeking refuge from the storm. They'd managed to find a Water Caller beforehand, who was able to warn us of the creatures, so there were only a few deaths on our side. Yamaria be praised."

"Has this ever happened before?" Ren asked, wracking his brain for any prior occurrences. "Creatures using the sand squalls to hunt prey?"

"Not so far as any Water Caller has ever recorded," the woman said. "But the use of poison and the methods of the killings, even by the creatures, reminded people of the Venomsting's work."

"You think this was premeditated?" Ren asked, shocked. "The storm did seem to come out of season," he reasoned. "If that's what's going on here, then it's horrid! At least show yourself and make your aggressions known before you end someone's life!"

"If only that were the way it was," the Water Caller replied with a note of melancholy. "Unfortunately, these assassins, for that is what the Venomsting are, rely on underhanded practices. It would not be the first time we saw innocents slaughtered by poison or stabbed in the back. In fact, their attacks have seemed to be on the rise in the past months. Some of our more paranoid members believe that there's some underlying cause behind this, but as of yet, there's no substantial evidence."

The Chillfang's attacks, combined with the trouble during the sand squall, are pretty substantial evidence if you ask me, Ren thought.

The elders had told the Water Callers about the attacks but made them promise that they would keep the news only to those who needed to know. Nobody wanted to cause panic by telling people that monsters from across the Eclipse had made it into the desert. The Water Callers had agreed, though they explained that even if people did know, it might be difficult to discern the nature of the creatures.

That much was true, Ren had to admit. Even among Fyroxi, only the name was really understood by all. Ren himself had failed to identify one that had been just outside the camp. It was clear that the race was not mentally equipped for the attack. This was something that the elders planned to fix in short order.

Ren sat in the elders' hut with Xio at his side. Her eyes were closed, and her tails rested on the floor, but her ears were perked attentively. Besides Amaru's duty of sharing missed information with Xio (which had grown increasingly less, as she pretty much went where he did) and being the face of the tribe, Ren had taken over a few other tasks. What lofty title did he earn? What new job did he have besides learning with Copernicus? Loyal masseur. Amaru knew that Xio loved getting her ears scratched while in fox form, and now Ren filled that role. As always, the girl shifted closer and almost seemed to purr.

A derisive snort from behind him caused Ren to pull his hand away, as Leif Kalix sauntered into the room. "Has Trinket already found a new item of interest? Amazing how Lover Boy is so quickly wrapped around another woman's paw." Leif chuckled scornfully. "He was so devoted to Amaru you'd think she was his one and only. Apparently not!"

Xio bared her teeth, her ears growing warm. She had become rather protective of Ren since they stood together watching Amaru walk away, and Ren feared she might try to attack the muscular male. There was a strange light in Leif's eye, and his expression clearly begged the girl to provoke him.

Ren doubted Leif would hesitate to attack like he had when Amaru was around. His hand crept over to rest on Xio's front paw. "Don't listen to him, Xio. H-he's just jealous."

Another snort from the larger male. "Me, jealous of you? Don't be stupid. What do you have that I could be envious of? Some lazy little woman with big ears? Oh, wait, I know now. I'm supposed to be jealous of you. Amaru's favorite little brown noser, who keeps random garbage as treasures."

"They aren't garbage," Ren growled, becoming defensive. "Each item has sentimental significance!"

"Oh, I'm sorry. My mistake." Leif chuckled, reaching down and snatching one of the pouches off Ren's side. He shook it, listening to the soft clinking sound before pouring out the contents. Four coins slid into his hand: one copper, one silver, one gold, and one a glassy material with a red dot of metal in the center. "Is this money? The hell do you need money for?"

It had been Amaru's parting gift to him, knowing that Ren had a collection of coins from the different people he traded with.

"Now you can say you've traded knowledge and people with Fyrestone. Only our gifts never made it, thanks to Chillfang interference."

"It's a token to remember the Fyroxi of Fyrestone by."

"Why do you want to honor people who failed in a battle against our enemy?" Leif asked savagely. "Acknowledging weaklings makes you become just like them." Ren shrunk back from the rebuke. "You're the perfect example of what's wrong with the Fire-Striders."

Ren was saved from answering by the elders coming in from the back annex of the hut. "You're late, Kalix," Sigmund snarled. "We have been waiting for you."

"I apologize," Leif swaggered sarcastically. "I had some business to attend to."

"You need to get your priorities straight, boy! And the first thing you do when you get here is to terrorize the other apprentices," Sigmund spat. "Sit down and shut your yap."

Leif grumbled under his breath but still sat down, away from the others.

Five elders sat in front of three apprentices. Ren felt in his heart that the others noticed the absence as well, and it weighed down on them like a stone.

"Do you have any idea why we've called you here?" Sigmund addressed the three.

"I'd think it has something to do with the Chillfang threat," Ren answered.

Sigmund nodded, regarding the young man with his one working eye. "Yes, we were idiots to stop teaching people about the Chillfang, but we thought they were long gone, behind that wall of magic. Trusting in magic was our first mistake especially after we lost its use—"

"But," Silque interrupted what was about to become a tirade, "whether we should trust magic or not is of no matter. What happened in the past cannot be changed now. All we can do is begin work to remedy the damage and prepare ourselves." She lifted an old tome from the table behind her. An ancient thing, pages brittle and yellow, leather cover worn and covered in holes. The papyrus crackled faintly as the pages were turned. "After we were cut off from the Chillfang, we stopped teaching our history, so lulled into false security, so foolish."

"Yes, we erred in the eyes of the Sun Mother," Purell said. "But she is a forgiving goddess and will not smite us, her dear children." The priest recited a bit of learned scripture. "Mikhail section 3 verse 1: 'The Fyroxi were the original children of the Sun Mother, and she loves them above all others. An injury to them is an injury to Yamaria, and she'll accept no repentance for such a sin.'"

Silque and Sigmund both rolled their eyes. "There is some debate over the original children part," the old veteran said. "Histories show records of life that go back further than ours do. But either way, splitting those hairs is pointless. Instead, we need to focus on the bigger picture. Now how much do you know about Moonwatch's religion?"

"Just as we here in Sun's Reach follow Yamaria, the goddess of the Sun, the people of Moonwatch pray to Gaarhowl, the Moon God," Xio replied.

Purell nodded. "Very well done, Xio. I'm glad you were at least paying some attention during prayer sessions."

Xio opened her mouth in what was meant to be a grin. "I may be asleep most of the time, but I keep my ears open, taking in information."

"That may be an instrumental skill in the near future," Sigmund said. "I'll likely be working with you to hone that instinct. Nobody suspects a sleeping girl as a spy."

Purell cleared his throat noisily. "Does anybody wish to speak more on Gaarhowl? Perhaps to his ways and methodology?"

Leif surprisingly actually had some input. Ren had expected him to sit sullenly throughout the meeting. "Gaarhowl is a god of overwhelming strength. His followers are known for being relentless in battle and won't stop until there is no way for their opponents to fight back." Nobody missed the admiration in Leif's tone, least of all Sigmund. "They only retreat in the event of a debilitating defeat."

"As is the way of the wolf," the scarred elder replied sharply. "Yamaria, being the embodiment of the fox, follows a less savage methodology. Foxes are sly and quick, and our style uses that to our advantage."

"Yes, because hiding behind long sticks and sling pellets is such a brave way to fight," Leif drawled sarcastically.

"Look, boy"—Sigmund was growing angry now—"I have been alive for much longer than you. I've met the Chillfang in battle many times. How the hell do you think I got all these scars? How do you think I lost my eye?" Leif started to comment, but the angry glare of the elder's remaining eye shut him up. "I used to be just like you, boy. I wanted to beat the Chillfang at their own game. But I'm older and wiser now, and that's because I had the sense to stop before it went too far." Sigmund shook his sleek head. "If you want to engage in an all-out battle with the Chillfang, then go ahead and get yourself killed like you almost did with that sand wyvern five years ago. Just know that this time, Amaru isn't here to save your sorry skin."

There was a tense moment of silence, Leif and Sigmund glaring at each other evenly, before Purell broke it with a nervous cough. "Anyway, back to the early days. Whether or not you believe that Fyroxi were the first people, all can agree that we came before the Chillfang. The Sun Mother created us to help colonize the lands and to spread awareness of her influence on the world.

"It is widely believed across many sources that Gaarhowl grew jealous of the praise and attention that Yamaria was receiving since most people slept during his hours. Gaarhowl didn't like being the passive god behind the scenes, so he created his own people to spread his religion. These people were the first Chillfang, sentient wolves granted the killing power of ice and cold. Appealing to the night owls and those who were discontent with the long hours they toiled during the day, Gaarhowl's support base began to widen. Over many hundreds of years, the two religions began to grow ever more divided. Eventually, they split into two nations, called Sun's Reach and Moonwatch. Despite the inhabitant's best efforts, Moonwatch still became the lesser power, and Gaarhowl grew angry with Yamaria for leading a more prosperous nation. That was when the attacks began.

"Now before this time, the Fyroxi were not a war-faring race. I'm sure, for them, the first attack came much like the most recent did for us. A complete surprise that left too many dead to hold the proper ceremony for."

Sigmund took over now. "When it became clear that the Chillfang wouldn't back down, we realized that we had to start adapting our ways to survive against their hatred-filled attacks. Back in those days, Fyroxi were still talented pyromancers, and that came in handy for fighting the Chillfang. And our more defensive fighting style allowed us to match even far superior numbers."

Copernicus picked up the story here. "Our ancestors appealed to the king of Sun's Reach for aid, and eventually, the entirety of both kingdoms became involved in our war. They made it into their own. As the battles continued and atrocities were committed in war, our hatred only grew, until our relationship blossomed into this flower of discontent."

Silque added her own two dims. "After Qrakzt the Mad Mage created his barrier, our people became too content and returned our focus to survival. Many of the secrets we once held were lost, held only by those mages who were killed by that savage spell. With so few of us left, it is possible we may never learn what we used to defeat our foes. The spear that Amaru took when she left was the last example of its kind in the tribe, and Weylin didn't know of any in Fyrestone's armory. Even if they were hidden, it's likely that they're now in the hands of the enemy. This puts us at a disadvantage in this battle against our old foe, but as we showed during the Hundredth Sunturn, a cornered and surprised Fyroxi fights hard. And that is what we must do, so that we, the last of the Fyroxi, can survive."

With that, they all agreed, even Leif, who despite his disappointment with his tribe, had no desire to die. If that meant he had to fight alongside weaklings for the time being, then so be it. Meanwhile, Ren and Xio both worried, for Silque's last line had them all scared. They were the last of the Fyroxi. Their race was in dire peril, and nothing could be done about it but to fight. They had to, or else they'd go extinct.

AMARU
To Heal a Friend

The awful sandstorm claimed many a life during its course, especially those without the foresight or ability to find nearby shelter. Tribes who hadn't prepared, or those who failed to properly anchor their tents in the loose sands found their handiwork more than matched by the ferocity of the ripping winds.

In the Scorched Waste, sand can be your life, the platform upon which your existence is based. But at the same time, that same material can be the cruel hand bringing death. Those who have lived many generations in the Scorched Waste understood this, and no matter the range of damage their homes experienced, they knew to work together to live and repair the damage done.

Over the following days, the Water Caller medics were busier than ever, and volunteers went out to help remediate the effects of the gale. Without knowing the full scale of the freak misfortune, Oasi Sanctus took no bets. The City of Tents shrunk significantly, as the healers traveled out to survey the damage. Only the necessary shelters remaining erect and a thin crew left to staff them. Travelers who'd been caught in the base or temporary visitors at Oasi Sanctus were left to watch over the unique patients.

One such man was Dalphamair Knollaxe, a dwarf who had traveled into the Scorched Waste, a man on a mission alongside a knight and a few trusted warriors. Now he sat on his hands, waiting for a woman to wake up. He stared at her prone figure, lying on the cot. She was covered in cuts, small ones, likely just from the sandstorm.

"You're either brave or stupid to come out here during a duster," Dalph muttered softly. The woman stirred at the sound, and the dwarf clamped his mouth shut. The High Servant's orders were to let her sleep after her ordeal. *She's one of the lucky ones*, he thought. *Many didn't make it to the City of Tents.* Outside, the winds had calmed down at last, the tent's walls no longer quivering. Through the crack of the entrance, the orange light of sunfall shone. Dalph pulled at his beard. *I hope this lass rouses soon. I need to feed Priscilla.* One of the other lads could take care of it, he supposed, but Dalph was particular about his Priscilla.

As he waited, he pondered the other strange thing he'd noticed. What was a Fyroxi doing wandering the Scorched Waste? Dalphamair wasn't knowledgeable about the desert or its people, but what he did know was that the Fyroxi weren't typically solitary people. They lived in tight-knit clans like the Dwarves. Though it wasn't unheard of for a dwarf to go somewhere away from his kind, it was rare. Take everyone's surprise at old Berdur Longshield when he put down his hammer and anvil for a mortar and pestle. Dalph would pay good money to see the look on his family's faces.

Speaking of faces, he spared another glance at the strange Fyroxi. She had a fair look, that was for sure. Dalph was far past the age where that sort of thing interested him. He had his mace and Priscilla, and what more did a simple dwarf need?

But that wasn't what had drawn his attention. The girl's face was moving. She stirred as she finally came to. Dalph straightened himself out. Wouldn't do to appear as a slouch in front of this lass. "Morning, lass! The sleeping draught worked well, I see."

"Where am I?" she asked groggily. Her eyes shot open as she recalled the events before her nap. "The storm, the monster! What happened?" She glanced at the blue fabric of the tent around her, half in confusion. "Is this Oasi Sanctus?"

"Aye," Dalph answered shortly. "You're safe for the time being."

"Thank Yamaria, we made it," she breathed deeply. "I thought we were going to die."

"And you would have, had we not heard the gnome!" An alarmed look crossed Amaru's face. "Don't ye be fearing. Celwyn survived just fine. She managed to send a message here, after the beast knocked her away."

"How many died in the attack?"

"A few," he replied. "Nothing major, thanks to you, I suppose. Though I did my own fair share." Dalphamair shrugged. "That attack gave us a surprise, but you and yer friends bein' out there saved us from death from an unseen enemy."

The Fyroxi girl sighed in relief. "Where's Alaric?" she asked. "The elf that came with me. Is he all right?"

The dwarf grunted. "Last I heard, he's stable."

"Stable? How badly was he hurt?" Dalphamair could hear the worry in the girl's voice, still thick with the fading effects of the sleeping draught.

"Sustained no small number of wounds. Fool of a man wasn't even wearing a weapon."

"I need to see him!" She began to stand, but her legs buckled underneath her.

"You just woke up," Dalph ordered. "What you need is to give yourself a few minutes."

The girl looked straight into the dwarf's eyes. "Alaric could be in danger, and I'm not going to sit idly by while he bleeds out. Not when I can help him. That creature we fought had venom, and if he was hit, he needs medical attention straight away. I'm no stranger to scorpion venom."

"Know medicine, do ye?" When she nodded, Dalph weighed his options. "Aye, I'll take ye to him, once ye wake yer legs up," he said finally. "Won't do to have ye falling all in the sand."

Amaru did as he instructed and changed into a new loose-fitting robe that had been left on the medicine chest. Dalphamair cocked his head when she bound up her tails and pulled a small turban over her ears, but she only gave a terse "force of habit" in reply, and the dwarf didn't question it. Her steps were still a little sluggish as the dwarf led her between the tents, pointing out ropes so she wouldn't trip. Residents of the City of Tents looked on curiously as the pair stumped toward the medical tent, but the purposeful look set on Amaru's face kept them from approaching to ask questions.

The healers' tent was the largest structure in the camp, a massive circular tent of green fabric, to set it apart from the others. The familiar scents of herbs wafted through the door, which was loosely tied with white strings. To be in a surrounding that she knew made Amaru feel like she was home, a pang of wistful joy hitting her heart. Dalphamair pushed through, and all the healers inside looked up anxiously. "Dalph, please tell me you don't have another one. Our beds are all filled up already."

"I've just got a visitor, though I'm sure there'll be more brought in before long. The scouts already located a few tents that weren't properly anchored, but no sign of their residents."

"Damn and blast. We always tell people to triple-check their stakes. We can't be wasting valuable tents and supplies on foolish mistakes."

"Now, now, Michel," an older man said with a chiding tone. "It is not for us to reprimand others, only to fix their injuries. I'm sure the pain they experienced will serve punishment and lesson enough." Michel blushed and turned his head to the floor. "I'm going to the supply tent," he mumbled. "We're low on lullroot, and some of these folks will start screaming again soon." He rushed out without another word.

Amaru cast her gaze over the beds. As Michel had said, they were at full capacity. Green-robed orderlies zipped around the room with cups of water, medicine pastes, and food. Most of the people in the beds had minor injuries, and as Amaru watched, their wounds were cleaned bandaged, and they were laid back to rest a bit. Such efficiency in healing put Amaru in awe. She'd seen Water Callers at work before but never in the ideal conditions of their home. She wondered again how the Fire-Striders were doing. With Vienna dead and she on the run, Purell would have to begin training a new apprentice in the ways of herb craft. She resolved to ask one of the healers about pilgrimaging to help out. The storm wouldn't have done the Fyroxi any favors either.

Finally, her eyes caught on a flash of pale brown skin and colorful clothing, and Amaru gasped. Running over to one of the beds, narrowly avoiding one of the healers, she looked over the prone figure of Alaric. As Dalphamair had said, he'd taken quite a beating. His superior senses, both honed and natural, might make him decent at fighting, but when you can't see, none of that makes much difference. And when the foe you're fighting is nothing natural, no amount of training can help you.

His face was bruised and beaten from rocks, and one of his eyes was black. His shirt was sliced open, baring his abdomen. One particularly cruel wound, a puncture wound in the stomach, seemed to be the most serious of the damage. Amaru realized at once that was where the scorpion creature had struck the elf. Alaric was lucky the blow hadn't killed him outright, just a little deeper, and…she cringed at the near possibility.

Amaru sniffed slightly, and a sickening scent assailed her nostrils. "Has anything been done to treat this wound?" she asked one of the orderlies.

"Poison of some kind," he explained, which was old news to Amaru. "We tried to treat it, but me thinks it's already too far in. He probably won't survive."

Amaru noticed then the black lines spreading out from the gash. The poison was working its way slowly through his veins. And once it reached his heart, Amaru had no doubt he would be dead. While she walked through the sandstorm, she had vowed that wouldn't happen. She felt his brow, warm and feverish. "What symptoms did he display when he came in?" She needed to know the specifics, to know how best to heal the wound.

The healers looked up in surprise, not expecting the question from some random girl walking in.

One of the orderlies who'd attended Alaric walked over. "When he came in at first, he was really shaky, having a hard time walking or keeping anything still. Ragged breathing, fast heart rate, and a couple of times, he started thrashing around, so we fed him some lullroot as sedation."

As Amaru had said, she was no stranger to scorpion venom, being one of the most common things a healer in the desert had to deal with. But this was no ordinary venom that the monster carried. The dark lines were spreading far too quickly. Putting him to sleep with the lullroot would have slowed the spreading process, but that would only work for so much longer. She would have to work fast.

Amaru called for a few herbs, water, and a chunk of soap as well as cutting tools. The skin around the wound was already infected and would need to be removed. She worked quickly and precisely; and the elder healer set two of the apprentices to assist her—crushing herbs, making mixtures, and gathering what supplies she needed.

Like Weylin's wounds, there was sand stuck in them, though walking through a sandstorm meant there was a much higher quantity than the Fyroxi could claim. While her assistants worked vigorously at the back table, she cleaned the wound and started cutting, feeding Alaric a mixture of lullroot and dreamleaf to keep him from waking or feeling the pain. A foul smell rose after each incision, but Amaru worked through it, knowing that time was short. Once the infected flesh was cleared away, she washed him with soap and water, flushing out any remaining toxins and infections from the outermost part.

She'd heard that in places near water, leeches were used to remove bad blood from wounds. Right now, leeches would be perfect, but they weren't available in the desert, so she would have to make do. Luckily, she had one advantage that all the other healers lacked. Something she was hesitant to use with so many people but would surely save Alaric's life: magic. Had they more time, Amaru would have sent for an antivenom to be created, but without a sample of the substance from that creature's tail, it would be pointless to try making one.

Still, she didn't want to make it too visible or go too heavy-handed on the healing. Memories of healing Leif popped into her head unbidden and what he'd become. Had that been a side effect of the magic or just pure coincidence? Until she knew for sure or learned better healing techniques, she would risk nothing. Rolling Alaric on his side, she leaned down to the freshly cleaned wound and lightly sucked on it, attempting to coax out the blood. As soon as she felt the tang of blood in her mouth, she sat up and spat, wiping her tongue with a rag. With one hand pressed to Alaric's stomach, she allowed the healing energy to flow slowly through her. As she watched, the black blood drained out of the wound, collected in a bowl by the orderlies, and the dark lines retreated away from the elf's heart. She lingered half a moment longer, switching the spell of expelling to one of mending, and allowed some of the flesh underneath the surface of the wound knit back together. It would be just enough to save his life, but hopefully not enough to be noticeable. Wrapping his stomach in a clean bandage, Amaru slumped back and breathed a sigh of relief, hearing Alaric's calm, steady respiration. Alaric would live!

In the excitement of having this skilled healer completing a task they all thought impossible, nobody noticed that the other cuts on the elf's body had also disappeared.

Amaru sat in solemn vigil next to Alaric's bed through the night. Most of the crew had left after her healing stunt, tired after having worked hard all day. Only a skeleton force of fresh apprentices remained with one full-trained Water Caller sitting in the back, ready to help if called upon. The short sleep brought upon her by the sleeping draught had been restful, but a couple of hours before sunrise, she felt herself nodding off. She figured she could rest for a couple of hours before the morning crew switched in.

ALARIC

Ruminations of the Heart and Mind

Alaric only allowed himself to crack open an eye once he heard Amber's breathing drop into a regular pattern. He gazed upon her fair features, illuminated in the soft glow of the braziers that smoldered at each end of the tent. He'd been awake for nearly an hour now, but he'd heard the others sleeping and didn't want to cause a commotion. Luckily, he was an outstanding actor; he didn't think that Amber had even noticed any change in his breathing patterns. Now she drowsed sitting up in the chair beside his bed. The elf felt a glow in his heart that gorgeous Amber had chosen to stay here next to him rather than go out. *Like she'd go anywhere else. I've already seen that she is hesitant to talk about herself with anyone.* His keen ears picked up that fewer tents were fluttering in the wind than the day prior, and Alaric gathered that volunteers must have been sent out.

As his mind wandered, he once again touched upon the main question that plagued his mind. Who was this girl that he traveled with now? Why did she remain so secretive? Alaric had a strange suspicion that things were not quite as they seemed to be with her. He'd been out of it for most of the time Amber had worked on healing him, but he knew he'd felt *something*. A sensation he couldn't relate to any herb he'd ever heard about. Alaric had no injuries on his arms or face, and his hands were not the raw, bloody messes they should have been.

Even the wound on his stomach didn't feel right; it wasn't nearly as tender as he'd expected. Alaric didn't care how good Amber's her-blore was; he had doubts that all this had a mundane explanation. He chuckled to himself, darting his eyes around to ensure he hadn't woken anyone. *It's like I forget that the Eclipse wiped out the gifted magics.* Wizardry, sorcery, and healing magic had all disappeared from the kingdom, thanks to fell ritual cast by twisted wizards. Notes of high mages had vanished, along with their authors. Only those without a gift, who had once been close acquaintances with some mage might have some knowledge of the lost arts. Neither Gnomes nor Humans possessed long lifespans, and most didn't share much, for fear of their work being stolen or vandalized by a rival, mean-ing there was little chance that one of these existed. Even the Elves, longest-lived mortals though they were, wouldn't have much knowl-edge to share. After that tragic event, only Lightstrider Vedalken had walked out intact, one of the last remaining unicorn knights of old and now the only living elven swordmage. Alaric wondered if the swordmage's gift hadn't been powerful enough to be considered by the soul-tearing spell or if that was just some unseen oversight by Qrakzt and his fellows.

But in less than three hundred years, the ancient hero would expire and, with him, all knowledge of the arcane on the continent. That would be a strange time, Alaric knew. He'd been born when there was still magic in the world, but by the time he had much clue about it, the Eclipse had already happened. *If magic was forever gone from Sun's Reach, would the continent continue to be separated for all of eternity? Would that necessarily be a bad thing?* his mind wondered. *I mean, other lands have magic, but at the same time, others don't, and they've progressed fine as far as I can tell. Sure, some of the biggest and best places were suffused with magical energy: Elyuneria, Seagap, Estrevaire. But then you have to consider Celebriant and Khascarve, which have never discovered magic.* Alaric thought that if he ever made it out of this desert alive, he would go to one of these places, travel and see what the world held, just like another famous elf, Arteni Galare.

The thought of leaving the desert saddened the elf though. Alaric watched Amber's pretty face, saw it tighten and contort as if she were having a nightmare. "I refuse to let that happen again," she'd said after the Venomsting made their first attempt to kill her. Alaric, like many of the Water Callers, doubted that the sandstorm was the work of Mother Nature, but the elf couldn't help but feel it had something to do with Amber.

*****

The next morning was heralded by the arrival of the day's healers. The girl in the chair next to him jolted awake as soon as they entered, startled by the sudden noise. She gave a deep yawn as she roused, glancing around the tent, before bringing those brass-colored eyes down to his face. "I'm glad you're alive," she said softly, noticing that he was awake.

"As am I," Alaric said, hitting her with his most charming grin. "I feared I wouldn't be able to look on so fair a face as yours again."

She punched him lightly on the arm. "Why do I feel you would say that to any girl in this same situation?"

"Can you really blame me for that?" Alaric shrugged, pulling himself to a sitting position. "When a pretty girl saves your life, a compliment, at the very least, is always in order."

"You bards are insufferable," Amber replied, shaking her head.

"I suppose we have our moments." Alaric grinned. "But you healed me, so you'll just have to suffer." He glanced to the side, his eyes lighting to find his lute sitting there. "But I won't make you do so in silence." He strummed at the cords with his long fingers, producing a melody that reverberated through the tent. It started off slow and sweet.

> Would that I could dance a jig.
> Or sing a sweet song to the air.
> For about me she gives a fig,
> My beautiful lady fair!

Then the tempo increased, Alaric's fingers flying across the strings.

> Perfect is her skin so bright, and golden is her
>   crown.
> Nothing impure could come of her, no darkness
>   weighs her down.
> And with a glance, to my knees I fall, whenever
>   we are alone.
> When we embrace, I'll say to her face that time
>   has ever flown.
> Though I may never be quite refined, I love a
>   lady who is so divine.
> Many men will fall at her feet, and many will she
>   rebuff.
> But call me the luckiest man alive, for she's prom-
>   ised: forever mine!

The entire tent waited in stunned silence as if to ensure he was finished. Alaric looked around with a nervous light in his soft brown eyes. Then the patients and medics alike began clapping and whistling. The elfin bard turned to Amaru. "Me thinks they liked it."

"I'd know those sweet strains anywhere," one of the medics proclaimed. "I should have recognized him sooner! That's Alaric Honeytone!" The volume now rose to an ever-greater clamor, and Amaru had to draw closer to Alaric to hear him.

"I told you I had fans." He tapped his nose and winked. "Though I'll admit, I'm surprised to find them here of all places. Never toured the Scorched Waste before."

"Water Callers come and volunteer from all over the kingdom," Amaru explained. "You never know quite where they're from unless you ask them." She looked over her shoulder and saw a small gaggle of girls approaching from across the tent. "I think I'll leave you to your adoring fans."

Alaric felt an urge to reach out and beg Amber not to leave, but before he had the chance, the girls were upon him. He amended his thought from weeks before in the monastery. *Perhaps there are more pretty girls in the desert than I thought. It's not so dry after all.*

His fans knew him as much for his deeds as his voice and were more than eager to sate his thirst, so to speak. But despite the relief that came as they dragged him to an abandoned tent, some small part of him felt like he was betraying something. Almost as if he was committing some crime against his own heart. How peculiar.

AMARU
Retribution and Rescue

Amaru got out of the tent as quick as she could while the horde of fans threatened to suffocate the elven bard. That was not a gathering she wanted to be a part of—far too many people, any number of which could clumsily pull on her robe by accident and reveal what she was. She planned to go back to the tent that Dalphamair had left her in before, where she could rest and make plans. Now that she was here in Oasi Sanctus, what was she going to do? A small part of her brain wondered whether the freak weather and attack that came with it had been planned for some specific reason. It almost seemed too convenient that after escaping from a Venomsting hideout and almost reaching Oasi Sanctus, some giant scorpion-man hybrid creature would appear to attack them. But how had the men escaped the cave? And if they had, they'd need to report to the higher ups of their group. Was there one close to Oasi Sanctus? "O great goddess mother of mine, if you could answer a few questions, I would be grateful," Amaru muttered under her breath. Beside the impetus to leave the Fire-Striders and that sense of protection during the sand squall, she had received no further clues as to her destiny. Was Amaru just supposed to run forever, or was there some greater part she was meant to play? No answer came from Yamaria herself, but someone did call out from behind.

"Lass! Wait up, lass!" She turned to see Dalphamair the dwarf running to catch up on his stout legs. She waited and allowed him to reach her, suppressing a small smile at the furiously pumping dwarf. "Goat's beard, you taller folk walk fast!" he complained.

"Is there something you need, good dwarf?" she asked politely, unsure what this man could possibly want from her. He'd been there when she'd awoken, but Amaru didn't know much about him besides that. Amaru continued walking toward her tent, now at a slower pace.

"Aye." Dalph nodded. "I saw you leaving the celebration and figured it'd be a chance to talk to you. I've a few questions and possibly favor to ask of you."

"I will answer them to the best of my power."

"Well, obviously, you had a firsthand experience with that scorpion creature," Dalph began. "How much do you know of them?"

"More than I'd like and less than I should," she said, using Ephraim's words. "I don't know what they are or where they came from, but I have feelings that they are connected to the Venomsting."

"Aye, that's about what I figured." Dalph scratched at his beard. "That brings up a few questions on its own. The Water Callers've never seen 'em afore this, and tha's worryin' if ye know what I mean."

"Having new threats appear in the already-dangerous desert," Amaru agreed. "Not a pleasant thing."

"Not in th' least."

Hopping lithely onto the edge of the bed, Amaru grabbed for her spear and stared at the engravings, as if trying to divine their meaning. Perhaps if she could read the engravings, she could get some clue as to what her mother wished for her. It had been, Amaru supposed, a subconscious message from Yamaria that had made her grab the weapon from the statue in the first place.

Dalph peered closer at the weapon, and his eyes winded. "Begging your pardons, but I doubt yer ever gonna figure out what those runes say."

Amaru raised an eyebrow at the dwarf. "And why not?"

Dalphamair let out a hearty chuckle. "'Cause we Dwarves are mighty secretive about our language! Especially the written stuff." Seeing the shocked expression on the girl's face, the dwarf tried to explain. "You see, I can't read everything on there since it's covered in several different languages. But a few of those writings are clearly in dwarven runes. And the supremely made haft? Clearly the woodwork of Hill Dwarves." He beckoned toward the spear. "Could I see it? I'll try to translate a bit for you." Amaru handed him the spear. The dwarf studied it a moment. "This line here"—he pointed to a small line that encircled the shaft near the point—"names this weapon Helios: Sun's Searing Tongue. We Dwarves name every creation of ours. Keeps things original." He patted the morningstar strapped to his back. "This thing's called Cryptfiller, and I have a javelin called Retirement, for riding."

Amaru smiled a bit. "Interesting names for weapons."

"Well, tha's one way to describe dwarven craft: interesting." He returned to his translating. "This string here marks this weapon as a symbol of the pact between the Dwarves and the Fyroxi against a common threat. I'd imagine that whatever these other languages are, it says much the same thing, seeing how they are stuck so close together." He shifted the spear around to get a closer look at the bottom. "And the final bit here just speaks to the history of the materials and the signature of the creator of the shaft. Thuldrosli Wargslayer." Dalph pulled at his beard. "Aye, that name's well-known. She was a real promising shield maiden and skilled at weapon making too, at least for a hill dwarf." The dwarf shrugged. "Anyways, that's a pretty fancy weapon, so I'm sure its wielder is no ordinary run-of-the-mill girl. So I'll ask now why you know the Venomsting."

"They tried to kill me. Alaric saved my life; that's why we travel together." Amaru saw no harm in telling the dwarf this. He seemed to be the reliable sort, and she guessed by his interest that Dalphamair already knew a fair deal about the assassin cult.

"And why would they be trying to kill you, of all people?"

"Darkness if I know," she half lied. "We were hoping to find that out ourselves." Amaru desperately hoped that it was a mistake, that the Chillfang hadn't already made allies with a group of assassins, but all the evidence seemed to point toward that possibility. Why else would they have attacked her before? If they were tracking Amaru, it was possible that they knew what she was or at least something about her. And who would have been able to tell them that, besides the Chillfang? "Why are you so interested in my connection with them?"

"Ain't it obvious, lass?" Dalphamair raised one bushy eyebrow. "If they're after you, then they won't stop till yer dead. That's their whole deal, bein' assassins. And it just so happens that I want to kill some of them!"

"What's your grudge against the Venomsting?" Amaru asked, surprised by the anger in the dwarf's guttural voice.

"They're the only reason I'm still in this thrice-cursed desert. I came here part of a group of men, head of which was vital to the kingdom. He was on some mission to kill a bunch of them, which he was pretty enthusiastic about. Well, you see, we cleared out a number of their smaller bases, but when we found one of their key forts, we faced more trouble than we were worth. Most of the men died, except for me, but I think that knight only got captured. I hope so 'cause I don't relish the person who has to tell the princess and the king that their knight is dead! But he should still be alive; Venomsting might be corrupt and evil people, but they're not stupid."

Amaru considered the possibilities. "If they want me dead, they probably won't stop just because I'm in a populated place. So attacking their base might be the only way to forestall them." She understood the logic. The entire reason for her leaving was to not endanger people. So if going against the Venomsting was the best way to keep others safe, then her mind was made up.

"Yep," Dalph said. "Ye seem t' understand. And if we can find that knight, it'll be the icing on the cake!" Dalph finished. "With you, that elf, Celwyn, and some Water Callers along with me, I might not get killed instantly, and you can get your answers as to why they want you dead and whatnot."

"And it shall go as the goddess wills it." Amaru folded her hands. "Praise Yamaria, glorious giver." The Sun Mother listened to her prayers and answered them. Her role in the ultimate plan began with this mission.

*****

Alaric's fans were deeply disappointed when he told them that he couldn't stay with them forever, but the elfin bard seemed almost relieved as he and Amber stood together in his tent. "Amber, where've you been these last two days?" He ran a hand through his long hair, which had not yet been bound into its usual ponytail. "'Twas a lonely time without seeing your face."

"I've been making plans with Dalphamair." She grabbed the duffel bag in the corner of his tent and threw it to him. "Besides, I doubt you were lonely at any point," she said pointedly. "You were preoccupied, so I decided to wait to tell you." There was a hint of amusement in her voice. "But we finally have a good lead on the Venomsting, and we are leaving tomorrow morning. I hope you haven't strained your singing voice too much. You've told me that your bardic magic can do more than just make pretty illusions. Well, here comes your chance to prove it."

"My fingers and my strings are at your command, my lady. Now as always and forever." Alaric stretched his long arms high into the air, the tips of his fingers brushing the top of the tent. "By Yamaria, I'm sore. I swear, those desert girls…" He whistled and shot a grin at Amaru. Without even any sign from his companion, he seemed to regret it. "Sorry, not a proper topic for such company. But know that I was not lying when I said it was lonely. None of them cared about talking to me like you do. They just cared about my vocal cords and…other parts. I thought I missed that old connection, but it didn't feel like it should have." Alaric seemed far more distressed than Amaru had ever seen him.

"That's sweet, Alaric. But for now, forget about it." Amaru patted her friend's shoulder to give him some small comfort. "Let's focus instead on the upcoming battle. Dalphamair is waiting for us to actually determine our strategy."

"Wait, you mean that we're actually going to make a plan instead of rushing blindly into the enemy's stronghold?" Alaric waved a hand dismissively. "I'm afraid I don't see the reason." The confused distress was gone from his eyes as if it were never there. She wondered if the emotion had even been genuine.

Amaru swatted his leg with the butt of the spear. "This is no time for jokes, Alaric. We are about to fight trained assassins."

He tapped his nose knowingly. "That's exactly the best time to tell a joke. If you don't keep light, then you'll be weighed down by your worry. And if you are distracted by worry, you'll find yourself stomach deep in a sword."

Amaru had to admit that the elf was right. "Come on, finish packing. We have much to discuss."

*****

By next morning, the crew was prepared to confront the Venomsting. Dalphamair had recruited a couple of the Water Callers and a few guards to join them in their battle. Celwyn couldn't be persuaded not to join, so she too stood at the designated meeting point when it came time to leave. Many who wanted to go had to stay behind, just in case the Venomsting decided to make a retaliation. "Besides, a smaller group will move faster," Celwyn assured the others. "It will be better for us to be quick in this instance, I believe."

"Now don't any of you go forgetting what we're up against." Dalphamair cracked his knuckles. "These people are damned sharp, and they're skilled assassins. When we went in last time, they corralled us into corridors and used murder holes to pour hot tar or poisoned arrows on us. I wouldn't suggest getting separated, but bunching up is a sure way to get yourselves killed."

"So we just need to stay the perfect distance apart and keep an eye out for everything that could possibly jump out to hurt us," Alaric said sarcastically. "Sounds simple enough. Anything else?" A small chuckle went up from the Water Callers.

"Bards." Dalphamair shook his head, that single word conveying more exasperation than a whole tirade ever could. "Absurd expectations aside, the Venomsting use outguards, starting a quarter mile outside their base. They'll be all sneaky like, so keep one eye behind you if you can. They still wear those chitin masks, far as I know, so look out for the gleam."

As the low light of the evening steadily rose into the morning glow, the team headed out. Amaru, Alaric, and the Water Callers all marched; but with Dalphamair's short legs, he needed a different mode of transportation. Luckily, his transport was also his steed for traditional battle.

They headed to the stables, and Dalph swung open the door to reveal the biggest goat Amaru or Alaric had ever seen. She had short cropped black hair in front and white in back, just barely visible through her leather armor. Thick horns sprouted from her forehead, making an impressive sight.

"Folks, I'd like you to meet Priscilla, my noble steed." Dalph snapped his fingers, and the goat stood with a slight groan. "We've been training together for years and can handle most anything. It's only by virtue of Priscilla that I got back here in one piece last time. Now we know what we're going in for, so we won't be fooled." Priscilla bleated in agreement and bent her knees slightly, allowing Dalph to swing on top of her. "Now let's go kill some murderous bastards!" Priscilla clopped out of the stable, and the team was off.

Dalphamair told them that he'd been lucky to survive last time, and if Oasi Sanctus hadn't settled so close to the old fortress, he might have succumbed to his wounds. "That also explains their creatures' appearance in the sandstorm," he grunted. "We'll see their fort when we crest that there dune. But if we can see them, they can see us, so be on your guard." The dwarf pulled out his javelin Retirement and held it close to him, the long point sticking out past Priscilla's neck. Amaru kept a tight grip on Helios, and Alaric had his fiddle poised, ready to break into song at any moment. Behind him, the two Water Callers had their shields up and hands in the material pouches they used for casting most of their druidic spells. The three guards had arrows nocked on strings and bows ready to be pulled up at a moment's notice.

Good thing too, as they crested the ridge and headed toward the first slope in the sand. There they encountered the beginning of the opposition. A masked man lunged out of cover in the dip and brought his knife up to stab at Dalphamair. Priscilla turned just in time, and the blade glanced off the boiled leather on her tall neck.

Within moments, the man was feathered with three arrows and fell to the sands, dead.

"And this is why I take point!" Dalph said proudly, patting his goat's neck.

The bowmen recovered their arrows, and they headed on. At each depression they came to, the team approached cautiously and struck downward. They managed to flush out and kill two more sentries before the others watching wizened up and tried other strategies.

"They'll know we're coming by now," Amaru said. "We'll have to be even more careful." They walked for a relatively long way without seeing anyone of note. Not far away, the stone building the Venomsting were using as a base stood in plain view, rippling slightly in the heat fluctuations. She wondered if it were an illusion, but she never had the chance to focus closer. Suddenly, Amaru heard the slight shift of sand behind her and tried to turn around. Before she could, however, a pair of muscular arms wrapped around her neck, and a knife appeared near her throat.

"Make sudden moves and girl dies," the owner of the arms growled in a broken version of the universal language.

"Drop her, or you get multiple arrows in the chest," one of their guards said tersely.

"You think you get arrow in me afore I slash pretty neck?" The man laughed and pulled closer to Amaru. "You skewer girl too!"

Amaru glanced around and saw all of them standing indecisively. The man had the right of it. If they tried to shoot an arrow, they'd be putting her in danger. Depending on where they shot the arrows, Amaru might be able to heal herself, but they would be wise to go for the heart, and she couldn't survive that. Those with melee weapons were likewise out of luck. By the time they reached the man, the dagger would be drawn across her throat. Finally, she looked at Alaric. He had a tortured expression on his face. The bow rested on the strings of his fiddle. Hands shaking, he met Amaru's eyes. He clearly had an idea but didn't want to risk making a move and getting her killed. She stared piercingly at the elf and nodded slightly, swallowing her own fear. She could faintly hear more shuffling feet. This man might sacrifice himself, but he would take her down, and his friends would have the rest of the team encircled, dead within minutes. Alaric must have heard it too because he squeezed his eyes shut, gritted his teeth, and wrenched a sharp note from his fiddle. Amaru expected to feel the cold steel against her throat, but nothing of the sort came. The man behind her cried out and dropped his weapon. Hands flew up to his head, but in another few moments, the magic finished its work, and he was dead.

"Behind you!" Amaru cried instantly. Everyone turned, and just as she'd expected, they were surrounded.

Weapons raised and determined expressions set, the team readied themselves.

"Charge!" cried Dalphamair, and on his signal, the battle began. Arrows flew from the bows of the guards. Quiet muttering from the Water Callers ensued as they entreated the elements around them to react. Their sounds were quickly drowned out by Dalph's war cry and Alaric's fiddle. He sang in a language foreign to Amaru, one that seemed mystical and flowing and put their foes in a trance. Amaru, however, felt the distinct moment of indecision as she had in her last encounter with these men. Because they were men, not animals. She had to kill animals almost daily to survive, and hunting for survival was different than this. She hadn't felt this during her battle with the Chillfang because they were monsters, but these were people, with reasons for doing what they did. She found it challenging to raise her spear to them. Unfortunately, her foe had no such qualms, as he rushed forward, long dagger in hand. Amaru raised her spear just in time and blocked the cut. She continued on the defensive, trying to persuade herself to strike. The man just smiled, seeing the indecision on her face. To him, this was an easy fight, and he would go to the heaven of his god in glory. Killing beautiful things made his lord happy. But before he could please his god, Retirement buried itself in his chest. Dalph trotted over.

"The hell was that, lass? Just gonna let him turn you to ribbons?"

Amaru tried to explain just what she'd been feeling, and Dalph held up a hand. "So you're not really the fighter type. That's annoying," the dwarf sighed. "Wish you'd told us that before. Woulda brought another couple of swordsmen. Just let us handle most of the fighting then. But if something breaks through, don't you hesitate, got me? 'Cause they certainly won't." Amaru gulped and nodded.

The enemies lay on the ground around them, and Dalphamair pointed them back forward. "More are coming out of that building! Let's meet 'em! Get around Amber and try not to let them through!" The group charged forward, crashing into the Venomsting with a yell. Priscilla knocked into the front ranks, tossing her horns to knock them off balance. In close range, the bowmen weren't much use, so they drew long daggers of their own and finished those that Retirement missed. Alaric played his music with aplomb, notes both sharp and flat pulsing through the air. The team pushed forward, growing ever closer to the stone fortress. Soon, it loomed up above them, an imposing structure of stone blocks, crowned with two short towers, like horns. Two walled wings came off the side, topped with barbed wire. The last enemy had been felled a short ways back, and the building stood quietly, too quietly. Dalphamair tried the door. Locked, of course.

"Nothing for it then." Dalph raised his mace and pounded on the wood. The dry slat rattled and creaked. A few more strikes left a sizable crack down the center. After that, it was a simple matter to send the shattered remains to the floor.

As soon as they did however, there was a powerful springing sound, and two arrows flew from the top towers, burying themselves in two of the guards. Both of the Water Callers began to chant frantically, but a dart embedded itself in one's neck, and he fell over, convulsing a few moments later as the poison within drained into his blood. A summoned burst of wind brought the dart thrower and one bowman crashing to the ground, and an arrow found the last. From behind the walls, there was another war cry, and six more men filed in front of them.

Dalph urged Priscilla forward. "Is this the last of your men?"

"Yes," the leader of the group said with surprising honesty. "You are stronger than we expected. But we have all the men we need."

"You ought to just surrender. We may be down in numbers, but I'm sure the elf and I could take care of you on our own, and he only uses a fiddle!"

"Getting overconfident, are we?"

As they talked, Amaru noticed that one of them kept glancing off to the side, where a thick patch of dead brush sat. Moving a little closer and pricking her ears underneath her hood, Amaru strained to listen. What she heard nearly made her gasp, but she smothered it just in time. A collection of low guttural voices, speaking in hushed tones, in a language that sounded much like Fyran. Her suspicions were confirmed, Chillfang and Venomsting working together!

"Heh, so that is an elf. That's good. I'm really hungry for some elf meat. I've heard they taste sweet here," one said.

"Yeah, moon elves leave a bad taste in my mouth. Whoever kills him gets the biggest portion, but we're sharing it," this voice seemed more forceful than the others. "None of us have been alive long enough to taste real elf or dwarf meat, and it may be a while before such a delicacy presents itself again."

Suddenly, the wind blew, and one of them sniffed. "Moons, boss. Did you smell that?"

"Oh, I did. I'd know the smell of succulent Fyroxi meat any-where. Gaarhowl has pulled strings to give us quite the feast today." The powerful voice cursed. "Wait, we can't just go killing the Fyroxi. What if it's the one our lord needs?"

Other swears followed this realization.

"Fine. Then we kill all the others, eat them, capture the fox, and bring it to our lord," another proposed. "And if it's not, then we make it suffer for fun while we kill and eat it." There were content murmurs following that. "Oh, and if any of the scorpion people try to kill her, eat him too."

Amaru felt deep fear pierce her soul. She could almost hear the wolves licking their lips. None of the men here had ever faced Chillfang before, and now they were going to die. Amaru looked down at her spear. This weapon was made to fight the Chillfang, but she wouldn't stand a chance. Even if Dalph could kill all the Venomsting, there were at least four wolves, one of which was strong enough to be called the boss. Amaru likened that to the elders back home, which would make him crafty and likely battle hardened.

"Sounds like they're almost ready," the wolf who'd first noticed her commented.

"About damn time," the boss voice said. "These humanoids spend way too much time mouthing off. I'm ready to dig my teeth into some bloody flesh. That knight in there got me all riled up, and they wouldn't even let me kill him."

So Dalph's knight was still alive. Not that it mattered, if none of them survived. She turned attention back to the men in front of them.

"Not going to run like last time, are you, little man?" the leader said. "Shooting at a moving target is fun and all, but I'd much rather the simple approach."

"All right, enough talk," Dalphamair said dangerously. "Time you learned your mistake in cornering a dwarf!" He dug his boots into Priscilla's side and charged forward. Weapons clashed, and the battle ensued once again. Dalphamair spoke truly about a cornered dwarf. He launched ahead with the fury of revenge, the horn and mace combo taking out two Venomsting before they even had the chance to react.

Alaric began to play his music, and the last remaining Water Caller whipped the sand around the Venomsting's feet, allowing the final guard to end him with an arrow.

Then the whistle sounded, loud and clear even above the sound of battle. The brush began to rustle, and out leaped the Chillfang. Two apiece went for the Water Caller and the guard, ripping them apart with ease. Crushing the druid's head in his powerful jaw, the scarred *boss* looked up at Alaric. The elf just watched with fear and confusion in his eyes while the huge wolf pounced.

For Amaru, time seemed to slow to a crawl. She dropped her spear and called out Alaric's name, reaching out her hand. The wolf flew through the air, ready to land on the bard and tear out his throat. Amaru knew she couldn't reach him in time; she was going to watch this man who'd saved her life and given her something to smile about die, and there was nothing she could do. Alaric seemed to glance sadly at her. His expression broke her heart, and her eyes squeezed shut, not wanting to see him ripped apart

Suddenly, some other presence seemed to fill her. Instead of fear, there was a strange calm. Instead of worry, only anger. Anger at the creature who would hurt this elf. Alaric, who brought happiness and joy to the world with music, this night-spawned Chillfang would not take him from this world! Time returned to normal speed. No scream came from Alaric but instead a high-pitched whine of pain from the wolf.

Amaru's eyes flew open. Her hands were still outstretched, and a ring of light encircled the elven bard. The Chillfang stood in front of the barrier, hackles raised, a low growl rumbling from his throat. The other three sat in amazement, not used to seeing their boss's attacks thwarted. The boss pounced again, and once again, he was turned. Alaric stood stunned for a moment, peeked at Amber, and then shook himself. Assured that he was still alive, Alaric launched into playing a particularly sharp and discordant tune, his hands trembling only slightly at his near demise, and the unforeseen deliverance by this strange, white-fire; it was magic, of that he was sure. The Chillfang behind began to whine, and the leader growled louder.

Amaru heard a calm voice in her head. *Now, Daughter, punish these night spawn for invading my land! They must learn their lesson!* Amaru nodded and clenched her hand, not allowing herself to marvel at the fact that Yamaria might have actually just *talked* to her.

Chillfang, like the scorpion creatures, were foes she had no reservation about killing. The glow of the shield increased and flashed. The Chillfang jumped back as if he'd been burned. Dalphamair took the initiative and charged at the other stunned wolves. He bashed in two of their heads and, with Alaric's help, now standing confidently within his circle of light, finished the other with little trouble.

"You"—the boss curled his upper lip—"you're the one that our Lord wants. How nice of you to come here to me."

"Your backup is dead, and you are surrounded," Amaru answered, her voice strong and confident. "I'll give you one chance to leave this place and never return." She pointed at the light around Alaric, and it turned into white fire. "Otherwise, you can die here."

"If I return home after seeing the Sun Wench, I'll not live long anyway," the Chillfang growled. "I think I'll take my chances!" He leaped, and Amaru raised one hand. The shield of white fire sprung up around her as well. The wolf collided with it and howled with pain. His thick fur caught, steam rising from it as the caking ice sizzled away. He tried rolling to extinguish it, but the divine flames stuck. "Gaarhowl will have you, Sun Wench! We'll never stop until this whole place is run over. Starting with your tribe!" At the word "tribe," a final yelp escaped his throat, and he succumbed to the flames.

The fire died down around her, and Amaru was glad that her mother was not the theatrical type. She didn't want any glow to set her apart now. She might be Amaru, daughter of Yamaria, but she didn't want to be anything special.

Unfortunately, that last hope was in vain. As a slight breeze, left over from a Water Caller's spell, ruffled through her hair, Amaru realized her head was uncovered, her ears visible.

Alaric staggered a few steps forward and fell to his knees at her feet. "Amber," he choked out, his voice filled with wonder. Dalphamair eyed her with even respect. "What's going on?"

Tears filled Amaru's eyes. "I'm sorry, Alaric. I'm sorry for lying to you! I had people hunting for me… But I-I didn't want to hide who I was, just keep you safe."

"Divines, Amber, I don't know what to say. But what do you mean 'lie to me'?" Alaric's breath spiraled out in a worried sigh. "Does it have something to do with what the wolf said? Gaarhowl is the enemy god of Sun's Reach, right? Why does he want you?"

"My name is not Amber but Amaru Sunbrand. As you can see, I'm not human but Fyroxi."

"I see that," Alaric mused. "But I've never seen a white-furred Fyroxi before."

"As you can probably guess by the fire, I'm more than a regular Fyroxi." Amaru felt a flood of relief. She could finally tell Alaric who she was, as she had desired back in the Venomsting cave. Amaru sent a silent prayer up to Yamaria for answering her prayers.

"I'll say," Dalphamair grunted, "so what the hell are you then, Sunbrand?"

"This may sound insane. I certainly wouldn't believe it if I hadn't lived it my whole life." Amaru looked each of them in the eyes. "I'm Amaru Sunbrand," she repeated. "Daughter of Yamaria."

Much to Amaru's surprise, neither Alaric, Dalph, or Celwyn reacted with surprise.

"Eh, makes sense to me," Dalphamair said. "What with the fire and the wolves. Those'll be Chillfang, right?" Amaru nodded. "Figures as much. Stupid barrier," Dalphamair spat in the general direction of the magical wall that was the Eclipse. "Works for a century and then starts letting things through. Great spell, my arse!"

"I can't say I saw it coming," Celwyn said. "But I thought you were hiding something. I'm just glad it's something amazing like this! I worried whether you might betray us, though you didn't seem the type."

Alaric had a different reaction. He whistled and looked pleadingly up at her. "I knew from the moment I met you, you were something special. And when you healed me, I was assured in my beliefs. But to see that I have traveled with a demigod"—the elf bowed his head—"I'm not worthy of knowing you."

"Don't say that, Alaric!" Amaru commanded sharply. "You have been my closest companion over these past months, and I have been glad for your presence." She crouched in front of him and touched his shoulder kindly. "If it weren't for you, I would not have survived as long as I did. Thank you, Alaric, for keeping me alive and sane."

The elf seemed to glow at the praise. "My sweet Amaru." He played around with the name in his mouth and decided he liked it even more than Amber. "Your praise does me more justice than I deserve. But though I may never believe myself worthy of being acquainted to one so wonderful as you, I will be your servant for all of the rest of my days."

Amaru shifted her hands from his shoulder and took up one of his bark-colored hands in her tan ones. "I have no desire for servants. Just continue to be my friend and companion. That is all I ask."

His eyes shone with tears of joy. "Forever and always, Amaru. Forever and always."

Dalphamair cleared his throat. "This emotional moment is sweet and all, but we should get a move on. I don't know if they have other bases in the area, but either way, I want to return to Oasi Sanctus as soon as possible. So I'd suggest we clear out this base and find that damn knight." Dalph pressed his heels lightly into Priscilla's sides and rode into the fort.

The inside was filled with cobwebs and rats and bugs. Chunks of rotting flesh were distributed over the floor, their sickly sweet smell permeating the air. Small piles of dry brush were scattered, which constituted as beds for the Venomsting. Multiple corridors shot off left and right.

"Most of those lead to dead ends," Dalph explained. "That's how they kill people who manage a breach. Get 'em to search the halls, cut them off from friends, and end their lives in small batches."

In the center sat a common room, where the Venomsting could sit around, drink, and sharpen their blades. Plates of food sat cold on the table, abandoned when it was told that they were under attack. Amaru found it surprising that notorious killers, who'd ended so many lives, had met their end by the hands of a small band of warriors. They were assassins, more suited to killing one person stealthily than multiple in open battle, she realized. Not like the Chillfang, who would use superior strength and pack tactics. Amaru recalled the night of the first battle against them. She and the two other villagers had been surrounded. Only Helios had saved them. The creatures had flinched away from the weapon. Dalph had said there were more weapons like this, forged together by the ancient people. Where had they all gone? Could their like ever be made again, or were their methods lost to the past, when Fyroxi were still pyromancers?

Dalphamair must have noticed her looking at the spear. "I see why you're not a fighter if you can do that sort of thing," he said, referencing the magic that she'd used to protect Alaric. "You'll be the protector type."

"That was mostly my fear working through me," Amaru answered honestly. "I'll have to practice before I can replicate that, I'm sure."

Dalph chuckled. "Goddesses are fickle beings, eh? Give you a taste of true power and then leave you to figure it out yourself."

After thoroughly searching the top floor, they found the stairs heading down. The dry wood crackled underneath her feet as she took the first step and the structure wobbled, barely holding their weight. "If you can get people to occupy this fortress, make sure to warn them about this. We don't want people getting trapped down here if the Venomsting decide to make a reclaiming effort."

Dalph nodded. "Aye. Or it can be used as another trap, as I'm sure the Venomsting planned it. Most of 'em can climb like spiders, so the stairs could be a false hope for people trapped down there. Once they start trying to escape, the weak stair would be dropped, and they could be slaughtered. And it's easy to build a shoddy staircase." He hopped off Priscilla's back and left her up on the first floor.

Down in one room, they found multiple shelves stocked with small glass vials. Liquids of various colors—from black to brown, red, purple, even transparent—filled them. "This'll be their poisons," Dalph commented, reaching for his mace. Amaru grabbed his shoulder.

"No, don't destroy them. Take them, and we can derive antidotes, learn how to better combat these foes."

"Aye, that's a smart idea," the dwarf conceded. "Leave it to the healer, I s'pose."

Alaric took the liberty upon himself. "We don't know what else could be down here. Allow me to carry the case." He pointed to a leather case stuffed with wool, with places for many bottles. "You've saved my life today, Amaru, and I shall take the example of the Gnomes and start repaying that favor." He shot a grin at Celwyn, but the flaxen-haired gnome was looking off to the other side of the room. She began walking that way.

"Where d'you think yer going?" Dalph asked. "The prison cells are this way; I can smell 'em!"

"I see something strange over here." She gestured absently for them to follow. "It looks like some sort of magic, but it's different from anything I've ever seen in my lifetime!"

Amaru, Alaric, and Dalphamair followed her, the dwarf with a bit of grumbling. Celwyn led them down a hallway; Dalph kept glancing up nervously at the holes bored in the stone, as if he expected something to pour out and kill them at any moment. Amaru patted him on the shoulder, reassuring the stout warrior that they'd cleared out the floor above.

"I don't see nothin'," Dalph complained when they reached the dead end. "Yeh lead us right int' one of their trap halls. Durned good thing there aren't any more Venomsting here!"

"That's precisely what they want you to believe," Celwyn admonished. "And you don't have gnomish eyes, dwarf." Cely stuck out one small hand and pushed it right *through* the wall.

"An illusion!" Alaric exclaimed. "Not unlike the one that we used to hide ourselves in that Venomsting lair, Amaru."

"Exactly!" Celwyn answered, glad that Alaric understood. She withdrew her hand. "It's cold in there." The gnome furrowed her brow. "Unnaturally cold." Cely waved them through and took point.

The sudden change in temperature was bizarre. To be standing inside of a sweltering stone structure in the Scorched Waste and then suddenly walk through a false wall and be in a room where the air nipped at exposed skin and frost formed on the walls made little sense to Amaru. She'd seen ice only once before, during the Hundredth Sun Massacre, and yet here it was, hanging down in tapering cylinders and hugging the sides of the room. The chamber was fairly spacious, though it was only one room, with no hallways or doors leading elsewhere. Straw covered the cold stone in places and chunks of red ice were scattered about, strewn over patches of ice that were also stained with the rusty red. Amaru recognized the color: blood, and lots of it. That would make the red ice chunks raw meat, which in turn would make this place. "The Chillfang lair," Amaru said decisively.

"That would explain the cold." Alaric nodded.

"And the magic," Cely followed. "They'd need both to keep this place habitable. The cold for the wolves and the magic to keep it cold. But the magic looks different, as I said before. It's not anything like bardic or druidic magic. And it doesn't look like your magic either," she said to Amaru. "Which only leaves the option of arcane!"

"Bah!" Dalph said. "There hasn't been arcane magic in Sun's Reach since this one was a youngster and ran barefoot in the forest." The dwarf made a vague gesture toward Alaric.

"It's unmistakable!" Cely said. "The fact that it's so foreign almost proves it!" She was searching around for some way to prove it, and her eyes finally alighted on a box in the corner. The box radiated magic, both a strain similar—to the gnome's eyes—to the cold and something entirely different.

She opened the cover and peeked within. The interior of the box was completely dry, and not a hint of frost showed anywhere. "There's a piece of parchment here." Cely picked it up and began to read, "We have reason to believe that the girl survived the sandstorm, though her companion may not have been so lucky. Undoubtedly, she will soon turn her wrath upon the Venomsting. When she does, be ready. Our plans in the kingdom will soon come to fruition, and the Sun Wench *must* be captured and delivered before it is too late. Your mission and your lives depend on it." She turned the parchment to face them, a worried expression on her face. "Then there is this strange symbol."

Alaric strode up and grabbed the paper; the bard scrutinized the symbol and looked back into his memory. As realization dawned in his eyes, horror and confusion dueled on his face. "B-but that symbol! It can't be, can it?"

"Spit it out, elf!" Dalph cried.

"That's Qrakzt's sigil!"

"Qrakzt?" Amaru asked, her heart plunging. "As in the same Qrakzt who set up King Algrith and killed all of those people, with the help of the other archmages?"

Alaric nodded, his mouth too dry to speak. First, Amaru told him that she was the progeny of a goddess, and now this? He wasn't sure if his heart could take much more of this.

"Let's not jump to conclusions," Dalph said cautiously. "Any idiot could be using the Mad Mage's rune to enforce a fear tactic. Though why he'd send that to the Chillfang is beyond me."

"Dalphamair is right," Amaru conceded. "Until we know more, we shouldn't panic. Though I admit this is all very strange, what with the new magic and the appearance of the Chillfang past the Eclipse. I'm sure that there is some connection, but this is something we should return to the Water Callers with. For now, we must find Dalph's knight friend. Something that the Chillfang said before they attacked makes me believe that he is alive in here."

"Finally, someone talks some sense. Go figure, it's the daughter of Yamaria!" With that, the stout dwarf turned on his heel and left the cold chamber, the others close on his tail.

As Dalphamair had said earlier, the prison cells were in the opposite direction. The mixed stenches of urine, feces, blood, and the peculiarly sweet odor of death filled the cage-lined hall. Dirt and grime slaked the stones, some of which were cracked. Multiple barred doors swung open, bits of dried flesh clinging to them, where prisoners had clenched the searing bars, ignoring the pain to beg for release. Amaru hated that any person, even the ruthless Venomsting, could subject someone to such awful conditions. Dalphamair's grunt and disgusted spit proved that he felt the same. He cupped his hands around his mouth. "Aye! Sir Leonidas! Are you in here? Is there anybody alive here!"

A weak, strained voice called out from a distant stall. "I'm here! Divines, it's good to hear common tongue again!" His voice suddenly grew wary. "Or is this just another one of your tricks! You won't get anything more from me, I told you!"

"Nay, you durned idiot, we're not the Venomsting. We killed them bastards, and the wolves too!"

"Yamaria's grace!" the voice answered, relief evident. "Dalphamair? Dwarf, is that you!"

The dwarf hurried over to the stall, the others close behind. The grimy stall was hung with chains, one set of which the man was secured to. A noisome set of urns sat in the corner, just in reach of the prisoner. The man was dressed in torn burlap, stitched together to make some facsimile of a beggar's outfit. His arms were stretched uncomfortably behind him, burned badly from the shafts of harsh sunlight that shone right into that spot. There were dark circles under his gray eyes, and a scraggly growth of a beard in desperate need of a trim covered the bottom of his face. Scars were latticed across his skin, angry and red. His otherwise handsome face was marred by a black eye and a long, thin scar that slashed diagonally across his face. "Dwarf," Sir Leonidas said softly, "you actually managed to survive! Did anybody else?"

"Nay, just us two."

"Yamaria," Leonidas breathed. "But you managed to survive. And you escaped, damn you." The knight's tone was scratchy but affectionate. "Thought you left me for dead."

"Not for a second did I think you dead, sir knight," Dalph said, making a quick sniffling sound. "I'm glad I wasn't wrong."

"By the divines, the tough dwarf actually can show emotion!" Alaric teased.

"I am not getting emotional, yeh daft bard!" Dalphamair said defensively. "It was just cold in that last room."

"Oh, I'm sorry," Alaric said ingenuously. "My mistake."

Dalph ignored the elf. "What the hell happened to you? Your pretty face is all mussed up; the princess won't be happy 'bout that."

"They tortured me for information, Dalph."

"And?"

"I think I held out pretty well," Leo said, maneuvering to scratch his cheek against his shoulder and wincing as he rubbed raw, burned flesh. "But there are still a few foggy parts. I hope they didn't get too much out of me." He nodded to the chains. "Are you going to release me? These chains are more than a little uncomfortable."

Dalph slapped himself on the head and busted the lock with Cryptfiller. He waddled over to the other side and made short work of the chains, smashing the mace on the fittings.

Sir Leonidas groaned in pain as his arms were suddenly released from the position they'd been stuck in for almost two months. He toppled over, lying on his face. Moaning as all his muscles protested, the knight rolled over so he could look them in the face. "I fear for the princess's safety. I must get back to the capital, and soon!"

"Yamaria, boy"—Dalphamair shook his head—"you were just tortured and kept in a prison cell. You're underfed, weak, and pretty gruesomely injured; and the first thing you think about is getting back to your job?"

"I was sworn to protect the princess at all times," Leo said dutifully. "I should not have left her side, but her father sent me here, and I was captured. With whatever they may have gotten from me, I can't trust that Emery will be safe. I must return at once to *ensure* her safety."

"I sent word to the palace about my survival. I didn't mention you, but I would bet my beard that your princess awaits your arrival," Dalph assured him. "Hell, we are a couple of months behind schedule for returning"

Leonidas tried to stand but stumbled, cursing under his breath.

Amaru walked over, crouched, and laid a hand on his shoulder, avoiding the burns. "As Dalphamair said, you are underfed, weak, and injured. You'll not be fit to walk, let alone ride back to the capital for weeks with the best medicine. Perhaps more than a month with what we'll be able to scrounge up from the Water Caller storage. And we'd have to get you back to Oasi Sanctus first."

"I don't have weeks," Leonidas growled, sounding very much like a disgruntled lion. "The royal family could be in danger as we speak!"

"I know," Amaru answered sympathetically. "I know you don't have time, and I wouldn't delay you if there was any other choice. Luckily for you, there is another choice. One that can see you on your way home by the end of the week, albeit still a bit sore and tired."

Leonidas looked Amaru up and down skeptically. "Who is this woman, Dalph? What nonsense does she speak?"

Dalph chuckled. "You should listen to her, Leo. She sounds like a madwoman, but I tell you, the things she can do are amazing. I've only seen a few things firsthand, but I don't doubt that she can fix you up just as she says."

"Who is she?" he asked again.

Alaric stepped into Leo's view. "This is Amaru Sunbrand, Fyroxi, desert guide, healer, and, most importantly, daughter of Yamaria."

Leonidas cocked his head, stunned for a moment. Then a low chuckle started in his throat, slowly rising into a weak laugh and then devolving into a fit of coughing, as particles of sand were sucked into his throat. When the fit was over, he turned up to meet Amaru's eyes. "I mean no disrespect, but I've never heard of the goddess Yamaria having children, and frankly, it sounds absurd."

"So I would think, were I not living it," Amaru said. That there was not a smile or a laugh in her voice made the knight peer up at her in shock.

"You aren't kidding?" Amaru shook her head. "By the divines." He shook his head in disbelief. "Please, lady, if you speak truly, then give me some proof, some way that I can be sure. For if you are what you say, then this land has received a miracle. You spoke earlier of a way to see me fit to ride?"

"I don't blame you for your disbelief. I'll admit it does sound crazy at first," Amaru said softly. For a moment, she concentrated, and her hand glowed with golden light, channeling the healing power that Yamaria had granted her. She lay her other hand on Leonidas's chest, pumping as much healing magic as she could. "Yamaria, Sun Mother, if this man's duty in this world is not yet finished, allow him to be returned to strength that he may deliver your word and fulfill the tasks you set upon him." The glow intensified, and Sir Leonidas gasped in surprise as his body began to tingle. Skin knitted over scars, and loose skin tightened; the burned skin cleared away, and new, stronger skin grew in its place, and the black eye vanished, alongside the other bruises. After they had been bathed in the golden light for many moments, it finally began to die down.

"By Yamaria," Leonidas whispered reverently. "That was…healing magic? One of the gift magics, the ones stolen during the Eclipse! And you just used it! You healed me!"

Amaru just nodded. "As I said, you will still be sore, and only rest will bring back your strength, but your major injuries are gone, and you'll not die from privation immediately."

"How did you come by this power?" Leonidas was taken aback and stunned. He had not expected to be rescued, at least not for a long time, and this was never something he could expect.

"I was born with it, I believe. The magic was placed in me by the Sun Mother, *my mother*."

"You…you really are Yamaria's child then?" Leo sounded convinced now.

"It is as I said." Alaric grinned. "Yamaria's light, given flesh."

He rose up on one knee. "I apologize for my rudeness. I should not have acted in such a manner. I beg your forgiveness, lady."

"Save your kneeling for the princess," Amaru said kindly. "It is my pleasure to help heal the wounds of others with this power. You said that you are close to the royal family?" Now it was Leonidas's turn to nod. "Then I will only ask for your ear, that I may tell you of knowledge the king needs to have." Leonidas stretched his arms, grimacing at the lingering aches but then gave Amaru his full attention. "You may be wondering why I, a Fyroxi of the Scorched Waste, am out in this territory, far from my own race."

"I'll admit, you did have me curious," Leonidas said. "With how reclusive your kind has become—rightfully, after the massive amount of death during the Last Astral War—I would not expect to see one of the Sun Children at large. Least of all with a dwarf, an elf, *and* a gnome as companions! Such a strange grouping, indeed."

Amaru smiled wryly at that. "You have the right of it. But my exile was not of my, or my tribe's, choosing. It was brought about by an attack. An attack of the Fyroxi's ancient ally."

Apparently, Leonidas knew his history. "The Chillfang? I thought I was going insane when I heard the howls and smelled the canine scent. I've never known Venomsting to train dogs, or at least not these ones. But how? The kingdoms of Sun's Reach and Moonwatch are separated by that barrier of Qrakzt's!"

Amaru made a soothing gesture. "We know only a little more than you, sir knight. We can't be sure as to their method of entrance but that they are here is a certainty. I fought them a couple of months back before I left, and we killed more outside when we arrived." The Fyroxi girl reached out to Cely, and the gnome pressed the note into her hand. Amaru, in turn, handed it to Leo.

By the distressed expression on his face, he also noticed the symbol belonging to the Mad Mage, and the news in the letter didn't please him. "The Sun Wench, that is their name for you?"

"Yes." Amaru was tense, remembering the night she'd first heard that name used. Alaric sensed her tension and squeezed her shoulders supportively. Amaru was once again very glad to have him around. The elf did give her a profound amount of comfort. "And I have no idea why they are chasing after me. They have mentioned that Gaarhowl has asked for me to be delivered alive to him."

"Then they plan to bring harm to you, either because of your birth or your magic," Leo said matter-of-factly.

"What I still don't understand," Celwyn said, running a small hand through her blond hair, "is how they could have known about any of that stuff beforehand. Heck, I traveled with her for a week, and Alaric for much longer, and he had no clue what she could do until just recently!"

"Good point, Celwyn," Dalphamair said gruffly. "However they did it, I don't like the implications."

"Neither do I," Leo said. He scratched his chin, dislodging sand and crusted blood from the mess of a beard hanging from his face. "But either way, I can see the danger and will do everything in my power to get my king to listen to what I have to say."

"Please do," Amaru very nearly pleaded. "My people are in dire straits; the Chillfang already infiltrated Fyrestone and killed the Fyroxi inhabitants. As far as I know, the Fire-Striders are the only ones of my race left. And not counting any attacks since I left home, there are maybe one hundred of us remaining."

Leo cursed under his breath, and his fists clenched, going white at the knuckles. "I've been gone far too long. I must get out and back home, and soon. Milady Sunbrand—"

"Amaru will do."

"Amaru," Leonidas corrected, "as I said, I will warn the king as to the danger. But I warn you, he can be a little…thickheaded at times."

Amaru recalled Durrigan's words when she'd asked about the king: *Well, he's a man.*

"I cannot promise any aid quickly, though I desire to give you all the help I can. If I didn't have to return to Searstar, I would stay here to guard you." Suddenly, something seemed to click in his head. "Perhaps, if I were to bring one of you with me, I could convince the king. If he has a testimonial from a denizen of the desert, he'll have to act! The king believes the Scorched Waste to be lawless territory, free from his jurisdiction, so Godfrey pays little attention to it. I must change his mind, and that is the best I could do. Especially if I want to convince him that there is a child of Yamaria in Sun's Reach!"

"I would rather you kept that on the quiet side. I'll not put more people in danger by letting others know of my presence. That is why I pretended to be human for so long with you." Amaru directed the last to Alaric, who nodded in understanding. "Furthermore, I cannot leave. There is more that must be done before I can even think about departing the Scorched Waste. I refuse to leave this place, which has the last remains of my family, until the threat has been dealt with or I have little other choice but to leave."

Leonidas nodded at the wisdom and loyalty. "I will not willingly separate you from family." Instead, he turned to the others, beginning with the elf. "I've not learned your name, but I can tell that you are a dutiful servant to the lady."

"Alaric Valyaara is the name that my father gave me, good knight," the elf replied with a deep bow.

"And yet you go by the name Honeytone."

"You know me?" Alaric seemed surprised. "I apologize, I'm just not used to having knights as fans! I'm mostly popular with the common folk and the ladies."

"It's not me; it's the princess," Leo said with a ghost of a smile on his face. "Emery Redwyn has desired to hear your music live for *years* now. To have you with me would be a great gift to her. Perhaps make her overlook my failures in this mission as well as allow me to have a personal account from the desert. What do you say, good bard?

Alaric scratched his chin, a battle of thoughts evident in his eyes. "It is all so very tempting. I've desired to go back to the capital for many years. The last time I was in Searstar, the princess was but a squalling babe. It would be an honor to play a show for her. I have heard many rumors, most of which say that the Her Highness Redwyn is gorgeous to behold." He hesitated just a moment before shaking his head. "Unfortunately, Emery Redwyn will have to wait a while longer to hear my music. At least until this issue we are having is over. I go wherever Amaru goes."

Leo understood the logic in that and regretfully let him pass. He entreated Celwyn but barely got the word out of his mouth before she was shaking her head. "I lived in the town of Fontain for quite a few years before coming here. I love the kingdom proper, but I am a Water Caller, and I will not leave that place which has become a second home to me."

Finally, the knight looked at Dalphamair, who shook his head as well. "Godly stuff was never my business, but I've wandered the realm with my Priscilla looking for a purpose for many years now. When you asked me to join you on your mission to the Scorched Waste, it felt like something higher was compelling me to say *yes*, though I'd have felt insane to admit it. Now I think I understand. This girl is more a healer than a warrior, and the elf is a bard. They need an actually skilled fighter. And if this girl is Yamaria's get, then I can feel assured that I'm doing the right thing protecting her."

"I see." Leonidas nodded and seemed to come to terms with the fact that he would not have any other aid. "So be it, getting inside will be much easier without foreigners to clear."

With that all said and figured out, the team returned to Oasi Sanctus, stopping only to remove the ceramic tags that each of the Water Callers and Sandward warriors carried. Celwyn explained to the others that the Water Callers had records of the tags and markings of every one of their volunteers. By returning the tag to the leader, it would be possible for their next of kin to be notified and whatever personal effects remained to be sent back home.

Already, vultures glided in slow circles above them, awaiting the departure of the living so that they might consume the dead. Before long, they would descend upon the corpses of those slain today and feast. Since the travelers had no way to transport the bodies with them, they would be left, as was so common. With food so scarce in the desert, any creature who died shortly became a meal for those as marked themselves scavengers. That way, the nutrients of the body could go to the sustainability of the other creatures.

When they returned to Oasi Sanctus, Amaru made sure that Leonidas ate and rested, very nearly standing over her charges' shoulder until he obeyed. "No matter how important it is to you to return home, you will do your princess no good if you die on the ride home." With a combination of foul-tasting potions and plenty of sleep, the knight regained some of his strength back. It would take training to return him back to his old physical condition, but at least he could ride. He could survive the journey to and along the Central Road and make his way back to Emery.

Finally, Amaru deemed Leonidas ready; and the knight was given new rough spun clothes, boots, and a map that would allow him to navigate to the oases on his own. One Water Caller would still join him, just to be sure that he managed to survive, but in the event of a tragedy, Leonidas would be able to save himself. The knight gave his thanks and final promises to Amaru and the others and clapped Dalphamair on the back in fellowship and farewell. Then it was finally time for him to leave, and the knight sworn to the princess was finally on his way once again.

REN

Ren the Hero

The Chillfang came again at sunfall.

Ren, Xio, and Leif had continued their training and learning. Sigmund practiced with each of them in turn, teaching them how to play to their strengths. Leif was the easiest for him, seeing as he'd trained with the boy since a young age. The battles between master and apprentice were always entertaining to watch. Leif nearly matched the old veteran in skill, having observed his methods for almost a century and coming up with counters to them. Leif knew all his master's tells, the tail twitch that meant he was going low, the flicking ear of a bite attack, or the blink of Sigmund's good eye, which was a dangerous pouncing maneuver. "Old habits die hard, boy," the veteran explained. "And everybody has their faults that make them predictable in battle. I didn't lose my eye from being perfect."

"That your own apprentice, who's lived less than half the years you have can beat you only proves the weakness in all of you," Leif answered. Sigmund stopped for a moment and glared at his apprentice. "What's wrong, old man? Did I hit a nerve?"

Without any warning, the old Fyroxi pounced, pinning Leif to the sand. The apprentice struggled and tried to bite at Sigmund, but to no avail. With seemingly limitless strength, the elder held Leif down until he finally tired out. Once the boy finally stopped struggling, Sigmund allowed him to come loose. "At any point there, I could have ripped out your throat or cut it with a claw," the elder growled. "You allow your ego to take over your judgment, and that will be the death of you. We need every competent warrior we have when these Chillfang return. That is the only reason we are tolerating your waxing on our weakness as a race. The power in our tribe has more to do with us as a collective whole rather than any one member. If you think I'm wrong, you can try surviving alone. When the poachers hear of a lone Fyroxi, there will be more than even you can handle. Then you'll wish you hadn't insulted tribe and family. Keep it up, and you may taste that feeling sooner than you'd like. Is that understood, Leif Kalix?"

Grumbling, the younger Fyroxi had reluctantly agreed and stalked off once dismissed. Leif rarely stayed around after his training sessions were completed. He missed a lot of valuable information, but the brash young man didn't seem to care. Ren saw the other elders muttering to themselves in the corner as Sigmund called him up to the ring.

"You know the rules, boy. We fight until you can't keep going or one of us is knocked outside the ring. Since you haven't done much fighting and this is training for a Chillfang attack, anything goes as long as it doesn't kill me or injure me beyond fighting ability."

With Vienna dead, Purell had to take a new apprentice for the learning of medicine. After seeing Amaru save Weylin, young Savannah had gladly stepped up for the task. She was a quick study and a bright girl, but she was still too young and inexperienced to handle anything serious. But small scrapes and bruises from skirmishes were just good training.

Ren nodded and stepped forward, tapping the pouches slung on his fox form's body. Usually, his bags contained treasures, but today he filled them with utility items that he'd received from the other people of the desert during his diplomatic missions. Working with Xio, he'd managed to reverse engineer some of them into weapons of a sort.

Sigmund looked appraisingly over the boy and nodded. "I wonder what little tricks you have for me today, Rienzi." Unlike Leif, who thought that hiding behind tools other than swords was craven, the elder praised the crafty use of items that Ren employed. "Not all men and women are made for swordplay or up-close fighting. That is nothing to be ashamed of. Using a spear is perfectly respectable for combat as Amaru did, and keeping your distance only keeps you alive that much longer."

Sigmund crouched low to the sand and barked once to signal the beginning of the battle. While Ren wasn't as knowledgeable about Sigmund's signals, he was quick. That served him well in this battle, as he slipped out of being pinned multiple times. While focusing on dodging, Ren searched for opportunities to use his other supplies. Unfortunately, being on a surface of loose sand, he couldn't make use of the glass marbles that the Sandmasons had gifted him, but he still had plenty of other tools. As Sigmund prepared to jump in for an attack, Ren pulled out a small thin-shelled berry capsule. Inside was a loose powder that filled the air. Throwing it down provided a screen for him to move behind. The elder didn't see Ren until the small male was on his back. The sudden roll that the warrior tried also played into Ren's plans. From his tail, he let drop a loop of rope. All of Sigmund's legs were together, trying to push Ren off, and with just a moment of maneuvering, the older Fyroxi was tied up and unable to move. Ren cut the rope and let the elder free.

"Well done, Rienzi," he said proudly. "You've come far, and the craftiness of the fox is within you." Xio smiled glowingly when Ren glanced her way. "Of course, that doesn't mean you can skip out on weapon training with the others in the tribe. We're meeting in an hour. Be there." Sigmund walked back to the elders, and Xio joined Ren on the walk home.

"Why do I never see you fighting with Sigmund?" Ren asked his friend as they walked. "He never calls you into the ring, and you're never at the drills."

"Well, usually, it's Weylin and Sigmund leading the drills, and someone has to watch over Jarrah and Savannah," Xio started. "Also, Silque started a few of us on other practices."

"Other than crafting?" Ren cocked his head. They'd tried to gather up materials for building some sort of border around the village, but there weren't enough trees or destroyed caravans in this area, even with the increasing Chillfang attacks. And nobody wanted to go too far from the village, with their foes creeping just out of sight. "What other things do you need to learn?"

"In the Hundredth Sun Massacre, a lot of the youngling's mothers were lost," Xio answered. "So she's teaching us the things we would learn with children of our own. Seeing as I've already been helping with the Fyrestone kids, Silque figured I was the right person to help teach."

"Oh, that's great, Xio," Ren congratulated. "When it comes time for you to be a mother, I bet you'll be great!" Xio blushed a deep crimson. "Also, I won't lie I'm glad that you're going to be safe with the children." Ren put an arm around Xio's shoulder. "I don't want to lose anyone else important to me."

Xio certainly understood his meaning. Vienna and Amaru had been good friends to both of them. But further, Xio couldn't imagine losing Ren. She wished she could tell him to stay behind from the battle, but after the massacre, she knew that nothing would keep him back. Besides, no matter how much Ren would like to pretend otherwise, Leif's comments bothered him. He didn't want to give the stronger boy any further reason to taunt him.

Xio wished she had the confidence to approach him about her feelings, but every time she tried, she was overwhelmed by nervousness. She didn't want to speak too soon when the loss of Vienna and Amaru's departure were too fresh. As they passed her hut, Xio bowed out; she needed to do some thinking.

It was while she was thinking that the sentries blew the warning note. One long reverberating call from multiple horns. It echoed through the village, notifying everyone that Chillfang had been spotted. Xio, following instructions from Silque, drew Jarrah and Savannah close to her and covered all of them in an old tarp. She hoped that the musty smells would mask their own and that they wouldn't shake too much. Xio knew that she was the prime suspect of this shaking, as the screams and howls pulsed through the orange-lit evening. She also knew that at this very moment, Ren would be out there, with all the eligible warriors, fighting to protect the younglings. *To protect us.*

*****

Ren was massaging his sore muscles as the blaring signal shattered the peaceful silence. Rushing to his chest, he grabbed his pouches, scrambling to fit as many on to himself as possible. There would be plenty of men and women with weapons out there. He would be far more useful at causing a distraction. Running out, he saw what he expected. The warriors of the tribe were separated among the four sides of the village, the four fronts from which the Chillfang were attacking. To the north, Sigmund was leading defense against the largest group of wolves, and to the east, Leif was controlling the battle, jumping in with gusto. The south had few Chillfang, as they had been sighted trying to sneak around and quickly dealt with by the sentries.

That left only west, and Ren rushed straight toward it. Caught up within the fervor of the battle, Ren wasn't aware of time passing. The only things he knew were the men and women fighting in front of him and the enemies attacking them. The Fyroxi used everything at his disposal: marbles were thrown underfoot, sand into eyes. He had a collection of caltrops from the Braavsand mercenaries, which lamed a great many enemies. Small pods that fizzled with a bright flash and snapping sound pulled Chillfang attention from the fight ahead and allowed his Fyroxi brothers and sisters to tear their foe apart. This time, as Amaru had said, they were prepared. The Fyroxi fought tooth and nail, their minds set on revenge for the Hundredth Sun Massacre.

*****

Ren woke up, head pounding from the fight. He tried to remember where he was. The air was hot and smelled ripe, meaning he was still in the desert, at least. His ears rang loudly, the result of a particularly nasty hit on the head. With mind clearing, Ren recalled what had led him to his current predicament. At some point in the battle, the Chillfang had broken through the south front. He figured it must have been near the end, a final desperate push to get into the center of the village and take the Fyroxi from behind. The screams from the southern defenders had warned them just in time, and Fyroxi had been sent from all other sides to handle them. Ren had been among them, and his supplies were getting very low. Without much left, he'd decided to wade into the fray, do whatever he could. Moving through the corpses in the center, something cold and hard hit his head, and everything had gone black.

Struggling to sit up, Ren heard the ringing start to fade. Some faint noise sounded in the background. Finally, he could make it out. A scared and growing-ever-more-tearful voice was crying his name. "Ren? Ren! Please, Ren, where are you?"

He tried to call out, let the caller know he was still alive, but the sound came out only as a faint croak. His entire body now began to throb with pain, as if he'd been trampled. Other corpses lay around him, those fallen in the middle meeting. Ren forced himself to sit up, and with all the strength he could muster, he called in answer. "Here! I'm here!" The Fyroxi heard a faint patter of feet, and suddenly, he was back on the ground. Instantly reacting, balled fists rose, but they dropped when he saw Xio's face hovering above his.

"Ren, thank Yamaria you're alive." The blond-haired girl drew him into a tight embrace, burying her face in his shoulder. "When you didn't return, I was so worried. I've been searching the dead ever since the sun came up." Xio's voice was thick with tears.

Ren's hands, stained red with blood, stroked her long blond hair. The girl was practically lying on him, knees digging into his stomach. "You're hurting me, Xio. Be careful," he complained, and she immediately hopped off, apologizing profusely.

"Can you stand?" she asked, gingerly looping an arm around his back. "We need to get you back to the tent. The others are waiting for me so they can finalize the count."

"I-I think so."

Xio helped Ren to his feet and supported him as they staggered back to the tent. Ren could hear the cheers as the Fyroxi celebrated their victory. Looking around, Ren could tell there weren't many bodies. Perhaps half of their last loss. Amaru had been right, surprise had been their main disadvantage in the previous battle. It had been over a century since the Chillfang and Fyroxi had been in open warfare. Although members of this tribe hadn't been in the Last Astral

War, they had dealt with a few stray strike units. The older tribe members knew what it was like to fight the Chillfang. Their enemy, however, was a notoriously short-lived race. Many generations had passed for them, and they only had stories of their battles. That must have explained their lack of attacks. They wanted to get a feel for their foe again.

Another thing resurfaced from the back of his mind. Throughout the battle, like before, the Chillfang had called for the Sun Wench. That made Ren feel a little better, at least they hadn't found Amaru yet. If she evaded them for this long, she must have found someplace safe.

Ren and Xio pushed through the flaps of the tent. As the remaining tribe members turned to them, a tumultuous roar overtook them. Men and women clapped as Xio dragged Ren to a bench and sat him down. Warriors chanted his name and raised their mugs into the air. The tent smelled like ale, which they must have opened again in celebration.

"What's going on?" Ren turned to Xio, who was smiling widely at the praise he received.

One of the warriors, a man named Bryndle, walked over and pat him on the back. "Can't believe you survived that, man! You really won us that battle!"

Ren was confused now. "All I did was stand in the back and throw stones."

"Maybe, but those were some damned good throws. Hit a bunch of 'em right between the eyes!" Bryndle pumped his fist excitedly. "And those spiky things? Even as the Chillfang retreated, they were getting them stuck in their feet. Plus, with the shiny powder you covered them with, they couldn't hide in the shadows. We couldn't have survived that fight without you!"

Ren couldn't recall any of this, but the fog of war was still thick in his mind, so he went along with it. If the Fyroxi wanted to call him a hero, who was he to object? "I'm just glad we survived," he said. "I think the real praise should go to the sentries, who alerted us in time."

"Yeah, they did! *Woo!*" Bryndle wandered back into the midst of his friends. "Three cheers for the sentries and for Ren!"

"Hip, hip, hurrah! Hip, hip, hurrah! Hip, hip, hurrah!" came the resounding cry from the lips of the Fyroxi. Even the elders joined in, Sigmund's voice loudest of all. Only Leif didn't take part, staring sourly at the cheerers and drinking deeply from his mug.

Leif was the first to leave, but people started to file out slowly, the weariness from the night without sleep and the battle taking them over and pulling them back to their beds.

Soon, Ren and Xio were the only ones left. The medicines she'd procured for him, combined with the alcohol and rest, had made all the pain he'd felt earlier disappear. Still, Xio insisted on helping him back to his hut and leaned her head on his shoulder the whole way. As she stood outside the doorway, preparing to bid him goodnight, he touched her shoulder. "Are you all right, Xio?" he asked tentatively. "You were pretty quiet today. Are you mad at me?"

She shook her head. "I can't think of anything that I could be mad at you for."

"Maybe because I took all that glory in the battle," he answered sheepishly. "It was kind of a... Leif thing to do. You know what I mean?"

"I suppose you have a point," Xio agreed. "But no, I'm not mad at you. Honestly, I'm just overjoyed that you're alive. I... I don't know what I would have done if you'd died out there." Her tone grew bolder, and she looked him straight in the eyes.

"Xio—" Ren started, but his friend cut him off.

"No, you wanted to know how I'm feeling, and I'm going to say my piece." She took a deep breath. "This is going to sound weird, but the entire time during the fight, no worries about my own safety or the rest of my family crossed my mind. The only person I thought about the whole time was you. I didn't want to deal with knowing that you died before I could tell you."

"Tell me what, Xio?" Ren's hand still lay on her shoulder, which shook with apprehension.

Xio's eyes were rimmed with tears and her golden hair with sunlight. "Do you really not know?" One hand moved into the crook of his elbow. "On the night of the massacre, I left because I saw you go off with Vienna."

"Oh," Ren said, now starting to understand. "Xio, did you want…"

"Yes, Ren." Xio pulled in close to him. "This whole time, I've been in love with *you*. But you kept turning to others: first, Amaru, and then Vienna. And you keep going into dangerous situations, and by some miracle of Yamaria, you keep returning alive. But I couldn't shake the feeling that you wouldn't return. I don't want that to happen."

Ren stroked his now-clean hands through her hair and pulled in a whiff of her sweet scent. "Shhh," he soothed. "It's all right, Xio. I won't let that happen."

"How can you just promise that?"

"Because I have too much to lose," Ren answered simply, lifting Xio's chin with a finger. "Honestly, Amaru was way out of my league, which I should have realized long ago. And Vienna was just the first one to ask me. Had you come up and said something…" Ren shook his head. "But I'm glad you weren't because then it would be you who died in Vienna's place. As you've proved over the past weeks, you are a darn good friend. I'm not sure I could have gotten through everything that's happened if I didn't have you around."

Fresh tears streaked down her face. "Do you really mean that, or are you just trying to make me feel better?"

"How's this for an answer?" He leaned in and kissed her lightly. "You and I are a team now. I promise that I will do whatever I can to keep you and the Fyrestone kids safe while also keeping you from worrying too much. I like staying in the back during a battle anyway."

"That makes me so happy to hear," Xio breathed. She blushed and turned her gaze to the floor. "Um, elder Silque says that soon w-we should start focusing on replenishing the tribe with new children." She felt so awkward just blurting it out, but she knew if she didn't now, she never would. "Before you said I'd make a good m-mother…" A pleading question filled her eyes. "Could we make up for the night of the Hundredth Sun Festival?"

"Not too nervous to ask this time, I see," Ren teased.

Her reply was to kiss him again, and finally, all the obstacles were gone. No more Amaru, no more Vienna, no more nervousness. Just Xio and Ren, together at last.

EMERY
Premarital Strain

As the week progressed, Emery and Tarus continued to meet during the day. Their conversations were short, and Tarus wasn't eager to give up much more of his history. Despite the secrecy, the princess could feel the young man growing on her.

The next morning was three days from the wedding ball, and the palace cooks made the most sumptuous breakfast Emery had ever seen. Piles of toast, soaked in egg wash and baked, plates of crispy bacon, bowls of chilled fruits in light cream, and more. Emery was amazed at everything that her father had done to prepare the castle for the Gardstars. Godfrey had seen to it that every wish these foreign travelers was fulfilled. The servants had been kicked out of the chambers they'd been allowed to occupy before, moved down to drafty corridors in the lowest part of the castle. Gardeners were called in to tend to the courtyard. Emery walked through there often, sitting outside during pleasant weather to read a book. She'd known every imperfection, and a part of her had been thrilled by those little mistakes. Now she figured none of them would remain. The princess planned to walk Tarus through the gardens this afternoon, thinking that they should spend some time bonding before the Rothsster-Leygrain wedding, where they would be expected to try looking like an actual betrothed couple.

Tarus looked like he wanted to devour the food in front of him with gusto, but glancing back at Lord Geurus frequently, he restrained himself. When Emery caught his eye, however, his gaze softened and broke into a wide smile.

The king was very proud of his cooks, of which he had many. Each had different specialties, and some even came from across the world, traveling to learn a new cuisine and drawn in by the king's heavy purse. From what little she knew about the culinary arts, Emery could tell that there were different flavors than customary in Sun's Reach.

As they ate, Cereos was chatting quietly with Queen Lysaria, who had been allowed to break from her paperwork for the rest of the week. Emery's mother's expression was utterly unreadable, despite Lady Cereos's smiles. The princess knew that her mother was judging every little word that the lady spoke, weighing its worth and searching for any secret meaning or contradiction. Lysaria was so prim and composed, a level of calm that Emery had never managed to replicate. From experience, she knew that her mother could make a conversation about sordid secrets look from the outside like a casual chat about the weather. It had been so when Emery had first told Lysaria about her feelings for Leonidas. They'd walked in the garden and spoke, the princess's emotions showing clearly while the queen had her cold mask, softened only by motherly pity. That ability to close off her feelings must have won her father, so concerned about his reputation. Lysaria would never let an ounce of her problems show to the public. Many a time, she wished it had been her mother who came from a royal bloodline and sat on the throne. Lysaria, like Emery, had genuine affection for their people. She would have made Sun's Reach a better place and not left quite so much of a mess for Emery to clean up.

"I know you haven't seen too much yet, but how do you like Sun's Reach so far?" Emery asked as she strolled arm in arm with Tarus later that day.

Tarus stretched and yawned. "Honestly, the little taste I have makes me excited for more. Though I doubt I'll ever get used to the lack of nighttime. The constant sun makes it hard to sleep, you know?"

The princess had to shake her head. "I've never had an issue with it. I don't understand why someone would *want* to have night. A city street or open field in darkness just sounds like a murder waiting to happen."

"Yeah, I suppose," Tarus agreed. "But that's just being overly critical of nighttime. Murders can happen just as easily during the daytime." The young lord drew a little closer. "Is it true that you have an organization of assassins here in the kingdom? They can pull off their job even in bright sunshine, I've heard."

"The Venomsting, yes, a brazen group that makes their headquarters somewhere in the desert," Emery explained. "I don't know much about them, but they are all very highly skilled and ruthlessly trained."

"So they're like my father's troops, except with a lot less honor," Tarus said. "I would almost like to see a battle between the two. Maybe if we end up getting married and you sit the Highsun Seat, we can work on arranging that together." He grinned wildly, white teeth glinting in the sunlight.

Godfrey announced that he would be taking Lord Geurus on tour around Searstar's walls, in hopes that he could set men to guard them. Even if no foe came to the gates, it would at least give the men something to do during their stay in the city. Tarus saw this as an excellent opportunity to see more of the capital. "If we get married, I'll be living in the castle and will have more than enough time to know every block. What do you say you show me around the places you like to go?"

So to the gates and down the stairs they went. Colorful tents were set up in the streets, run by the vendors for the wedding because a little more money was never something to scoff at. Strains of music flowed through the air, adding a little spring to everyone's step. People gathered around the musicians, belting out the lyrics to songs they knew.

"Things aren't always festive, but you came at one of the best times of the year," Emery told Tarus. "Midsummer and harfestival are the two best-known affairs in Sun's Reach. I've been told that in the past, we used to celebrate a winter holiday as well, but since the

Eclipse, winter and summer have the same temperature, and there's never any snow…"

"There was no way to continue those traditions," Tarus finished. "My father says he misses snow most of all from home. Even though we got cooler temperatures during 'winter,' there was never much that accumulated."

"I've never known it in my lifetime, but like with the debate about the night we had earlier, I think we have the better deal." The princess indicated her arms and legs, uncovered in the comfortable day. "Soaking in the sun's rays is just so pleasant, and I couldn't imagine living without the warm breeze."

"It's lucky for you that we will get to stay here in your kingdom once we are married," Tarus said.

Emery couldn't help but notice how often he mentioned that they were to be married. It was as if he was absolutely sure of the result or trying to reassure himself of the fact. To be fair, with the way King Godfrey was acting, it was more than likely that Tarus would be correct.

"Meanwhile, I have to learn how to survive in this sweltering heat!" He tugged uncomfortably at the neck of his shirt but flashed a grin to show he was being overdramatic.

"I'm curious, Tarus," Emery asked, deciding to bring up one of her doubts with the boy. "How do you feel about marrying a girl you barely even know?"

"What do you mean?"

"You know what I mean," Emery sighed. "We only just met, and more than likely, we are going to end up married. Wouldn't you rather have the choice to marry someone that you care about?"

Tarus thought about this for a moment. "I understand where you're coming from. I guess it would be frustrating to be forced into a marriage against your will." His brow furrowed. "Do you find the idea of marrying me unpleasant?"

"I-I don't know," she answered honestly. "As I said, I don't know you well enough. But I feel that marriage should be a thing of the heart rather than politics."

Tarus frowned and caressed his chin. "But unfortunately, that's not how things are in this world. If everyone married who they wanted, then we would have nobles and swineherds hooking up, and *that* would just get awkward."

"I don't think so," Emery said and separated herself from the blond boy. She saw two familiar figures strolling through the market, admiring the wares. "Reyna! Arcadia!" she called. "Are you ready for the ball?"

Reyna lit up upon seeing the princess. "Emery, it's been a while! Father keeping you busy with wedding preparations?"

"Of a sort," she said, gesturing toward Tarus with her head.

"That's one of the visitors from the other day," Arcadia stated, sinking deeper into her cowl. "His father came in with a bunch of men, a nasty-looking lot. What are you doing with him?"

Reyna looked worried. "Is everything all right, Emery?"

"Well, you asked before if I was going to be tying the knot. The answer to that is behind me."

"One of those arranged things, I imagine," Arcadia said darkly. "I don't like the look of him."

"Now, now, sis," Reyna chided, "no reason to judge someone solely on appearances."

"You mean like he's doing now?" Arcadia pointed one bony finger at Tarus, and the others looked back. A muscle twitched in the cheek of the blond boy as he stormed over. "It appears like he's taking exception to our presence."

Tarus's hand rested on the hilt of his sword. "Step away from the princess, demons," he spat. "Or else I'll be forced to do something drastic."

"How nice of our gracious visitor to threaten innocent city folk," Arcadia drawled, "really displaying that nobleman's charm."

The sword flashed out of its sheath, leveled at Arcadia's throat. There was a hard glare in Tarus's eyes and white teeth ground in his mouth. "Nothing about your kind is innocent," the blond boy growled. "I should kill you both right now." Tarus drew back his blade. "Rid the city of your scourge." He was about to thrust, but suddenly, Emery was in the way of the point, arms splayed out protectively. "What are you doing protecting these beasts, princess?"

"Put up your steel, Tarus," Emery commanded. "You are not to hurt my friends."

"You consider these...these"—he searched for another word—"these monstrosities your friends?"

"Yes, I do," Emery answered. "And if you bring them any harm..." She left the threat hanging heavily in the air, leaving Tarus wondering just how far the princess would go for the two.

The foreigner hesitated, the tip of the blade wavering angrily. Finally, with a strained, forced-looking movement, Tarus shoved the sword back in its sheath. "Figures you would become friends with the unfortunate," Tarus grumbled. "I hoped when I met you...but no, it seems they were right. I'm going back to the market. When you're done associating with those...girls," he said the last word with some difficulty, "you can meet me there." With that, he turned on his heel and strode back into the thick crowd. A couple of people who had stopped in surprise at the sight of naked steel turned away, muttering. The three stood in silence, Emery dropping her arms and head.

"So that's your new husband-to-be," Reyna supplied at last.

"I told you I didn't like the look of him," Arcadia said matter-of-factly.

"Everyone has their faults," the lighter Khindre said. "But that was rather surprising, wasn't it?"

"That's one word for it," Arcadia snorted. "Are you all right, Princess?"

Emery had been quiet, which was understandable given what had just happened. Reyna looped an arm around the princess's shoulder. Her orange skin was warm to the touch. "I know I barely knew him, but I thought he was a good person," the princess mumbled.

"He still might be, though perhaps his quick action was unwarranted," Reyna said soothingly. "I think you just need to talk with him."

"But you did hear what he said at the end, right before he stormed off," Arcadia mentioned. "Who was he referring to? Any clues, Princess?"

"None whatsoever," she replied. "I've known Tarus for less than a full week."

"So I was right," Arcadia said unhelpfully. "It is one of those arranged marriages."

"Yes." Emery walked over to the wall and sat down, not heeding the dirt that was coating the back of her sundress. The Rainclaw twins joined her, one sitting on either side. "I was feeling unsure about it from the start. Now I'm just confused."

"You sound just like Caitrial." Reyna laughed. "She hasn't married yet because she wants to find someone who will accept us. Unfortunately, Princess, most of the world shares an unfavorable opinion about Khindre like us. Don't let that common perception taint your opinion of Lord Tarus."

"You speak as if he didn't just threaten your life!" Emery said, bewildered. "How can you so easily do that?"

The gorgeous Khindre smiled brilliantly. "I've been told that I often give people the benefit of the doubt." She rested her forehead on Emery's. "Just as you do. Answer me this. I know that you have little knowledge of him, but do you think you could, at any point, of your own free will, love him or marry him?"

The answer came immediately to the princess's throat. "No," she said and meant it. "If this weren't forced upon me, I wouldn't willingly choose him."

"There's another," Arcadia stated. "I can tell by the tortured look in your eyes."

The secluded alcove they sat in was devoid of people besides them, so Emery allowed herself to nod and felt tears jump into her eyes.

"I knew it!" Reyna exclaimed. "I knew there was some reason that you were bothered by our questions about marriage. And it wasn't hard to notice the difference that came over you since Leonidas left."

"You've known all this time?" Emery was shocked. "And you never said anything?"

"I didn't want to pry," Reyna answered sheepishly. "But perhaps I should have."

The two stood up abruptly. "If you stay too long, your friend there might get angry," Arcadia said. "We'll see you at the ball. And Yamaria grant you good luck."

When Emery finally caught up with Tarus, the boy was tapping his foot impatiently. Talking in hushed tones, they walked back toward the castle, the princess avoiding Tarus's grabs for her arm.

"What was all that back there about?" she asked crossly.

"They're Raethwyr," he said as if it answered everything. "Demon kin."

"Technically, *Khindre* are devil children, not demon children," Emery argued, puzzled by his strange terminology. "There is a difference."

"Does that really matter, Princess?" Tarus fumed. "I honestly can't believe you are defending them!"

"You've never met Reyna or Arcadia," Emery countered. "You don't know anything about them. Yamaria, I thought you had some sense!"

Tarus looked wounded by her anger. His expression softened, and he reached out a placating arm. "I'm sorry, Princess. Perhaps you're correct. I didn't mean to anger you. Please forgive my rashness. I've just had bad experiences with their kind."

Emery was put off guard by the sudden change in attitude. "Maybe one day, you'll feel comfortable talking about them," she offered warily. "But I won't ask you to relive them now. I'll leave you to your thoughts. It's never a good idea to ask two people who just met to spend all of their time together."

With that, she walked off, leaving Tarus on his own. He floundered for some sort of reply and reached out an arm, but the princess didn't look back.

*****

The next morning marked two days until the wedding of Mia Rothsster and Ferrin Leygrain. The princess woke up early, feeling hopeful for some indeterminable reason. At her request, Tarus had left her alone last night, and he was still locked in his room, asleep. Emery went out to one of the balcony paths that circled around the drum-shaped castle center. It had been many days since she'd roused early enough to see the dawning of a new day. From talking to Berdur and others, Emery learned that the sun rising from the low position above the land wasn't as impressive as watching the night dissipate as the great ball of light climbed into the sky. She thought back on the conversation with Tarus the day before. *I wonder if having nighttime is better than I first imagined.* She couldn't shake her bias toward the golden sun, but that didn't mean that she had the right to put down the silver moon, which Tarus seemed to find more impressive. *Perhaps one day, he and I will go traveling. He could take me out of the zone of magic that keeps the sun and moon acting so strangely here. Then I can experience night and a genuine sunrise.* Sailors who traded goods with other kingdoms had confirmed that the strange cycle of daylight that Sun's Reach experienced was a local event. To see what it was like most everywhere else in the world, that would certainly be interesting and well worth the trip.

Where would Tarus Gardstar be able to take her? she wondered. If they came from an island, he must have ships, which meant the whole world was open to them. Thoughts of far-off lands, new horizons, and strange people swam through her head. With them, the realization that she'd still not seen most of her own kingdom hit her hard. A few times, she'd visited the Sunne Steps below Searstar and once she'd gone to Cendrillion in the very center, but nothing farther. And even on that trip, they'd taken the Central Pass, which wasn't known for its sights, only its speed. Another goal to write on parchment, that list just seemed to grow longer and longer. At least the most recent one could be solved during the wedding tour. Emery was unsure how to feel about that: a journey of the kingdom with Tarus, their driver, and guards as her only companions. Given his prejudice against Khindre, the princess doubted young Lord Gardstar would permit the Rainclaw twins to join them.

*****

Staring over Searstar, her city, made Emery feel calm and comfortable. Below her, people worked and played. The midsummer festival swarmed with activity, and the gates were open to any delayed visitors for the wedding. Emery knew that the rest of Ferrin's family would be among them, their servants kept busy at home with tending to their farms. Occasionally, the portcullis blocking off the castle would be opened, and a few figures would meander inside, emerging from the end of the tunnel and making their way to one of a variety of places on the castle grounds.

As she watched, Emery slowly made her way down the balcony ramp, sliding her hand absently down the golden balustrade. As she descended farther down the sloped pathway, she started to hear the tinny edge of faraway voices. Those voices belonged to the castle guard, still men loyal to King Godfrey. However big a fool the king was and no matter how infatuated he was with Lord Geurus, Godfrey had guaranteed that the foreigner's men stayed out on the walls and street patrols until their alliance and mutual trust was affirmed. With the massive girth of the drum tower and the leisurely pace at which she walked, it took Emery over an hour to reach the stone tiles of the base level. As she neared the bottom, a light sheen of perspiration on her fair face, there came excited voices from the men on the castle wall. The portcullis was dragged open, faster than it had been for any of the other guests. Emery wondered what all the excitement was and hurried down the rest of the way, the soles of her shoes landing on the springy grass of the courtyard. She gazed at the end of the tunnel, wondering who was going to come through. *Who could have made the guard so excited? And nervous*, Emery thought, wincing as the metal gate crashed down beyond the tunnel. Suddenly, the reason was revealed to her, and the princess's feet started to move on their own, running at top speed toward the visitor. She proffered a cry to the air, which caused the figure to turn just in time, as Emery threw herself into the arms of the knight.

Her knight: Leonidas Braveheart. He was alive! And more importantly, he was home!

Emery was overcome with emotions: joy, sadness, a slight twinge of anger, affection, some she couldn't even put a name to. Her arms grasped as much of his well-toned bulk as they could, pulling herself tight to his chest. There was a moment of shocked paralysis before the knight recovered. He encircled and lifted her body with his muscular arms, which trembled with exhaustion but still found the strength necessary.

The pressure against her back, combined with her feet leaving the ground, imparted a giddy sensation to her head. Unable to find words to say, she buried her face into his thick beard. It smelled like sweat, but it also held that heady familiar musk that she could only describe as *Leonidas*. Finally, turning her head up to meet his eye, she found words. "You need a shave," she said, keeping her eyes steadily on his.

"Nice to see you too, Princess," he replied, a ghost of a smile appearing on his face. He really did look tired. Emery didn't know much about his journey, but to see Leo like this, she surmised that he'd ridden from wherever he had been with little rest. She was right, of course. In all of Leonidas's haste to return to the capital, he'd traveled for days on end, switching horses whenever he could find a stable and barely giving himself the rest that his body now certainly craved.

Suddenly, as if the walls she'd built had all come crashing down, water started to well in her eyes. All the tears that she'd repressed for the sake of looking strong came flowing out at once. Leonidas sank to one knee, gently resting Emery's feet on the ground. He patted her on the back, listening to her as she regurgitated a tearful tumult of words. She doubted that there was a single coherent phrase in the whole lot of it, but there didn't need to be. It conveyed to Sir Leonidas well enough that the princess needed comfort. He'd been gone for quite a while, and by the sound of her, Emery must have had a rough time of it.

The knight blamed himself for being careless enough to be captured and causing his princess any amount of grief. Eventually, the word storm ended, and the tears subsided. Looking down affectionately at his princess, Leo decided to speak. "Are you all right, Emery?"

She nodded wordlessly, her eyes shining. "That's good." He raised himself up, touching the large wet spot on his grimy shirt. "I think it's long past time I made my report to your father. When I'm done with that and probably a long nap, I'll come to see you. I feel like we have a lot to catch up on."

Emery released him reluctantly, wishing she could stay in his arms all day, as she used to when they were younger. But they were older, more mature now, and the knight was right, his debriefing was long overdue.

AMARU
Revelations and Decisions

Amaru, Alaric, and Dalphamair sat within the mess tent, awaiting the pleasure of the High Servant. The de-facto leader of the Water Callers was a very busy man, heading all the rejuvenation efforts across the desert. Dalphamair was aware of just how much time it could take for a request to get approved, after having to sit on his hands for weeks to get people to join him on his mission to save Sir Leonidas. But to his credit, after the successful rescue attempt and how the Fyroxi and elf had alerted the City of Tents to attack, the High Servant was relatively quick in arranging their meeting. So it was that a few days after Leonidas left, an old man—with untrimmed gray hair, bushy eyebrows, and a prominent nose—walked into the room muttering to himself.

"Ah, good, good. You're here on time."

"Of course, sir," Amaru replied. "You asked us here at this time, so here we are."

"You might be surprised at how hard it is to make the younglings act so promptly in this day and age," the old man sighed and laughed at the same time. "And please, young lady, just call me Rovinald."

"Rovinald then. I imagine you remember why we wished to meet with you?"

Rovinald scrunched up his brows, which formed a single thick monobrow in the center. "Something about talking further about the Chillfang threat, which if I remember correctly, the knight Leonidas had something to say about it as well. I thought it was outlandish when he said it; perhaps he'd gone senile from the Venomsting's poisons. And apologies, but I don't know either of you two all that well. But, Dalphamair, I know, is a trustworthy man, completely sound of mind. And Celwyn has worked faithfully here, and though she may not be the wisest gnome around, she has her uses."

Amaru wondered whether Rovinald would have said that if the gnome had been here. At this very moment, Celwyn was busy traveling to a close-by settlement, ensuring that they could get back on their feet following the sandstorm and creature attacks. Then she wondered if Cely would even care. Knowing her, the gnome would have just laughed at the joke.

"I don't know about all that sound-o'-mind stuff." Dalph chuckled. "I've taken my fair share of knocks to the head."

"But you've survived and pulled off a rescue attempt, and purging that should have been impossible."

"Not without a cost though," Dalph grumbled.

"The men who were lost will be sorely missed," Rovinald said, twining his fingers together in prayer. "But going up against such odds, some loss was expected. And if what you claim is true, then their sacrifice will be for the greater good of the desert, if not the whole kingdom. Whatever happened, I now have word from someone I trust that a creature that I know only from story is threatening lives, not to mention those scorpion creatures. Yours are not my only reports of strange happenings involving large dogs. I thought at first that they were just jackals that people mistook for something more fearsome. Desert heat can put you in the mind of some strange things, after all. But if Dalphamair says that it is Chillfang, then by Yamaria, I believe."

Dalphamair couldn't believe how perfect of a segue he'd been delivered. Without the dramatic touch of Alaric behind him, the dwarf had been wondering how he might broach this next topic. "If you permit me, Rovinald, I'd like to stretch the limits of your belief even further." He pointed at Amaru. "What if I told you that Yamaria sent us a sign, directly from above? Not only a sign of danger but also one of hope."

One thick eyebrow raised against the High Servant's forehead. "The girl?" he asked. "What does a human girl have to do with Yamaria?"

Alaric spoke up now. "With all due respect, Amaru here is no mere human." He snapped his fingers, and Amaru pulled back her hood.

Rovinald had been in the Water Callers' service for most of his life, and he'd seen his fair share of the Fire-Striders. So the look of shock that registered on his face was not from her race but rather her coloration.

"Introducing the gorgeous and mystical Amaru Sunbrand, daughter of Yamaria."

Amaru blushed at the introduction but stared forward evenly all the same.

Rovinald nodded. "A white-furred Fyroxi is certainly not commonplace. In all of my years of service, I've never once seen one with fur such as yours. Daughter of Yamaria, you say? Makes sense since the Sun Mother is often depicted with radiant white fur in her true form."

"Y-you aren't going to argue or say that we're insane?" Alaric asked, surprised by the unexpected belief.

"Nope," the old man replied with a smile. "It would also explain why I keep getting letters from different people about a lost Fyroxi friend that they would pay dearly to see returned to them. My guess is that they aren't friends at all but people who want you for some sort of god thing." He tapped two fingers on his lap to an indistinguishable rhythm. "And I also guess that this is not something that you want."

"Very astute, Rovinald." Dalphamair nodded sagely. "I imagine that you gave them no answer?"

"One of them actually showed up in person to ask about you, girl. They must want you desperately. A worrying thought honestly. If they find out that we are actually harboring you—"

"Too much risk of innocent life," Amaru finished, flexing her hands in her lap. "I can't allow it. I'll have to leave again."

"That would seem like the best option," Rovinald started to say, but then he shook his head. "But no, I will have to forbid it. I've not risen to this position by not being able to protect my own. And if you really are something sent to us by Yamaria, then I would be foolish to let you go out into the proverbial jaws of the wolf."

"But I'll get all of you killed!" Amaru protested.

"Do you remember nothing about my promise to you, Amaru?" Alaric admonished. Amaru looked at him in astonishment. "I told you that you aren't allowed to put yourself in danger alone anymore." He touched her shoulder gently. "I know what you're feeling. That you think about that shows just how wonderful of a person you are. I love that about you, Amaru, but Rovinald is right. You can't just sacrifice yourself for the sake of others all the time. Be a little selfish, if not for you, for me."

Dalphamair nodded. "Fleeing'll get you nowhere, girl. And remember what I just said, yer the hope that Yamaria sent. And I ain't lettin' that hope leave us in her dust 'cause she wants to be a martyr of sorts."

Rovinald looked on with sympathy. "Like your friends, I admire your bravery, Lady Sunbrand. But I believe that you are mistaken about the scale of this event. As I said earlier, I've received many reports about both these Chillfang and the scorpion things."

"Chitinites, Yamaria called them," Amaru supplied.

"Chitinites, a strange name." Rovinald scratched his beard a bit.

"She says to use that name, as most people would be unable to pronounce their ancient title."

"Hit me," Alaric said, confident that no word could best him.

Amaru looked keenly at him. "Takrincahalarkhae," she said, pronunciation crisp and perfect.

"Could I get that in the common tongue please?" Alaric asked sheepishly.

"Chitinite," Amaru answered without breaking stride. Did Alaric detect a hint of smugness there? The elf was proud.

"Chitinite it is then," Alaric said, thoroughly humbled.

Rovinald chuckled. "Anyway, as I was saying, these creatures are doing more than just targeting you. They've been causing trouble all over the Scorched Waste, and I doubt that they're going to stop here, especially if they don't get you." He held up a finger to forestall

Amaru's rebuttal. "But failure to capture you might delay them a bit. Perhaps long enough for Leonidas to tell the king about what's going on. Then people will be prepared, if Yamaria sees it in her to put some sense into that old fool!"

Amaru gasped. "That's treason talk!"

"Girl"—Rovinald looked down his nose at Amaru—"Godfrey doesn't even recognize us as part of the kingdom. So by his rules, we can't commit treason against him. Besides, I'm just stating the truth, as I'm sure Leonidas told you something similar."

"He did," Amaru conceded. "So what is your plan to keep me away from the Chillfang if I'm not allowed to protect you by leaving?"

Rovinald looked glad that Amaru wasn't going to argue that point any further. "That's what I was hoping you would help me figure out."

"What I said to Sir Lion wasn't just a bunch of empty platitudes," Dalphamair said. "My mace is yours, and I say we go stick it right up the Chillfang's lupine arses!"

"Are you insane, dwarf?" Alaric exclaimed. "You would just deliver the bastards what they're looking for! Should we take some of those fancy desert sashes and wrap her up like a pretty little package too?"

"And what would you have her do?" Dalph countered. "You just said we weren't going to let her run around the desert, waiting to get killed."

"Do you think I don't realize that? At least my plan gives her a chance to escape!" Alaric suddenly flared up in anger. "Just because your preferred solution to things is smashing heads doesn't make it the smartest option! In fact, it's the dumbest possible choice! What she needs to do is leave the desert, get as far away from the Chillfang as possible."

"Damnable elf, cowardly as ever!" Dalphamair taunted. "Why don't you go back to your forest?"

"Cowardly? Why, you little bastard. You ought to return to your hill," Alaric countered. "Or do you even belong there? You've got the build of a mountain dwarf, and yet here you are doing hill dwarf things! Your battle lust makes mountain life too boring?"

"Boys!" Amaru raised her typically serene voice to a level denoting that she was fed up. "Will you both stop bickering like children?" She glared fiercely at the both of them. "Yamaria, you'd never guess you were both more than a century old," the Fyroxi girl sighed. "You both raise good points." She addressed the dwarf first. "Though I agree that the Chillfang need to be destroyed, Alaric is right; we shouldn't just charge in blindly. At least not with what we currently have available. I'd say wait until we have a better clue about what we are facing and perhaps until Leonidas convinces the king to send aid." Alaric smiled smugly, and Amaru turned the glare on the elf. The grin immediately shriveled. "When I started this journey, I expected to spend my life on the run from the Chillfang. Then I met you, and I realized that perhaps I didn't have to do that. Perhaps, I thought, I could make some difference, have a life that wasn't lived in constant fear. That being considered, remember what I told Leonidas. I will *not* leave the desert, not until I know that its people are safe or as safe as they can be."

"Then we are at an impasse," Rovinald said. "Luckily, I believe I have a solution. One that allows us to keep tabs on you and also face our threat at the same time. You folks know the most about our foe, little as that might be, so my thinking is that you stay here with the Water Callers and guide us in how to best remedy what they've done and, if it comes to it, fight them."

All three of them considered the plan. It seemed like a sound one, fulfilling all their needs for now, and if they waited as Amaru suggested, they could get the soldier power they needed to strike definitively against the Chillfang and Venomsting.

"Aye, it makes more sense than either of our plans," Dalphamair admitted. "I like it."

Amaru had to agree. "It seems the best option," she replied an unintentional mirror of Rovinald's earlier words.

"Besides," Alaric said lightly, "I think my fans might rip me apart if I tried to leave for good. It's amazing how being deprived of good music makes its reappearance so sweet!" The bard had amassed quite the fan base among the Water Callers, and as Celwyn had predicted, he rarely had a day off playing, not that he minded of course.

"Great!" Rovinald exclaimed, clapping his hands. "That's all decided. Feel free to kick back and refresh for a few days; you've all earned it. I'll start getting people ready to defend. I know some of our Sandwards are getting pretty bored, so I'm sure they won't mind." He stood and crossed to the door. "Whatever endeavors we face, may Yamaria grant us success."

Dalphamair stood, stretching his stout legs, and followed Rovinald to the door. "Aye, I'm glad that's all figured out. I'm going to go feed Priscilla now." The dwarf turned and left to feed his goat, leaving Amaru and Alaric sitting in the tent.

"What a crazy few days, hmm?" Alaric said when they were alone. "First, we have a magical sandstorm with creatures that nobody has ever seen except in their nightmares. Then we find ourselves in the City of Tents and off to rescue a captured knight. We learn that you are, in fact, the most magnificent Fyroxi that Yamaria has ever blessed this continent with. And now here we are, selected as the heads of a salvation effort for the Scorched Waste!"

Amaru was reminded of Durrigan, who called her the Fyroxi's salvation. Had Yamaria actually called her that? Was she the saving grace for their dying race and perhaps even more?

"We're like the desert's Lightstriders!" Alaric concluded.

Amaru smiled at that. They were definitely the desert's deliverance, at least in Alaric's eyes. "We've not heard much about these Lightstriders here in the desert. To be sure, none of them come around here. Would you mind telling me about them?"

"Given what Sir Leonidas and Rovinald said about Godfrey's view of the desert, that doesn't surprise me. It's unfortunate since one of them came from the desert. Now how best to start." The elf snapped his fingers in sudden realization. "I wrote a song about them, which I could sing to you if you'd like."

Amaru smiled and nodded. "I'd like that quite a bit." She loved listening to Alaric sing. His voice was just so beautiful and full of passion. She could tell that the bard cared about his music and put his all into every piece he wrote and performed.

"Well, it just so happens that I like nothing more than serenading you," Alaric said, pulling out his lute from its travel bag. "Prepare your ears for the 'Ode to Striding Light.'"

O! Hail, Lightstriders, what a grand old band
    they are.
A land beholden to them, as they fight and travel
    far.
Sun's Reach has never shone any brighter
Since their forebears led the wars against the
    Nighters.
To protect people is their troth. To their blades,
    our foes shall fall.
To this land they swore an oath, forth they come
    to answer the call.

Leader of all, protector of king, this man stands
    proud.
Casinius Brightblade, born from a line of heroes.
His allegiance to this land has been firmly avowed.
With ancient family blade in hand to the top, he
    rose.

O! Hail, Brightblade, do your land an honor.
Break the shields of foes and fiends,
Heedless of what danger means!
Any forced to fight with you will surely be a goner!

Born from a desert tribe, stern and fierce as could be,
Galbraith Severesse brings fury to all who do wrong.
When she comes to enemies, they beg and take
    a knee.
For they know when great axes do throw, life
    shall not be long.

O! Hail, Severesse, do your land this honor,
End your foes in mindless rage,
Then we can turn the page!
Any forced to fight with you will surely be a goner!

Coming from the race of elf, long of life and long
    of spear,
Smiting foes with spear and spell, Vedalken rides
    forth!
Mounted upon unicorn grand, this elf has seen
    many a year.
To see him is to know the force that strikes fear
    in all the north!

O! Hail, Spellstroke, do your land this honor,
Cast foes up from darkest depth,
Give them fate they must accept.
Any forced to fight with you will surely be a goner!

Call forth Dwarven Shield Maiden, a hero from
    the hills!
Raerizen the Beardless, for whom no death knell
    tolls.
She needs only hammer and spit, no wish in her
    for frills.
Foe nor food can best her; to Yamaria, she sends
    their souls.

O! Hail, Devourer, do your land this honor.
With a thirst for fight
Or hungry might,
Any forced to fight with you will surely be a goner!

Last but not least, the soul without flesh,
Tinco Anar, the man avenging ancient past.
Given a new steel body, may skills stay fresh!
Unknown and unbowed, from this day to the last.

O! Hail, Steel Revenant, do your land this honor,
Go forth, Metal Sun.
Until battle, you've won!
Any forced to fight with you will surely be a goner!

Alaric repeated the first stanza one last time, before finally dropping off. "Pretty much tells you everything you need to know about the Lightstriders on the surface. That's one of my most popular songs," he said proudly. "And it was a devil to write."

"I can imagine," Amaru said, shocked. "It truly was a powerful piece. Are you sure that you wrote that?" she asked teasingly.

"My lady, you wound me." Alaric placed a hand flat on his chest. "I am more than just a pretty voice and a pair of handsome legs." He tapped his head. "I have many a song fragment floating around up here. Perhaps one day, I can write a song about you." Alaric shrugged, then let out a long, thin sigh. "I really wish you would consider my offer, though I understand why you won't. I just really think you would like the kingdom proper. Haven't you ever wondered what's out there?"

"Perhaps a few times," Amaru admitted. "But the situation is dire here; I cannot leave."

"I know I wouldn't expect you to be the kind to galivant around while people are in danger. It's one of the things I love about you." Alaric squeezed Amaru's hand. "Maybe, whenever all of this is done, we could go on a journey together, see the sights. I really want to show you the five cities."

Amaru smiled and gave Alaric's hand a squeeze in return. "I would like that, Alaric. It sounds like an interesting time, to say the least. I've enjoyed showing you around the place I grew up, and I'm sure that we'll both be seeing even more of the desert before long. It would be only fair to let you show me some of your favorite places." The girl nodded. "Consider the journey planned."

Alaric suddenly felt as if his mind was buzzing, and his heart was strangely in his head. Not trusting himself to form a response, the usually loquacious bard smiled and bobbed his head a couple of times before standing to leave. He had some thinking to do.

CAITRIAL
A Fateful Meeting

Caitrial Rainclaw slipped into the lavender dress that had just recently come in from Barnio's shop. The day of the noble wedding and ball had finally arrived. The crisp purple fabric felt foreign against her skin, so used to scratchy wool tunics and leather. Despite her reservations at first, she had to admit that it felt good to wear this sort of clothing. Walking over to the closet, Caitrial dusted off the tall mirror that her parents had gifted her when she moved out. It had been put in storage during the moving process for safety's sake and never came back out. Arcadia didn't like being reminded of her appearance since it made others hate her so much, and for her own part, Caitrial never saw the need to stare at herself. Working at the smithy left her toned and muscular but often covered in soot. Besides, she heard enough from men that she was attractive that she didn't need to look for herself. *And that's without making an effort to look good*, she thought wryly. Almost as foreign as the dress was the woman who stared back at her in the glassy surface.

Today, in preparation for the reception, she had spent nearly an hour in the bath, scrubbing out soot that had been ground into her skin for years, it seemed. Her long brown hair, no longer blurred by the dust and ash, glistened in its single braid, snaking down the center of her head and down her neck.

The garment was flattering, she had to admit. Her lean muscles played underneath the long, slim sleeves and flashed out of the small slashes that Barnio had removed as a final touch. It was a wonder that the man didn't get more business. "Arcadia! It's almost time to go," she called across the hall. "Are you ready?"

"Almost" came the rasp from the other room. Adorning a silver bracelet that had been one of her first successful projects at the smithy, she went downstairs to await her sister. Finally, down she came. At first, Caitrial wondered whether she'd even changed her clothing, a long almost-robelike gown colored black and silver hung around the Khindre's bony frame. It was only when she saw the ribbons on the shoulders that she knew it was, in fact, Barnio's dress.

"You look great," Caitrial assured Arcadia, who still looked uncomfortable.

"There will be many who know us there," Arcadia said. "I'm glad that Barnio did so well on this, but it doesn't mean I like the idea of going to this…celebration. Were it not Emery who invited us, I might have declined."

"Now, now," she chided, not knowing just how much like Reyna she sounded, "everything is going to be okay. Not even the most radical fool would consider hurting you, given who requested your presence." She decided not to mention her own apprehension to Arcadia. Caitrial was sure that the men who'd tried to court her would be among the guests, and the thought of facing them without a hammer on hand to dissuade them perturbed her.

She took her younger sister's cold hand in her own warm grip. "Come, it's not a short walk to the castle." Caitrial disliked the thought of walking the city streets in this clothing, for risk of damaging it, but she supposed that was what she got for not being noble. However, when she opened the door, much to her surprise, there was a carriage waiting. The horse attached to the front sneezed, and the driver looked down.

"Ah, good," he said. "I was beginning to wonder if I'd gone to the wrong house."

"You're here for us?" Caitrial asked, surprised.

"You *are* the Rainclaw sisters, right?" he asked, checking a memo by his other side. "I'm here to pick you up and bring you to the party. Special orders from Princess Emery." Caitrial felt a surge of affection for the princess as she climbed into the back, helping Arcadia onto the step. "She said there were three of you. Is that why I have a second address?"

"Yes," Caitrial replied. "Our other sister lives with our parents still."

"That's the second Khindre, right? Lives at Cynderstone?" Caitrial gave an affirmative gesture, and the driver nodded. "Just need to know my clients." Caitrial wondered if it had been just luck that their driver didn't have an issue with Khindre using his services or whether that had been arranged by the princess as well. They pulled up to the bar, and Reyna quickly stepped out of the door.

"I've always wondered what a gathering such as this would be like, though I never expected I'd actually get to experience one." Excitement shone in the golden globes of Reyna's eyes. "How do I look?" The blue-and-pink backless dress looked wonderful on her svelte sister. It had been crafted from a light and airy fabric and accomplished without fault the purpose Barnio had intended. Caitrial was sure that the nobles would be infatuated with her, even as they were mentally cursing her race. "I've no doubt that your feet will be sore from all the dancing you'll do tonight."

Reyna smiled glowingly and turned to converse with Arcadia. While they talked, Caitrial reflected on how glad she was that there was no bad blood between the twins. When Sardan and Cos had shunted Arcadia from the house and slandered her name, Caitrial had been extremely worried about the two. Given the nature of Arcadia's magic and the origin, their older sister had expected a rift to form. But no such thing had happened. The twins were still close friends, and Caitrial knew that they helped each other in dealing with their magic. Reyna had always had difficulties restraining the innate power, so strong was it in her blood. It was part of the reason why she practiced so often, to let out the pressure that formed. Arcadia, on the other hand, had no trouble restraining it, but the dark nature of the magic seemed to gnaw on her from the inside. It explained her reclusive, subdued personality. Caitrial tried to keep Arcadia from getting angry, fearing what might happen if the young Khindre snapped. Her younger sister had just barely managed to contain herself when Grayson Redwyn had hurt Reyna. The prince had been lucky to get away with only a slight nip from the shadows.

Suddenly, she looked up, and there was the castle, standing tall and magnificent in the late afternoon sunlight. Their driver maneuvered the cart around the others, flashing a pendant with the phoenix symbol to the other drivers and the guards patrolling the roadway. "Being friends with the princess gives you benefits for sure," he said, as he tugged on the reins. "Y'all have a good night now but don't dance too hard; you'll still need feet to make it back to the carriage. Name's Blake, by the by. Ask for me when the thing's all done; save us both a lot of trouble." He allowed the three girls to step out and safely away before setting his horse back in motion.

They'd been left by a separate hall, connected by a corridor to the main building. Although the castle had five towers, which drew the eye, several smaller structures were splattered around, joined to the Roost with shorter rays. The music that flowed from the hall along with the general hubbub around the entrance called to the guests. The three sisters walked forward and got into line, which moved along steadily. At the two large doors, guards stood with lists in hand. They were Lord Geurus's men, clad entirely in their black armor, helmets and all. As the sisters approached, the man to their side stared down at them as if expecting something. The two guards in front of the doors had their spears crossed, barring the entrance. There was a moment of silence, Caitrial unsure what the man was expecting or what the list was for. Finally, someone hissed behind them, "Say your name," then in a quieter voice that was clearly meant to be inaudible, "stupid peasant."

Caitrial decided to save her withering glare; nothing was going to ruin tonight. She was at a high-class event, and damn it, she was going to have a good time. She stated their names to the guard, and he nodded. The spears uncrossed, and the wedding was open to them.

Walking into the hall where the whole affair was taking place was like moving into a dream. Like Reyna, Caitrial had heard tales of the massive parties that King Redwyn was famous for throwing, and she'd always been envious of the nobles. *And now here I am. All I had to do was be sisters with a couple of Khindre*, she thought wryly.

The ball was everything that she'd ever imagined, music played from the balconies, the lights flashing and swaying along with the tune. The high ceiling sparkled with dim points of colorful lights, in a pattern that looked like the stars her masters had talked about. *Lord Geurus's doing no doubt.* The foreign lord had been seen at the king's side speaking to and advising him in what matters no commoner woman would know. Young servants scurried around the room, carrying pitchers of drink and plates of food. They slipped in and out of the crowd, weaving between legs with the ease that came only with practice. Caitrial picked something off a platter as one ran by, a slice of millet bread covered with melted cheese and olives, and popped it into her mouth. It was delicious, the cheese oozing off the bread and filling her mouth with flavor.

Small cliques of nobles had already formed around the hall; most everyone had a glass of wine in their hand and were socializing while waiting for the premier event to start. Caitrial looked and saw that the stage had been transformed into an altar for the occasion. Flowers lined every inch of the platform, and a pedestal faced outward, holding the *Solari Sancturi*, the book written by a Fyroxi priest long ago, with lessons and stories displaying of the Way of Yamaria within. Caitrial looked around for familiar faces but saw only her sisters. The Khindre both stuck by her side, away from the glares that were cast at them.

Finally, after what seemed like an eternity, doors at the back of the hall swung open, and in strode the most highly honored guests. Jovial King Godfrey looked to be half drunk already, with how he laughed at everything that Lord Geurus beside him said. Arm in arm with him was his weary queen. She looked as if she hadn't slept properly in weeks. Caitrial knew the look in her eyes, even though all the skin-deep imperfections were covered by makeup. It was something she had seen in her own eyes once upon a time. When she'd begun work as a smith, she'd stayed up all night, multiple days a week, working out any flaw in her weapons or shields. It wasn't until her masters noticed her rate of work and impressed upon her the necessity of sleep that she took a rest. They had admired her fierce determination however, and thus, she'd lasted there longer than any other apprentice.

Lord Geurus and his wife Cereos were resplendent in their dark raiment; and both looked sober, strong, and healthy. Caitrial couldn't help but wonder what others were thinking about this sight. Their own king wasn't making too good a show whereas the new foreign couple seemed immaculate. Their daughter Velara came with Grayson beside her, though the prince looked uncomfortable with her presence. His eyes searched the crowd, taking advantage of his higher perch. They seemed to light up with joy and relief as they looked toward the Rainclaw sisters and Reyna waved at him. His resting annoyed face cleared into a smile, and with a willing nod from the Khindre, a tacit promise for at least one dance was made.

Then, of course, came Emery, with Tarus beside her. Like everyone in the room, Tarus couldn't seem to keep his eyes off the princess. When Caitrial had seen it in the shop before, the gown had been gorgeous. Now that it was fitted and worn by the princess, it was, as Emery had said, perfection. Tarus looked positively dull next to her in his stark grays. Emery gave a small turn, and the frills on the bottom spun, appearing as flame. The audience gasped in tandem at the visual illusion, and Caitrial wondered if Reyna might have cast a spell on the princess. But the sisters were just as in awe as everyone else.

Behind the princess, tall and imposing, was a face that Reyna quickly recognized with surprise. "Sir Leonidas?" she whispered. "He actually returned!"

Caitrial looked over this knight, who'd been off on a mission for the longest time, and apparently, he must have found his way back. Caitrial envied Leonidas, as he could go out on adventures while Caitrial was locked down by her work and by keeping Arcadia safe. And of course, a lack of formal training never helped. When last she had seen the knight, he'd had been clad in castle-forged steel, plain and dull, like everything that Jorjen made. Now he seemed to have lost some weight, and the bushy beard that once clung to his chin was gone, revealing a handsome face with robust features yet a gentle disposition. Though Emery walked in with Lord Tarus, it didn't escape Caitrial that she stuck closer to Leonidas. Out of respect to

Emery, Arcadia and Reyna had actually kept the fact of Emery's love for the knight from Caitrial, so the smith just figured that Emery wasn't quite used to Tarus Gardstar yet.

It seemed that most of the money had gone into the party and entertainment, as the marriage itself was simple yet sweet. It was clear that Mia Rothsster and Ferrin Leygrain loved each other deeply. Their vows were heartfelt, and the kiss they shared at the behest of the priest was long and genuine.

After the wedding itself was over, the feast began in earnest. A bountiful variety of foodstuffs flowed out from the castle's kitchen. Even living in a relatively wealthy tavern, the Rainclaw sisters saw more food passed around than they had in most of their lives. Caitrial sampled only small bites of everything, to ensure that each dish could be tasted. Crispy chickens, fresh bread, salads of fresh greens, and steamed vegetables were piled on their plates.

After the meal came the dance so everyone could work off their dinners. Caitrial found herself passed between many different men. All the single men and some of the married ones took the opportunity to comment on her beauty. She ignored the compliments, her mind focused elsewhere. She was a fighter and a smith, not a noble. Though none was foolish enough to say it to her face, Caitrial heard the mutters of "commoner" and "kin to devils." Like the slights before, they went ignored.

She might have done at least marginally better had she been paying attention to the dance itself. But her eyes wandered, taking in the sights. Tarus and Emery did the first dance together, but afterward and seemingly much to Tarus's displeasure, they found other partners. Emery danced most with Leonidas, hogging him, to the annoyance of the other women on the floor. The princess looked utterly at peace with the knight's hands on her waist and shoulder and leaned in a little closer than she perhaps intended to. When the song ended, Leonidas said something to Emery and broke off, starting in on the queue of people awaiting a turn with him.

As was expected of the married couple, Mia and Ferrin danced with the other members of their lover's family and enjoyed every minute of it, most of all when they were pushed back into each other's arms.

Arcadia stood in the back of the room, watching the festivities but refusing to take to the floor herself. She spoke a few words to the servant boys as they ran about their work. Looking at her other sister caused Caitrial to smile. Reyna and Grayson stood close together, the Khindre's arms around the human boy's neck. The prince stared down the entrancing half devil next to him. His eyes showed only admiration and love. They stood very close, Grayson's arms wrapped all the way around Reyna's waist. Reyna gladly smiled up at the prince. Caitrial had heard from Arcadia that the young man spent much more time around Cynderstone and not often drinking. Caitrial had to admit that it felt good, in a perverse sort of way, to see the prince defying expectations. She wondered whether they noticed the daggers in the eyes of the nobles around them or if they cared at all.

Suddenly, she was aware of someone next to her and spun around, to find herself face-to-face with Sir Leonidas himself. He bowed cordially. "Milady, would you do me the honor of a dance?"

The previous song had just ended, leading into something slower. "I'm afraid I'm not skilled at the dances," Caitrial apologized. She was stunned by the smile that spread over the knight's face.

"Do you think I am?" One of his eyebrows arched high. "I'm a warrior, not a dancer. I learned these steps practicing with the princess rather than on my own initiative." Caitrial was struck by how similar his words were to her own thoughts.

"I'm sure it wouldn't do either of us any harm then," she conceded and allowed him to move in and take her arm and waist. "Let's dance."

Leonidas and Caitrial danced around the room, stumbling and awkward, occasionally bumping into other couples, but they didn't care. The knight laughed good-naturedly as he nearly tripped and the smith's arm shot out to stabilize him.

"Most women wouldn't be able to support someone of my bulk," Leonidas commented, nothing mocking in his voice. "It's rare to see a woman in this city who would work on their muscles rather than their hair. It's honestly rather refreshing. Reminds me of Tara…" he trailed off wistfully, and Caitrial recalled something she'd heard from city gossip in the market. Leonidas had been married once, to a girl in the village where he was born. But she had apparently died, which drove Leo to become a knight. She was curious to learn more about this story, but this was not an occasion to talk about death.

"So is it true that you only recently returned from one of your missions from the king?" she asked instead.

"Yes, though I'm the only one who did," Leonidas answered mournfully. "Our force was overtaken by skilled adversaries. The king underestimated what we would be going up against, and I made a mistake that cost most of my soldiers their lives."

"Well, nobody's perfect," Caitrial said, deflective. "Don't let it bother you too much. It would be better to celebrate their lives than mourn their deaths. Did your mission at least come with some success?"

Leonidas nodded, waves rippling through his chin-length brown hair. "After my rescue, I learned something about possible enemy movements and dangers to the kingdom, which I hope to convince the king to act upon. Let me ask you, Caitrial." The smith was surprised that he knew her name. "Do you believe in the divines?"

Caitrial unconsciously reached for her back, where a broadsword would be fastened at most any other time. On it was inscribed "In the divines, we trust." "I suppose you could say I do."

"I saw some bizarre things out there, in that desert. Some things that I wouldn't believe possible had I no faith in Yamaria." Leonidas shook his head. "Whatever happened there, I'm glad I went. All it cost me was my armor and hammer."

Seeing an opportunity, Caitrial grasped onto that idea. "Your captors stole your armaments?" Leo nodded, and the smith smiled. "Perhaps I could go about making something for you."

The knight's eyebrows rose again. "I was planning to go to Jorjen to get my work done. It'll be as plain as ever, but that serves just fine."

"Leonidas Braveheart"—Caitrial shook her head admonishingly—"a man such as you shouldn't be content with plain armor."

"Plain armor works just as well as any other," he commented, looking a little less sure.

Caitrial nodded at that. "True, but you are the captain of the royal guard, Princess Emery's personal guardian. I feel like you ought to stand out a bit, as your beautiful princess does." She gave the knight a sincere smile. "Besides, if I'm honest, I'm just trying to get more work. Making only construction equipment, tools, and wagon parts all day can get a bit dull."

"I would imagine," Leo conceded, a large white-toothed smile revealing itself now. "And I'm sure that a suit of armor would be a handsome payday for you."

Caitrial's grin was not at all sheepish. "That it would be! Though, I must admit, I'm an admirer of your skill and what you do for the people. It would be an honor to craft armor for someone so bent on helping folk such as us. Me thinks you had a good influence on Emery, made her learn the right way."

Leonidas blushed and pushed his long hair away from his face. "Such praise, milady," he thought for a moment and nodded. "Very well, I'll trust you to make my armor and weapons. Either tomorrow or the next day, I shall come by so that you can take the necessary measurements. I'll admit that I've been curious about your masters' skills for a while. It would only be right to support you and your sisters with my gold rather than Jorjen and the king, both of which have plenty as is."

Caitrial bowed her head in thanks. "I'm curious, Leonidas. Why did you approach me for a dance?"

"Besides wanting to give everyone a fair chance to dance with all the guests? I wanted to meet you, seeing as you are the protector of one of the Rainclaw twins."

"Oh, really." Caitrial was intrigued now. "Why would my protecting Arcadia interest you?"

"Many reasons." Leonidas spun Caitrial out and pulled her back in, as the dance required. Caitrial thought it was rather strange to be having such a serious conversation during a dance like this. The thought almost made her laugh. "Unlike many, I don't see the issue with Khindre. I've been to Carrion Cove, where many of them... I'd say where they live, but that's not exactly the right description for what they do. It's a shame what they have to go through. I'm just glad to see a kindred spirit, is all."

"I've been treated to many surprises this evening," Caitrial admitted in wonderment. "The princess sent a carriage over to pick us up. The driver was kind to my sisters, and now you as well. Why is it that you care so much about Arcadia and Reyna?"

"Honestly?" Leonidas looked into Caitrial's eyes. "Your sisters support Princess Emery when she's down and gave her comfort and company that I couldn't provide when I was imprisoned. For that, I will be eternally grateful. But even before that, they make her happy, and that makes me happy."

"You really care about the princess, don't you?" Seeing how tightly Emery had stuck to the knight, Caitrial couldn't help but pry.

"Her father gave me a new chance at life when he took me into the guard. I appreciate the king because of this, despite any short-comings he may have. And in protecting the princess, I found a life-long duty guarding someone that I enjoy the company of. I suppose I have grown fond of the princess, yes." He spoke with pure respect and reverence for the royal family.

"Emery is lucky to have you," she said at last. Before he could reply, the music cut off abruptly, and the dance ended, as King Godfrey Redwyn and Lord Geurus Gardstar took the stage.

"Good evening, ladies and gentlemen," the king began. "I hope that you've all had a fantastic night at this wedding between the great houses of Rothsster and Leygrain. Before I dismiss you all so that you can sleep off the wine I'm sure you have all drank copious amounts of, I—no, we—would like to make one final announcement."

Lord Geurus raised a hand for silence, quelling the murmurs that had overtaken the crowd. "I'm sure that many of you have won-dered why it is that I have come to Searstar with my family. It would take a blind man to miss the stares! I do not blame you for any suspi-cion you may have, but tonight we will be answering your questions once and for all.

"In the past months, I have been searching for a good young lord for my beautiful daughter to marry," Godfrey announced. "I received many an offer, but none so enticing as what Lord Geurus had. You all have seen his men around the city, here to protect you in the case of trying times."

"My family and I came here to seek out the possibility of an alliance with the king of Sun's Reach, and though we only have a short time meeting in person and several letters as experience with each other, we are certain that this is the right move to make," Geurus stated, patting the king's shoulder in a friendly gesture.

"As such, we have decided that it is time for us to make the official announcement." Godfrey swept his arms out. Caitrial had to admit that the two played well off each other. She couldn't help but wonder if this had all been rehearsed. "My daughter, Princess Emery Redwyn, will be married to Tarus Gardstar before the summer is out!"

"I can't wait for the day when my son sits the Highsun Seat," Geurus began before Godfrey cut him off.

"Don't forget, milord, that it will be Emery who has the throne, royal blood and all." The king had a laugh in his throat. "But Tarus will fit perfectly alongside her."

The eldest Rainclaw sister felt the temperature in the room decrease by a few degrees, as the foreign lord gave the king a quick icy glare. Then Geurus laughed. "Of course, of course! My mistake, my king. It must be the wine, some of the finest I've ever sampled, for sure." Geurus managed to save face and returned to his previous energy. "I think that everyone would agree that after dessert, we must retire for the night. Most of these fine men and women still need to work in the morning! With this joyous news in our hearts, let us return to business as usual!" There was a general murmur of consensus, as people returned to their tables.

Caitrial looked around the room. The Rothsster and Leygrain families looked shocked at this announcement. Apparently, they hadn't been told that the thunder from their wedding would be stolen. Besides them, mostly joy filled the room. Some of them had the chance to meet with Geurus, and they could see why the king enjoyed him so. Lord Gardstar was a persuasive man with a wealth of experience on top of his soldiers. They were glad for the match and the long-awaited marriage of Emery.

The only one who didn't seem quite so happy about the announcement was the princess. Caitrial was confused. Wouldn't the princess have a say in her marriage? Was she being coerced into the match? Despite what she'd heard about the king being a fool, she didn't want to believe that he would disregard his daughter's wishes.

Emery walked over to the pair, barely paying attention to the people wishing her congratulations. "Leonidas," she said faintly, "I need some air. Would you please come with me?"

Leo released himself from the smith. "I shall be back shortly, Caitrial," he promised, slipping one arm gently around the princess, who leaned into him.

The smith wondered if this new marriage announcement would allow them to meet again. Caitrial hoped so. Kindred spirits indeed! It would be more than pleasant to see the knight again, for he seemed to be both honorable and wise. If nothing else, she could ask Leo when he came for his armor fitting. And if their schedules didn't match, Caitrial wouldn't deny the possibility of changing. She could always use another friend, especially a friend like Leonidas Braveheart.

LEONIDAS
Affection Uncovered

Leonidas nodded to the men who were guarding the garden door, luckily his own men rather than the strange, silent ones that Geurus had brought. As the knight and the princess stepped out from the stuffy ballroom, Leo looked down at his princess. Emery had her head against his side, almost leaning against him for support. She stared blindly ahead, he could tell, by the vacant expression in her eyes. The girl trusted Leonidas to guide her to the right place, and he figured he knew exactly where to go. In the center of the garden complex, there was a small pavilion with a latticework roof. Shafts of red-orange light shone through the gaps, peppering the floor with its radiance like a volley of arrows. This was one of Emery's favorite places to sit and read, with the fountain bubbling nearby and the sweet aroma of flowers around her. Leonidas guided his princess over to the bench in its center and lowered her down onto it. Emery's eyes were downcast, her fingers fidgeting in her lap.

"Is everything all right, Princess?" Leonidas asked, moving over to the fountain. His soldier training on top of the short time he'd spent in the desert had taught him to always carry a waterskin with him. He filled it with fresh, sweet water and brought it over to Emery. "I know it's warm in there. Perhaps that's getting to you. Take a drink; it will refresh you."

The princess followed his orders dutifully. It was a beautiful night for the wedding. A few clouds formed in the sky, providing brief splotches of cover from the sun, so the exquisite costumes wouldn't be ruined by too much sweat. Leo gazed down at the garment made by Barnio. A beautiful dress, for sure. He knew that the princess had been so happy to see everyone's reaction. He also knew something that few people did. His first meeting with Barnio and his son, Barnibus, had marked him as different than the Humans or Elves that Leo had met. First, there had been suspicion because he didn't want to think about what a moon elf was doing in Sun's Reach. But meeting and talking with the clothier had revealed that his family had been trapped on the wrong side of the barrier after the Eclipse. Leonidas felt sorry for the man. It must have been difficult to hide his identity from a land where all the residents would be more like to string you from a post than serve you lunch.

Emery puffed out a long shuddering breath, and Leonidas returned from inside his head. He wrapped one arm around the princess, and she put two around him, sobbing softly into his shirt. "Hey," he soothed, running a hand through her red hair. "I know you aren't used to having so many nobles staring at you, but it's hardly something to cry about."

"That's not why I'm crying," she said softly, Leonidas needing to lean down to hear. "And I think you know it."

"True, but I don't know why you're crying, so I had to think of something off the top of my head," Leonidas defended. "Would you have preferred it if instead I asked if you were possessed?"

Her shoulders shook silently with laughter. She turned her red tear-streaked face up to his. "No, I think I would know if I were possessed."

"Or the spirit inside of you could be a skilled actor," he pointed out, and both cracked smiles. Neither of them believed a lick of the rumors that spirits from the other planes could inhabit mortals, so it was a go-to for Leonidas when he needed to cheer Emery up.

"Fair enough, but by that logic, how do we know that you aren't possessed, hm?" She dropped off and gazed into Leonidas's eyes. He smiled down at her.

"Princess?" Leo called tenderly, "I'll ask again. Is everything all right? Why were you crying?"

"It's the marriage announcement," she said after an uncertain pause. "It was just very sudden."

"Didn't your father tell you?" Leonidas asked, puzzled.

Emery shook her head. "I figured he would ask me, but he never did. And now he goes and makes this announcement."

"Well, that doesn't seem right." Leo's mouth stretched into a thin line. "I'd say you should definitely talk to him."

Emery perked up at the suggestion. "Yes! I think we should talk to him." She moved in a little closer. "Maybe we can get him to change his mind."

"I figured you would want that to be a private matter." Leonidas scratched his head. "But I suppose I could go with you if it is what you wish."

"It is all I wish," she answered quietly. A long shuddering sigh escaped from her throat. "I—I love you, Leo." Suddenly, the princess pressed her warm lips against his.

Emery had imagined this moment at least half a hundred times since Leo had returned home. In her most recent version, they were out in the woods, just the two of them on a horse ride. The warm sun beat down on them, but neither of them cared. Finally, they reached a clearing and let their horses graze while they set out a blanket on the springy grass. What was in the basket always changed, but that barely mattered. After they had finished eating, Leonidas had gone through his exercise drills, with his sword in hand. Muscles flexed against his shirt, and sweat glistened on his forehead. She'd asked to give it a try, and Leo had guided her through the motions, his body enticingly close to her own. As she attempted the simple jabs and cuts, his hand guiding her arm, Emery tripped on a loose stone. The princess fell back, directly into his arms. She'd looked up into the knight's eyes, heard his rumbling laugh, felt the pressure of his hands on her sides, and then felt their lips meet before the vision faded.

Things are always different in your imaginations, she reflected. This wasn't a forest clearing but part of the palace gardens. It was nighttime after a dance, though Leonidas still tasted faintly salty from sweat. She'd been crying from an unexpected announcement rather than laughing at a clumsy mistake.

And in her dreams, Leonidas had always kissed her back.

The knight's body was as rigid as a stone, his expression unreadable.

"Leo?" Emery whispered, wondering why he'd gone so still.

At length, he spoke again, "Princess, you are soon to be a married woman, this is no time for such jests. Mayhap you drunk a bit too much wine." Emery's expression was so wounded that Leonidas realized that this was no idle joke. The princess's eyes were clouded with confusion, but they were still clear of the bleariness of alcohol. "By Yamaria, Princess," he muttered, pushing his hair behind his ears, "I don't know what to say."

"Don't let a lack of fancy words stop you." Emery's tone was full of painful pleading. "Just say how you feel."

"I feel… I feel that you've taken my fondness for you for something else," Leonidas began. "I do love you, Princess, but it's because you remind me of my little sister when she… I don't… This isn't… I'm sorry, Emery. You are going to be married to Tarus Gardstar."

"B-but, Leo," Emery sputtered, desperately searching for some way to convince him, "I don't love Tarus. I-I love you! I know you lost your sweetheart to bandits before you came here. And I know you haven't chosen to love again. Let me be your wife, Leo! You could be king, and together, we can destroy all of the bandits this kingdom has. You would be a good king; I know it in my heart of hearts!"

The knight was stunned. "Princess, I am ten years your senior and only a knight. I'm far too low ranking; people wouldn't take kindly to such an arrangement." Leonidas shook his head. "A match between us, I couldn't see it working. It would be resisted by most every noble. And if I were king, I couldn't go out to fight the bandits. I would be an up-jumped knight, sending people out to die for my personal vengeance. I couldn't do that."

"I don't care a shade about your class or your age. You should now that, with how I've treated the people of Searstar. I've been in love with you for years now! Are you going to tell me that it was all in vain?" Salty tears streamed down her face, which burned red.

Leonidas extracted himself from Emery's grip. "I hate causing you pain, Princess; you know that," Leonidas prefaced. "However, I must say this now. I care for you like family and as my liege lady who I am proud to serve. I await the day when you sit the Highsun Seat, and I can be your guardian and advisor. But if you harbor dreams of anything more, I'm afraid you'll be disappointed." There was great sadness and worry in his eyes. He chastely squeezed her shoulder with one hand and walked back to the ballroom, leaving Emery outside, clutching at the shards of her broken heart. The arrows of sunlight felt as if they had pierced and shattered it.

EMERY
The Sting of Love's Arrows

Emery was unsure how long she sat there, eyes burning with tears. Had she actually mistaken all his affectionate acts? "You remind me of my little sister." Was that all that his support had been, familial kinship for the girl whose father had hired him? She didn't want to believe that those years of comfort and support hadn't been anything more. With her heart on fire and a roiling wave in her stomach, Emery stared forward, barely seeing anything. She watched as the nobles streamed out of the dance hall, watched Mia and Ferrin going off to enjoy their marriage bed, and felt burning jealousy. If things had gone the way Emery had wanted tonight, she and Leo would be doing something very similar right now. She'd desired nothing quite so much as to hold Leonidas Braveheart in her arms, to invite him into her bed, if she could. But her dreams weren't reality, and now the Princess Redwyn felt like she was living a nightmare.

After many long minutes, the flood of people turned into a trickle, and one last carriage came up. Emery recognized the insignia on it: the wagon she'd procured for Caitrial and the Rainclaws. From her seat in the gazebo, she saw five figures walking out of the dance hall and heard the doors slam shut behind them. Arcadia walked by Caitrial's side, and so did Leonidas. A few paces behind them were Reyna and Grayson. The two were close together, the prince with his hand on the small of Reyna's back. As the others reached the wagon, the two turned to each other, talking softly and affectionately she knew, though Emery couldn't hear from a distance. The Khindre went on tiptoes and pressed a soft kiss onto Grayson's lips, striding back toward where Caitrial was waiting. The prince swooned a bit as if he were drunk, though the princess doubted he'd had much to drink tonight.

Emery wanted to feel proud of her brother or glad for her friend, but she couldn't. At least most of the Redwyns got what they wanted tonight.

Grayson and Reyna were together; Queen Lysaria had a night off from the king's paperwork, and Godfrey had his daughter's wedding all set up. "Congratulations, you're finally getting married," she said to herself. "Just not to the person you wanted." Emery watched as Leo gave his chivalrous farewells to the smith. She'd looked on from afar all night, as the two had talked and danced, seeming to hit it off well. Emery knew she should be happy for her best friend's sister making a new acquaintance, but her shadowed heart put a dark twist on it. What if Caitrial had something to do with Leonidas's rejection? *No*, the hopeful side of her answered. *There is nothing between them besides a new friendship.* The princess could see it in the way they walked, not close like lovers. Leonidas was just his usual chivalrous self, holding the door for Caitrial and her sisters, helping them up into the carriage.

As the wagon rumbled off and Leonidas returned to the castle, Emery continued to sit there, hurting and crying until no more tears came. The garden blurred around her, and the princess was only faintly aware of the crouched darkly clad figure that led her back to her chambers.

ALARIC
Tension and Fondness

A few days later, Alaric stretched his arms, wrapped in protective clothing, into the air unconsciously. The sun beat down overhead, and the elf could already feel sweat beading on his forehead before drying instantly, though he wasn't paying much attention. He was busy thinking. It was amazing how the Scorched Waste, which he'd thought of for so long as being the prison that Taliesin Valyaara had placed him in, had become one of his favorite places. All because of one person: Amaru Sunbrand. And therein lay the elf's most confused thoughts. From the moment Alaric had seen Amaru outside of the Solgaele Monastery, his eye had been caught. On that day, he'd labeled her as the most beautiful woman in the world. To this day, that remained true, but there was something else. Amaru was unlike any other woman he'd ever laid eyes or hands on. She was so kind and pleasant and amazing. Alaric never got tired of talking to her, and at times, he wanted nothing more than to be around her, even when there were other pressing matters to deal with. He'd had many lovers in his life; but it was thoughts of Amaru that made his hands itch, ache, and search for any excuse to touch her. Then a crushing wave of inadequacy rolled over the elf. He felt differently about Amaru than he had any other woman, but she was no ordinary girl. *She's a goddess! Or at least the child of one.* But it was close enough, and it hurt Alaric to think that. When he'd expressed his doubts of his worth before, Amaru had been quick to squash them, but they still remained. What was he? Just some bard, from a family of Elves that didn't even recognize him as part of the family. What did he have that would benefit Amaru? Nothing, he was nothing.

Alaric wondered briefly if his father even thought about him. "Probably not." Alaric shrugged. "After all, he has my sister, who's everything he wanted from me and more." As he walked, without guiding himself, he found himself by the stables and hitching posts for the camels. Standing there was Dalphamair, next to Priscilla as usual.

"You have a terrible habit of talking to yourself," the dwarf grumbled. "Almost as bad as your near-constant humming. You kept Priscilla up all night the other evening with your roving and noisemaking."

"What can I say? I'm a bard, and I need to keep the creative juices flowing."

"You need something, all right," Dalph answered.

Alaric recalled their little spat earlier that week in the tent and chewed on his lip. "I've noticed that we always tend to end up in arguments, Dalphamair." Alaric crouched down to look in the face of his dwarven ally. "I'm not sure if you can tell, but I like people. I'd rather we not fight, especially if we're going to be living and perhaps traveling together for the next...who knows how long!"

The stout man sighed and leaned back against Priscilla. Alaric imagined. "I think it's got something to do with the fact that you have her ear," Dalph grumbled.

"Who? Amaru?" Alaric was taken aback. He'd been expecting a history lesson on the Dwelven Wars, tens of hundreds of years ago. Back before there were classifications like Hill Dwarves and Wood Elves, the two races had been close friends, fighting against common enemies like the monsters that roamed the Sulfaari Expanse. Different historians had different versions of the betrayal that had caused the allies to turn, but Alaric's favorite version had to do with a small group of Dwarves and Elves that had fallen in love, creating the wholly disappointing and reviled race known as the Dwelves. Nobody had seen the Dwelves in many years, and most presumed them extinct, to few people's displeasure. "Is that really what's both-

ering you? Excuse me for laughing, but that seems like a silly griev-
ance to have."

"You heard what Amaru said. She trusts your opinion wholeheartedly," Dalph explained. "She always turns to you first, before
anybody else. You are just a bard, whereas I'm the one with actual
combat experience. I fought in the Last Astral War, and I just think
it would be nice if she'd take my thoughts into mind every once in
a while."

"I see how that could be obnoxious," Alaric admitted. "But she's
known me for longer than you, and anyone would trust a friend over
someone they'd only recently met. Besides, in the most recent case,
Rovinald had a better solution."

"Hmph, the difference between an acquaintance and a friend is
about a century," Dalph muttered an old dwarvish proverb. "But I'll
just get used to it. Just be careful. I know what people like you are
after. Don't trick her into making any rash decisions." He tugged on
the lead rope and strode off to the mess tent for supper.

Alaric was wounded that Dalph thought he would let his attrac-
tion to Amaru get in the way of his judgment, but he had a point.
Emotion clouds minds, unless you have the skill to separate the two.
But he'd had plenty of years of building that skill.

He started walking again and saw Amaru standing at the edge
of the tents, staring into space. "Dueling with unpleasant thoughts?"
he asked.

She startled at the unexpected voice but relaxed when she saw it
was only him. That made him happier than he could imagine. This
nearly unattainable girl was growing comfortable around him. It was
as Dalphamair said, Alaric had her ear.

"Not exactly," Amaru said. "Though I have been thinking about
my tribe, the Fire-Striders. I left them at a vulnerable time, and part
of me wants to go back and make sure they're still safe."

"We could always go back and check," Alaric offered. "I'm sure
that Rovinald wouldn't mind having you go see them again. In fact,
I'm sure he's planning on it. If the Fire-Striders really are the last of
your kind, they'll need all the help they can get. And more people

with us, especially skilled hunters like Fyroxi, will only be a bonus if we need to fight anything."

Alaric was right, of course, and Amaru smiled, glad to know that the elf understood. "I know that this is going to sound strange, but I don't feel like our meeting was a coincidence, Alaric. I feel as if Yamaria might have pulled a few strings so that I would meet someone like you. Someone who could help me achieve some greater destiny...whatever that is." Amaru laughed, her bright, lovable laugh making Alaric's heart swell. "I'm sure anyone would say I sound mad, going on about destiny."

"I wouldn't say so, milady." Alaric guided her toward the stables as they talked. "I believe that you are correct. Until you, I'd never had any experience with the divine, but I do not doubt that you will bring great succor to Sun's Reach, even here in the desert. And as you say, you don't know where your path will lead. To me, that's the best part of the whole adventure."

"You're right, Alaric." Amaru patted him fondly on the arm. "I'm glad that we joined together for this venture, wherever it leads us."

The elf felt his heart skip a beat. Divines above, this woman was amazing. He sent up a prayer of thanks to Yamaria that she'd sent down Amaru Sunbrand, who, as he said, he had no doubt would save many, many people, himself included.

EMERY
The Wedding

Emery found herself thankful for her mother's lessons on not displaying her outward emotions. She found this skill being ever the more useful as the days slowly crept by, advancing inevitably to her marriage to Tarus Gardstar.

After the official announcement had been made, the young lord had actually opened up a bit more, becoming more friendly to Emery and joining her in her daily affairs. For the most part, Emery was glad for his presence. Having him to talk to at least distracted her from the deep recesses of her mind. Had it not been for her mother's teachings, the princess would have sunk in the pit of despair that threatened to swallow her up, made even worse by the continued presence of the handsome knight as her guard. Leonidas was no different with her after that night, as if he had put the events in the gazebo out of his mind completely. Emery wished she had that ability, but no, her aching heart refused to give up what she felt for Leonidas Braveheart. She'd known and cared for him for far too long to stop loving him. It was foolish behavior, she knew, to be thinking about the captain of the guard when her husband-to-be was sitting right in front of her, but at least she had one reprieve. Her heart and mind often argued about whether it was a good thing or not, but Leo spent much time over at the smithy where Caitrial worked. When asked, Leo told Emery that she was forging his new armor and weapons, and he sparred with the eldest Rainclaw to help her improve in the arts of weaponry. Every once in a while, the princess would go down to the lot where they trained and watch them. Caitrial's dummy broadsword versus Leonidas's makeshift hammer and shield clanged off each other in long strings before one of the combatants finally found an opening. It was an impressive sight, and every time, even when Leo lost the melee, Emery was proud to have him protecting her.

As for Tarus, Emery found him to be a strange subject. She'd noticed before how he seemed to act differently around his father, and the more time they spent together, the more evident this difference became. Whenever Lord Geurus was around, Tarus changed to a completely different person. The young lord became sterner and answered his father with absolute respect, to a level even Emery never managed when her father was still a respectable man. Neither smile or smirk crossed his face, which became like an iron mask, rigid and cold. When it was just him and Emery, on the other hand, Tarus would tell tales from his father's homeland, of hunters that had taken down magnificent beasts or heroic berserkers who defeated pirates on the sea. One particular story of a man named Nodram, who had killed many of the dire wolves that raided the land, struck a chord with Emery, reminding her of the things that Leonidas had told her about. Wolves in the desert killing more of the Fyroxi. Reminded her of Fyrestone and the unavenged tragedy over there. Yet another damper to her mood.

When she wondered aloud at the similarities, Tarus had just shrugged, saying, "The cold northern lands often have big wolves, or so I've heard. I've never been to Moonwatch, so I wouldn't know much about it. Their 'Chillfang,' as you call them, could be completely different from our dire wolves." His explanation seemed reasonable enough, and it did seem that his family had no knowledge about Moonwatch or Sun's Reach. Either way, his stories were entertaining, if a bit grisly for Emery's taste.

For her sake, Tarus even stayed calm near the Rainclaw sisters when Emery went to visit. His face would morph into the mask he wore when his father was around, but at least he wasn't forbidding the princess from being near her closest friends.

After the night at the dance, Reyna and Grayson also spent more time together, her brother occasionally joining their forays through the woods or the city proper. Her resentful heart was a bit upset to see her brother getting the affection of the one he wanted while she couldn't, but she refused to let it taint her opinion of Reyna. The two did make a good couple, and if Grayson spent a bit more time at the bar than usual, at least he didn't come home smelling as strongly of booze.

The end of summer was quickly approaching and with it, Emery knew, her official marriage to Tarus Gardstar. Lord Geurus and Godfrey were already hard at work planning they had been for some time. Things would be all set very soon. Already, the nights were growing cooler, and the wind had a slight chill to it, so the king and the lord didn't have much time to bring their promise to truth.

Emery continued to spend time with Tarus, hoping beyond hope that perhaps she could fall in love with the boy. When he wasn't all business with his father, there were a few things that made it possible for Emery to, if not love the boy, at least enjoy his presence more than she ever expected to.

His vulnerable smile when he was assured there was no authority around showed a soft side that Emery related with. That side loved how she donated money and time to the poor, loved how she would spend hours in the garden just reading or conversing quietly. Perhaps, if he learned to bring that side out more often, Emery could convince herself that this betrothal was right for her. And Yamaria knew she spent plenty of time doing just that, trying to believe that she could forget Leo and marry Tarus without it being a farce. The princess wasn't sure if she was up to acting out a happy marriage to the citizens when their love was hollow.

As the first month of harvest season came to its midpoint and the preparations for harfestival started, the work for the royal wedding was already well underway. Emery and Tarus practiced their dances and wrote their speeches. The general mood around the castle was uplifted with the sounds and scents of celebrations that flowed in from the city streets.

It was suggested by Lord Geurus that the vow portion of the ceremony be held atop the bell tower that stood over the sizable city square. "That way, more of the city people can experience this world-changing event. We could fit nobles and craftsmen alike and a few commoners to spread the tale to their friends."

King Godfrey liked the idea of more spectators for the solidifying of such a powerful alliance. He set Queen Lysaria and a handful of scribes to work on writing out the invitations. Emery was sad to see her mother working so hard and spent whatever free time she didn't dedicate to the Rainclaws with her.

The queen prepared Emery for marriage and spoke to her of the duties of being a wife and eventually a mother. "Hopefully, Lord Tarus will be more capable than your father, but seeing as you have the blood of the Redwyn line, if anything, you can force him to do this drudgery. But I wouldn't suggest it unless you wish all of the love you might have for each other to evaporate like morning dew."

"Don't worry, Mother," Emery soothed. "I won't be foolish enough to follow in Father's footsteps. He has brought us to a precarious position if anything I've heard from Sir Leonidas is true. And I will take it as my personal duty to help bring Sun's Reach down from the ledge."

"You have what it takes to be a great queen, Emery." The worrying creases on her mother's face dissipated. "I hope that I live longer than your father so I can get a glimpse of the life ahead of you."

While the overall mood of the castle was an anticipation for the upcoming wedding, some people were a little more nervous than others. Surprisingly, Tarus was among them.

"Milord." Emery curtsied to her betrothed, who stood out on the balcony, the morning sun streaming down into his blond curls. Not expecting a visitor, Tarus whipped around quickly, hand falling to the hilt of his sword. His eyes were wild and searched for something that wasn't there. "Tarus? Are you feeling all right?" She retreated a step and remained ready to bolt.

The young lord heaved a heavy sigh. "I'm sorry, Emery." He reached a hand out to lay on her elbow. Since it was the same hand that had been on the sword, she moved back to him and allowed him the contact he wished. His eyes almost seemed to beg for it and didn't calm until she was near him. "I never expected that I would feel so anxious. But this marriage has my heart in my throat." He hesitated for a moment. "It's just…you're perfect. All that I could have asked for."

"Oh, Tarus." Emery felt her face heat up. "Well, it's only a week away. And have no fear that I will refuse you. When I first heard that we were going to marry, I thought *absolutely not*! But that was just because I didn't know you. Now that we've spent some time together"—she swallowed the lump in her throat—"I-I want nothing more," she lied. "I've grown quite fond of my…handsome Lord Gardstar." Emery hoped her smile was convincing and looked at Tarus to see his reaction. His eyes were far away, staring off into space. Emery wondered what he was thinking.

"That is…good to hear, Emery." He turned back to the open air, staring at the courtyard. "I've been having nightmares, where… where you denied our marriage before the ceremony, canceled the entire thing, and ran off with someone else."

Emery felt a pang of sadness and guilt. On the night of the Rothsster-Leygrain wedding, she had been ready to do just that. The princess would have eloped with Leonidas if he'd allowed it. *And I would still do it in an instant,* she thought. *If the other would have me.*

Though all of what she'd said to Tarus was true—she *was* fonder of him than she'd been—Leo still had a grip on her heart. "Don't worry about that," she assured him, *lied* to him. "There is nobody else. There never has been, and there never will be." She did it as much for her own sake as his.

"Good." He pondered for a moment. "Have you decided what you're going to wear for the wedding?"

"I was thinking to use Barnio's masterpiece like I did for the Rothsster-Leygrain wedding," she replied. "I think it would be an inspiring image to evoke: the phoenix of Redwyn and the astral knight of Gardstar."

"I love it," Tarus breathed. "This wedding will be worthy of the bards." Emery almost thought she saw him cringe as he turned but waved it off as a trick of the light.

*****

The day finally came. The whole palace was running amok, servants preparing the two families for the wedding. Lord Geurus had his guards set up in a border around the city square which Emery was sure was already filled with people. She and Tarus were kept apart, being prepared by servants and family alike. Queen Lysaria fussed over every little detail of Emery's look. Despite the stress, Emery could see the joy on her mother's face. Godfrey had given his wife and Lady Cereos command over this whole event, and the queen wanted her daughter's special day to be perfect. Emery hadn't told her mother or anyone for that matter about the events after the last wedding ball, so Lysaria didn't have any clues about the doubts that still raged in her heart. She had to set those aside, the princess knew. Tarus would be a great husband, and Emery couldn't afford to make a fool of herself by accidentally saying the wrong name during the ceremony. *Or tonight*, she reminded herself. Emery hadn't thought until recently about the wedding night. A red-hot blush shot to her face. Tonight she would have to consummate the marriage between the two houses. Having never lain with a man, except in her dreams, the princess wasn't quite sure what to expect. She hoped that Tarus had some skills in the arts of romance. That would make everything much easier; she could just withdraw a bit and think while it happened. Emery knew that wasn't the right attitude to have, but she couldn't help it.

Many wedding gifts awaited her from different noble houses. Gloves made of luxurious fur, bowls of exotic fruits, books that were written by a famous elven author named Arteni, including his travel guide of both local and faraway places. Arteni had traveled all across the world by ship and foot in the three hundred years he had lived and seen so many beautiful sights.

> Though words on a page cannot begin to describe the natural magnificence of Sorvaire island in Seagap or the manufactured beauty of the gilded cities in Gildergrant, I understand that not all have the time or money to travel. As such, I will describe such things to you just as best I

can. Just keep in mind that, especially for the shorter-lived races, taking at least one trip to a foreign land will give you a new experience that you are likely never to forget and provide a new meaning to your existence. This planet of Keylis has a great variety of lands, maybe even some that have yet to be discovered. Stay adventurous, my loyal readers! (Arteni Galare)

This book had been sent by the Rainclaw family. Emery had confided in Reyna and Arcadia her desires to travel multiple times. Knowing how she was tied to her kingdom, they decided that this would be the best way to give her some reprieve. Emery wondered how many people had read Arteni's books across all the lands. It was rumored that the elven writer had more money stowed away than all the great houses combined.

She had dressed in Barnio's dress once again, and her escort came to lead her to the carriage. Emery wasn't the only one who'd received a gift.

Leonidas was clad in the new armor made for him by Caitrial and the forge masters. Shining silver plate accentuated with gold adorned his whole body. Snarling lion heads glowered down from his shoulders and chest, and scalloped steel covered arms and legs. Curved sheets of metal protected his neck from arrows on three sides, and the mail beneath the plate would keep him safe if that failed. A royal blue cape trimmed with silver flowed behind him as he walked. On his belt hung a silver sword, the pommel another lion head, with three flaming hearts embedded in the hilt. On his back, the war hammer was slung, a dangerous chunk of iron, with pyramidlike ends and a tall spike on the top. Leonidas looked so regal that it made Emery's heart ache. He smiled down at the princess. "Caitrial did an amazing job, wouldn't you say?" He turned his gaze all over the magnificent suit.

"Yes," Emery breathed. "She did, and you look stunning. You look like a genuine Lightstrider." She strode over to him and lay a hand on his, wishing that he could trade places with Tarus. Well, she couldn't marry him, but there was still something she could do. Something that would give Leo what he deserved and give Emery the option to keep him near when her heart desired it. "When I am queen, you will be named Lightstrider, if you will accept the honor."

Leonidas's eyes widened, and his mouth hung open for a moment. "It is more than I deserve, but I will gladly accept the position." He drew his new gleaming sword from its sheath and lay it at the princess's feet. "This may be a bit premature, but Emery Redwyn, I vow my sword to you, from now until the day that I die, to serve and protect you until I can do no more. I promise to do you no disservice and bring honor to your name everywhere I go. This I swear by the eternal light of Yamaria."

Emery had learned these words from her mother as well. "And I promise to ask no service of you that would taint your honor. I will listen to your counsel and respect your opinion. For as long as you live, my hearth and home will be yours as well, no matter what may befall us. I accept your fealty by the eternal light of Yamaria." The princess managed to keep her voice from catching. It wasn't the oath she'd wanted from Leo, but it was still very touching.

"Well, I'm glad that whole affair is settled," a new voice called, entering the room a moment after Leonidas swore his oath. Godfrey Redwyn swept in, his round face alight. Resplendent in vibrant red-and-orange garb, the king was even happier than she'd ever seen him. "Finally, Emery, my dear, today is the day you get married. I couldn't be more pleased!" The king clasped his daughter's smooth hands between his own sweaty palms. "With you and Tarus, the Redwyn legacy will now be solidified. He will give you healthy children to which the crown may pass, and his men shall keep you safe until the end of time."

"As you say, Father," Emery said. She wanted to believe it; she had to believe it. It was her life now. "I am glad to see you in such good health. You've finally been getting some sun recently." It came out a bit harsher than she'd intended, but Godfrey didn't seem to notice.

"Yes." He chuckled, his stomach shaking. "Lord Geurus has had me tour him around the city multiple times in the past months. And he's assured me that he has men patrolling every street. That host he brought is going to make everyone so very safe! Especially if what Sir Leonidas says is true." He turned to the knight. "I know you have been waiting a long time for those soldiers to go out. But the time finally comes! They have been armed in proper desert gear and horsed and are on their way out to the Scorched Waste now. We have Lord Geurus's men in place, so I can allow my warriors to go."

Emery raised her eyebrow at this and saw Leo do the same, but neither dared say anything to burst the king's bubble. Lord Geurus's men did seem disciplined at the very least.

"But now is neither the time nor the place to talk of such affairs." The king reached into his robe and pulled out a ring. "This ring has been passed down through the Redwyn family for years and years as each young man and woman were married. Each part was forged by a different race as a pledge of allegiance to the first Godfrey Redwyn, for whom I and the four others before me were named. Now I pass it to you, Emery, a little spark of the undying flame that lives within each of us." The king gave a throaty chuckle and wiped at a tear. "I am so very proud of you, Emery. I only hope that this marriage brings you as much happiness as it brings me!" He strode toward the door, where the royal wain awaited. Leonidas climbed in with Emery, with Lysaria and Galbraith behind them and King Godfrey with Casinius in the front.

*****

The people cheered and whistled as the royal family approached, carts open to show the crowd their smiling faces. Emery saw people of both noble and common descent mingled in the massive mob. Encircling the whole group was the black-clad knights of House Gardstar, standing impossibly still with spear butts to the cobblestones. The black steel of their weapons reminded Emery of Ignis Duskwalker, and the princess realized that she hadn't seen the Secretkeeper once in the past weeks. Emery had not seen hide nor hair of the strange man. She wondered what he was up to, what facts he was learning at this very moment.

The wagons pulled slowly to a stop, and Leonidas climbed out, offering his hand to the princess. Emery grasped the leather glove, feeling the heat of the knight's hand underneath. Leonidas guided her around the back of the bell tower, where a servant waited at the entrance. A massive spiraling staircase led up to the top, where workers would ring the bells as the sand clock dictated. Today, the bells were to be rung from a different tower, as not to bring harm to the royals. It occurred to Emery that no such thought was given to those who worked here, save strips of cloth for tamping into their ears, which she saw lying on tables. She would ask Leonidas about that after the wedding. With the deafening noises on the battlefield, perhaps the army might hold something to remedy the effects.

Emery strode proudly up the curving steps, holding her skirts and tassels in the air so she wouldn't trip. If a stray tassel broke free and found its way under her foot, Leonidas's hand would be on her back almost instantly. She trusted in her beloved knight not to let her fall.

When they reached the top landing, Emery saw that Tarus was already there. Her husband-to-be was standing in an alcove talking to his father. That signature cold mask slid into place, neither eyes nor twitch of muscle betraying how he felt. Lord Geurus slipped something to Tarus, who dropped it into his pocket. Heartily patting his son on the shoulder, the lord left the room in the same mood as Godfrey. Emery approached Tarus, who was dressed in flowing robes of black, white stars speckling them. A sword rested on his belt.

"Part of the astral knight costume, to make this more realistic," he assured the princess when her eyes flitted toward it. "Are you ready for this?" He offered an arm to Emery, who looped her own through. Their fingers entwined; his were cool to the touch. She could feel the slight vibrations of his skin; the young lord was shaking.

"Are *you* ready for this?" She turned his own question back around on him.

"Sorry, just a little nervous about what has to happen." He allowed a smile to grace his features. "I've never been married before, but I didn't expect it to be so nerve-racking." His eyes lingered on her face for a moment, eyes now showing a duel between thoughts while Emery turned away to study the balcony where they would say their vows. A long way from the ground, the royals would have to project to be heard by the entire crowd. Emery knew from her time walking in the square that there were other lower balconies, where Lord Geurus, Lady Cereos, and Velara would be standing, joined by Grayson and Galbraith. Already, the soldiers of House Gardstar lined the platform. They bowed to Tarus and Emery as they approached. One of them halted the group at the door. "Now we wait for the king, as he is to go first onto the balcony to make his speech. Then while he speaks, you will go and prepare to proceed with the wedding."

At some length, Emery heard puffing from the stairs, as Godfrey achieved the top landing, supported by Casinius and Queen Lysaria. "We simply must get some sort of pulley and winch system in here, if we are ever to use this tower again," he was saying, wiping at the perspiration dripping from his chins.

With one final puff of breath, he walked forward, urged on by Casinius who said, "Quickly, my king, I'm sure the people are growing restless. Some have been here since early morning to secure their space."

"Yes, yes. They have been here long, but they can forgive their king for his weak knees and wobbling belly, can they not?"

"As you say, my king." Casinius bowed his head. The lord captain of the Lightstriders discreetly nodded to the guard at the door as he passed, his face unreadable. Like the king, Casinius's age had begun to get to him. Wrinkles lined his face; his downturned mustache was going gray, and his goatee was now sparse. The red helmet on his head covered the balding spot in his short brown hair. His family's ancient sword was slung in its sheath, the only thing still in perfect condition, preserved in the way that magical artifacts from the past were. Emery found it interesting that Qrakzt the Mad Mage hadn't thought to take the magic from artifacts, along with people. Perhaps he hadn't had the power to do all of it.

Emery's heart began to pound as her father started to speak and she was led out onto the balcony. Lysaria gave her hand a quick squeeze before joining Casinius on the other side of the platform. Leonidas took his place behind her, and the guard from the door, who Emery could now see wore a more ornate set of armor than the other guards, went behind Tarus.

"Ladies and gentlemen of Searstar, proud people of Sun's Reach!" the king began. "Today we gather to celebrate the wedding of Emery Redwyn and Tarus Gardstar from the North." There was a murmur as people below wondered where from the north Tarus actually came from. Emery realized that she didn't have that answer either. Perhaps she would pry it from Tarus's lips this evening. "Lord Gardstar has provided us with many a great thing. As you can see, you are under the protection of his troops at this very moment. He has given me counsel in many troubles, and I hope that this partnership will continue to provide both of our families with great boons!"

He waited a moment while the crowd cheered, before raising a hand for silence. "Now, if you will excuse an old father's rambling, I would like to talk about my daughter." His voice caught at the end, but he cleared it away. "Emery Redwyn is the one thing I am most proud of since the moment my wife delivered her as a squalling babe. When I first held her, I knew that I had the perfect heir cradled in my arms, and I'm gladdened to see that my premonition was correct. I could be no more satisfied with my beautiful daughter." Godfrey cleared his throat. "I am not so blind that I cannot see my own failings. I know I've not been the most effective king and that I grow old. But trust me, people of Searstar and Sun's Reach at large, the ascension of Emery Redwyn will mark a new age, a *better* age for all involved." Emery felt her eyes misting at her father's kind words. She stared straight ahead, not trusting herself to keep from crying in front of others. "Now that I have Lord Geurus and Lady Cereos here, I promise that the short remainder of my rule will be better than ever before. I foolishly precluded my daughter from learning how to rule until only recently. I pledge to have her taught the ways of proper rulership, and once I am gone, you shall all have the queen that you desire. I promise…"

Emery was only half paying attention, so focused on keeping the tears from flowing, on Tarus's hand in hers, and on Leonidas's presence directly behind her. She only faintly noticed that the king had finished speaking. Then somebody screamed. The princess's eyes snapped up, and she looked at Godfrey. The king had a shocked expression on his face, eyes wide and mouth, forming soundless shapes. Looking down farther, Emery saw what the issue was, and her heart nearly beat out of her chest.

Her father was swaying and clawing at his throat, where a crossbow bolt protruded! Many others below began to cry out, and Emery joined them. She tried to go to him, but Tarus gripped her arm.

"Whoever shot that bolt may have another loaded. You are *not* going over there, Princess," he said sensibly. "I couldn't stand...to lose you." There was an uproar from the crowd below as the audience tried to find the person who had shot the king.

At Tarus's words, the shock finally hit Emery. King Godfrey Redwyn was dead, killed by an assassin at his own daughter's wedding. Confusion and fear battled within her. Who could have done this and why? She looked across to her mother, who was restrained by Casinius. Tears streaked down the queen's face, and she was shouting something, though it was lost in the cries from below. She beat on Casinius's armor fruitlessly, delicate hands becoming bruised by the ordeal.

Leonidas moved up and encircled her with shield and hammer. Emery gratefully pressed close to her knight, huddling against his silver-and-gold chest plate. She saw Tarus, shaking and staring at the king, whose corpse had finally stopped twitching and now lay in a puddle of crimson.

"An awful tragedy to be sure" came a cold yet amused voice from behind them. Emery whirled and saw a sweeping black robe. "There is nothing quite like murder to spoil a wedding."

"What do you want, Geurus Gardstar?" Lysaria asked venomously. "Was this your doing?"

"Oh, how very perceptive of you, Queen Lysaria," Geurus drawled mockingly. "Yes, I ordered your failure of a king killed."

"Father!" Tarus sounded shocked. "Why would you do this? On the day of my wedding no less?"

Geurus tsk-ed and wagged a finger. "Tarus, my dear boy, I'm sure this must come as a shock to you, but sometimes these things must happen. If you'd taken in any of my lessons, you might understand the reasons why it had to go this way. I couldn't afford another disappointment." He looked sharply at his son. "But my actions today will set in motion something great, beginning with my ascension to the throne of Sun's Reach."

"If you think that killing the king gives you the right to take the throne," Lysaria growled, "then you're as much of a fool as my husband."

"So you admit that Godfrey was a fool?" Geurus laughed. "I've only done a favor to the people of Sun's Reach!"

Lysaria clenched both fists. "Casinius, your king is dead, and the one who ordered his assassination is standing right in front of you." Her voice dropped dangerously low. "So why don't you unsheathe that magical sword of yours and *sever this problem at its head*!"

Geurus chuckled again. "Yes, Casinius Brightblade, fulfill your oath. Slay the problem!"

Casinius nodded and drew his family's ancient blade. The runes gouged in the sturdy metal glowed crimson. "I am sorry," he said. "But I have a duty to protect both king and country. Seeing as I failed my first directive, it only stands to reason that I deal with the second." His face stern and unreadable, the Lightstrider took a step forward, away from the queen. "I will do what is best for the people of Sun's Reach." The aging knight took a deep breath and raised his blade, pointing it at Geurus. The lord continued to smile and looked Casinius straight in the eye. Then in a nearly untrackable movement, Casinius turned on his heel and swung. The blade flashed and swished through the air and sliced through the queen's neck like a hot knife through butter. Emery felt Leonidas tense behind her, gasping audibly. Lightstrider Casinius turned back around, his face grim but proud.

Geurus clapped and gestured to the head of Queen Lysaria, which had rolled a few feet away, near her husband's corpse. "Well done, Casinius. I think she was clueless up until the end, by the surprise on her face!" He laughed. "I wonder what her final thought was, with the honorable Lightstrider Casinius chopping off the head of his own queen!" One of Casinius's cheek muscles twitched at the comment, but he said nothing, just wiping his blade on the queen's thin scarf and resting it at his side.

Emery wasn't sure how long she screamed for, but when she came back to focus, she saw that Leonidas was standing in front of her, threatening Casinius and Tarus at her side, his eyes narrowed at his father and one hand hovering over the hilt of his sword.

"Put your weapon down, Leonidas," Casinius ordered. "I am Lightstrider, and you are only a palace guard. I have the higher authority."

"All of your authority was forfeit the moment you betrayed those that you swore your life to!" Leonidas growled, hefting the hammer. "You have no honor, but I will give you the chance to die in a duel rather than rotting in prison!"

Casinius shrugged as if that hadn't occurred to him. "I suppose you have a point, but that point is moot. I have no quarrel with you, but if you insist on fighting, you will quickly learn the difference between the training we were each given." He flicked his sword casually. "I might not be as fast as I used to be, but I could still kill you in mere moments."

"Stand down, Leo," Emery cried. "What he did is unforgivable, but I won't have you throwing your life away!"

Leonidas hesitated a moment as if he still considered going in for the attack. Then he shook his head and lowered the hammer, walking back to guard his princess.

Geurus clapped once more and turned to his son. "Well, I have other business to attend to, so I suppose we should get this wedding back underway, for the betterment of the kingdom or whatever it was that Godfrey said." He walked back through the doorway, Casinius directly behind him. The old Lightstrider gave Leonidas one last lingering glare and followed Lord Geurus back down the stairs.

Everyone stood shock still for a moment, the confused roar of the crowd echoing beneath them. Tarus knelt beside the princess and wrapped an arm around her. "By the stars," he huffed, "I'm so sorry."

"You're sorry?" The princess was bewildered by the apology. "Your father just killed both of my parents, and you are going to apologize?"

Tarus tensed beside her. "Emery, look at me." She did. His eyes were red rimmed and full of pain. "Emery, I didn't know that this was going to happen. I wouldn't have allowed it to happen if I did." His voice rang with sincerity. "All I wanted today was to get married to a beautiful, kind, generous girl." Tarus helped the princess rise and led her toward the balcony so that they could look down on the people.

The crowd looked up fearfully but waited for something else to happen. A few dead men and women were strewn on the edge of the circle. A few of Geurus's men's spears were bloody, and one had a corpse hanging from it. The man had deeply tanned skin and held a crossbow in a death grip, his arms hanging limply. The people gasped when they saw their crown princess walk up with Tarus. They wouldn't have seen Lord Geurus up on the balcony, so they were confused.

"Emery, nothing about what happened today changes my feelings. You are perfect, Emery, and I love you." Tarus nearly choked on the words as he wrapped one arm around the princess's waist and stared deep into her eyes.

For a moment, Emery searched the young lord's eyes, probing for any sign of deceit. Finding none, she sighed and nodded. "Tarus," she started uncertainly, "I can hear the sincerity in your voice, and I know that you would never wish harm upon me." Her voice grew stronger, loud enough to carry down to the people below. "However, your father, Geurus Gardstar, just ordered the deaths of both the king and queen of Sun's Reach." She heard the people gasp in surprise. "How can I be expected to marry you, given the events of today? To marry the son of my parents' murderer would be nothing less than an insult to them and a betrayal to my family!" Emery's eyes glistened with tears. "Geurus Gardstar was a skilled manipulator and liar. He promised his troops to help protect us, and yet here they stand with my citizen's blood on their spears! I cannot marry you, Tarus, not today or ever. Your father will be imprisoned and sentenced to death as he is a vile man—" Suddenly, Emery felt a sharp pain in her stomach. She looked down and saw a dagger embedded there. She lifted her eyes to stare calmly at Tarus, who looked both horrified and grim.

"And it seems that you are no different," she spat, coughing up blood. She shifted her gaze over to Leonidas, who was standing stunned, his eyes wide. "Leonidas Braveheart," she said affectionately, now only loud enough for those on the balcony to hear. "Leo. My lion, *I love you*. I want you to know that hasn't changed, and it never will." Despite the blood staining the bottom of her face, her voice was only slightly strained, kept steady by pure force of will. "If you still hold any affection for me, then follow this last order: don't get yourself killed. I don't think my soul could take it to know that you died because of me. Do that for me please." Those were the last words that Emery could choke out as Tarus's arms gripped tighter on her waist and hoisted up. It wasn't until she was already falling that the princess realized he'd lifted and tossed her from the balcony.

Emery barely had time to register what was happening as she fell. The dagger wouldn't be what killed her. But when it was discussed later, nobody would be sure if it was the dashing of her head against the tower wall that did her in or whether she was still alive until her fall ended at the bottom with a sickening crunching sound.

The people hadn't loved the king all that well, and his death had still made them angry. But *everyone* had loved Emery Redwyn, and her death sent the denizens of Searstar into a rampage. They surged at the guards around them like a shockwave. The spears came down and impaled the charging masses. When the crowd had spent their rage, many lay dead on the ground, and blood washed over the cobblestones like a red tide. And all the while, the dead eyes of Princess Emery Redwyn stared up at the tower blindly.

Tarus stared numbly down at his hands, his face a mixture of shock and horror. He finally glanced up at Sir Leonidas, who was grinding his teeth. The knight shot a quick look at the guards around him, all of which had their swords bared. "You are damned lucky that I follow Emery's orders," he said dangerously. "Elsewise, I might not leave here alive, but rest assured, you wouldn't either."

Like that was supposed to make his rest any more comfortable. Tarus waved for his guards to put away their blades, and Leo slung his own hammer over his shoulder, looking around warily, as if he half expected the warriors to attack anyway. "I'm glad," Tarus said shakily. "I've seen enough good people slaughtered today." Leonidas gave Tarus a queer look but received no further answer.

Tarus barely trusted himself to speak; he turned to the ornately armored guard. "Cousin Tavindre, send a letter across the Eclipse. Sun's Reach has been won." Tavindre saluted and headed off at once. Head hung low, Tarus walked off the balcony and back to the carriages.

Epilogue

The people of Searstar were forced to stand and watch, kept contained by the guards belonging to Lord Geurus, as the murderer of their royal family made his speech. Casinius Brightblade, their trusted Lightstrider, stood proudly by his side; but quiet yet dangerous Galbraith Severesse had two dark hands clenched on her hand axes.

Prince Grayson, the only living member of the Redwyn royal family, knelt despondently on the stones in front of Lord Geurus. "Boy, repeat after me," he instructed. "I, Grayson of House Redwyn, renounce all claims to the Highsun Seat."

Grayson ground his teeth angrily, but the ax-wielding guard above him persuaded him to comply. "I, Grayson of House Redwyn..." he hesitated.

"Come on, boy, we haven't got all day," Lord Geurus prodded, nodding toward the big man. This man had to be an executor by trade; Grayson was sure of that.

"Renounce all claims to the Highsun Seat," Grayson finished, in a growl.

"Good." Lord Geurus smiled thinly. "Is there anything else you'd like to say?"

Grayson's hands balled into fists. "I also endorse Geurus Gardstar as the new king of Sun's Reach, long may he live," he spat at last.

"Thank you, son. You are free to stand now." When Grayson didn't move, Geurus shrugged. "Or don't. It's your dignity, not mine," he snapped, and two guards dragged the man formerly titled prince back besides Galbraith.

"Men and women of Searstar, you all heard your prince," Geurus began. "I am your new king." A quiet hiss ensued from the crowd. "It doesn't matter whether you like me. You will obey me." He indicated the guards around the circle, as innocently as if he were a child showing off the sculpture he made from twigs and grass. "Godfrey Redwyn was not a good king: he hid many things from you and was a wastrel with your money. I'm sure that you are sick of his empty promises. Instead, I will give you information! Something that Godfrey knew for quite some time but did not deem important enough to share with any of you." He paused momentarily for dramatic effect. "You people may see me as your foe, but at this very moment, there are real enemies within your border! They are raiding in the Scorched Waste at this time, but they will not stop there. Soon, they and their allies, men and monsters alike, shall start their incursion of Sun's Reach proper. Direct not your ire at me but at them, who would slay your kin and destroy your resources! Your five cities need the food that comes from the Sulfaari Expanse. If they are harried by our foe, then you shall all starve. We are all citizens of Sun's Reach now, and a civil war will do us no good!" Geurus's words got the crowd muttering, which was precisely what he desired. "Know that at this moment, I have yet more warriors wandering the kingdom, ready to protect you all. I have also dispatched a large number of troops to the Scorched Waste to try heading off our foes there." He received a few isolated cheers, which quickly quieted down as their neighbors looked sharply at them. "In time, you will appreciate what I have done, as you hear the stories of those who don't earn my protection. Until that day, feel free, have your opinions, but don't forget that any direct act of insubordination will result in punishment as will the breaking of any law, just as normal." The new king of Sun's Reach turned back into the building, his wife Cereos by his side and Casinius behind him, leading Galbraith and Grayson, who still hung between two guards.

*****

While the people were still focused on the events in the square, a man poked his head out from the shadowed corridor. He'd chosen not to attend the wedding, as he had far more important things to worry about. Back pressed flat against the wall and hair hidden under a black hood, he skirted the edges of the buildings, sure to stay out of sight of any guards still doing their patrols. He doubted that being caught would turn out favorably for anyone involved. Reaching the sunlit street, he could now see the tower where the wedding had taken place. He circled around through the shadows and shuffled along the tower wall. Now the man could see what he was looking for. Right in front of him was the corpse of Emery Redwyn. The combination of smashing into the tower wall and impacting the ground had turned the back of the princess's head into a bloody mess. It had been crushed like a watermelon, both juices and little chunks of gray-red flesh sprayed out in a corona. Her lower body lay in a pool of blood, which trickled out from the knife wound. The offending object still stuck from her stomach, a cruel crescent-shaped blade made of white metal. The handle was ivory, and black rocks decorated it. A very fancy dagger, made of rare, unique metal, he knew. The new king would be sore wroth to find it missing. He wiped it clean, stuffed it into one of his empty sheaths, and stared grimly down at the princess's pretty face for a moment. "Everything goes according to plan," Ignis Duskwalker muttered under his breath. "Though quite the unfortunate ending for the Redwyns. Certainly doesn't feel like a victory." During his talks with Princess Emery, Ignis had grown rather fond of her. The girl reminded him of his own daughter, who he hadn't seen in many months. "Well, Princess"—he moved his arms under her body, feeling Emery's fading warmth—"I hope you don't mind because now, the real fun starts." Using a thick old cloak, he wrapped up the corpse and applied pressure to the princess's head and torso so that no leakage would give them away. Then he lifted and cradled her in his arms. She was surprisingly light, and Ignis found her an easy load to bear. With nary a look back toward the castle or the tower, the Secretkeeper clicked his heels together and suddenly vanished from sight, carrying the princess back into the shadows he knew so well and out toward the gates of Searstar.

END

About the Author

Spencer Steeves was born and raised in Plainville, Connecticut, and lives there to this day, attending school, working, and writing whenever time allows. Spencer enjoys biking, playing *Dungeons & Dragons*, reading, and writing. He is fascinated by the worlds and stories that fantasy writers create and dreams that one day his works might inspire other aspiring writers too.

CPSIA information can be obtained
at www.ICGtesting.com
Printed in the USA
JSHW031150140721
16792JS00001B/1